Praise for R.C. STEPHENS

"A sexy NHL player, a sassy heroine, and a heartfelt romance that kept me engaged from beginning to end!" — *NYT* bestseller Mia Sheridan on Big Stick

"From first kiss to major plot twist... two solid love stories for the price of one... a sweet romance about new beginnings."
- Kirkus Reviews on HALO

"Myles and Flynn's chemistry is ice-melting hot in this fast-paced, friends-to-lovers romance sure to warm your heart. Another R.C. Stephens SCORE!" - Julie A. Richman, USA Today Bestseller on Big Stick

"I knew in Big Stick I would love Oli's story, and after getting to know this sexy giant in the pages of Butt Ending, I now think I love him more than Myles… so, therefore, I claim them both!" ~ A.M. Madden USA Today Bestselling Author on Butt Ending

THE TRUTH ABOUT US

R.C. STEPHENS

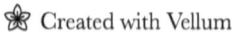

Prologue

Christmas

Ten years ago

Two days till Christmas and I wait anxiously by the window. When will he be here?

I stand up and sit back down. Excitement courses through me. It makes my heart beat fast. As I stare out the window small flakes fall ever so slowly. It's so pretty, adding a magical essence to this time of year.

The gloomy wintery day isn't a downer at all because Griff is home visiting from College in Florida. We will be able to sneak time alone together. That is, if my family stays out of the house. If my brother Logan ever caught on to what was going on between Griff and me, he would lose it. Griff has been his best friend since kindergarten. And if Daddy ever found out, all hell would break loose, but we are careful . . .

I text Griff. Everyone left more than an hour ago. This is quality alone time for us.

When are you coming? Dad is out of town.

Griff was my first kiss junior year of high school. He was a senior. That kiss locked our fate. Since then, I've only wanted to kiss him.

Not a good idea. I see your brother all the time. He's my roommate. We need space from each other. I can't just come over and hang with you. Even though I can't wait to kiss you.

Grr.

Logan isn't home and neither are Jenn and Mom. Everyone is out for the day.

Now that changes everything. See you soon!

Yesss!

I squeal. I've crushed on him since I was young. Never in my wildest dreams did I think he would fall for me, the simple sister. Jenn is beautiful. A human version of a Barbie doll with blond hair and blue eyes. I am simple with my chocolate-brown hair, green eyes, and naturally tanned skin. We barely look like siblings, but that's because Logan and Jenn look more like Dad with his Scottish background, and I look more like Mama with her Italian heritage.

I jolt from a knock on the door and stand quickly from my seat. As I bolt toward the door, my smile spreads across my cheeks. Excitement gets my blood pumping hard and it feels like I'm going downhill on a roller coaster, my breaths coming fast and my heart beating rapidly.

OMG. He's finally here. I haven't seen him since he left for college with Logan at the end of August.

I fling the door open and gasp as Griff stands tall and handsome in the doorway. His aquamarine eyes sparkle. His lips tug up at the corners.

"Jojo," he says breathlessly, taking a step inside.

"No one's home," I assure him, taking him by the hand and pulling him over the threshold. My family isn't expected back until tonight.

He's shivering. "C-Close that door so I can get my lips on you," he says, his voice horse. Boston is experiencing an abnormally cold winter and Griff doesn't own a car.

"You're ice." I wince.

"So warm me up." He sticks his hands under my shirt, resting them on my hips. They are so cold, I squirm out of his reach.

"Hey, get back here." He laughs. "I want to kiss you so bad."

I can't resist snaking my arms around his neck. Our lips touch and a familiar heat sparks inside me, spreading like wildfire through my body. His cool hands run up and down my back but I no longer care. I want to kiss him into tomorrow. Kissing Griff is the best drug. It's been so long.

He breaks the kiss and gazes around with anxious eyes. "Where's your dad?" He is always paranoid when we hook up at my house, but we don't have many options for privacy.

"Out of town, I told you, and Logan is out with some friends. Said he wouldn't be back until much later."

"Yeah, he texted me earlier. Some of the guys from the team were getting together," he explains.

"Didn't you want to go see them?" I ask, knowing better. I just want to hear him say the words.

"There's no place I'd rather be than here." He kisses me again, kicking off his shoes and backing me deeper into the house. My eyes open as he walks me toward the family room.

"We are going to need more privacy than this," I say into his lips.

"Oh yeah? What did you have in mind?" he asks with a hint of intrigue.

"For starters, we need to go to my room and close the door. You know the neighbors can be nosy." I remind him, because Mrs. Saloway is constantly on the deck in her backyard even in winter and somehow, she is always looking around. Mom just mentioned to me the other day that she asked her about the new plant on the left-hand corner of the room.

"Your room, huh? I'm liking the sound of that." Griff's grin closely resembles that of a Cheshire cat. It floods me with need. I grab his hand and take the stairs quickly to my room.

"Eager much?" He laughs.

"You have no idea." I smile deviously. I wonder what his reaction will be when he finds out what I have planned.

After climbing on my bed, I place my head on the pillow, and Griff cuddles up beside me.

"How's school going? You have a lot of work to do over break?" he asks.

As a senior, I've been working my ass off. If I want to get into Harvard to do an undergraduate degree in history, I need to have top marks.

"I've got work," I answer, not wanting to get into details. "But I was hoping we could focus on other things right now," I say, using my finger to caress some exposed skin on his neck.

His face flushes, and I'm sure his blood is running south.

"I'm liking the sound of that." He smiles, his voice low and gruff.

It takes mere seconds for our bodies to meld together. Our lips brush and heat overtakes us the way it usually does. He rolls on top of me and uses his arms to prop himself up so I'm not crushed beneath him. He smells like fresh shower gel and Griff. I inhale, marking his scent to memory, knowing he'll be leaving soon. Two weeks of break will fly by, and I'll have to wait for Easter to see him again. For more stolen moments.

His tongue sweeps inside my mouth, wet and messy. My hands run up his back and lower to his behind while his hand skates under my shirt. His eyes open when he finds me bra-less. His thumb gently rubs my nipples, giving attention to both of them, and I let out a moan.

"You have no idea how much I missed that sound," he says. "I'm rock hard." He winces, as if he didn't mean for the second part to escape. "I'm sorry."

"Don't be. Knowing you want me makes me crazy." Sparks of heat shoot between my thighs.

He slides his finger inside my flannel pajama pants. "Fuck, you are so wet," he growls.

"Yes," I moan, moving my hips. I need him so much. I reach for his belt and unbutton his jeans.

"Jolie, what are you doing?" His tone is scolding, but I'm five weeks away from my eighteenth birthday and I want this.

I blow out a breath.

"What?" he asks.

"I want us to sleep together." There, I said it, and I feel so much lighter. His eyes widen. He needs some convincing.

I press my pelvis into the hardness of his crotch. He groans and rubs at his eyes.

"I love you. Is that not enough?" I ask with a pout.

He stares at me, his gaze filled with agony. "I would love to sleep with you, Jolie, but not yet. I want to be something, establish myself when I make you a promise of forever."

"You already made me a promise of forever," I remind him playing hard ball.

"I did," he agrees, rubbing my back.

"I'll be eighteen soon enough," I preen. "I'm ready. I want you. I need to have something to remember you with when you're away at school. I want to feel you inside me."

An animalistic rumble vibrates his chest and leaves his mouth. "To hear you say those words . . ." He flips me on my back and presses his hard length into my belly. "You're going to be the end of me. I can't say no to you." He grinds his length into me and I whimper. I manage to read between the lines of his words.

"My dad is on another continent. We have the house to ourselves all day."

We grind into each other. I moan.

His resolve weakens as he cups me behind my head and brings his lips to mine. We've always been hot for each other, but now it feels like a new fire has been lit and burns wild between us. As we kiss hungrily, my breath is sucked away. We work frantically to get each other's clothes off. Naked, we continue to dry hump. Why are we dry humping? Our clothes are off. Still, it's such a turn-on feeling his skin rub against mine, and I think I may come so I take a breath and look down. I've never seen his penis. It's bigger than I thought.

"What?" He laughs.

"It's big." I have no frame of reference. His is the first penis I've seen.

"Having second thoughts?" He cocks his left brow.

"No." My answer is fast.

I slowly touch him, and he groans. I wrap my hands around his cock and pump.

He groans and gyrates his hips beneath my touch. "Jesus," he hisses. "You're going to make me come."

He places his hand over mine to stop the movement and flips me on my back, hovering above me. My nipples strain beneath his stare. He doesn't leave me hanging long as his hot mouth connects with my nipple. My body feels too hot. Need throbs painfully between my thighs as I run my fingers through his hair.

"Griff," I moan, needing something.

"I know," he answers with a raspy voice. His kisses move lower and lower . . . until his lips connect with warm flesh. I moan so loud I'm sure the house rattles.

"You sure we're alone?" he asks, looking up to me from between my thighs.

I blush, and I'm unable to formulate a sentence. He has never gone down on me before and his warm tongue against the most tender parts of me makes me detonate like fireworks on the fourth of July. I am going to explode as my heart pumps fast, and my skin is slick with sweat. "Don't stop," I groan.

Griff chuckles. "Wasn't planning on it."

Colors. . .lots of beautiful colors and rainbows fly past me as I climax.

"I want inside you. Problem is I don't have any condoms." He frowns.

"I have a box," I say, and his eyebrows almost hit his forehead.

"What?" he asks, as if he didn't hear me right.

"I told you on the phone I wanted this." I don't know why he is so surprised.

"I thought I was dreaming," he answers with a snicker.

"No." I lean away and reach into my side table where I have a full box of condoms I bought from the pharmacy last week. I pass him the box, and he cusses under his breath as he sheathes himself. I watch him intently. With the condom on, he hovers above me and kisses me softly, tenderly.

"I love you so much," he whispers.

"I love you," I answer.

"Forever," he says.

My heart bursts because college hasn't changed him. He is still different from the rest of the teenage boys I know. He doesn't only want in my pants. Our hearts are connected in a way that's hard to describe.

We were friends first. He's been there at so many important moments in my life and we are here now, sharing this special moment.

"Forever," I say as he slowly enters me, and a slow burn of pain crawls up my spine.

"I'm sorry. I'm trying to be gentle." He grits his jaw tight.

"This is perfect," I assure him even with my eyes squeezed shut and my breath held. If I tell him it hurts, he will stop.

"You're perfect and mine, always." His movements quicken, and the burn I felt before turns to white sparks. Need like I've never felt before blazes through me and I begin to move with him. I take what he is sharing: his love, devotion, everything, us, forever. My orgasm comes spiraling, surprising the hell out of me. Just as I let go, Griff falls with me. We fall together.

I'm so sore, but I also know I have him for a limited time. He gets up briefly to dispose of the condom and I watch the clench of his bare behind as he walks to the trash can next to my desk. Everything about him is perfect, from his heart to his muscular build, and when he turns around and smiles, my heart bursts a little further.

He climbs back into bed and I lie in his arms, sated, for I don't know how long. I roll on top of him and we begin to kiss. His arms wrap around me and with our naked bodies pressed together I feel him lengthening and that blazing need I felt before returns, but he doesn't initiate anything more.

"I want you again," I assure him.

"I don't want to hurt you," he sighs.

"You won't. I need you," I say.

He groans. "You don't know how much I want that."

"So have me. We don't get a lot of alone time together. We need to take advantage." I try to convince him. It isn't hard. He flips me on my back and his head dips down between my legs.

His tongue caresses my clit back and forth, and it doesn't take long for me to writhe beneath him. I begin to moan.

"I want to make you come like this but I am greedy." He stops and pulls the condom box off my side table. I watch him roll the condom over his length as my insides contract, and I feel bereft of his touch.

He rubs me with his fingers a little, spreading my wetness, and then he thrusts inside me and my eyes snap shut. His movements are hungry and both our bodies are coated in a sheen of sweat. My hips begin to move with his and my chin tilts back, and I come. The feeling is euphoric. Griff picks up his pace and stiffens inside me. I open my eyes and watch him come undone before me. I revel in the thought that I can make him completely come apart.

"How am I going to be without you until Easter?" He falls on the bed beside me, panting.

"I don't know." I can't imagine him leaving to go back to school. I want him more now than I did before. "Maybe I can come out there to visit for a weekend?"

He cocks a brow. It's my senior year and I've been working extra hard. Logan is his roommate; it was a far-fetched thought.

"I wish you could." He kisses the tip of my nose.

"I should get up." I sit and throw the blanket off me, and my eyes widen at the sight of blood between my legs.

Griff hisses beside me. "I'm sorry," he says.

"You have nothing to be sorry for," I answer fast. I don't want him going inside his head; he has a tendency of tearing himself down.

"Let me grab you a warm cloth," he says, and he climbs out of bed and heads into the washroom attached to my bedroom.

He returns with a warm cloth and slowly cleans off my thighs before cupping me between my legs. His touch is gentle, and the warm look in his eyes makes me fall even harder for him. "I hope I didn't hurt you. I feel bad for making you bleed."

"I'm pretty sure bleeding comes along with taking one's virginity and you shouldn't be sorry. Today was perfect." I lean forward and press a kiss to his lips.

"We should probably get these sheets in the wash," he says.

"Definitely." I don't want Mom coming home and finding them. I spring into action, throwing the pillows off my bed and gathering the sheets.

I put on the T-shirt I was wearing before and the pajama pants, and I saunter down the hallway to the laundry room. I start the machine right away.

When I return to my room, Griff has his clothes back on.

"I better get out of here. I hate to leave you but we both have these stupid smiles on our faces. I want to stay and say hi to your mom but she will know we had sex." Griff laughs, looking a lot more relaxed.

I walk over to the mirror in my room. He's right; my cheeks are a healthy pink and I'm grinning from ear to ear. "I look like I just got lucky." I giggle.

"I'm the lucky one, Jolie," he says, making my heart feel so full. He kisses the side of my neck and shivers roll down my spine. "When is your dad expected back?"

"I don't know the exact time. Mom said he was on a late flight, and he would be taking a cab home," I answer. It is only five in the afternoon. We have plenty of time. "Today was perfect."

"It was. I plan on having more perfect moments with you over break," he says, and we begin to kiss again and that sparks fire..

When my fingers thread through his hair, he pulls away. "I better go. If I kiss you like this a little longer, we are going to end up back in that bed, and I'll have you whimpering under me."

I want to tell him I'm too sore for a third round, but I don't want him feeling bad. Today was perfect.

I kiss him and slide my tongue in his mouth. He moans.

"I need to go. I have to leave." It is taking all of his willpower not to take me to bed again and that makes my ego soar.

"When will I see you?" I ask.

"Stevenson is throwing a party tomorrow night," he says. Mark Stevenson was on the football team with Logan and Griff. I'd heard he had stayed in town and went to Boston U. "I wish you could come with me," he says, rubbing his hands up and down my waist. "Your brother will be there."

"Will Jenn be there too?" I ask, trying to hide the bitter taste I feel on my tongue. Jenn gets to hang out with college guys and do fun things while I will be stuck at home watching some old nineties movie. If only my friends wanted to go to parties too.

"I'm guessing she might be," he says sympathetically.

"Why does she get to go and I don't? It isn't fair." I cross my arms over my chest, knowing I sound whiney but not caring.

"Logan expects her to get drunk and act like an ass. And if you're there, I will want to be with you. I don't have to go," he says.

"It's not like we can hang out anyway," I answer. "Dad will be home. He hasn't been home in a week. I'm sure he'll want to spend time with Mom," I say, even though that isn't always the case. Sometimes Dad is gone for a week or a few days, then comes home and spends most of his time in his office at the university. He and Mom don't have the most romantic of relationships.

"Maybe we should just tell Logan the truth about us," I suggest.

"What if he tells your dad?" Griff sounds terrified. "I don't want to think what would happen then."

Logan is Dad's clone. He looks like a young Chris Hemsworth. He also idolizes our father and wants to be a Harvard professor like him. Dad isn't home often but when he is, Logan tries to do everything to soak up his attention.

"You have a point. I don't know that my brother can be trusted." I grunt.

"I'll see you Christmas Eve. Your mom invited me over," he says apologetically. I know he wants to spend more time with me. Our situation sucks. "I should go. I hate to leave. I wish we didn't have to hide . . ."

"I know." I can read his nerves. If Dad comes home, this won't look good.

Dad doesn't like Griff hanging around me. He made that clear when he found Griff teaching me how to slow dance in our basement when I was in eighth grade. Griff had been a freshman and he was just a friend helping me out, but maybe we had always been more than friends and Dad saw it.

"I love you." Griff presses his lips to mine and closes his eyes like he's cherishing the moment. I close my eyes and enjoy his lips on mine.

"I love you," I answer. "Come, let's go eat something," I say, knowing Mom always has home-cooked food ready in the fridge. Griff grew up with an alcoholic father who did a shit job at taking care of him. He probably doesn't have food at home now, and being a student, he is on a tight budget.

We sit in the kitchen and I warm some of Mom's mac and cheese. The way he quickly eats tells me he is hungry. I hate knowing he hasn't eaten, and internally, I chide myself. I should have brought him to the kitchen before taking him to my room. He didn't even say anything, because he probably wanted to spend our alone time together in private. At least if someone comes home now, it won't look so bad.

When he finishes eating, I pack him a ham and cheese sandwich for later tonight and walk him to the door. We kiss and say goodbye. I am sure we will sneak more perfect moments over Christmas break.

Only we don't, because on Christmas Eve, when he is supposed to join us for our usual festive dinner, he doesn't show.

Logan gets a text saying Griff is back in Florida. Apparently he had applied for a job at Universal Studios and it came through early. He started work right away.

Griff doesn't answer my calls or the million text messages I send. He's vanished from my life and I don't understand why . . .

Chapter 1

Ten years later

"Hey, Jolie, how about we go to that hot new bar tonight? The client that was just here invited me, but it's not a date. I could really use you as my wingwoman." My best friend Michelle pushes out her lower lip.

"You know a hot new bar isn't my scene." I scrunch my nose at the mere thought of having to get dressed in some trendy outfit and wear high heels. The last time I was out was approximately three months ago, for my twenty-eighth birthday. Michelle and our other friends literally tricked me into going out with them.

"So the wingwoman argument isn't working?" Michelle's lips quirk on one side.

"Sorry, babe." I shake my head and smile. She's a good friend for trying to get me to go out, since I have a tendency of staying home all weekend. "I have fifteen minutes until my next client. I was going to grab a cup of coffee and snack. I'm exhausted. I got caught up in a really good book last night about a highlander pirate." I waggle my brows.

"Bleh. You and your books." She waves me off. While I like to read about happy ever after, Mich is out there trying to find hers. I think it's great but after everything I've been through, a book boyfriend is playing it safe, and I like safe.

A customer walks up to the front desk, a credit card in hand. Mich's disappointment with me transforms into her full-wattage smile. I'm thankful to be saved from one of her lectures on how I'm throwing all the good years of my life away by reading books and not living life. I don't see it that way.

I lived to the fullest. I married young. My husband was an NFL star who unexpectedly died too young. Now, I prefer to spend my time working as an aesthetician at a posh Manhattan spa. My job isn't the most fulfilling but it gives me a stable income.

After grabbing a quick coffee and power bar, I head back to my room to prep for my next client who has booked a one-hour massage.

I go through my routine of laying out fresh sheets and towels, and I light an aromatic lavender candle. My life is predictable and stress-free, just the way I like it.

"Mr. Reynolds is on his way to you." Mich's voice comes through the intercom speaker on the phone in my room.

I press the red button so that she can hear me talk. "Thanks Mich."

"He's so hot," she says with a long drawl. "Like seriously. Holy shit. It isn't fair you get to touch all that male hotness," she whispers, and I shake my head as a slow smile forms my lips.

Mich is twenty-nine and single. She moved to New York City five years ago from a small town in Nebraska. She wants to settle down with a man, but so far has had no luck finding someone suitable.

The spa has a strict policy about employees dating clients but Mich just likes to look and not touch, which explains why she is drooling over the client about to enter my room.

I press the red button again. "You're incorrigible and he'll be here any minute, so buzz off," I say playfully, and just as I release the red button, the door to my room opens and there stands Mr. Reynolds, all piercing blue eyes and muscles that go on for days.

With a towel wrapped around his torso, not much is left to the imagination. Mich is right. He's a hottie. As a single female who hasn't gotten laid in more than three years, my jaw should be dragging along the floor. My heartbeat should kick up a notch, and my woman parts should say, 'Hello there. Come to mama.' I should be flushed for sure- and I feel nothing.

"Hello, Mr. Reynolds, I'm Jolie. I have you booked in for a one-hour Swedish massage," I confirm then smile. Taking a step back, I allow him to climb on my table. His towel remains wrapped around his waist and I'm relieved, since some clients prefer to remove it. I usually don't mind because it's a part of my job, but Mr. Reynolds is a very handsome man. What if I do suddenly develop an attraction to him based on the feel of his tense muscles beneath my fingertips. Shit. That can't happen.

My thoughts make me anxious and I cough to clear my throat. "Excuse me," I say, and then I begin to work his neck and shoulders. "Let me know if you would like more or less pressure."

"That's perfect. He smiles, flashing perfect white teeth. My husband was also a handsome man but given he was a professional athlete, his teeth were far from perfect. It's been two years since he died. I wish my thoughts didn't somehow always lead to him but how could they not?

I nod and apply some heated lotion to my hands in order to warm them up. Starting at his shoulders, I try to release his tension with my fingertips.

"You have a good touch," he says, and for the next hour, I work on his tense muscles. He remains quiet and my own mind drifts to more mundane things, like the highlander book I am reading, what I will make for dinner tonight, and my cat Sasha. My quiet and simple life makes me content.

At the end of the hour, I realize he's fallen asleep.

"Mr. Reynolds," I whisper while wiping my hands on a towel.

His eyes flicker open and clear aquamarines stare at me causing me to startle. A color like his is rare and for a split second, they remind me of Griffin Campbell's, my first love.

My heart skips a beat. I take a deep cleansing breath. That's weird. I haven't thought about Griff in years. I try not to think of him at all. Logan is still in touch with him and he will sometimes mention him but I never ask. Even though my brother will just throw things out there, like the fact that Griff moved to LA or that he has some big job in Hollywood. Good for him. My family never knew we had a thing and after the way he left, I didn't want them thinking poorly of him even though I shouldn't have cared.

"Sorry about that." Mr. Reynolds smiles bashfully. Something about his looks are so similar to Griff it makes me feel uneasy. This has never happened before.

"Don't be. It means I did my job." I grin.

"You definitely did. I'd like to book with you again?"

"Sure."

He stands, rooted in his spot. This is the point where he is supposed to turn and leave only he isn't leaving. His brownish-colored brows bunch together.

My eyes sweep over his body. It's smooth and sculpted to perfection. Something resembling attraction sparks inside me. So what if he's my type. This is definitely not happening. I haven't been on a date since my husband passed. I'm not ready. Even the slight attraction I feel right now causes guilt to claw inside me.

"Can I ask you out?" he says shyly. It surprises me that a guy like him can be shy about anything. It makes me think that maybe he's a nice guy.

"I'm sorry. We aren't supposed to date our clients," I answer, figuring it's the easy way to let him down. He isn't the first person to ask me out at work, and other than with a few persistent guys, my excuse works like a charm.

"I can ask for someone else next time. That way I won't be your client," he suggests.

That's sweet of him. But my tattered heart is in too many pieces to even try to date. I have never been one for one-night stands so Mr. Handsome and I aren't happening.

"That's sweet, but I'm not available," I say carefully. This is my second line of defense.

"Okay, well maybe I'll see you around then and hopefully by then, you'll be available," he says and smiles, and a cute dimple pops on his cheek.

"You never know." I smile to keep things friendly. I still hope he'll leave me a tip on his way out, and I don't want to get in the way of that.

I'm not going to tell him that I don't think I will ever be emotionally available again, even though that's the truth. I'm happy living a simple single life. I have good friends and a cat who loves me, and that is all I can handle.

"You have a great day Mr. Reynolds," I chime.

"You too." He grins and leaves through the door.

I quickly prepare for my three o'clock. My cell buzzes in the front pocket of my pants. I usually don't answer the phone while working but a quick peek tells me it's Mom. Shoot. She knows not to call during the day.

I ignore the call and change the bedsheets, then warm the wax. My cell phone continues to buzz. It's a few minutes before three, so I quickly pick up the phone.

"Mom I'm just about . . ." I whisper when I hear a loud gasp.

"Oh dear," Mom cries. Her sadness seeps through the line and my heart sinks. *Oh no.*

"What happened? Are Logan and Jenn okay?" I ask frantically about my siblings.

"It's Kip," she croaks, referring to my stepdad.

"Mom what happened? Is Kip okay?" My heart beats too fast. I had a similar phone call when my husband died. The familiarity causes a cold sweat to break over my body as the memory of Mason's mom calling me, frantic over the phone, surfaces.

"He had a heart attack. He died. He was playing squash at the club and just fell. Didn't open his eyes again," Mom continues to weep and it feels like someone has speared me in the chest. Breath is sucked from me. Bitter memories of death surface in my mind as Mom sobs for her husband.

My client enters the room wearing a robe.

"OMG, are you okay? You look as white as a ghost," she asks. She is a twenty-something woman I wax on the regular. Her father owns some posh hotel chain, and she's a bit of a spoiled brat.

"My apology." I swipe at tears I didn't realize were falling. "I . . .uh." My brain isn't working enough to tell me what to do.

"You know what?" she says, sounding nasal. "I'll just come back another time." She points to the door behind her and turns on her heels and leaves the room.

Shit!

"Jolie, are you there?" Mom's voice breaks through my muffled thoughts.

"Sorry. What can I do? What should I do?" Gah! I feel like a helpless wreck. When did I become this much of a mess?

"I need you to come home. I have to plan a funeral," she cries some more. "I can't believe this is happening to me again," she bellows. Dad died unexpectedly in a car crash. We had all been sideswiped.

"I'm so, so sorry." I snap out of my daze. "I'll book a ticket. Do you have anyone with you?"

"Rick and Agnes are here at the hospital. They are going to take me home," she explains, and I'm relieved she's with friends.

"Okay." There isn't more to say.

I remember people telling me how sorry they were when Mason died. He had been a big star, and his death was all over the news. Nothing could comfort me back then.

I have to go to Mom. "I'll get there as soon as I can. You take care of yourself."

"Thanks, Jojo bear," she says, calling me by my childhood nick-name. And with that, she ends the call.

I tidy my room and shut off the wax warmer like I do at the end of a shift. I gather all the dirty linens and put them in a bin, and head for the reception to find Mich.

When she sees me, her brown eyes brighten. "How was Mister Tall, Dark and Handsome? Did you see the color of his eyes?" Her tone bleeds excitement until she really looks at me, and her face falls. "What happened? What's wrong?"

I swallow, rubbing the back of my neck, trying to keep my shit together. The waiting room is full of patrons. I walk behind the front desk and over to Mich, and whisper in her ear that there is a family emergency.

"I need to leave," I say.

"Okay. Take care of you," she answers, rubbing my shoulder.

"I also want to quit," I suddenly say, surprising even myself.

"Um, what?" Her brows furrow.

"I don't want to work here anymore," I say to her, since she is one of the managers of the spa which is owned by a hotel chain.

"Sweetie, why don't you go take care of your family thing? We can talk more about this another time," she says softly so no one can hear.

I blow out some air.

Hearing of Kip's death, so sudden, without warning, makes every synapses in my body fire on alert. My husband died without warning and my father did, too. It reminds me how unpredictable life is, and I don't want to spend another minute wasting mine or living a life I don't love. I may still be hurting from everything I've been through, but living a safe simple life isn't making me happy.

"Mich, I appreciate that you're letting me go, but I am telling you right now to find someone to fill my spot," I answer, because even though I hate to leave her hanging now, she needs to know she has to find a new aesthetician.

"You're in shock. It's understandable. Go take care of your family and we will talk soon," she says, but she is starting to look at me like I've lost it, and I begin to think maybe I have. Having to face so much death is draining and sad, and makes me want to curl up in a ball.

"I will call Heidi to come get you," she says, referring to one of our friends who works at a restaurant nearby.

"I'm okay," I assure her. "I'll head home and make arrangements to fly to Boston."

"Okay. Call me and let me know when you arrive," she says.

"Will do," I agree. I don't think she has taken my resignation seriously, but I need to leave.

My heart beats fast as I look out the cab window on the way to my apartment. Mom must be crushed.

Her and Dad had what I think of as a loveless marriage. It isn't something we openly speak of at home, but there were signs, like Dad working all the time. They didn't do couply things like some of my friends' parents, but they didn't fight either. My parents' marriage had solidified my thoughts about true love being nonexistent if people could fall so easily in and out of love. Love wasn't real.

Then Mom went and married Kip. I didn't spend much time with them, but I knew enough of their relationship to know Mom began to blossom and I began to believe again.

After Griff ripped my heart out and stomped on it, I'd begun to think that maybe what we'd shared wasn't love—maybe it was just lust or a bad crush. My entire senior year of high school had been spent reliving our last moments in my mind while barely trudging through school. Dad had been on my case about my grades, so I still tried to get on the honor roll. By spring, I had admittance to Harvard.

I'd stumbled upon Mason one night over spring break—or more like he stumbled upon me. We became quick friends. Then Dad died and I did a one-eighty. I applied to Brown and left with Mason the following September.

It took time for our love to sprout. It was different than what I had felt for Griff. It was rooted in mutual adoration and respect, and I'd thought it must be true love. But he didn't make me burn the way Griff did. Mine and Mason's chemistry wasn't scorching hot, but it was real, dependable. It was true love because what Griff and I shared wasn't, and so, in my young mind, it all made sense. Funny how death has caused old memories to surface.

I usually take the subway home from work because it's more cost efficient. This cab ride is going to cost me a nice buck.

The cabbie pulls up in front of my apartment building. I pay him and exit the car. In the elevator heading up to my apartment, I pull up Google. I quickly search for flight options.

Sasha greets me at the door, rubbing her face along my leg. She purrs as I pat her head. Leaving my front door open, I walk to see my neighbor, Mrs. Montgomery, two doors down. She is an elderly woman who is lovely to talk to, and she loves Sasha. Her own cat died last year, and when I need to head out of town, she's always up for babysitting her.

Sasha follows me, and I knock on her door. She doesn't leave me waiting.

"Jolie." She smiles. Her long white hair is twisted in a bun at the back of her head. "I just made some fresh banana bread. Can I offer you a slice?"

"I would love to but I'm kind of in a bind." My nose scrunches. "I need to head back to Boston. My stepdad passed away unexpectedly."

She gasps, palming her heart. "Oh dear. That's terrible. Do you need me to watch little Sasha?" She speaks of Sasha like she is a little baby, and I love that.

"Please. I don't know how long I'll be gone. My mom needs me. I just bought a large bag of food so she should be good for a few weeks," I explain. "If I'll be gone longer, I can order more and have it shipped."

"Of course, but how long do you plan on heading out of town for? I mean, I don't mind taking care of Sasha, but don't you need to get back here for your job?" She raises her brows.

I may have mentioned to her how I left for Brown with Mason on a whim decision when Dad died, and I left Texas on a whim decision when Mason died.

But this isn't the same thing. Kip and I weren't close and . . . I'm doing it again. I'm running.

"I quit my job," I mumble, because she is onto me. She can see I am running and now, through her wise eyes, I see it too. I still don't want to talk about it right now.

"I thought you liked that job," she persists, sounding like a concerned mom.

"I did." My voice rises a few octaves too high. "I can't explain now, but I will. My mom is on her own, and she sounds like she is a mess. I need to go to her."

"Okay, dear, but think hard on it and consider your options

before making rash decisions. You've been happy here, and don't worry about little Sasha. She will be well taken care of."

I lean in for one of Mrs. Montgomery's hugs. The woman hugs with her whole heart, wrapping her arms around me firmly while rubbing my back in an assuring way. Her hug manages to make the loneliness I feel dissipate for a short time while instilling strength in me.

"You'll be just fine, Jolie. You are one of the strongest people I know," she says and I want to believe those words because she is wise and has so much life experience. "You may be crazy for quitting that job. It paid well, but you're resourceful. You'll figure something out."

Her confidence in me makes my heart warm. There is a reason I am quitting my job. I want to follow my dreams and even though it's a rash decision, my dreams were made when I was a little girl. I just put them on hold, and hearing about Kip's death reminds me that life is too short. The time has come to do something for me. Mrs. Montgomery's right; I will figure out a way.

"Thank you, and that's the plan," I finally pull out of her embrace and give Sasha's head one last rub. I swear it's as if she knows I'm leaving her.

I speed walk back to my apartment and pull my suitcase out of the main closet. The last time I used it was a year ago when I went for a girls' weekend with my friends to the Hamptons.

I open my suitcase on my bed and begin to dump my summer clothes inside, along with all my bras and underwear. There is no way I would ever want to move back to Cambridge, Massachusetts. The town holds too many memories of my childhood. Too many good times I spent with Griffin Campbell. Even now, a whole decade since he walked away, I can't wrap my head around why he would leave me the way he did. It was so cold and callous. Something I didn't believe he was capable of, but then again, I may have just been a bad judge of character.

This trip home isn't going to be easy. That's the reason I've stayed away.

With my bags packed, I call the airline. It takes forever to be passed through to an operator. When I finally get through, the news isn't favorable. All flights are booked. The representative recommends heading out to the airport and trying to get a standby seat.

I change out of my work uniform and throw on a pair of jeans, a white T-shirt, and my yellow chucks. I don't have time to shower because I could be missing an opportunity to catch a flight, and I am anxious to get to Mom. I still smell of the lavender oil that I used on Mr. Reynolds. Hopefully it isn't too strong, I barely notice it anymore.

I cab to the airport and head inside. A loud yawn escapes me, and I look to my cell to see it's five o'clock in the evening. My eyes tear up. I start my day by jogging the streets at six a.m. By this time of day, when I usually leave work, I'm ready to pass out. I need coffee or maybe an extended nap.

A coffee stand catches my attention, and I dash straight toward it. Standing in line and having to wait for caffeine is a nuisance but it is also my top priority.

My eyes feel as if they will lull shut. The emotional weight of all the stress is causing me to crash.

I people watch as I wait my turn. My gaze lands on a tall man who reminds me of Griffin. I haven't thought about him in so long —I don't know why today, of all days, my mind is playing tricks on me. Maybe it's because I am heading home for the first time in years.

While waiting for my coffee to be made, I watch the tall man talking on the phone. He's dressed to the nines in a three-piece suit. Griffin was always the laidback type, but he was also a student back then.

Geez, I really have to stop thinking about him. He's part of my past I've worked hard to forget. Going home now is about Mom, not me facing old demons.

The man turns around and his eyes search around and lock on mine. Air is sucked from my lungs as the most piercing blue eyes I've ever seen take me in. He's just as shocked as me. His head tilts to the side and he blinks too many times. My heart begins to hammer in my chest.

This. Can. Not. Be. Happening . . .

I'm not ready. I pull my gaze and completely ignore him like I would a stranger. After not seeing him for ten years, that is what he is to me—a stranger.

Chapter 2

Griffin

When Kathy Bryant calls, you drop everything and answer. I'm pretty damn sure she is a saint, calling me still at least once a week to check in even if I haven't been back to Boston in a very long time.

That's why when my cell rings just after four in the afternoon, I answer. I had been taking a nap after a tiring meeting with a producer this morning. We are going to be meeting for a business dinner this evening, and I just needed a power nap to recharge.

"Dear." Her voice trembles.

"What is it, Kathy . . . I mean, Mrs. Armstrong? Are you okay?" She changed her last name when she married her second husband after Mr. Bryant died in a car accident.

"I . . . no . . ." she murmurs, scaring me. She is the only mother I have a clear memory of.

She accepted me, despite strong objections from her late husband, who believed I was a bad apple and shouldn't hang around their kids.

The Bryants had been my substitute family since my father

married the bottle when Mom left. The Bryants may not have been a picture-perfect family, but they were all I had.

"What's going on? Take a deep breath," I urge. My heart ricochets in my chest.

"Kip . . . he . . . Kip . . . I'm still at the hospital," she mutters. Kipton Armstrong was a knight in shining armor. He had been best friends with Mr. Bryant, and after Mr. Bryant died, he became a shoulder for Kathy to lean on. I didn't know the man personally because I left Boston before they got together, but he always sent his regards to me by phone, and Kathy always told me great stories about him.

"Is he okay?" I croak.

"No . . ." She pauses. "He died. Heart attack. Was playing squash at the club and just fell. He's gone, Griff," she cries into the phone, and I spring out of the hotel bed. I swoop into action, and head straight for the three-piece suit I have hanging in the closet.

"I'm so, so, sorry." I stop, staring into the darkness, not knowing what else to say. "I'm coming to Boston. I'll be there soon." I rub at my eyes. What a fucking disaster. I haven't been back to Boston in years. I never planned on heading home. Ever. Why did I offer to go back now? My mind is spinning but the answer is clear. Kathy needs me, and she's the only family I've got.

"Thanks, dear. I do appreciate that," she whimpers.

"Of course." I'd give her my left arm if she needed it. The woman kept me alive as a child. I wouldn't be where I am today without her.

Dressed in my suit, I leave the luxury hotel suite behind. My head is foggy and my heart is hurting. It's not going to be easy to go back home. Memories of the place are cloaked in me trying to survive my childhood. Even with all the good times with the Bryants, I'd rather have the past remain buried.

In the back seat of the limousine, my finger hovers above Logan's name. Kipton had been a hard pill for him to swallow, with him being his deceased father's best friend. When Kathy announced her engagement to Kipton, Logan had been furious.

Kathy had married him in a private ceremony to save the heartbreak of her children. None of us have been back to Boston since. I only know that because on one of the many phone calls I've had with Kathy, she let it slip that no one's returned home. She didn't say it but I can tell it breaks her heart. Now I need to be there for Kathy like she was for me. Only it's easier said than done.

My chest feels tight. Even after years of therapy, my father's cruel words and Mr. Bryant's clear disdain feel like an open wound. Fuck. My stomach turns when I think of how long it took me to understand what it meant when Kathy scolded Mr. Bryant about not keeping his pants zipped. By the time I got to high school, the meaning clicked. He had been too friendly with his female students at the university. Crazy thing is, their kids never caught on. They lived in blissful oblivion.

I'd envied the Bryant kids because they were sheltered. The only thing they weren't sheltered from was me, according to Mr. Bryant. I was the dirty poor boy who wouldn't amount to anything.

How wrong he had been.

Chapter 3

Jolie

Past

"Hey Griff, I need your help with something," I whisper, not wanting Logan or Jenn to hear my problem. Griff has always been more understanding than Logan.

He peeks his head out of the fridge. "Your mom made mac and cheese. You think she would mind if I had some?"

My stomach twists when he asks for food. I've overheard conversations between Mom and Logan about Griff being hungry, not having enough to eat at home.

"You know you don't need permission. Mama said to help yourself whenever." I frown.

He has started to get really tall, and he is looking thin. I know the only reason he is asking was because Dad makes him feel unwelcome.

Griff pulls the tray of mac and cheese from the fridge.

"Just heat all of it. I'm starving," I say, which buys me a wide smile. A smile that makes his aquamarine eyes twinkle and my belly do flips.

We sit together and devour our meal quietly.

"What's bothering you, Jojo?" He pauses mid-bite.

"I . . . uh . . . need some help with something," I mutter.

"Sure. Name it." Griff is always so helpful.

"You promise you won't laugh?" I cringe.

He gives me a look that says, 'Come on.' I know he won't laugh. Even though he is Logan's best friend, he and I are secret friends too.

"There's a dance party at Kate's house Saturday night. Tatum said there will be slow dancing, and I don't know how to do that." I say too quickly. I am sure my cheeks look like two bright red apples.

"Why would I want to teach you how to dance with other boys?" He gives me an incredulous look.

"So, I won't look like an idiot." I raise my brows, thinking the answer is obvious.

His eyes narrow on me. He goes back to eating, and so do I.

When we are done, he motions for me to follow him. Logan is up in his room. He is talking on the phone—I can tell by his show-off tone that he is talking to a girl.

I follow Griff to the basement where we have a CD player with all of Dad's favorite CDs. Griff is into music. He likes to sneak down here and listen when Dad isn't around.

Griff pops a CD in the machine and a slow song starts. The singer's voice is low and scratchy.

"Put your hands on my shoulders," he says.

I do what he tells me. He is only a couple inches taller than me even though he is a freshman and I am in eighth grade.

I wait. For some reason, he looks nervous.

"I'm going to put my hands on your hips," he warns me.

I laugh. "'Kay."

I pull my lips straight when I realize the moment isn't a funny one.

"Now, you move to the music."

We begin to move.

"I like this song," I say, grinning from cheek to cheek. Griff is so cute. Adorable, nice funny. My heart beats funnily.

"It's Eric Clapton's 'Stairway to Heaven.'" He grins.

I want to say that I feel like I am in heaven but hold my tongue. We continue to dance, and Griff moves in closer and my head presses to his chest.

"IT'S A LONG SONG," he says. That makes my insides warm, I don't want this moment to end.

The basement door swings open, and I flinch, moving away from Griff. I squint. The sound of heavy footsteps causes my heart to pound. Daddy comes into view. My happy heart grows fearful as I see the angry look on Daddy's face. I wonder if he's seen us dancing.

"Did you just have hands on my daughter?" Daddy snarls.

"Daddy, it was my fault. I asked Griff to . . ." I try to explain but Daddy's nose flares, his eyes wild and angry. It is like he doesn't see me there—only Griff.

"Hush now." He returns his attention back to Griff. "You do not ever put your hands on my daughter again. Do you understand me, boy?"

He stares him in the eyes and Griff bows his head.

"This girl here is royalty, cream of the crop, and you are rotten fruit. Are you getting what I'm saying? Those two things don't mix in the same bowl. For crying out loud. Where is your mama?" Daddy spins around and looks me in the eyes. His are filled with disappointment. What he doesn't know is that I am disappointed in him. I don't know why he is so cruel to Griff, but Griff doesn't deserve it. I love Daddy, but sometimes, I don't really like him.

"Sorry sir," Griff murmurs, his head remaining bowed. "I'll leave," he says, heading for the stairs.

"No," I cry out, taking a sharp step forward.

"You let him go, Jojo bear. Trust me; it's for the best."

Griff goes home that night. He comes back the next day and stays over. Daddy was out till late. I begin to like it more and more when Daddy doesn't come home, because then I get Griff, and he is sweet like sugar.

Chapter 4

Jolie

Present

A rush of adrenaline has me awake and alert. I spin around and head for the airline booth.

"Hey, wait up," Griff calls from behind me.

He can't seriously be following me, can he? This day keeps getting worse and worse.

I ignore him and head to the airline booth, but with coffee in hand, a purse on my shoulder, and a medium-sized suitcase rolling behind me, I'm not as fast as I would like to be.

"Jolie, wait." The way he says my name pierces me in the chest. My heart is beating fast as sweat pops on my forehead.

I make it to the American Airlines booth and walk up to the attendant. "Hi, I would like one standby ticket for Boston Logan please?" I smile and dig into my purse for my credit card.

"Sure, let me check that for you." The lady smiles at me when I feel a presence looming behind me. The attendant lifts her head and grins. "There's a flight leaving in forty minutes."

"Jolie, please," Griff says, his blue eyes pleading. Last time I saw him, he was a boy. Now, he looks like a sophisticated man, and it has me on edge.

"W-what do you want?" I ask. I haven't seen him for ten years. He's stayed in touch with my mother and my brother, for goodness sake. He could have found me at any time. Why is he stalking me in the airport?

"I'm heading back to Boston too," he says, surprising me.

"M-mom called you?" Geez! Why can't I speak?

"Yes. I'm heading home for the funeral," he says, and he watches me.

This is just great. I wasn't expecting Griff to be called home. I mean, he obviously didn't show for my husband's funeral, so why now? He didn't even know Kip.

"Um, miss." The airline attendant pulls my attention from Griff. "You'd have to clear security and make it in time to board in about thirty minutes. I need you to give me an answer now," she says. Griff still stands beside me. Can't he fly a different airline? What is he doing in New York? I thought he lived in LA.

"Thank you. I'll take it." I pass my credit card.

"One second . . . I'm sorry." She frowns. "There are only two business-class tickets left."

"We'll take them." Griff extends his hand with a credit card. Is he using me to cut the line now? This is not happening.

"Uh! No thank you." I make a decent living, but not one that can afford me a seat in business class.

Griff watches me with his brow cocked. Logan mentioned he was some Hollywood big shot. His expensive tailored suit and Italian-looking shoes and briefcase scream wealth.

"I got this, Jojo." He winks, calling me by the nickname my brother and he used for me as a child.

"You're not paying for my ticket, Griffin Campbell," I shoot back. "And there is no way in hell you're calling me Jojo." Only my family calls me that.

I cross my arms in front of me. When I turn my attention back to the lady behind the counter, she's fighting a smile, and batting her lashes at Griff. He looks like he just stepped off of a movie set. He's perfectly groomed, and his chocolate-brown hair is mussed enough to look sexy and not messy.

"Can you please find me one economy ticket? I don't care if I have to sit at the back of the plane. There has been a death in my family, and it is important that I make it home as fast as possible," I say with an assured nod. *I also want to sit as far away from this man as humanly possible.*

My heart beats fast from having Griff this close. He's familiar in some ways and a stranger in others. Still, I need to keep my cool. I'm not going to let him ruffle my feathers even though my insides feel very much in turmoil. I'm supposed to hate him after the way he left and didn't look back, but there is a tenderness in his stare, and he looks so good it's confusing.

"One second, ma'am." The airline attendant types away. "I have a ticket and yes . . . it is at the back of the plane." She smiles wide. Great I'll be smelling the bathroom the whole way to Boston.

"Don't be stubborn. Besides, I could use the company." Griff's smile is easy and welcoming, like an old friend. *He ripped your heart out, Jolie. Don't sympathize with the enemy.*

"One economy please." I set my coffee on the counter and pass the lady my credit card, and she sets me up with a seat. With my boarding pass and coffee in hand, I stalk off without so much as a sideways glance at Griff. I know I will have to face him at Mom's, but that's a couple hours away.

I walk quickly toward security, and I'm relieved to see only a small lineup. My body screams from exhaustion. My earlier rush of adrenaline has caused me to crash again and my eyelids grow heavy. All I want is to do is sleep the whole hour-and-fifteen-minute flight and not think of him.

As I sit back in my seat, I take a deep, cleansing breath, allowing my head to rest against the headrest. I close my eyes.

"Pardon me, excuse me . . . pardon me . . ."

That voice. It grows closer. I crack one eye open.

Fuck no.

Griff places his briefcase in the overhead bin.

"I've got the aisle seat." He winks.

"You gave up on first class to sit back here?" I ask, flabbergasted. His lips tilt ever so slightly. His aquamarine eyes, clear as the Caribbean Sea, see through me. No matter what happens between us, this man who was once a boy has somehow imprinted himself on my heart.

I sigh, defeated. "Fine. I'm not talking to you."

An uncontrollable, loud yawn escapes me, and I clap a hand over my mouth.

His smile is slow and spreads his cheeks. "You're adorable, Jojo bear."

They are the last words I expect to hear, yet I'm too tired to deal with him. Instead, I allow my eyes to drift closed.

Chapter 5

Griffin

I am freaking the fuck out. What were the chances we'd arrive at the airport at the same time?

I haven't had any time to think this through. I should have known I would see her eventually . . .

This is fine.

I will head back to Boston, show Kathy my support, and fly back to LA.

No complications.

Fuck.

Who am I kidding?

I shift in my seat and swipe a hand over my mouth, looking down at the only girl I've ever loved. When I asked the attendant at the sales desk if she could offer the person sitting next to Jolie an all-expenses-paid business-class seat, she was hesitant. But I had to sit next to Jolie, no matter the cost. We need to talk.

Thankfully, the attendant finally agreed. Only I hadn't banked on Jolie falling asleep that fast. I've never seen someone fall asleep on a plane so quickly. We haven't even taken off.

Why does she have to still be so beautiful?

This is a mess. My life is complicated. I just need to know that she will be cool around her mom and Logan. I don't need her blurting out anything about the past while we stay under the same roof. I mean, why would she, really? I've spoken with Kathy and Logan a lot over the years, and they've never dropped so much as a hint about anything that has to do with me and Jolie or me screwing Jolie over. My anxiety is clearly unwarranted, which means I just scored a seat beside her because I want to be next to her.

No! That can't be right.

After all this time, I won't be thinking of her in that way. Just because she is the kindest most beautiful girl . . . I pause to stare at her. She's a woman now. A feisty, stunning woman. *Jesus!*

I take a deep breath. She fell in love and married another man. I have to remind myself because my emotions are suddenly in a fucking tailspin.

Panic.

I'm fucking panicking.

I close my eyes and try for slow, deep breaths. I can do this. I can go to Boston and support Kathy through a funeral, then head back to LA. Piece of fucking cake. *Not.*

I turn my head and watch her sleep. Watch her breathe. Slow breaths. Her chest rising and falling.

I take in the contours of her face. High cheekbones, golden skin, beautiful brown hair. How do you shut love off? I can't. It's been a decade since I've seen her and still my heart beats for this woman. Why did I stay away so long?

I tried to cleanse her from my system years ago and now, with one meeting, all my hard work trying to forget her has been erased. All. I. See. Is. Her.

Problem is, I broke her heart and mine. She won't look at me now. When I finally wanted to come back for her, she was dating a football jock who she ended up marrying. There was no point sharing my reasons for leaving when she'd already given her heart to another man. Besides, for many years I bought her father's bullshit and believed I wasn't good enough.

My body is wound tight as my past collides with my present. Returning home isn't easy. I told myself that this would be a quick trip, but who am I kidding?

I open my laptop and draft an email to my assistant, Annette.

To: AnnetteThompson@GCworldstudios.com

Heading to Boston for family funeral. Had to cancel dinner with Patrick Wild in NYC. Please reschedule any appointments from Wednesday onward. I feel bad asking, but can you please go to my place and pack me a suitcase of casual clothes? I mean jeans, T-shirts and shorts, not LA casual.

Thanks, Annette.

I will be in touch again soon with the address to send the suitcase.

Griff

I press *send*.

My cell rings. Annette's name lights up the screen, and I can only imagine she is ready to cuss me out. We have a big week at work and meetings with new producers who are potential clients. My phone buzzes and buzzes but I don't answer.

Annette is not only my assistant but my best friend. Telling her I left New York for Boston will make her ask a million questions I can't answer, especially with Jolie passed out beside me. And then there is explaining this mother of a fluke that I am on the same plane as Jolie and heading back home.

The phone continues to buzz and the pilot comes on the intercom. We are getting ready to take off. I take a few cleansing breaths and power off my phone.

What the fuck do I do about Jolie? She is so beautiful. So perfect. I watch her sleep and remember a time I wished to have just one more chance with her. When she married, I gave up all hope, and when her husband died, I felt bad, but I didn't want to see her. I wasn't going to be anyone's second choice. The way I feel right now is unexpected, to say the least. I have been through years of therapy. I have my shit together. I'm happy with my life in LA. I have a beautiful home in Beverly Hills, and good friends, and that's all I need.

I look down at a sleeping Jojo. If being around her for less than an hour has me feeling this way, I'm in bigger trouble than I thought.

Chapter 6

Jolie

Past

Spring is my favorite season, signaling new life and beginnings. The trees and flowers blossom anew. The air is sweet and dewy from the rain, which gives life to all the blooming greens in Mom's garden. Tonight, Mom and Dad went out for dinner. A rarity around here. Jenn is also out somewhere, and Logan is over at a friend's house, which means Griff and I are alone. This doesn't happen ever, and I'm more than excited. Mom left a note saying we should warm the meatloaf, one of my favorite dishes.

"Do you want to eat out back?" Griff asks, taking the warm platter of meatloaf from the oven. He's already a senior. He's been taller than me for a while, but recently his shoulders have broadened, his jaw looks more chiseled, and his chin and jawline are speckled with hair. He looks deliciously handsome tonight in an old grey T-shirt and worn-in pair of jeans.

What started as an innocent crush for me has grown into so much more. My heart beats fast every time he's near. My cheeks flush, and my body buzzes from his closeness. I've always liked him, but recently, something has started to change. A fire in me sparks at just the thought of him.

"Squirt." He waves his hand in my face, using a nickname that only my brother tends to use.

Shoot. *Was I staring?*

How embarrassing.

"Yeah, it's perfect weather. I could use some fresh air." To cool me down.

I smile, trying to hide my attraction. I'm pretty sure my blush gives me away. He smiles back, and then his brows draw together. What must he be thinking? That I'm a silly teenage girl with a crush? We've known each other too long for me to be blushing.

He takes the meatloaf platter outside, and I follow with mashed potatoes, a set of plates, and cutlery. We've shared many meals together over the years, but my family is usually around. Tonight is different. I think it's because we are alone.

"Your dad would just love to know it's only me and you for dinner," he scoffs, a pained laugh escaping him.

"How many times do I have to tell you not to pay him any attention? I don't know why after all these years he can't drop it. I want to say he's being protective. I love my dad but he's an ass when it comes to you," I say, looking in Griff's eyes, knowing how my dad's lack of acceptance is a sore spot for him.

"Whatever." He waves it off. "Let's eat. I want to enjoy this time with you while I have it." His lips twist, and he looks me in the eyes. His aquamarine eyes are so clear, I squirm like I usually do when he looks at me this way.

He smiles wryly. "Do you want some meatloaf?" he asks, ready to serve me.

I rip my gaze from his gorgeous smile and wide shoulders and swallow. "You know it's my favorite."

"Mine too," he agrees.

We sit in comfortable silence, enjoying our food. I don't feel the need to talk as I breathe in the fresh spring air. Mom designed our backyard with a stone patio surrounded by flowers and plants. Now, the flowers are in bloom, giving the air a sweet smell. Little tea lights hang above us providing a romantic glow. It's a perfect night. I stare at his lips and wonder what it would be like to kiss him. To have his hard body pressed to mine. Having him here alone, eating a romantic meal while the sunset provides a perfect glow in the sky, feels magical.

"It's a nice night. I'm glad we got a chance to eat together," he says with that deep voice of his. He looks up for a brief moment and our eyes meet. That electric buzz I constantly feel around him returns.

He must feel it too.

He's looking at me expectantly. What did he just say? He's happy we get time alone together? Jeez. Remember to answer the boy. "Me too." I can't pull my gaze away from his. I'm feeling mesmerized. Tonight is different. He *is being different.*

"Yeah?" His brows raise and his eyes twinkle with an excitement. He's looking at me like maybe our dinner for two is more than a friendly event.

Something in his glare causes a jolt of bravery to zip through me. Before I can think too hard, I find myself on my feet, closing the distance between us. He leans back in his chair, watching me like I'm a goddess, and he doesn't know what to expect. We've always been so comfortable with each other. I take a seat in his lap.

"Jolie." His deep voice cracks, and his cheeks flush.

"Griff." My voice is shaky.

He swallows hard while saliva pools in my mouth and my heartbeat quickens. He doesn't miss a beat, wrapping his arms around my waist. His hands on my body cause a flush of heat to flow through me.

"What . . . happens now?" he asks, and I know it's out of respect for me. He doesn't want to do something I'm not ready for. His throat bobs and I see it in his eyes. He wants me as much as I want him. We've been building up to this for years.

"I kiss you," I say breathlessly, looking into eyes that suck the air out of my lungs.

"Is that so?" he answers, sounding intrigued.

I slowly move in, pressing my lips to his. I'm an amateur, a girl who at age seventeen has never been kissed. I've saved my first kiss for Griffin Campbell.

Relief washes through me as he springs into action. His tongue coaxes my lips open. My lower lip drops, allowing his tongue entrance, and liquid heat moves through me, settling between my thighs, causing a throb. My heart beats erratically as the kiss intensifies. Our frenzied tongues move together in a hungry dance. Heat continues to surge through my body from head to toe, and that burning pulse between my thighs grabs my attention once more. My hands stay on his shoulders. His hands move up and down my back. My body feels like it's burning, and this average spring night suddenly feels too hot.

I shift so I can straddle him, and that's when I feel something long and stiff sitting between my thighs. My eyes pop open. The kiss stops abruptly. Griff must feel my apprehension because his eyes open wide as he looks to me with alarm.

"I'm sorry," he apologizes, moving his hands in the air like he's surrendering. The chair jerks back.

"For what? Giving me the best first kiss ever?" I grin, enjoying the feel of my swollen lips and preening over the thought that it was Griff who made them this way.

He looks frozen as he says, "I just gave you your first kiss?"

He shifts me off his lap, stands, and paces nervously.

I walk over to him, getting in his face. "What's gotten into you?" Anger flares inside me because I can't read him. If I'm not mistaken, he looks regretful.

He pauses, staring at me, and that's when I see he's filled with fear not regret. "Your dad is going to kill me. I'll never see you again."

His fear makes my stomach roil. I hate that Daddy has to be brought into this perfectly memorable moment.

I take Griff's hand in mine. "I don't plan on telling him about this and honestly, I've wanted that kiss for some time now," I confess.

He looks me in the eyes and swallows. "I know. I've been burning to kiss you too."

"Really? Why haven't you tried to kiss me then?" I'm offended. "I notice the way you look at me," I say, wanting to bite my own tongue.

"I'm not going to deny it," he says taking a step toward me again and capturing my lips with his.

Oh! He tastes so good. My head tilts up and I run my hands down his back. He groans into my mouth, pulling my hips into him. I moan too, taking what I can. We kiss until we are both panting. Until my body feels like it will combust if he doesn't touch me more. Problem is, he keeps his lips on mine and his hands respectfully at my waist even when I push for more.

"This will be our little secret," I say as our kiss slows and our heavy breaths mingle.

"Our secret," he agrees.

"I want this to happen again, a lot." I laugh, whispering against his warm lips.

He presses his forehead to mine. "Me too, squirt."

"You can't call me that anymore," I chide him. It's so unsexy.

He chuckles. "Okay, Jojo." He continues to brush his lips to mine and groans. "I've wanted this a long time. I was waiting on you to grow up," he says, and my chest warms knowing I read him right —we both want this.

"I was ready for a first kiss like two years ago." I snicker. I'm probably the only junior at my school who hasn't been kissed.

His light eyes darken as a wave of pain crosses his face. "I wasn't going to make the first move. We shouldn't be doing this at all. I . . ." He looks away.

My heart cracks. "Don't you dare say another word, Griffin Campbell. That was the best first kiss a girl could ask for. I will never let anyone but you kiss me." My finger presses to his lips. His forehead creases. I know there are parts of Griff that are hurting, that are beyond me to heal, but I also knew he holds a smile just for me.

"We have to be careful. If your dad ever found out . . ." His words trail off, and I know the meaning of his warning.

"We'll be careful," I assure him, even though my insides shudder at the thought of Daddy ever finding out. He hates Griff, and it makes my heart hurt.

———

Present

Shake. Shake.

I'm jolted from sleep.

"What?" My eyes open and my heart drops. I've fallen asleep on Griff's shoulder. "Sorry."

"Turbulence. There's a storm over Boston. Pilot says we're going to have a rough patch now," Griff explains calmly. I, on the other hand, am not so calm. It makes me nervous not being in control and turbulence just escalates my anxiety.

"Everything will be fine. You're safe." Griff pinches his lips together. It reminds me of all the times he's made me feel safe.

And then he left. Disappeared from my life, gutted my heart, and left me feeling empty.

I nod and straighten out, holding my breath as the plane bounces. My bladder is full from the large coffee I drank but I'm too scared to get up and use the restroom. Besides the seat-belt sign is lit. Instead, I squeeze my eyes shut and pray. I find it's the only thing that soothes me in these circumstances.

Griff touches my hand and I flinch. "I just want to comfort you. It was a natural response," he says, and his words cut deep. He stares into my eyes and a slight fissure runs through my heart.

"Don't, okay?" I can barely speak with the anxiety of turbulence and the emotions he stirs inside me.

"Okay," he says, and turns away. He looks straight ahead to something playing on the screen in front of him.

I wonder why he's finally decided to return home. He didn't come back when my husband died two years ago, or when Mom married Kip. I didn't invite him to my wedding. I'd made amends with never seeing him again. I'd found a way to move on but now, sitting here beside him causes all those fiery emotions to rise inside me like a tidal wave. I've only ever felt this way about him.

It doesn't matter. I will head home for a few days. Focus on Mom. Spend time with my brother and sister, who I barely see, and head back to New York City. I have nothing to offer Griffin Campbell so he can stop looking at me with such longing, because if I thought I was broken when he left me, I was very wrong.

My husband shredded whatever was left of my trust and heart.

Chapter 7

Jolie

"Would you just get in the cab?" Griff waves me in, huffing out a heavy breath. He clearly doesn't understand that I don't want to be near him.

I tilt my chin up and walk away, rolling my suitcase behind me.

"You do realize how ridiculous it is to pay for two cabs when we are going to the same place?" he shouts after me.

Outside, the airport terminal is flooded with cabs and limousines. I don't answer him as I walk up to a cab parked in front of the one Griff is about to take. I tell the driver where I am headed. He agrees to take me and pops his trunk.

As I place my suitcase in the trunk, Griff walks up to me and places his suitcase and briefcase in the trunk too. "This is my cab," I say pushing out my lower lip, knowing I sound like a pouty child but I can't help it.

"Yes, and we are sharing it." He winks, closes the trunk, and walks over to the driver's side of the backseat. I blow out a puff of air. Just great. He clearly doesn't understand that I don't want to be anywhere near him.

THE TRUTH ABOUT US

I enter the cab on the passenger side of the back seat. I close my door, cross my arms over my chest, and look out the window.

The driver pulls into traffic and we are off to see Mom. I quickly shoot her a text that I have landed and am on my way. It shows up as read but she doesn't respond. It makes me worry. I hope she's holding up okay.

"You will need to talk to me eventually," Griff says from his seat beside me. A quick side glance gives me a view of his long muscular legs in that perfectly tailored suit he's wearing. His knees are touching the front seat; he's so tall. He shifts and I feel his stare burning into me. "Jolie, your mother doesn't know what happened between us, I'm guessing. I'd prefer to keep it that way," he says.

His words ignite the flame that was already burning inside me. "Are you freaking kidding me? You are worried about me telling Mom now? She just lost her husband. Revealing to her that you're a grade-A asshole would only break her heart further."

"Well, good. I'm glad we are on the same page. I came back here to support Kathy too," he says.

"How thoughtful of you." My tone bleeds sarcasm even though I don't mean it. It's nice of him to show up for Mom but after the way he screwed me over and didn't look back, I'm wary about any of his intentions.

The driver pulls onto the freeway and I pray that Griff will just stop talking. He does, which gives me time to think. I need to at least be cordial to him in front of Mom. I don't want to be sending any red flags.

Every few minutes I notice that he turns my way and just watches me. I can see him doing it from my peripheral vision and it makes me uneasy. Why is he just staring?

I'm grateful when the driver pulls up in front of Mom's house. I reach into my purse for money but Griff beats me to it and pays.

"I've got it." He gives me a smile that reaches his aquamarine eyes, and my stomach sinks, because why does he have to be so good-looking?

"Thank you," I answer curtly and leave the cab.

Griff meets me around the back of the cab and lifts my suitcase out of the trunk first. I take it and walk up the driveway to the front door.

I ring once and wait. Griff comes up beside me with his suitcase. I can't believe this is happening. Us being here together. My parents' house holds so many memories, good and bad.

"Do you have a key?" he asks, when it's clear no one is coming to open the door.

"No." I haven't been back since my husband's funeral and before that, it had been years. Why would I have a key?

Griff rings the bell twice and we wait. I don't know where I will go if Mom isn't home. It's not like I stayed in touch with anyone after I left.

The door swings open and Mom stands in her robe. The dark strands of her hair look unruly and she has clearly been crying.

"Oh Mom." I lunge into her arms and hug her tight.

"Jolie," she whimpers.

"Kathy." Griff steps into the house, and Mom releases me and gives him a hug that is just as fierce as the one she gave me.

"I'm so happy you both could make it," she says to Griff and me. Her brows furrow. "Wait. Did you two arrive at the same time?" She looks between me and Griff.

"Craziest thing. Griff was on a business trip in New York and we both got standby seats on the same flight," I explain, my voice too cheery. I hope I don't come across as unhinged as I feel right now because a part of me wants to get in Griff's face and make him tell me how he could be so heartless and cruel.

"That's a real coincidence." Mom uses the tip of her finger to dab at her eyes. "Why don't you two get settled in upstairs? I will turn the kettle on." She turns toward the kitchen.

Griff and I both take off toward the staircase. As I take the first step, so does he, only there isn't enough room for both of us to pass with suitcases in hand.

He coughs. "Sorry." He takes a step back. "Let me help you with your suitcase," he says and reaches for it.

"I've got it," I say, and lift the dang heavy thing up the long flight of stairs. By the time I reach the top, I am puffing out air. I

THE TRUTH ABOUT US

packed a lot. I didn't know how long Mom would need me to stay and now that I've quit my job, I could be here all summer.

I head to my old bedroom and don't look back but as I stare at my old room, it doesn't matter that Griff is no longer in sight because this room is filled with memories of us on the bed, talking, making love, hanging out, and listening to music. The overwhelming feeling pushes me from my room.

I head down to Mom like I'm ready to run a marathon. I find her in the kitchen.

"All settled in?" she asks.

"Yes. How are you holding up?" I ask.

"I'm not." She pours a shot of whiskey into her coffee.

"Uh hi." Griff waves like he feels out of place.

"Come have a seat. Coffee or tea?" Mom asks.

"I'll have what you're having," he says, tilting his chin to the whiskey on the counter.

"Me too," I say because I could use something to settle my nerves. I take a seat at the table beside Griff.

Mom pours a healthy amount of whiskey in our mugs and walks over to the old kitchen table.

"To Kip." She raises her mug.

Griff and I clink mugs with hers and we both say, "To Kip."

Before Mom takes a sip, she breaks into a fit of tears. Her shoulders shake and her coffee spills over the rim.

I stand and wrap my arms around her. "I'm so sorry, Mom. I don't even know what to say. Nothing helps, but time does heal." That much I know.

"It was just so sudden. Dammit," Mom snaps and sobs some more. I've never heard Mom swear, let alone use the word dammit. I rub her back.

"I'm angry." She pulls out of my embrace and stands from the table. "I want to smash every dish in this house. That's crazy, right?"

Griff looks to me sympathetically. He doesn't know what to do.

Then, through her tears, she breaks into maniacal laughter. "It's funny but I was just complaining to Kip about you kids never coming home to see us. It broke my heart and Kip said he'd think of something, of a way for me to have all my kids home, and now here you are, and Jenn and Logan are on the way. Even from death, he gives me what I need. I don't know what I am going to do without him. No clue." She waves her hands in the air.

She takes a seat back at the table and so do I. Both Griff and I stay quiet. I use the coffee thermos to refill Mom's coffee and add more whiskey.

We drink in silence for what feels like an eternity. A pin drop could be heard in the kitchen and the uneasiness inside me builds.

I wish I had better advice for her but I never felt about Mason the way she did about Kip, so I have nothing.

"It takes time. Just give yourself time to grieve and know we are here for you. I only took a few days off work, but if you need me here longer I will make it happen," Griff says and reaches for her hand, giving it a squeeze. I know Mom took care of him as a kid but I hadn't realized they were so close.

"Thank you." She blinks. "I think I will go rest. It's late," she says.

I look at the clock and see that it's already ten p.m. Why on earth did I drink coffee? I will never get to bed.

"Good night." I stand to give her a hug and she gives my back a light rub.

Griff hugs her too. She looks between us and her head tilts to the side.

"What is it?" I ask.

"Nothing." She pinches her lips together, shrugs, and walks up the stairs.

Griff stands in the kitchen and we both stare at the door Mom just went through. When I turn to look at him, he's looking at me. *This is so awkward.*

"We need to talk about what happened," he says.

"No, we don't."

He looks up to the ceiling then back at me. "Why are you so stubborn?"

"Because I am." It's a stupid answer.

A slow smile spreads his lips. It's so . . . sexy. Dammit.

"I'm going for a walk," I say, because I am not going to get to sleep now.

"I'll come with." He walks up next to me.

"I want to be alone," I say, and if I am not mistaken, he sulks. Why does he do that? He's the one who left. He shredded my heart and self-esteem. He left me broken. He has no right to sulk. I side-step him.

"Jolie please," he says, but I am already a few steps away from the door and I don't look back, just like he didn't ten years ago.

Chapter 8

Griffin

Jolie Bryant is the most stubborn, annoying, beautiful woman I have ever seen. Not much has changed since I last saw her. The last time, she convinced me to take her virginity. She was so adamant about it too. Now she is hard-nosed about letting me explain why I had to leave. I can't push either. I don't need Kathy getting wind of the drama between us.

It's been a hard two days because Jolie has basically ignored me. It's good Kathy's friends come and hang out all day because it takes her attention off me and Jolie, so I don't think she's realized we actually do not talk to each other.

I head down to the main room on my way out of the house. I haven't even seen Jolie yet this morning. I'm pretty sure she is holed up in her room again, like she was for most of the day yesterday.

"Where are you off to?" Kathy catches me just as I am about to walk out the door.

"Oh . . ." I rake my fingers through my hair. "I was going to check on my dad." Just the words leaving my lips are enough to make my body feel cold and cause an acrid taste to fill my mouth.

Kathy frowns. I never talk about Dad. Even during our weekly phone calls, he's never mentioned. He's my dirty secret. The man neglected me and verbally abused me, and now I take care of him because he is my only blood relative. I love him, despite everything. I hate how he's been withering away in that apartment of his.

"H-how is he doing?" she stutters. I've clearly thrown her off. Maybe she thought I had written him off.

"Well . . . I can afford doctors for him now." I pause as I contemplate how much to devolve. "He's bipolar. He was sick. He didn't get the right medication when I was younger," I say, because somewhere deep down, I feel the need to defend him.

"Oh Griff," she sighs, palming her chest. "I'm sorry you had to go through any of it."

"Yeah." I swallow hard. "He uh . . . still drinks, but he's more cordial now," I say because that is what the doctors have told me.

"Of course. He wasn't well. You know my own father left us when I was quite young. My mother never spoke about him. Later in life, I learned he started another family. The only reason I found out was because my half-sister contacted me after he died."

"I'm sorry," I apologize, because I understand what it's like when a parent walks away and doesn't look back. "I've always wondered about my mom. I imagined her with a new life and new son. I used to think it was my fault she left. Today I know that isn't the case. My dad kept me with him despite his illness; maybe he did the best he could. You know?" I don't mean for the last part to come out like a question.

"I think I do. I mean, with Gary, things were far from perfect, but he did the best he could."

"That's a really positive way to remember someone," I say. Especially someone like Gary Bryant. He was a cheater and an asshole.

She gives me a half smile, her tired eyes crinkling at the corners.

"Well, I should get going. Logan said he'd be here around two. I should be back by then." I grin.

"Oh, before I forget. That suitcase over there arrived for you early this morning," she says, tilting her chin to a medium-sized suitcase off to the corner of the living room.

"Ah. Thanks. I had my assistant pack me some more stuff. I only planned to be in New York for a couple days. I don't have much with me," I say.

Kathy looks down at my feet and smirks. I'm wearing my suit shoes with a pair of shorts. It looks ridiculous. I totally forgot what I had put on. My nerves were so bad about seeing Dad, I was operating on autopilot.

"I'll change my shoes." I smile wryly. I walk over to my suitcase. Annette is the bomb. I have everything here. I pull out my leather flip-flops.

"It's super warm today," Kathy says, making a face. The weather is very humid here compared to LA. I don't miss it here. "You can take my car if you like."

"Thanks, but I think I would rather walk. Give me time to think and get my nerves in check."

"Good luck, and remember, whatever happens, you are an amazing person and your dad doesn't define you." She gives me a pat on the back.

Her words hit a deep hole inside me. A spot where my insecurities flutter around, reminding me that I am never good enough. Even with all the money I've made and spent on therapy, that small flutter still exists.

"Thank you," I say, all choked up.

"I had to tell myself the same thing for years." She laughs.

"Okay. I shouldn't be too long." I blow out a breath.

"See you soon." She nods. She seems to be doing a little better than she was the first day I arrived. Maybe being surrounded by Jolie, me, and her friends is helping.

I head into the warm summer air. Even though I take care of Dad financially, I haven't seen him in the last ten years. I send nurses and doctors to take care of him, and they update me. I have groceries delivered to his house once a week but we haven't spoken since I left town. There isn't much to say.

The fifteen-minute walk seems like it goes by too fast. As the old supermarket comes into view, my chest grows tight. Memories of the past assault me, causing my stomach to tie in knots. Dad's sorrow. Him taking it out on me. Me getting home from school and opening the fridge, only to find it empty.

Remembering the hunger causes nausea to stir inside me. Why did I come back now? It only causes the pain I've worked so hard to bury to rise to the surface. Sweat breaks out on my forehead. It's not the humid summer air that has me sweating. Dammit. My legs feel like jelly as I grow nearer and nearer to the supermarket. Why am I putting myself through this hell?

I know why. My life in LA is pretty amazing. I live in opulence and make lots of money, but it's also void of love. I'd always craved materialistic things and now that I have them, I want more. Kathy called and I came running not only to support her but so that I could feel a connection with people who loved me before I was rich, before my name meant something. The Bryants have been that for me, and Jolie . . . she was my everything. I take a deep breath as an image of her enters my mind. Long chestnut hair, green vibrant eyes. I remember the way she used to watch me as a little girl and then I think of the woman who looks to me with disdain now, and a shiver rolls down my spine. *How did we come to this, Jolie?*

I walk around the back alley of the supermarket. The familiar smell of garbage rotting in the summer heat wafts up my nose. I head up the rusted steel staircase until I reach the door to my old home. Do I knock? I have a key. I bet the old man hasn't gotten around to changing the old locks. Gah! I want to hate him so much but knowing he was unwell has changed things for me . . . a little.

I knock and wait. Nothing happens, so I knock again.

"It's Thursday . . . go away." I hear my father's voice, and my heartbeat picks up pace.

"Um . . . Dad, it's Griffin," I shout through the door, my voice shaky and uncertain. Why do I feel like a little helpless boy all over again?

The door swings open and there stands my father. His hair has greyed. He's wearing a white top, and a pair of grey slacks that have seen better days.

"Hi Dad," I murmur and wave. *This is so awkward.*

His brows that had once been dark are now white, and they

bunch together. "Griffin?" he asks with a hoarse voice. He walks away and leaves the door open.

I assume it's my cue to enter. The place smells musty as I take a step inside. The pungent smell reminds me of home but I don't feel a sense of comfort.

My father walks over to the old khaki-green couch that had once belonged to my grandmother who lived here way before I was born. My father stares at me without breathing a word.

"May I take a seat, sir?" I ask, pointing to an old armchair. I have never called him Dad or Father. He'd always preferred I called him sir.

He nods, and I take a seat. I'm suddenly not sure what to say. I came here for some sort of closure. I wanted to face my past so that I could move forward.

"I want to thank you, son." They are his first words. They shock me and cause me to suck in a breath. He doesn't sound as angry or hostile as he used to. It's like all that negative emotion has melted away and what is left is a shell of a man.

"You don't need to thank me," I answer softly.

He watches me, biting the inside of his lip, looking like he's contemplating something. "I was mean. I may have been drunk, but I remember a lot . . . most of it, really . . ."

I want to say he sounds filled with sorrow, but his tone is more indifferent.

"You weren't well. I'm glad you're getting the help you need," I say holding my breath in fear I may say the wrong thing and set him off.

"I am . . ." He stands from the couch and walks over to the fridge.

When the door swings open, I have a clear view of the inside. It's filled with food and beer. My stomach sinks as Dad grabs a beer for himself.

"You want one?" he asks.

"No thank you," I answer, thinking it's a little early to be drinking. The doctor I hired to care for him told me he still drinks, but hearing it and seeing it are two different things.

Dad cracks the bottle open and chugs nearly half of it, then he belches and walks back to the couch. This may be where I came from, but it's not who I am.

"Why you here, Griffin?" he asks, getting to the point. There's no warmth in his tone. What was I expecting?

"My friend's stepfather passed away. I'm here for the funeral," I explain.

Dad nods. "The Bryant kid."

"Yeah," I say, my voice filled with shock. I never really spoke about Logan. When I would leave the house as a child, I would say I was heading over to the Bryants', but I figured Dad was too drunk to pay any attention.

"Don't look so surprised, kid," he says. "Kathy Bryant used to come over here."

"W-what do you mean?" I stutter, confused by his words. Is he drunk already?

"She would stop by when you were at school, saying she wanted to check in, but she would also warn me that you were looking thin, or she that child services would take you away if I didn't get my act together. With her warning came a little money, so I let her say her piece." He shrugs and laughs, giving me the sense that he thinks Kathy is a stupid fool. My stomach turns. I sit in silence as his words process. Kathy had come here to try and talk some sense into Dad. She gave him money.

Dad begins to laugh, and his shoulders shake. His head tilts back and it feels like he's mocking me. I'm not really sure why I remain silent. As a kid, I trained myself not to agitate him. I guess that hasn't changed.

"She wanted me to give up drinking, but it appears nothing can make me do that. I just don't have it in me. Your mama ruined me, and looking at you just makes me remember why I chose the bottle." His words are meant to sting, but they don't hold the same venom they used to. Maybe it's the years of therapy I've been through, or maybe I just believe in my own self-worth today. Looking at him now, through the eyes of an adult, I see a mean old man and I wonder why I ever gave his negative words any power at all.

"I don't know why you say shit like that. You're responsible for yourself. I sure as hell am not driving you to drink, and neither did Mom. I get you were sad when she left but that didn't give you the right to be a grade-A asshole." I stand from the chair as my father gapes at me with his bottom lip dropped.

I head for the door and grab the handle. "I don't know what I was looking for by coming back here." I turn to look him in the eyes. "Maybe I wanted to see if you had changed. Maybe I wanted to come to terms with the fact that this place doesn't define me. What I can tell you is that we all make choices, and we all have to live with the consequences. I will still send you food and take care of your medical bills, not because you deserve it, but because that's who I am. I'm willing to give of myself without expecting anything in return. I can't say I learned a hell of a lot from you but maybe you can take that small lesson from me."

I step out the door without giving the man who fathered me a second glance, and I slam it shut behind me. I take the steps fast and when my feet hit the concrete of the back alley, I begin to jog. My pace picks up until I'm running. I'm used to running in the heat back home, but right now, I am wearing a pair of flip-flops. They smack against the ground as I realize that I stood up to my father. I had never done that before in fear his cruel words would transform into physical abuse. Today, I didn't care. Today, I wasn't scared, because he has no power over me anymore. He can't hurt me.

I replay the scene in my mind. My father wanted to blame everyone but himself for his problems. I run faster down the sidewalk, as if I'm being chased.

As I run, Jolie's face comes to my mind. As a kid, I had believed that Dad broke from love. That he loved my mother so powerfully it ruined him, and because of that, the way I felt about Jolie scared the shit out of me. I was terrified of breaking like my father.

Only I'm not going to break. I am not like him. I am strong, a fighter.

I stop at a convenience store and buy a large bottle of water, then I walk back to the Bryants' brownstone. All I can think about is how Jolie can't even look me in the eyes. When she stares at me, there is a coldness in her glare, like she doesn't know me. I know how we got to this point, but suddenly, I want to do everything in my power to change her opinion of me. To tell her the truth about us.

I know I can't undo the past but I can set our future in motion.

Chapter 9

Jolie

I'm pretty sure I heard Griff leaving, so I head down for a late breakfast.

"There you are." Mom catches me on the way to the kitchen. "I was starting to think you were never going to leave that room." She purses her lips together.

"I'm sorry." By trying to avoid Griff, I've accidentally avoided Mom. I'm surprised she isn't curled up in a ball in bed. I'm grateful she has such a supportive group of friends. It makes me feel a little less guilty for not coming home.

"What's going on?" she asks.

"I was just going to make myself something to eat. I'm starved," I say.

"Was that you who left the house at five thirty this morning?" she asks.

"Sorry." I frown. "I didn't mean to wake you. I went for a run." I head over to the cabinets and take out a pan.

"What do you want to eat?" Mom asks.

"I was going to scramble some eggs and toast." I shrug, heading to the fridge.

"Let me make you something. I can do an omelet," she offers.

"You take it easy. I got this. You wouldn't believe this, but I can scramble eggs without burning them." I laugh.

"I'm glad." She gives me a half smile. "I need something to do. How about you sit at the table and I'll make you something. I can't sit and stare out that front window anymore. I feel like Kip is about to walk through the door any minute."

"Oh, Mom." My heart breaks. "I don't even know what to say. Everyone says they're sorry and they mean it, but it doesn't fill the gap in your heart, does it?" I hope my words are helpful but I'm not sure.

"You would know, my sweet girl." A lone tear rolls down her cheek. "This family has experienced so much tragedy. When will it end?" Her voice cracks. "All I want now is for you and your brother to settle down. Maybe you can give me some grandbabies to keep me busy."

"Mom. You have Kyle," I remind her. Kyle is Jenn's four-year - old son. They live in LA, but Mom has been out there for visits.

She's never pressured me for grandbabies before but I guess having grandbabies would fill the void she feels in her heart and keep her busy too.

She turns to look at me, wide-eyed. "They live on the other end of the country." Her lips turn down. "When you were younger, I always thought you and Griff would be together. I guess having you both home . . . I don't know. I feel hopeful." She shrugs.

Her words cause air to get sucked from my lungs.

"W-where is this coming from? Why would you think Griff and I . . .?" I'm not sure what to say.

"Don't seem so shocked. I'm your mom. Do you not think I know that you used to have a little crush on him?" Her words ease me a little, and my rapid heart rate slows. She doesn't know we have been together and now, more than ever, I think it's better it remains a secret. *Don't want to get her hopes up.*

"Um. . ." My face scrunches.

"If you aren't interested in him, that's fine too," she says, shrug-ging. *But it isn't fine, Mom. I haven't been able to stop thinking about him since*

I saw him in the LaGuardia airport two days ago. Being back home and watching him from afar makes my heart beat in a way it only does when he is close.

I keep my thoughts to myself. This is so messed up. He hurt me in ways that changed the course of my life. I can't overlook it. Even if my family considers him a part of the family, I don't have to.

"Sorry. I've forced you to go inside your head, and that isn't my intention," Mom says. "I'm just in a weird mood. Life is short. I want you to make the most of it. Griff is a good man. Maybe he could make you happy." She gives me a small smile.

I walk over to her and hug her. "You don't need to worry about me. I'm doing good." I pull away.

She turns away and opens the fridge. She pulls out some asparagus and zucchini. It looks like I'm getting a healthy omelet. She also takes out the cheddar cheese. Hopefully that will mask the taste of the asparagus.

"Was I dreaming or did you tell me you could stay the summer because you quit your job." She eyes me curiously.

"I did mumble something to you the other day. You were busy with Agnes I shouldn't have slid it into the conversation," I say apologetically. Agnes asked me how long I was here for and I said the whole summer.

"This isn't you running away, is it?" Shit. Busted. Why do moms have to be so intuitive?

"Um . . . yeah. It's nothing to worry about. I have money saved," I explain.

"I wasn't worried about money. I don't like you not finding something you are truly passionate about or hopping around from city to city. I was hoping you would have laid some roots by now," she says.

She cracks some eggs in a bowl.

I head over to the freezer to see what kind of frozen goods she has. She used to always freeze things after baking too much.

"Try the multi-grain rolls. They turned out great, and I added some dates for a little sweetness," Mom says.

I find the rolls and pop a few in the oven to defrost. "I've been in

New York City two years. I've planted roots there. I have a cat, remember?"

"Sasha. How is she doing?" Mom asks.

"Good. She's staying with Mrs. Montgomery."

"You're lucky to have her," Mom says. "But you know what I mean by roots. Every time something tragic happens, you pick up and make a life-altering decision. I'm seeing a pattern with you."

She isn't wrong. Daddy died, and I ran off with Mason. Mason passed, and I picked up and moved to a new city, made new friends, and found a new job. I wasn't even close with Kip and it looks like my instincts to run have kicked in.

Damn. She has a point.

I fall into one of the chairs at the kitchen table. I rest my elbows on the table and brush my hand along my forehead. "I can't argue with you, Mama. You know me too well. Things are good in New York but I want something . . . more."

"What does that mean exactly?" With all the ingredients cooking on a low simmer on the stove, she comes and sits across from me. "You know I don't like to tell you what to do, but I like to know you're safe and happy. I lived most of my life in a loveless marriage. It wasn't until I met Kip that I began to feel, to find my passions. I may not make money from my art, but my soul is content when I go into my studio upstairs and paint."

"I'm so sorry you lost him." I give her hand a squeeze. I don't know what it's like to lose the love of your life because Mason wasn't mine. I loved him dearly but he didn't stir things inside me like . . . I can't even think his name.

"He gave me so much. He taught me to run after my passions, to live life to the fullest. He may be gone but his legacy will always live on. His love will always shine down on me," she says, and tears fill her eyes. "I'm sorry."

"Don't be. You're so strong. You're doing so much better today than you were even a couple days ago. I've been watching you. You will get there and honestly; you seem different in general. You are stronger; you have this inner calmness about you that I never saw before," I say, holding her hand.

"It's Kip. That was his gift to me. I just can't allow myself to break. He wouldn't want it," she says.

It makes me think of Mason and the way he died. No one knows that we hadn't been living together before his death. It was a secret we kept from the world.

"I'm thinking of returning to school," I blurt, even though I've been pondering the idea for months now. There was just never a good time to take the leap.

Mom's green eyes widen. "Really?" Excitement laces her tone.

I finished college when Mason was drafted but never continued to graduate school. His career was just so much bigger than mine could ever be. "Really. I want to get my master's degree. I don't know if I'll want to teach like Logan or continue to a PhD program."

"Oh, Jolie." She takes a big breath and she smiles a real smile. Through all her pain and sorrow, she is happy for me. "This is great news."

"Thanks, Mom. I don't have anything sorted, but I was thinking of attending NYU. I'm not sure yet but I have a plan I want to follow through on."

"That's great news." The smell of burned food wafts through the air, and we both look over to the pan at the same time.

"Shoot." Mom stands abruptly.

"You sit. I got this." I walk over to the pan to see her little concoction has smoke rising from the pan. "I'll just fry up some eggs," I say. "You relax."

"Thanks, honey." She remains seated at the kitchen table while I fry eggs. I take the rolls out of the oven and set them on the table.

The front door chime rings, indicating someone has entered the house.

"That must be him," Mom whispers, referring to Griff.

"Please don't do anything embarrassing," I plead.

She peeks out the kitchen door and my eyes follow hers.

It is Griff. His shoulders are slumped and he's covered in sweat. He walks straight up the staircase, and a door slams shut. I think it was the bathroom, but I'm not sure. Mom winces and so do I. She closes the kitchen door and turns around, bumping into me.

"Oh," she says. I guess she hadn't realized I was snooping right behind her.

"He went to see his father. By the looks of it, things didn't go too well." Her lips pinch into a frown.

"No," I agree. My heart drops into my stomach as I think of a younger Griff struggling just to have his basic needs met, and yet he always found a way. In the midst of all the chaos in his life, he was this sweet, loving boy. *What happened to you, Griffin Campbell? What made you run?*

I don't voice my thoughts. Instead, I scramble some eggs and sit with Mom at the kitchen table, eating a quiet meal. I should get closure where Griff is concerned because, whether I like it or not, he's a part of this family and I can't avoid him forever.

Chapter 10

Griffin

It doesn't matter how much time I spend under the showerhead; I still don't feel clean after leaving my father's place. I've been assaulted with memory after memory of feeling hungry and tired. Feeling beat down by his words and life.

I step out of the shower and wrap a towel around my waist. Thinking of hunger makes me want to eat. The same thing used to happen to me when I first left for college. I suddenly had access to lots of food, and even though I wasn't hungry, I would eat *just in case* because in the back of my mind, I had to fill myself up in fear that later I would starve. I give my head a good shake. It's been a long time since I felt this way.

I walk out of the bathroom just as Jolie is walking down the hall.

"Hey." I smile.

She comes to a halt, her gaze sweeping over me for the briefest of seconds. Her eyes lock on mine and grow narrow, and she lifts her chin and walks past me. I take her gently by the arm. "We need to talk. I know I fucked up. Let me explain," I say softly, pleading with her.

Her chin tilts down and she gives me a look that I think says she thinks I have a real nerve. "Not now. Logan will be here any minute."

She walks away and I stand out in the hall, watching her descend the stairs. I can't say I blame her for being harsh with me.

I throw some clothes on and dry my hair with a towel, then I head down to the kitchen. Thinking of food, and my earlier run, has me ravished.

"I'm baking a tuna casserole. It should be ready soon." Kathy smiles.

"That sounds great. Thank you," I say, even though it's not my favorite.

"Jolie said she was going for a walk. She passed on her serving." Kathy smiles.

"Ah, just like old times." I chuckle as I remember coming over here sometimes after school and getting two helpings since Jolie never liked to eat hers.

What isn't like old times is the part where Jolie hates me now.

I take a seat at the table. Kathy opens the oven and inspects the casserole, then she removes it. She places a plate of casserole in front of me.

"Are you eating too?" I ask, not wanting to be rude and start without her.

"No, my appetite hasn't been great, but please eat."

I dig in and take a few bites.

"How did things go with your dad?" she asks, her face scrunching up.

"Not great. I don't know what I was expecting . . ."

"I know what you mean."

"Dad said you had gone to visit him when I was a kid. I really appreciate you doing that," I say. I want to offer to pay her back, but I know she would be offended.

"I'd hoped my visits inspired him to look after you better, but I'm guessing that wasn't the case." She sighs.

"No, it wasn't." My chest tightens as I think of my father's evil sneer when he told me he took her money. "I'm happy I went to see him though. I always worried about being like him in some way, but today I saw it wasn't the case."

"Definitely not the case," she agrees, and it makes me feel a warmth in my chest I can't describe.

"Have you and Jolie had a chance to catch up?" she suddenly asks, throwing me off.

"Not exactly, no," I say, worried that maybe Jolie said something to her. Over the years, Kathy's never mentioned anything specific to me about Jolie during our weekly calls, so I assumed she never shared what I did. I also don't think she's caught on to the tension between us now, even though Jolie's barely left her room since we've arrived and when she has, it hasn't been to talk to me.

"She's been through a lot. Give her time," Kathy says.

That makes sense. She lost her husband. I hate that just the thought of him causes my old jealousy to spark. Even though I hurt her, I never understood how she fell in love and married. I was never able to.

I sit back in the kitchen chair across from her. If I'm not mistaken, it looks like she wants to share something now. I watch and wait.

"Oh! Come on," she insists. She gives me a look that says *who am I kidding*. "Jolie had a crush on you since she was in kindergarten. I was never oblivious, Griff. I may have made some poor decisions, but I know you two had feelings for one another." Her words are so matter of fact, there is no room for argument.

I cough, trying to release the tightness in my chest. "Uh . . ." I'm at a loss of words.

"I thought staying with Gary was the right thing for my children. Divorce didn't seem right at the time. I grew up without a father. I figured the kids were happy, so why rock the boat? And I was scared too." She shakes her head from side to side. "As a stay-at-home mom, I didn't have a lot going for me. It would've been hard to find a job, and Gary didn't want a divorce." She sighs, and takes a deep breath.

Who am I to judge? She was comfortable, and after growing up hungry, I know how important it is to have basic necessities met.

"He was hard on you and I felt helpless to stop it. A stronger woman would have stood up to him." Kathy's brows pinch together, forming a line between her eyes. Does she know what happened? The real reason I had to leave? No, that couldn't be.

"You shouldn't be apologizing. If anything, you kept me alive. I wouldn't be where I am today without you. You have no idea how grateful I am. I should've come back sooner but . . ." I don't have a good excuse. Silence makes more sense.

"My mistakes are mine. They cost you," she says.

I want to ask her what she knows. It would be such a relief to share my side of the story with someone from this family so that they could understand that I was forced to leave and not look back. Maybe if Kathy knew, she could tell Jolie and help me win her back.

"You didn't cost me anything," I answer. I want to add *it was the asshole Gary Bryant who cost me,* but I keep my mouth shut.

"Maybe you and Jolie would have ended up together if you hadn't left. Then my daughter wouldn't be in the pain she's in today."

Okay, so Kathy doesn't know about what Gary did. But hearing Jolie is hurting causes a pinch in my chest.

I want to say that we most definitely would have ended up together, but I don't know what would have become of us. I want to believe we would have found a way to stay together. Maybe we would have gotten married and had kids by now.

I can't allow my mind to go there.

"What's going on with Jolie?" I ask, hoping to learn something about the woman she is today.

"You know she was widowed two years ago." Kathy frowns.

I shift in my seat, remembering when Logan called to tell me Jolie's husband died. He came home for the funeral and left right away. He was hoping I'd meet him here, since he didn't want to come on his own.

"Yeah, I was sorry to hear about it," I say, rubbing at the scruff on my face while feeling guilty that I hadn't come to support the family through a difficult time. I just couldn't bring myself to watch the only woman I've ever loved mourn another man even if he had passed.

"It was tragic but she is still not over it. She doesn't date. She barely gets out. I just . . . I worry for her."

It makes me sad to hear Jolie is still hurting. That she isn't moving forward.

I wonder why Kathy is sharing this information with me.

"What do you think I can do? Do you want me to talk to her?" I ask. I have been friends with Jolie since we were little. She used to come to me when she had problems in school and she didn't want Logan or Jenn to know.

"I was thinking more along the lines of maybe taking her out. You aren't dating anyone, are you? Last time we spoke, you said there was no significant woman in your life, and well, you are here, and Jolie is here, and she had the cutest little crush on you when she was small. I just thought . . ."

I blink twice. I wasn't expecting Kathy to play matchmaker. Gary Bryant used every ounce of his power to keep me away.

"Um . . ." I'm at a loss for words. I can't exactly say, 'I stole your daughter's virginity and never spoke to her again, so she basically hates me and won't give me a second glance.' *Think, Griff. Say anything.* "I mean. I can try to talk to her as a friend . . ." I mutter. "I made bad choices. I haven't stayed in touch. She hasn't been very friendly toward me, and I can't say I blame her."

"My daughter is stubborn but so are you," Kathy says, throwing me off again. "I used to see the way you looked at her. By the time she was in middle school, you couldn't take your eyes off her." She eyes me like I've been caught with my hand in the cookie jar.

I swipe a hand over my mouth. "Was I that obvious?" I say, sheepishly. No point in lying now.

"Yes," she says, blatantly.

"We haven't been in touch in forever." She married another man. My heart races and I don't know what's happening, but this woman is filling me with hope. I can't dare to hope. Can I?

My heart thuds. *Hope. Hope. Hope.* She's pouring it inside me, and

THE TRUTH ABOUT US

it's seeping into my pores and pumping through my entire body. I can't . . . no, I won't allow it.

When I heard of Jolie's engagement, I was a fucking mess, drinking myself into oblivion. It was Logan who helped me to get my shit together. He didn't even know my bender was because of his sister. He just thought I was dealing with shit when he said to me, "Griff, you are better than your old man. Don't go acting like him." Something about his words got me to pull myself together. I sobered up and moved on with life.

"My daughter is hurting. She's been through a lot." Kathy looks me in the eye, and her soft voice holds a sternness that tugs on my heartstrings. *She approves of me. Thinks I'm good enough.*

"I'm home." Logan's voice carries through the house.

Kathy rolls her eyes. "He always did like to make a grand entrance."

I laugh. "Sorry," I apologize to Kathy, because this is a sad time.

"Don't ever apologize for that smile." She gives me a small smile too.

"Let me also remind you that your son will lose it on me if I go anywhere near his sister." I choose my words carefully out of respect, but Logan would go fucking ape shit.

She tilts her head from side to side. "Jolie is a grown woman who can make up her own mind. Her big brother is going to have to accept that she's all grown up. It's his only choice."

She stands from the table and so do I. She walks over to me and wraps her arms around me, then whispers, "I'm glad you came back, son."

My heart beats faster as warmth pumps through me. After my meeting with my dad this morning, I bite back tears.

"Of course I came. Anytime you call me, I'll come running," I say, my voice choppy and filled with emotion.

She looks up to me, her eyes creasing at the corners. Her appearance looks like an older version of Jolie. Kathy turns to leave the kitchen to greet her son. I remain behind to take a few slow breaths and gain some composure back. Her words run through my mind, both soothing and piercing.

I shake off my emotions and head out to the front door to greet my best friend. We met up in Vancouver this past winter and did some skiing up in Whistler, but it's been a good six months since we've seen each other.

Logan works as a teacher in Iowa. He is almost a carbon copy of his dad. Instead of becoming a professor, he became a history teacher and moved to Des Moines, Iowa—the small town where his dad grew up. When he died, Logan lost his hero.

I wait while Logan hugs his grieving mom and apologizes for not being able to get here sooner. The funeral is tomorrow. At least he'll be here for that.

"Hey man." He turns his attention to me and gives me a bro hug. "So weird being back here," he mutters so only I can hear.

"Yeah, man," I agree. If only he knew how weird it was.

He walks deeper into his childhood home. I follow him as he gets settled in his old bedroom.

"Roommates?" he asks.

"Yup."

"Cool." He blows out a harsh breath. Being back here isn't easy for him either.

"Why didn't you come sooner?" I ask.

He rolls his eyes. "Chick problems."

"Do tell." I rub my palms together.

"You remember that woman I told you about? Audrey?" he asks, no doubt waiting or my mind to jog.

"The hot single mom," I say playfully.

He nods. "Things have gotten complicated." He opens his suitcase.

"Complicated how?" I ask.

"We kissed, and her daughter is in my class this year. I kissed a parent of one of my students." He sighs.

"Is that so bad?" I ask, because I hear Audrey is cool and hot as hell.

"Yeah, there are strict rules at school about a teacher dating a parent, but I don't want to talk about it." He stares across the room. "Where is Jolie? I thought she was here."

"I think she stepped out," I say as Jolie walks up to the bedroom door, holding a cup with some green concoction inside.

"Hey there, squirt." Logan runs up to her, hugging her and lifting her feet off the ground.

"No calling me squirt," she bites back with a laugh.

I peek out the blinds in Logan's room. His faces the street. A cab pulls up to the front of the house, and Jenn and her kid get out.

"Jenn's here," I say to Logan and Jolie.

Jolie turns away from Logan and screeches, "I finally get to meet Kyle." She dashes down the stairs.

"Mom, Jenn is here," she shouts.

Logan and I head down the stairs. A smile tugs at my lips from just watching Jolie's excitement. From what I understand, she hasn't seen Jenn in a heck of a long time.

Jolie heads straight for the curb where Jenn is wrestling a whole lot of suitcases out of the trunk.

"Go greet your nephew, Uncle Logan." I chuckle, nodding for him to follow his sister.

Jolie seems back to her bubbly self as she hugs her big sister and nephew.

"Do I get to see Kyle too?" Kathy cuts in. She has gone out to LA to visit Jenn and me a few times, so she's met Kyle before.

"Hi Gran." Kyle smiles.

Jenn gives me a quick hug. She still carries a chip on her shoulder. I can tell by the way she is with Jolie. While Jolie is full of excitement and warmth, Jenn is cool, calm, and has her nose tilted to the sky.

"Now that I have you all here," Kathy cuts the reunion short, "I'd like all of us to head out to the Cape after the funeral tomorrow," she says, and I look at the Bryant kids to see Jolie's jaw is dropped, Logan's eyes are wide, and Jenn is grinning.

Kathy's mom left her a beach house in Cape Cod years ago. I'd gone up with the Bryants when they spent the summer there on a number of occasions.

"Mom . . . don't you want to stay here for a bit? Um . . . I'm sure Kip's friends will want to drop in after the funeral," Jolie murmurs nervously, like her mother's suggestion is way out of left field.

"Hon, if I can get through that funeral in one piece, I'd like to leave right after. Logan, Jenn, don't unpack your bags. I want to leave town as soon as I can," she says before stalking off.

"Mom, wait," Jolie calls out, and Kathy turns around and looks at her. "What is this about?" she asks quietly, as if she's tiptoeing, not wanting to scare off a mouse.

Kathy takes a few steps toward her. "This is about reclaiming my family. I've stayed in touch with all of you all these years, but I know you haven't been good at staying in touch with each other. You and Logan speak often, Jolie, but I also know that calling your sister at Christmas or Easter isn't enough. You don't speak to Griff, who I consider my own child, and I know I am to blame. When I chose Kip, I pushed you all away, and that was selfish of me, and I truly am sorry. My life was . . ." She shakes her head, and it looks like she's biting her tongue. Her life was awful with Gary Bryant, and she wanted to feel happy for once.

"Mom, you weren't selfish. I'm sorry." Logan steps forward. "I was hurt about Kip at first, but I should have gotten over it."

Kathy goes up to him and hugs him. "We can't take back the past, but we sure as hell can define the future of this family. You are all my legacy. I want you close," Kathy says with a stern voice.

"You're right, Mom," Jolie says. "I'm in."

"Me too," I say, still feeling choked up about her referring to me as her child.

"Me too," Logan says, and we all turn to Jenn.

"Whatever. I mean, if you are all going, then Kyle and I will join," Jenn says, sounding indifferent. It's so annoying.

"Good. It's settled then." Kathy gives an assured nod, turns and walks away. She was never so outspoken when we were growing up, but I am liking this side of her now.

"Okay, pack your bags." Logan looks to me, then Jolie. "We leave for the Cape after the funeral tomorrow," he says, having the last word. We all nod in agreement. Jolie follows Jenn to her old room with Kyle. Logan and I head to the kitchen.

I internally give myself a pinch, thinking I'm living through some fantasy. Jolie and me, back on the Cape. This trip is about to get a lot more complicated than I'd originally expected.

I need to come clean to Jolie and finally tell her the truth about why I had to leave. I only hope she can find a way to forgive me.

Chapter 11

Jolie

While Kyle and my sister get settled into her old bedroom, I rush back to my own room, shut the door, and dial, Michelle, back in New York.

She picks up after one ring. "How is it going? I tried calling you," she says, her tone laced with worry.

I fall back on the bed. "Hello to you too."

"Jolie," she chides.

I rub at my eyes. "Sorry. I didn't mean for you to worry. Being home is complicated . . ."

"OMG, he's there, isn't he?" she says. There are only three people who know mine and Griff's story, one being my deceased husband, the second my good friend Tiffany Miller, back in Texas, and the third being Michelle.

"He's here. He was on the same damn flight as me from New York . . ."

"What do you mean? I remember you saying he lived in LA," she says, sounding confused.

"He was on a business trip in New York City, of all places, when my mom called with the news. We were on the same damn flight, sitting next to one another," I say.

"What are the fucking chances?" Michelle says. "So how was it? The big reunion."

"It hasn't been a reunion. I've been avoiding him. I just can't imagine he has a good enough excuse to justify his shitty behavior. What's the point in dredging up the past anyway? We lead different lives. I'm here for a few weeks." My mind runs with a list of reasons why I should not give Griff the time of day.

"Still, Jojo, I mean, won't a part of you always wonder why he left the way he did? It can give you closure." Michelle means well, but I can't do it. My mind has been replaying so many childhood memories since I came to town. I did the same thing after he left, trying to find clues as to how he could just walk away the way he did. There were no warning signs. Now, my emotions feel mixed up because how can I feel anything for him at all after the way he left me? It makes me feel crazy that I can still be attracted to him.

"I already have closure. I moved on. I was a happily married woman," I remind Michelle. It's a lie.

"I want what's best for you. If you think staying away from him is the right thing to do, then I'm behind you," she says assertively.

"Thank you, and all would be smooth sailing except for the fact that my mom is playing matchmaker suddenly and wants to set me up with him. She wants everyone going to our family beach house in Cape Cod tomorrow. She said she needs to get away from the city, but I'm calling bullshit. Mom has a plan up her sleeve." I groan.

"Go, Kathy," Michelle cheers. "So this means he's single, right?"

"I don't know but I'm guessing Mom does, and if she wants to set us up he must be," I answer, *with the way he looks, I can't imagine he would be single*.

"You can ask Logan," she suggests.

I snort. "Logan never knew about us, and there's no way I'd ask him about Griff."

"Damn you're stubborn," she snickers.

"Tell me about it," I say, knowingly. I take a deep breath. "Give me advice here. What am I supposed to do? Do I say hello and goodbye, and be courteous to him like I would any stranger on the street? Do I ignore him? No . . . Mom wouldn't like that. It's always important for her that we all get along."

"Um . . . I am still on the phone," Michelle cuts in. "Or do you want me to let you go and you can continue speaking to yourself."

"Just tell me what to do," I whine.

"Describe him to me," she says, and I picture her sitting on her bed, rubbing her hands together in anticipation. She loves paying attention to detail.

"Hmm?"

"Griffin. How does he look?" she asks.

"I don't know. He's tall . . . maybe six two. Built. Wide shoulders. Used to play football. He's got brown hair and the lightest blue eyes you've ever seen. Like seriously, they look the color of those photos you see of the ocean in vacation magazines for Fiji or Tahiti. He's got this sexy smile where his lips lift on one side. It's subtle but panty-melting," I say.

"Jojo?" She says my name like a question. "Don't kill me for saying this, but is it possible you still have feelings for him? I mean, it's been a decade, but you guys were tight."

I cringe, knowing she's right. There must be something seriously wrong with me. I can't even look at Griffin Campbell without my pulse racing and my cheeks heating.

But there is no way I'm admitting that out loud. Not even to Michelle.

"That's not it. I'm turned off by him. He completely ripped my heart out and stomped all over it. There is no way I can be attracted to a man like that." *Lies. So many lies.*

"If you say so. I have to head out but keep me posted. Honestly, it sounded like you were describing Chris Hemsworth, and you know I love Chris. I wouldn't blame you for not being able to keep your hands to yourself."

"Mich, come on," I chide.

"What? I'm more than curious to know where this goes. And Jojo, you're young, vibrant, beautiful, and single. You're allowed to find love again."

"I'm a widow," I remind her. The thought of setting myself up for potential heartbreak is so unappealing.

"I know," she says softly. "But you're only twenty-eight. You can't just give up on life."

"Okay, Mom," I answer jokingly.

"Take care of you," she says.

"You too." And with those last words, we end the call.

Since my husband died, guilt isn't only stopping me from dating —it's holding me back from living. And it isn't because I've felt like I was betraying my deceased husband. My reasons for harboring guilt run much deeper. They are reasons I've only shared with my therapist back in New York City.

I push off my bed and begin to repack my suitcase. I can't tell Mom I don't want to go to the Cape. I just have to find a way to survive the next few weeks with my heart still intact.

Chapter 12

Jolie

I loved this beach house as a child. It still has a nostalgic, romantic feel with the cottage-style furnishings that were chosen by my grandmother. Each wall is adorned with some sort of picture of the Cape or Nantucket. Little souvenirs collected from fishing trips Dad took are settled along the coffee table, side tables, and dining table.

There aren't any pictures of our family on these walls. Mom removed those when Dad passed, but I still love each little memento holding a memory of its own, a small slice of a happy childhood.

Kip's funeral had passed in a blur. At least, for me it did. I'd had a hard time staying present as my own father's funeral buzzed in my mind, followed by Mason's. I'd been relieved at how well Mom kept herself together. Of course, she had shed tears, but she'd been strong and resilient. I envied that about her.

Now, I am breaking on the inside from constantly having to be close to Griff. A part of me wants to attack him with questions while another part of me fears his truth.

"Where you off too, Jolie?" Mom's soft voice comes through the darkness, a whisper. My eyes follow the source of the sound until I spot her curled on the armchair at the corner of the main living room.

"Oh! Geez, Mom, I didn't see you." I palm my heart as I take in my fragile-looking mother with her pale face and red-rimmed eyes. "You okay? I'm sorry."

I walk over to her, concern filling my insides.

"Couldn't seem to sleep. Leaving Boston hasn't stopped me from thinking about Kip," Mom sighs and swallows a garbled laugh. "I mean, I knew running away wouldn't ease the pain. I'm just . . ." She stares blankly, like she isn't seeing me at all, her green eyes looking clear and vacant.

I take her hand in mine, feeling how frail she is. Her skin is soft and cold. "You're numb," I say knowing the feeling all too well.

She nods, blinking. A soft sigh escapes her.

"It takes time. He died so suddenly," I say, and she rubs nervously at her neck. "You didn't have a chance to say goodbye." I bite back tears, knowing exactly how that feels having experienced it first with Griff and then Mason.

Mom's lips turn down. "I didn't . . . I should've known death comes knocking whenever it wants to. I knew from your father and Mason but . . ." She pauses, looking me in the eyes. Her stare says more than words ever could. She was a great mom, but she never did anything for herself until Kip came along and whisked her away on travelling adventures around the world. He inspired her to paint, and she found she had real talent. She found herself, and she was truly happy.

"I know, Mom. You can say it. You were really in love with Kip. I'm sorry you have to face another tragedy." I struggle to hold back tears. I don't know if it's for her sake or mine. Both of our sakes.

"I loved him dearly." She nods. And I think she wants to say he was the love of her life, but she doesn't, maybe because she doesn't want me feeling bad. I always thought Mom was so brave, allowing herself to fall in love a second time. Her and Kip just fit.

"You two were the perfect match." They are the only words I have for her.

"We were. And so were you and Mason, but Mason's been gone

two years," she says. "I know you loved him dearly, but you need to move on. You are young and beautiful. You need to make yourself a life."

Huh! Michelle's words echo in my head.

"You're right," I reply. She is, sad as it is. I don't want her worrying about her youngest daughter becoming an old maid. Mom smiles, and that makes my chest warm.

"I love you, Mom," I say, wrapping my arms around her.

"Love you too, Jojo Bear." She rubs my arm.

"I'm going to go for a run." I straighten and point my thumb to the front door.

"Sure, but maybe you should eat something first," she suggests, her gaze taking a quick sweep of my body. In a sport tank top and runner's shorts, there isn't much to hide. I've always been a slim build, but with all the running I've done during the last two years, I've become quite trim.

"I'll eat when I get back." Most of the time, food tastes bland to me. Everything in my life feels bland. If anyone could understand that, it would be Mom. Still, she has her own husband to grieve. I don't want to add to her plate.

I turn the knob and leave through the front door. The warm summer air fills my lungs, along with a humid albeit salty freshness from the ocean. The sun has just begun to rise as my feet hit the pavement.

The Cape always felt like my home away from home. As I watch the waves hitting the shoreline, I move to the sand, since I don't have this option back home. With earbuds in, music fills my mind. The perfect runner's high. Even with the loud noise of music, my thoughts drift to Mason. How can they not? We met here on this very beach for the first time. And still, two years after his death, I am feeling empty. People didn't know our marriage wasn't what it appeared to be.

I glance down at my smart watch while slowing my run, focusing on the way my feet move against the hard sand. A familiar burn climbs my calves. My lungs ache with tension. There is no way I'm making it back to the beach house without a break first. The sun is fully up now, and the stores that line the boardwalk have their lights turned on and their doors open for business. I trudge over to an old bakery I frequented as a teenager, happy I tucked some cash into my waist pouch. After ordering a warm croissant, I take a seat in the outdoor patio so that I can watch the serene roll of the early morning waves. My mind drifts to the first time my path crossed with Mason Amos. He was so full of life, handsome. He had everything going for him. I was this shy, quiet girl who had suffered a broken heart . . .

My family came up to the Cape for a week to enjoy spring break. Mom went to Nantucket to visit a friend, since Dad took an overnight fishing trip. With no parents at the beach house, Logan and Jenn have decided to throw a party. Blech.

I head into the kitchen that holds a thousand memories of Griff and me sitting at this very table late at night when everyone was asleep. We talked about everything: life, love, our plans . . .

I reach into the fridge and take some leftover roast chicken Mom left, thankful the guests aren't allowed in here.

The loud thump of music vibrates through the dark space, but at least I'm alone. The feeling has become all too familiar now that he's gone.

I eat my chicken and dread having to walk through the main room of the house filled with drunk high school kids, even though they are around my age. I push through the swivel door and spot Jenn climbing the stairs, holding hands with a handsome boy. He's some football jock from back home. Rumors are flying all over about him making it to the NFL. His grandmother owns a small bake shop nearby.

Why can't I be more like Jenn? Carefree, fun, outgoing. She's had sex with many boys and her heart is still intact. I had sex with one boy—a thief who stole my heart and never returned it. He shattered me.

I slip into the main floor washroom to clean the chicken off my hands. I leave the washroom and just look at the craziness before me. Teenagers drinking until they don't know their names. This scene has never enticed me. Most of the teenagers partying in the house are locals so I don't really know them, but I guess Jenn and Logan do.

It's freezing here this time of year. I don't know why Dad insisted it would be a good idea for us to come.

I head to the closet and grab my heavy winter jacket. At least the tempera-tures have been above seasonal this year.

I slip out the front door, worried maybe Logan will tell me to get back inside, but he's too busy talking animatedly with a group of people. I slip back outside and head straight for the sand, my mind whirling, my chest aching. All I want is for this feeling of heartbreak to end. All I want is to feel happy again.

The cold night air causes a shiver to roll down my spine. My parents don't like us being out here alone at night, but it's better to have some peace and quiet than a noisy house filled with drunks.

I pop a squat in the sand. It's freezing so I tuck my jacket under my behind. I don't think I will be able to stay out here long. Listening to the waves roll to the shore somewhat relaxes me.

I'm still grinding the whole Griffin Campbell fiasco in my mind. I thought at some point he would message me and explain himself but that hasn't happened. It just doesn't add up. I know Griff has parts of him that are broken. Parts that cause him shame, but I never thought he would leave me.

I don't know how long I've been sitting here when the sound of footsteps yanks me from my thoughts.

"Hey, should you be out here by yourself?" the voice says, sounding deep but friendly.

I turn my head up to see who it is. The guy who followed my sister to her room stands with a bashful smile, his hands tucked into his jeans pockets. His dark brown hair is long at the front, flopping over his face, and his hazel eyes seem friendly and sincere.

"I'm Mason. Nice to meet you." He extends a hand.

"Jolie. Jenn's younger sister," I clarify, thinking it's needed since he has just been with my sister. I swear he winces a little. Still, I offer my hand, not wanting to be rude.

"Mind if I keep you company?" he asks, surprising me. "Party is getting too much for me."

I stay quiet, watching him and trying to figure out his angle. He's Logan's age but hooked up with Jenn, who is a year older. Of course he would want her. She's beautiful and easy. He looks tall and built, like one of those football players I watch on television.

"Sure, go ahead." I shrug, thinking he just wants time away from the party like me. I want to add that I won't be good company, but I keep my lips sealed.

He smiles and sits in the sand about a foot away from me. "Do you not like the party?"

"No, definitely not my thing," I snicker, staring out to the ocean. This is so awkward. Why is he sitting here with me?

"What is your thing?" he asks, and I feel his eyes bore into the side of my head. My stomach lurches. I'm lonely and upset, yet I know better than to be hanging out with a boy who hooked up with my sister.

"I don't think we should really talk or whatever this is," I say pointedly, surprising myself. I am mostly shy around boys.

"You mean because of Jenn," he answers knowingly.

I nod.

"That meant nothing. It's nothing personal, but your sister just likes to get around. There were no feelings involved." He shrugs.

Gah! It irritates me how easily the kids at my school can just hook up with people. I'm not built like that and Jenn isn't even in high school anymore. Can't she hang out with people her own age? The answer is no, and I know it.

"Do you like astrology?" he asks, changing the subject.

"Yes."

"With binoculars, you can see Mercury on some nights, Venus, Mars. There's this website—"

"I have binoculars in my room back at the house. Tonight, it's Mars," I say.

"Can we go to your room and get them?" He sounds excited.

"Is that code for something? Because if it is, then, no." I retort, matter-of-factly.

"It's only code for binoculars, Jolie. That is a really pretty name." He chuckles and covers his mouth with his hand. "I just like to see the stars at night. I'm a dreamer," he says. His hazel eyes sparkle in the darkness as the moon casts a glow over the water.

"I'm a dreamer too," I say, and he smiles again. I feel a tiny connection with him beginning to build.

After that night of stargazing, Mason and I became fast friends . . . and I needed a friend after Griff left. I couldn't stay living inside my own head trying to figure out where we went wrong. Why he'd left the way he had. I'd been making myself crazy and Mason had turned out to be the perfect distraction. He hadn't pressured me. He'd just been happy to find someone who liked the things he did outside of football. We had so much in common, from loving astrology to reading fantasy books to listening to Mason play the guitar. He had so many talents.

We became best friends that spring break. He hadn't filled the void Griff left behind but he'd made my heart beat. He'd inspired me.

My mind comes back to the present. After eating and drinking, I don't feel as weak, but I decide to cab it back to the beach house since the sun is fully up and the air is humid.

As I walk through the front door, everyone is awake. Chattering draws me toward the kitchen. My brother and Griff are eating breakfast at the table. Griff has a laptop set up in front of him, and my heart clenches. It squeezes in a way it only can when he is near.

"Thanks Annette," he says, and snaps his laptop shut. *Who is Annette?* I shouldn't care, but how can I not? After everything we've shared and felt, I can't stop caring. I wish it was an emotion I could flick off with a switch.

Griff's attention fixes on me. I hate that I like it.

"Look at you, squirt." His aquamarine eyes are hooded. I'm still in my running gear, my skin damp, my hair in a ponytail.

Logan eyes him. Griff has never been so blatant about his attraction to me.

"Cut that shit out," Logan warns. It doesn't matter that I'm a grown-up. My brother will always see me as his little untouchable sister.

"What are you up to today?" I ask my brother, figuring we should hang out.

He's too distracted by something on his cell phone to even hear what I've said.

"Logan," I repeat, my tone bleeding irritation. I need a distraction from Griffin, and Logan is the perfect candidate.

"Huh?" His head snaps up. "Sorry, what did you say?"

"I asked your plans."

"Oh, uh . . . I just plan on chilling by the pool. I figure I should get some of my lesson planning out of the way. The principal assigned me to a senior course for next year that I haven't taught before." He pushes his glasses up his nose.

When did he become so responsible? Last time we hung out, he was an immature college student who was partying and messing around all the time.

"You suck." I push out my lower lip.

He rolls his eyes playfully. "Totally. This adulting thing is so messed up," he says, using a mock teenager voice that I am sure he hears his students use.

"Oh whatever." I wave him off playfully. Logan returns to messaging someone on his phone.

"All right then," I say to myself. Even though Griff is watching me, I don't ask what he's up to today because just seeing him splits my heart in two. I can't imagine what spending time with him would do to me.

I grab a cold bottle of water from the fridge and head out back, where we have a swimming pool. Mom is watching Kyle in the water.

"Where's Jenn?" I ask, looking around for her. Until the funeral, we hadn't seen each other in so many years. A trip to the beach house might mean spending quality time together.

Mom's lips purse. "She's asleep."

I look to my watch. It's nine o'clock. I don't know much about kids, but I figure they wake early, which means Jenn should have too. Mom gives me an *I know* look.

"Hi Aunty Jojo," Kyle calls out to me from the water. Mom has him in a life jacket.

"Hey there. Would you like a swim partner?" I ask. The cool water looks too good to pass up. I remove my runners, socks and money pouch, and drop them and my phone on a lounge chair. I dive in with my clothes on.

"Why don't you go take it easy, Mom?" I suggest from inside the pool.

"Maybe I should get started on dinner," she answers. I'm surprised she isn't in bed curled up in a ball. That's where I was for a long while when my husband died.

"You don't need to do that. I could probably whip up something quick. We have all day," I chuckle.

"That's a nice offer. Although I'm guessing your idea of whipping something up would consist of a green smoothie." Her nose wrinkles. "Not sure Kyle, Logan, or Griff would give it their seal of approval." A small laugh escapes her.

I'm in awe of Mom right now. The way she's able to continue on with her life—she's so strong. "Very funny." My lips twist.

"I want to cook. It relaxes me." She shrugs, standing. "Besides I haven't had you all together at my table in a long time. I need this. Cooking is cathartic for me." She attempts another smile but the sadness peeks through.

"If you put it that way . . ." I smile, ". . . who am I to get in your way?"

"Kyle, are you hungry?" She turns her attention to my sweet nephew, who is treading water beside me.

"Yes."

"I'm going to go put on a bathing suit and head to the beach. Want to join me?" I ask Kyle. I'd like to bond with him on my own, and by the twinkle in his eyes, I'm guessing I just made him very happy.

"Yesss," he cheers, then pauses, looking to his grandmother for approval. "Can I go, Grama?"

"Of course," Mom answers, holding a towel up to wrap him.

I stand dripping wet beside Kyle. "Hey, don't I get the same special treatment?" I joke.

Mom looks to me thoughtfully. "You absolutely do, Jojo bear," she says, calling me by my childhood nickname. She takes a towel from one of the lounge chairs and holds it up for me too. I step toward her, and she wraps me up like I am a little girl.

"Thanks, Mom." I blink for effect and give a wide smile.

"You know you will always be my baby." She grins and gives me a hug.

"I'm going to get you all wet," I chide.

"It feels so good to have you here after all this time. I'm going to take advantage of every minute of having my three kids home."

Her words cause guilt to flood through me and I feel terrible for staying away so long. Just because I was hurt doesn't mean Mom should have suffered. I vow to be a better daughter.

She pats my back and turns her attention to Kyle who is sitting in a lounger, all wrapped up in his towel. "Can I make you a quick peanut butter and jelly sandwich? That used to be your mom's favorite."

"Blech!" Kyle's face scrunches up. "I don't like peanut butter. How about a grilled cheese sandwich?"

"Grilled cheese it is." Mom smiles down to him.

I go up to my room and slip on a bikini and cover up, then I head back down to the kitchen.

"All ready?" I ask Kyle.

He beams at me, putting the last bite of grilled cheese in his mouth.

Jenn trudges into the kitchen, looking like she had a rough night of partying.

"Good morning, Jenn," I say. We got in late last night. Jenn went out right after she settled Kyle into bed.

Her face contorts, and what seems like an attempt at a smile looks more like a frown.

Griff stares up from his laptop. "Where you headed?" He's looking directly at me.

"The beach," I say rigidly. It's so hard to talk to him.

He looks between me and Kyle, giving my nephew an easy smile. "Mind if I join?"

Kyle nods emphatically. I get the impression he isn't used to all this attention. I don't have it in me to tell Griff I would rather be alone with Kyle.

"Great." Griff snaps his laptop shut.

"Where's Logan?" I look around for my brother, hoping he can act as a buffer. With Logan around, Griff won't get into anything with me.

"I think he went upstairs," Griff says.

"He's been very pre-occupied," Mom says.

"I noticed that too," I answer, then I look to Griff. If anyone knows what is going on with Logan, it would be him.

He shrugs. "I think it has to do with a woman but I can't say more. You know, bro code and all."

"If it has to do with a woman, that's a good thing. If there is something to share, I'm sure he will. I mean, the boy has never brought a girl home. It will have to happen eventually, right?" Mom looks between me and Griff.

"I have a feeling this one is special. Now let's change the subject." Griff winks and walks over to the kitchen table where a fruit platter is settled in the middle. He takes a grape and pops it into his mouth. "Ready to head out?" he asks.

My gaze drops to his full lips that are a little wet since he licked them after eating the grape.

I swallow. "Yup."

While Kyle waits by the door, I grab some beach towels and sand toys from the front closet. Griff, Kyle, and I leave the beach house together and head across the street to the beach. My chest feels tight from nerves as I try to convince myself that this day should be about getting to know Kyle, and not dwelling on a past I can't change anyway. I turn to look at Griff. He's wearing a plain white t-shirt that hugs his chest and shoulders and makes his muscles pop. His board shorts hug his fine behind and mirrored glasses cover his pretty eyes and all I can think is that I am in bigger trouble than I realized because I am still attracted to Griffin fucking Campbell.

Chapter 13

Jolie

Kyle makes a run to the shoreline and starts to build a sandcastle. Griff lays out his towel next to mine. I reach for my cover-up and pull it over my head.

Griff lifts his sunglasses and watches me intently. Is it pain I see in his aquamarine eyes? Or lust?

"Stop watching me," I chide. He's making me self-conscious, even if I am comfortable in my own skin. It took me time to get my self-esteem back after the way he left, but Mason was a pro at making me feel good, and after a while, I began to believe in my own self-worth again.

Griff's Adam's apple bobs. "When you have a chance, I'd like to talk."

"Isn't it a little late for that?" I snap, then regret it. There's no point fighting over or rehashing our history.

He drops the sunglasses back over his eyes. For some reason it feels like a barrier between us and I breathe a little easier without his crystal clear blue eyes boring into me. "I'm hoping it isn't." He sits on his towel, his legs bent in front of him and his arms resting on his knees.

The smell of his expensive cologne and sunscreen wafts my way. Even though he doesn't smell the way he used to his demeanor and presence still feel so familiar. A lot of our time together was filled with happy loving moments and now my body betrays me by reacting to him. I inhale deeply. "Not now, okay? I'm here for Kyle," I say, because at age four, he knows to go play by himself in the sand quietly. Something about that irks me.

"How about I help you make a castle?" I walk toward Kyle and plop myself down in the sand.

"You don't mind getting dirty?" he asks, surprised.

"What do you mean?" I begin to gather a mountain of sand.

"Mommy doesn't like to sit in the sand," he explains. *Sounds like Jenn.*

"When your mommy was a kid, we used to build sandcastles on this very beach." I smile, remembering the past. Daddy used to join us in building fortresses.

"Really?" His eyes grow wide like I just told him we were going to Disneyland or something.

"Yeah, we used to sometimes bury each other in the sand, then rinse off in the ocean."

"That sounds fun. I don't have any sisters or brothers but a lot of the kids in my preschool have them," he says working the sand.

I grab two pales. "I think we need some water. Want to help me?" I pass Kyle one of the pails. His loneliness seems to be tugging on my heartstrings.

"I want in," Griff says, standing.

He follows close behind us to the water and I can't help but envision a life we could have had if Griff hadn't left me. Would we have been here on this beach with our children?

My heart splinters. After Mason died the idea of me having children died too. I'm not sure a child really would have fit into his lifestyle, but it was something I had hoped for down the road. I hate to think that a little bit of resentment bubbles inside me now about Jenn not giving a damn about the precious gift she's been bestowed.

Griff splashes us. The cool water is a shock to my skin and I yelp heading in a little deeper so that the water hits my knees. He follows us in and splashes Kyle too and suddenly, we are having a water fight. Kyle giggles as he fills the bucket and throws it at Griff.

"Good one." I high five Kyle and he's right there offering me his palm, laughing so hard his whole body shakes.

"Oh! You think that was good?" Griff warns us. Suddenly, he's charging toward me, I run sideways not wanting to go in any deeper only he catches up and lifts me. "Griff. . . please. . . don't."

"Come on the water is crisp it will be refreshing," he says mischievously. If he drops me from this angle I won't be able to catch myself and the water is freezing. I hate swimming in cold water. He gets ready to drop me right in. This feels like déjà vu.

"Griff, come on. Don't . . . the water is cold. I hate cold water." I whine like a little girl.

"Exactly," he replies, and he lets me go. My body falls into the water first I put out my hands to stop my head from completely submerging but a wave rolls in and knocks me over. The jolt of cold sucks the air from my lungs but I quickly scramble to my feet and charge toward him.

"You're going down," I warn playfully. "Come on, Kyle. Help me bring down Griff." I wink to my nephew.

He winks back at me. I have the urge to squeeze his cute cheeks. he's just so adorable.

"Now I'm in trouble," Griff says walking backward deeper into the water.

Kyle runs up to him and grabs his arms trying to stop him from going deeper. Only Griff looks like a tall giant with loads of muscle next to Kyle. Kyle needs my help, so I climb on Griff's back. "There's no escaping now," I say with an evil laugh, and Griff falls down into the water only he holds my legs, taking me with him. *Jerk.*

"We did it, Aunty," Kyle cheers.

"We sure did." I smile. Now that my body has adapted to the water temperature, it doesn't feel so bad.

"That was fun. Mommy never plays with me at the beach," he says, causing my stomach to turn.

"Anytime you want me to hang out with you on the beach, let me know. You're a cool kid," Griff says, ruffling the hair on Kyle's head. Why does he have to go and be sweet like that? It reminds me of the boy I fell in love with. A boy with the biggest heart I knew.

"Thanks." Kyle smiles.

"How about we finish up that sand castle?" I suggest, because I need space from Griffin. If he is so loving and kind, then why did he leave the way he did? It was so callous.

"Okay," Kyle says.

Griff follows close behind Kyle and me. I kneel in the sand next to the castle we began to build, and feel Griff watching me. I wonder what he's thinking.

It's warm enough that the hot sun dries us fast. I smile to Kyle.

"Aunty, we need more water," he says.

"Go ahead," I say, and keep my eyes on him as he reaches the shoreline.

"Something is really messed up with your sister," Griff says quietly and fast.

I eye him and see the worry lines forming on his forehead. "We don't know that. Just because she doesn't like the beach doesn't make her a bad mom," I say trying to defend my sister.

"She's neglecting him, Jojo. I can feel it," he says, and my broken heart develops another fissure. Griff's mom left him, and his father neglected him, but we don't know for sure if Jenn is failing at her parental duties.

"Griff, don't jump to conclusions. I'll talk to mom and see what she thinks. I'll touch base with Jenn too. Maybe she just needs a break from being a single mom," I suggest. Jenn was an irresponsible teenager but I can't believe she would neglect her own child.

"Maybe you're right," he rubs at the scruff on his chin. It used to be a nervous gesture. I don't know if that's changed. "I am worried. Keep me updated I want to know what Kathy thinks," he whispers as Kyle returns with the pail.

"I'll talk to her later. Promise." I end it there, not wanting Kyle to catch on to the conversation.

"Logan was saying you work as an aesthetician," Griff says.

"Yeah," I answer, not adding the part that the job is history. I keep the conversation between us light and courteous but not too friendly, despite our little fake fight in the water. There is no way Griff and I are becoming besties.

He nods. "I just always thought you'd do something with history like Logan," he says, and his words irritate me. I don't want to answer him, but I also don't want to create tension around Kyle.

"I'm actually planning on heading back to school," I say quietly. Why does it feel like he's looking at me with longing? It makes me feel uneasy.

"Really? That's amazing. Good for you."

"Thanks. And you? I hear you work in the film industry." I leave out my brother's description about him being a Hollywood hotshot.

"I make movie trailers. I love my job. I'm grateful to have come this far," he says, sounding humble.

"That's really great." I smile sincerely.

"Thanks." He gives me a thoughtful look that holds a hundred unsaid words. "So where do you plan on going to school?"

"I haven't thought that far ahead," I answer curtly. This feels so awkward. It's weird to think how close we once were. Now we are like strangers, forcing conversation. I just want to get away from him.

We extend the sand castle to a long row, each of us working hard. I'm relieved Griff has ended his attempt at small talk.

My mind drifts again to the first night I spoke with Mason. He had come back to my room to get binoculars while the party was raging at the beach house. We'd sat on this very beach in the sand and watched the stars.

"I love stargazing," Mason says. "The universe is just so big, and we are so small in comparison."

I can see his breath. The air is so cold. Still, it is better to be out here than back at the house.

"Yeah." I sigh, feeling blissful that a high school quarterback is hanging out with little old me. "I'm the baby of my family. Everyone is always fussing over me, which is great because I get spoiled but also overbearing because I get too much attention. I shouldn't complain, but sometimes I wonder what it would feel like to be a small speck in the sky."

"Exactly," Mason agrees, looking into my eyes with awe. He watches me

the way Griff used to. "Everyone expects so much of me. I'm quarterback. Coach really thinks I can make it big, so he works me harder than everyone. My family and teachers see me as this star. They're sure I'm going places, and they don't let me forget it for one minute."

"That must be hard. Having to shoulder that kind of responsibility."

"My family doesn't have a lot of money. Sometimes they talk quietly about me making it big and helping them live a better life." He looks out to the water, his gaze intense. "Sometimes I feel like people are my friends because of football. Because they think I'm a star. It's annoying. I actually hate having attention on me."

"But you love playing football," I say, because why would he work so hard if he didn't?

"I more than love it. It's why I put up with all the other bullshit." His lips quirk on one side.

I smile. "I get that. When you're passionate about something, working hard isn't a big deal. I'll probably become a history professor like my dad."

"Oh yeah?" He looks at me like I amaze him. "What kind of history?"

"I don't know. I love learning ancient history but then I also love learning about American History and British history," I mumble quickly, a familiar excitement filling me when I speak about history. "I have time to decide anyway."

Mason watches me like I am a wonder. "I'm glad we met, Jolie. You seem to get me more than anyone else I know." He grins wide.

I am happy to make a friend. I can't think of Mason in any way but platonically. Griff broke my heart when he left but my heart still wants him, my lips still ache to kiss his, yet there is also anger that stirs deep in my belly. Him leaving me feels like a betrayal and from what I understand from Logan, Griff has no intention of ever coming back. He wants to start a new life. Logan says he deserves a fresh start. I don't disagree with that, but that fresh start was supposed to include me.

"Hey, where did your mind just go?" Mason says, interrupting my thoughts.

I give my head a good shake. "Sorry."

"Don't be. Who broke your heart?" he asks, and my stomach sinks. Am I that obvious?

"It doesn't matter," I answer. "He's gone now."

"As in, dead?" Mason asks, causing my heart to jolt.

My eyes widens at those words. The idea of something bad happening to Griff guts me.

I take Logan's words to heart. I have to let Griff go. I don't know why he left the way he did, but he deserves a chance at a good life. I want that for him more than anything.

"I wanted to kiss you, but I see your heart is already taken," Mason says, surprising me.

A blush crawls up my cheeks. I am only used to Griff, who has been a constant in my life. When the time comes, I don't know how I will bring myself to kiss another boy. "My heart was stolen."

"That bad, huh?" Mason gives me a knowing look.

"You know something about that?" I ask, because the look on his face tells me he did.

"My mom is a widow—suffers from a broken heart. She says she can never love another man again since my dad passed."

"I'm sorry." I frown.

"Yeah, my dad taught me to throw my first football." His lips turn down and he looks to me curiously. "You're too young to give up on love and I'm patient," he says, and just like that, Mason Amos becomes my best friend, even though he doesn't hide the fact that he likes me or that he is waiting for my heart to heal.

Eventually, I develop feelings for Mason, with a heart that is still broken beyond repair, and he accepts me.

MY MIND PULLS me back to the present. The sand castle is almost finished. Griff is working hard, and Kyle seems to be eating up his attention. Griff is a natural with him, and I hate that I've gone back into my own head, as I usually do.

"All done," Kyle says, standing proud.

"That is one great sandcastle," I praise my nephew who is smiling wide.

"Can I go for a swim?" Kyle asks with hopefulness in his eyes.

"Sure." I walk over to the water's edge with him and Griff follows close behind. "Don't go too deep."

"I know. I only go up to my knees," Kyle says back.

"He's bright for a four-year-old," Griff says.

"Yeah." I look at Griff and my heart squeezes.

Silence falls between us. I never really got over him. I learned to live without him but he took a piece of me I never found again. I don't know how to behave around him now. My emotions are like a hurricane, swirling in every possible direction.

"We need to talk," he says adamantly.

"I know." I exhale a long breath. This talk is a long time coming. Yet learning the truth scares me. My life took such a different turn to the one I envisioned as a lovesick teenager. I almost don't want to open old wounds.

It won't change anything anyway. But Griff is a member of my family. We can't run from each other forever. My wishy-washy feelings make me feel dizzy.

I think of my conversation with mom back in Boston. She figured out that Griff and I had feelings for each other way back when. And the way he looks at me now, I can see he's hurting.

I owe it to both of us to hear him out.

Chapter 14

Jolie

"Dinner is delicious, Mom." Logan smiles, shoveling mashed potatoes and brisket into his mouth. It's the most words we've exchanged the whole meal, besides Kyle telling everyone how much fun he had with Griff and me at the beach today.

"What is up with you kids?" Mom asks, frustration leaking from her tone. She has every right to be upset. She worked hard in the kitchen making this meal; the least we can do is be civil, but there is something missing. I don't know if it's because it's our first meal here at the beach house without Dad, or if it's just the long period of time we've spent apart from each other that has created a rift. "There was a time when I couldn't get you to stop talking, even when you had food in your mouths." Mom laughs, possibly trying to break the tension at the table.

Jenn drops her fork on the plate. It makes a loud clattering sound, and all attention is drawn to her. How some things never change. "I'm going to head out for a bit," she says and stands with her plate, walking it to the kitchen sink.

Logan eyes me and Griff does too.

"What is going on with you?" Mom snaps.

Jenn has been anti-social and just weird since we got here but leaving in the middle of the meal is plain rude. Typical Jenn—we are here to console Mom, yet somehow, she makes things about her.

Mom's worry for her is transparent on her face.

Jenn went to design school in California but never finished when she married Husband Number One. He cheated on her and they divorced. Then she married again and had Kyle with Husband Number Two. A year later, they divorced. She had small weddings both times and didn't invite us. She only told us she was married after the deed was done.

"Nothing, Mom. I'm just going through stuff." She drops the plate in the sink. Logan side eyes me, clearly wanting to know what's up with her. I shrug my shoulders.

Jenn leaves through the swinging kitchen door. "I'm heading to the Frog's Den," she shouts, loud enough that we all hear.

"I'll drop by later to say hello," I holler back just as I hear the slam of the front door. I wince. My attention is drawn to Kyle as I worry how he must feel about his mother's outburst. His head is dropped and he has stopped eating. I look to Griff who is sitting beside him and he raises his eyebrows in an I told you so way. I nod to him. Maybe he's right and Jenn isn't being a good parent.

IT'S BEEN a long time since I stepped foot in the Frog's Den. The place still has an old rustic feel. The bar is still covered in all brands of neon beer signs, although it looks like more exotic beers have been added over the years. The original owner was a woman named Sally. Her husband was a fisherman, and she ran this bar. They lived inland.

I used to come in here with my dad during the day and get Sally's famous clam chowder soup. It was mine and Dad's thing that we did together. I miss him so much it hurts.

I spot Jenn by the bar nursing a beer. A man is leaning over the bar next to her and they seem to be deep in conversation.

"Hey there." I knock my shoulder softly into hers and give her a friendly smile. If she needs help, I'm willing to give it.

She gives me a flustered smile and the man she was talking to turns his attention to a football game on the television.

"What's got into you Jenn? We haven't seen each other in ages. I was expecting a warm welcome. Not the cold shoulder." I stare her down, waiting for an answer.

A puff of air escapes her and she rolls her eyes. "Little Miss Jojo, always saying what's on her mind," she says, and she's being mean. Growing up she wasn't the world's best big sister, but she wasn't mean either—more just indifferent. I'm not sure where this current attitude is coming from.

On closer look, I notice her eyes are glazed over. She's drunk already?

"Hey, what can I get you?" The bartender walks up to me.

"You remember Jojo. Don't you?" Jenn cuts in and asks.

"I do," he answers with a wide smile. He looks to be about my age, maybe a little older. "Michael. Sally's son. Nice to see you." He extends his hand to shake mine.

"Sorry. It's been a while since I last saw you." He looks nothing like the boy version of himself.

"No worries. Good to see you again." He smiles, and I shake his hand and look over to my sister. She rolls her eyes at me. What is up with her?

"How is Sally?" I ask to deflect attention away from my sister's rudeness.

"She's good. Retired. I run the place now."

"I'm glad to be in a familiar place. I used to come in here with my father and have your mom's clam chowder soup. It was my favorite," I say, smiling at the fond memory.

"We still have the old recipes. I can grab you a bowl if you like," he offers, pointing to the back of the bar where the kitchen is situated.

"Thanks. I'm good. My mom just made a big dinner and I'm stuffed. Can I just get a Bud Light?" I ask.

"Aw! Little sister drinking beer," Jenn says, taunting me.

I look at her, wide-eyed, irritation clawing at my insides. "I'm twenty-eight years old. I've been drinking beer since I turned twenty-one," I say with my jaw loose.

"Why am I not surprised you waited to be legal," she scoffs. Before I can answer, she turns her attention to the male suitor beside her.

The man smiles wide and leans in to her. My insides cringe. I'd never be able to pick a guy up at a bar. I still believe a kiss should mean something. Not Jenn though. It seems things are just the way I remember back in high school. Certain men are like magnets to her and she gives herself too easily.

"Jenn," I snap, because this ridiculous behavior has to end. She is a mom to a sweet four-year-old boy. She needs to start respecting herself more, for Kyle's sake.

Her head swivels around and she gives me a lazy smile. "What is it? I'm busy, if you haven't noticed."

"Tell your gentleman friend you're busy right now because you need to talk to your sister who you haven't seen in more than five years," I say gritting my jaw tight.

"Sorry, honey." Her smile is saccharine as she pulls her attention from me and places her hand on the gentleman's forearm, smiling to him seductively. "What do you say we get out of here?" Her voice purrs and bile rises in my throat. At age thirty and being a single mom, I'd have thought she would have grown up.

The man she's propositioned looks just as shocked as I feel. Problem is, he also looks game.

"Sure, baby," he answers her. *Slime bucket.*

She stands from her stool, swaying slightly. I internally argue she's drunk and isn't making a logical decision, but this is Jenn, and this is how she behaves.

She takes off, and I sit by the bar and sip my Bud Light, alone.

Michael's cheeks flush as he tries to look away. I don't even have words to explain what just happened.

"Hey."

A gruff voice pulls my mind from racing at dangerous limits. When I look up, Griff has taken a seat on the stool beside me.

"Hi." I turn my head to look for Logan too. Someone needs to talk some sense into Jenn.

"Where's Logan?" I ask. I'm too worked up over Jenn's behavior.

"Said he wanted to chill at home. I think he didn't want to leave your mom alone. She was pretty upset about Jenn's behavior," Griff answers.

"Mom really doesn't need Jenn's drama," I say.

"No, she doesn't, but when has your sister cared? Did you get a chance to talk to her? She just waved at me when she left with that dude," he says and it looks like he cringes.

"Not exactly. . . I think you may be right about something being off with her." I hate to think Jenn hasn't grown up but she is acting so irresponsibly it sickens me.

"You want to grab a seat at a table?" He looks nervous. I think.

"Oh! I wasn't planning on staying," I answer quickly. I'm not ready to face the past just yet.

"We can just talk about Jenn if you want," he says, clearly reading my distress. How does he know I'm freaking out? I haven't seen him in a decade. "I'm scared too," he says, surprising me. "But when we do have that conversation, I need it to be in private."

I nod. What harm can it do?

I am curious about him. I've thought about him more than I would like to admit over the years. And when the time is right, hearing the reason he left the way he did may give me closure or cause me to wring his neck.

I stand and take my beer with me over to a table. My heart beats differently when I'm near him, which isn't a good sign, and I hate that the emotion bubbling inside me resembles attraction, desire along with confusion and hurt.

"I came in after she propositioned that dude. Fuck that is messed up." He shakes his head, staring me in the eyes. "What? Why are you looking at me that way?"

"What way?" I lean against the backrest of the booth, needing space between us so I stop paying attention to the way he smells and the way he watches me with those clear eyes. I once thought he was so transparent but then he proved me wrong.

"I don't know. Bewildered, shocked . . . does that sum it up for you?" His lip quirks on one side. Does he act like Jenn when he's not on the Cape? With the way he looks today, I'm sure he has a long line of women, and he clearly is a liar. He told me he wanted to marry me and have kids together, and then he was gone.

I snap my mouth shut. I hadn't realized my thoughts were transparent on my face. "Um sorry. I figured that was something you did too. I mean, pick up random chicks." I scrunch my nose. Maybe *honesty is the best policy* isn't the most appropriate method for right now. I'm not looking to fight with him.

He gives me a wry smile. "Never been my thing." His answer is curt, leading me to wonder. "I don't think you want to get into that now."

"Why not? I assume you're like my brother. Unable to keep a girl longer than a month." I don't know why I am pushing him this way. None of it matters. Only somewhere deep inside me it does. Why did he promise me everything and leave? The wound is still open and raw.

"Okay, so I haven't been in a relationship that lasted longer than three months, but that's because I haven't been with the right girl. When I find my match, I plan to stick," he says.

Yeah. I call bullshit. He was supposed to stick to me and he didn't. His words pierce my heart. "This was a bad idea. I should leave." I shift off the bench and get up.

"Wait." His hand lands on mine on the table, stopping me. If I'm not mistaken, he looks confused. We stare into each other's eyes.

A beat passes. "I'll come with you then." He stands from the booth.

"You didn't order a drink yet," I say, because space is what I need.

"I didn't come to drink. I came for you," he says with a deep, gravelly voice.

"Griff . . . I . . . ." I'm at a loss for words.

"Let me just walk you back," he pleads.

It feels like I'm holding my breath underwater. I finally nod. "Okay."

"Okay," he repeats, sounding hopeful.

Suddenly, I recognize the song playing on the speakers. "Stairway to Heaven" by Eric Clapton. My breath hitches and Griff just stares at me. We don't move, like we are both frozen in time as the words come through the speakers, seeping into my soul, reminding me of the day Griff taught me how to slow dance in my parents' basement.

"We had a lot of firsts," he says, his voice raspy and his eyes watery. I open my mouth to say something but I'm still frozen. Feeling overwhelmed, I spin on my heel. I walk over to the bar to pay for my beer.

I place a ten dollar bill on the bar.

Michael walks over. "No worries. It's on the house," he smiles.

"Thank you," I force a smile while battling my nerves.

"Come back again," he grins.

"Will do." I turn and head out the front door of the bar. There are speakers outside too and without the loud chatter, the song is louder, clearer. Griff is a few steps behind me as I take a few ragged breaths, trying to slow my thumping heart.

"May I have this dance?" he asks, extending a hand toward me.

I don't move. It feels like I'm not breathing.

"Jolie, you need to believe that I would have never left you of my own free will. Things happened. I would like to tell you what, but right now, I want to dance with you." His voice is smooth, sultry, and filled with so much emotion the icicles around my heart melt. Or perhaps one of the many fissures he caused in my heart a long time ago heals. Either way, I don't have it in me to say no.

He takes a step toward me, and we are moving together on the sidewalk in front of the Frog's Den. It doesn't matter that people are walking by, smiling as they watch us, and it's not totally weird that we are dancing out here on our own, because in Griff's arms, I feel at peace. I haven't felt this way in a long time. As we move, I smile, remembering just how long the song truly is. A million memories run through my mind and when the song ends, my last memory of him enters my mind too. The day he left me . . .

"Hey. Where did you just go?" he asks quietly, looking at me intently again.

"Sorry." I give my head a shake.

"Don't be sorry. Tell me what's on your mind." He seems concerned, but a lot has changed.

"I . . ."

"You once shared everything with me," he says, and my heart, the one that had been numb for years, cracks all over again.

"Things have changed since then. Should I remind you that you walked away and didn't look back?" I snap. I take a quick breath. I can't allow him to get under my skin. As familiar as he feels, we are damaged. That isn't something I can overlook. Not when he was an integral part of my life.

"Then let me tell you what happened. You need to believe I would never willingly walk away from you," he says, his words cutting me deep.

"I've heard you say that with no explanation." I look him in the eyes, and he holds my gaze. Nervous butterflies take flight in my stomach, and I place my shaky hands by my side.

"Let's walk and talk," he suggests.

"I've made a million excuses in my mind about what happened to you, from getting abducted by aliens, to being wanted by the KGB because your father had been a secret agent. You left for Africa to join the Peace Corps." My tone bleeds hurt and anger, but he just watches me with a pained expression.

"Unfortunately, none of those are true." He lets out a heavy breath.

His cell rings. He ignores it.

"The truth is. . ." His cell rings again and he checks the screen. My brother's name lights up the screen.

"You should answer," I say, and not because I'm not completely curious about what he's going to say, but because I'm terrified that whatever he will say won't justify his actions and then it will mean our past meant nothing to him.

Enough time has passed that it shouldn't matter. We live separate lives and yet here we are, thrown back together under the same roof. *Thanks, Mom.*

"Hello," he answers. "Yeah, she's here with me. She followed Jenn here, yeah . . . No, she took off . . . yeah man I don't know what to say. . .with a guy," he says.

I hear my brother's cursing from the other line.

"Chill you don't want to worry your mom," Griff says. "Okay. . . yeah. . .obviously." He ends the call.

He turns his attention to me. "Your mom was worried about Jenn."

"I figured," I answer.

Silence blankets us for a few moments, and I take in the salty night air, a brisk breeze providing some relief from the tightness in my chest.

"It's harder than I thought . . ." Griff breaks the quiet. I turn and look up to him as we continue walking, not understanding the meaning of his words. "Telling you why I left. Things were so complicated . . . I was a boy. I had nothing and no one to fall back on," he explains, sounding apologetic.

"You had me," I remind him.

"I always loved you but, in that instance, love wasn't enough," he answers. I would argue that notion but a large part of me feels it's the truth, a sour lesson I learned from my husband.

"I won't argue with that." I wince because I used to be that girl who believed in fairytales.

Griff's eyes turn wide. "Really?" His surprise quickly morphs into sadness. The deep lines of his forehead crease together. "Life hasn't been a walk in the park for you. I'm sorry for that. I'm sorry for all of it. I wish I could have done things differently but given my circumstances, I was stuck between a rock and a hard place."

"I can't lie and say you aren't making me completely curious, but it also feels like you are hiding something intentionally," I say, analyzing his demeanor.

He chuckles, dry and throaty. "You can still read me."

"Can I?" *It's been a decade since I last saw you.*

"Yes, very much so," he answers, seeming deep in thought. He tucks his hands into the front pocket of his jeans as we reach the beach house. He stops and we turn to look at each other. A part of me is not ready to hear what happened. "I never wanted to leave you," he begins and just like that I'm left with no choice but to face the truth about our past.

Chapter 15

Griffin

"I never wanted to leave you," I begin. "I loved you so much. I remember you as a girl." I smile at the fond memories of us playing together. We had been good friends. "You were always so kind to me. Sometimes it felt like I fascinated you and that made me feel so good inside."

Her eyes fill with tears and it shreds my heart.

"Logan was always my best friend but the bond we shared was special to me. You know how guys are. We aren't emotional with each other. Logan and I were a team. He knew my dad drank too much and my mom wasn't around but we didn't discuss it. Then there was you. You were so attentive. I hated to see how you looked up to Jenn and she never gave you the time of day. I knew how that felt," I pause knowing I should get to the point but she needs to know how I saw her. She was such an important part of my life that it ripped me apart when I was forced to leave after she gave me such an intimate part of herself.

"Yeah, you're right. Logan was always big on protecting me but he didn't want to spend time playing with his little sister and Jenn has always been pre-occupied with herself," she shrugs. "We share this strong past. That's what made it so hard for me to believe you had really left. I was sure you would return by Easter, but you never came back. I was filled with anger and resentment. Those emotions were so foreign to me. I hated that you brought out such negativity in me. I hated that you agreed to sleep with me and left me like I was nothing." Tears stream down her cheeks, but she watches me carefully. She isn't turning away from me which tells me that this is it. I never believed this day would come but it's here.

"I wanted to come back so badly. You have no idea. You were my everything. The fact that you trusted a kid like me with all your firsts. . ." my voice cracks. "I was practically an orphan. I had no one to care for me at home. I wore these dingy clothes. Your mom cut my hair herself. I probably hadn't showered enough. I believed your father was right to keep you away from me," I say.

She takes a step toward me and I am not sure what she is going to do. Slap me, hug me, scream? She points her finger in my face. "Don't talk like that. I always told you my dad was a jerk. I didn't see a dirty orphan. I saw a boy with crystal clear blue eyes that had a heart of gold. I saw a boy that liked to spend time with quiet and boring me. And I saw a boy that I trusted enough to go to when I needed help. We grew up together. You were in my bloodstream, a part of my life I always expected to be there just like any of my limbs. You taught me a very sour lesson when you cut me off." Her shaky finger drops and her shoulders sag. I see a defeated woman.

"Jolie. . .I . . .don't want to shatter everything you know to be the truth. I don't want to tear down the walls of your perfect castle," I answer as my heart beats erratically.

"Don't pull that shit on me. I'm not a princess. My life has been far from easy and if you think you are sparing me something you're sorely mistaken. I'm not the same girl you left behind. My glass castle was shattered a long time ago," she says and her cryptic words send a shiver down my spine.

I take a step toward her. My emotions running high. I place each of my palms on her shoulders and look into her eyes. "What happened to you?" Her green eyes turn round and her mouth drops open like she is ready to speak but she stops and snaps her mouth shut.

Chapter 16

Jolie

A part of me wants to tell him everything. Purge every deep dark secret that remains locked inside me but I can't. My stomach turns as my mind goes to my marriage. Mason and I married the year he had been drafted. We had just finished undergrad. Life was busy. I didn't get a job right away, deciding it was more fun to travel with my famous husband and attend games with some of the other players' girlfriends and wives.

After the first year, I'd had enough and started working for a software company in Texas. Mason and I spent less time together, with all his away games. Most of the guys on the team were cheating on their significant others. I knew Mason wasn't the type. Our problems stemmed from something else entirely.

"Please talk to me. Tell me what haunts you," he pleads, his eyes dropping to my lips as if his stare will force the words out.

"I can't," I turn my head to the side and pull my gaze from his. Staring into his baby blues is just too painful.

"Fine. Then let me tell you the truth. Let me purge my own demons," he says sounding broken and desperate.

I return my gaze to his. "I'm all ears."

His shoulders slacken. "Your dad never liked when I came over. I don't think he had a problem with me hanging with Logan, but he sure as hell hated when we played together or as we got older hang out," he says looking at me with what I am guessing is sympathy. "I would try and lay low when he was home and I was over. Lucky for me he wasn't home a lot," he laughs sadly.

"I remember thinking that I preferred you to be over than dad to be home as I got older. It makes me realize that since he died Logan, Jenn and I had him painted in this perfect image but it wasn't our reality. He was self-absorbed and not attentive. The image we painted was a façade," I say and I'm not sure why. Maybe because I hate hearing the way daddy made him feel, but as I think of my own words I know they're true. Daddy wasn't there for mom or us kids. Looking back on my childhood from an adult view makes me see things so differently. My parents did a good job of keeping us sheltered but all we saw was a loveless marriage and a man that was married to his job.

Griff clears his throat. "I uh. . .once heard him and your mom arguing about your father acting indiscreetly," he says and his face scrunches. "I'm sorry. I never thought it was my place to say anything. I still don't. The last summer I was here, I accidentally overheard your dad talking to another woman on the phone. He said lewd things and I tried to stay quiet, but I dropped your grandmother's vase on the floor, breaking it. He guessed I'd heard him," Griff says, looking at me with a sheen over his eyes.

"I remember when the vase broke," I say, remembering how mom had been upset.

"I tried to convince him I didn't hear a thing. He seemed to accept my answer," Griff says.

"Are you saying my father threatened you?" I ask because I had witnessed daddy threatening him more than once.

"Not exactly." He moves his head from side to side.

"Is my sister putting on her big girl pants? Because I can't believe you are going to pop Jojo's perfect little bubble," my sister's voice is sweet and perky and causes my head to snap around as she walks up behind me. As my gaze zeroes in on her I realize she's swaying.

"I'm having a private conversation. Do you mind?" I snap at Jenn shocking even myself. She really ticked me off earlier the way she left with that stranger and this whole conversation with Griff has me so on edge that I don't need her sarcastic remarks. Her words suddenly register and I feel like I do a double take. *Did Jenn know that dad was a cheater?* "What did you say?" I narrow my gaze on her. If she thinks Griff is going to pop my so called bubble it means she knows something about dad's indiscretions.

She lets out a garbled laugh and sways as she nears. "Aw. Aren't you all adorable. Look at that heartbreak on your face Jojo. Imagine how I felt? I caught Daddy getting off with another woman on the phone when I was fourteen."

I gasp and Griff curses under his breaths.

"For crying out loud! Jenn, why didn't you come to me?" I say as my anger toward her fizzles and is replaced with heartbreak and sympathy.

"Seriously? You want to know why? Okay." She clicks her tongue. "Daddy said it had to be our secret. He was sorry I had to witness his poor behavior. He said he would go to church and confess, and that it would never happen again. Only I knew. He was cheating on Mom." She begins to cry. "Shit! I think I'm going to be sick." She wobbles past us to the bushes that line the front of the beach house and vomits. I quickly rush over to her and hold her hair and rub her back.

"Well, that explains a lot," Griff mutters.

Jenn wipes her mouth with the back of her hand. "You all have a good night." She leaves us and walks toward the beach house, as if she didn't just drop a bomb.

"I should make sure she's okay," I say, to Griff. I follow my sister inside the house and up to her room where her sweet son sleeps on a single bed. I'm itching to get back to Griff. I was just on the cusp of finding out his reason for leaving. I can't imagine what daddy's indiscretions have to do with us.

"It wasn't fair for Dad to burden you with his problems. You were only a child, for goodness sake," I whisper as she undresses into her pajamas.

"Thanks, Jolie. That's nice of you to say. I haven't been all that kind to you to deserve your understanding." She slides into the other single bed in her room.

"You've been just fine. We can talk more in the morning," I whisper, not wanting to wake Kyle.

"I'd like that," she answers, and I give her a small hug. She smells like sex and tequila. "Get some rest."

I walk quietly through the house and back outside, where Griff is pacing up and down the sidewalk looking at the ground. My blood races through my veins as I anticipate what he will say next. I don't have a clue.

He walks toward me. His lips tipped in a frown. He takes a deep breath and I brace myself knowing that whatever Griff is going to tell me will change everything.

Chapter 17

Griffin

"I'm freaking out here," I say, looking into the eyes of the only girl I've ever loved. I thought my confession would rip her world apart. For years, I pondered how I would ever tell her the truth without destroying everything she knew to be true about her family. Only the woman standing in front of me now is strong; she isn't shaking or falling apart. Which also gives me the sinking feeling life has toughened her up.

"Tell me what you have to say. I can handle it. I'm not a porcelain doll that will break," she says, wrapping her hands around her middle.

"I can see that." I pause. "Okay, here goes . . . when I was away at college, there was a group of guys and I selling textbooks to students. The textbooks came from Russia. They were copies of the texts that weren't copyrighted. It was illegal, and I knew it, but I was finally making some money and it felt good not to worry anymore. I'd always worried about my next meal growing up; I went hungry more times than I care to remember," I say, and I watch a shiver run over her.

"I know you were hungry. I know Mom tried to help, but there was only so much she could do. She didn't want you to end up in the system," Jolie explains.

"Your mom kept me alive. I'll always be grateful to her." I almost say that's why I'm here now, but it wouldn't be the whole truth, because I'm here to tell the woman standing in front of me that I didn't leave her of my own free will. A part of me wants to blurt it all out and kiss her into oblivion, but things don't seem so straightforward. She's broken, and it's not like we can pick up where we left off.

She gives me a small smile.

"I got caught," I continue. "One of my professors figured out I was selling textbooks and he could have turned me in, but he didn't. Instead, he wanted to speak to my father. He wanted to make sure I would stop selling because I was jeopardizing my future, and he thought me to be a good kid. I was also on the football team, and we were doing well, winning games, and I was part of that success. No one wanted to see me kicked out of school." I pull my gaze away from Jolie and look to the curb. Even after all this time it is still fucking hard reliving the worst time of my life. "Can we take a seat?"

"Of course," she answers thoughtfully. I take the seat next to her on the curb, wishing I could reach out and hold her hand.

"I couldn't give my professor Dad's number because he didn't pay the phone bill often, and he could have been drunk and told him to fuck off. I gave him your dad's number and I called your father and asked him to do me a favor." I curse inside my head, remembering that awful day. I should have told my prof I didn't have a dad and given him Kathy's cell. Things would have played out very differently.

"Did Daddy talk to your professor?" she asks, so hopeful.

"He did. He spoke to my prof and saved my ass." I smile but it falters fast. "Christmas break I came home to see you. The day after we made love, I was hanging out with Logan. You were running errands with your mom. I overheard your dad on the phone. It was an inappropriate phone call. I tried to move away fast, but our gazes connected, and he knew I knew. He told me to leave your house and never come back. He said he knew there was something going on between us and he wouldn't have it. He warned me he would go to the police and have me charged for selling the books. He asked me to leave town that day, and he threw a few hundred bucks on the floor for a plane ticket." I still remember how the money had floated slowly through the air as my chest felt like it was splitting in two. I hadn't wanted his money. "I only wanted you and he made it impossible. If I stayed, I could have gone to jail. He said if I ever told you, he'd find a way to have me arrested." As those last words leave my lips, a burden is lifted but when I look over at Jolie, her head hangs between her shoulders and my stomach sinks.

She's quiet. Too quiet.

"Say something." My words are a plea.

She lifts a finger. "I need a moment," she whimpers.

"I'm so sorry." I don't know if she wants my arms around her, but my arms wrap her up and she begins to cry into my shoulder.

"I know," I whisper.

"In a million years, I never thought this would be the reason you left—not because of my father. He couldn't be responsible for ruining my life," she finally croaks out.

"It was more than my fear of going to jail. I feared my knowledge would destroy the only family you knew. I didn't want that for you. We were young, and I had no one to confide in. I was on my own," I mutter, wanting to make her feel better somehow. It had gutted me knowing that she saved herself for me and I had to leave with no explanation. I'd thought about telling Logan what had happened, but I'd been scared of his reaction. I hadn't trusted that my best friend would support me because my self-esteem had been low, and I'd figured he would agree with his dad. I wasn't good enough for Jolie.

"I'm so sorry. So very sorry," she repeats.

A garbled laugh escapes me. "*You're sorry?* I took something precious from you."

"Is that why you didn't come to the funeral?" she asks referring to her father's funeral.

"I couldn't pay my respects to a man who completely upended

my life and yours. He thought I would never be good enough. My self-esteem was never great, but it worsened after everything went down. I thought your father was right. I would be a good-for-nothing jerk like my own father. I've spent years in therapy. I would never want to be away from you intentionally," I say, taking her hand in mine. She doesn't pull away. It has to mean something. "When I found out you were with Mason, I figured it was for the best." I grit my jaw, remembering the day Logan told me Jolie had a serious boyfriend. I'd thought I was going to lose my shit. I hadn't been able to believe that not even a year had passed and she could be with someone.

I'd known Jolie. I'd known she didn't connect with people easily, and if she had, it had to mean she was in love.

"Mason was there for me through a dark time. We had become friends. I waited for you to contact me and you didn't. Then daddy died and you didn't show. After that I knew you were never coming back," she explains and I better understand how she could move on. Damn, it's still a hard pill to swallow, but now, looking into her eyes, I say, "I'm here now. I want to earn your trust again."

We stare into each other's eyes. My heart is beating so fast, and my mind is whirling. I want her to be mine again but I'm terrified to breath those words so I said earn her trust. After all these years I don't want to be rejected.

My revelation isn't so surprising. Ever since I saw her in that airport back in New York City, I've been feeling different. My heart has been beating weirdly, and this sense of hope keeps springing up inside me.

"This is a lot to take in," she says, turning her head. Dammit. I need to look in her eyes. It gives me some idea of what she could be thinking. "I wish I could scream at my father and tell him how much his actions have hurt me. How he side railed my life in a way he couldn't possibly have understood. It's frustrating and heartbreaking."

"I know," I say, hoping to find some way to console her, only she pulls her hand from my grasp. *Don't walk away. Please don't walk away.*

"I need time to process this," she says, standing.

"I get it. I mean, it's not like I thought I would come out here and we would fall back into each other's arms," I snicker. It sounds like such a lie, because that's exactly what I thought.

"Griff, I'm not the girl you left behind. I've experienced things that . . ."

"You've been through a lot. I just . . . want to get to know you again. Maybe we can spend some time together as friends. Being with you today on the beach was nice." I force a smile despite my disappointment.

"It was," she answers solemnly.

"I'm sorry I had to tell you at all. I never wanted to paint your dad in a bad light. I know he was a good father to you and Logan even though he really messed up where Jenn is concerned." I blow out a heavy breath. I hadn't expected Gary to treat his own daughter so badly. "He went too far."

"He did. It's hard to come to terms with all this. I mean, poor Jenn." Jojo looks up to the sky. "She must have been in so much pain, and none of us realized it was her acting out. My dad was not a good father. A good father would have never put his fourteen-year-old daughter in that situation. If he wanted to screw around so much, he should have left Mom. I just hate that he isn't here right now, because I want to scream at him."

"It's important you know that I didn't want to leave you," I reiterate. "You were always my favorite memory and my biggest regret."

"But you never came back. Not even after he died. You stayed away. That was on you," she says, her voice shaking.

"You're right. Like I said, I was broken. I heard you were with Mason and I didn't have it in me to see you with another man," I say.

"He's been dead two years." She swipes tears from her eyes.

"I didn't know how to face you. You married another man." It's hard to hide the hurt I feel over her finding love again. I blow out a heavy breath, needing to cool down because she isn't to blame. I left her broken. "I'm sorry. I don't mean to snap. That is all in the past," I say, remembering how I lashed out at the news of her engagement by fucking my way through too many girls. I'd thought it would ease the pain, maybe numb me, but it only made me feel worse because no one could replace the connection I shared with this woman. "I don't want to fight. I want to repair things. Honestly, when your mom called about Kip, I was on a short trip to New York to meet with a producer. I came back to support Kathy, but the moment I saw you in that airport . . ." Words can't express what I felt. "I may have convinced myself I was here for your mom, but deep down, I had to see you. Know you," I say, hoping with everything in me that she will understand and maybe find it in her heart to forgive me. It's taken me years of therapy to forgive myself. "Please say we can spend time together. Just friends . . . I'll take anything you're willing to give."

"I'm feeling overwhelmed by . . . everything. This is a lot," she says, and I read between the lines. She was the type of girl to kiss you because she loved you. She doesn't show her affection easily. I'm glad to see that hasn't changed.

"That's one of the things I've always loved about you," I say.

"Griff." She pauses, and it looks like she's deep in thought. "I don't know how . . ." She shakes her head. "I'm feeling over-whelmed. I've . . ."

"Whatever it is, you can tell me." I give her what I hope is a reassuring smile. When she was younger, she came to me for things she couldn't share with others.

"I . . . can't. I'm sorry. I need to go inside. I need space to think." She looks like she is on the verge of tears.

I try to place myself in her spot—her leaving me the way I did after we made love and never coming back.

I should have come sooner. I should have shown up at her wedding and told her not to marry the guy. Her father was gone by then, but I didn't. I fucked up, and I have to give her time while I try to find a way to make amends.

"See you in the morning?" I raise my brows and press my lips into a thin smile, not wanting to seem too hopeful.

"Yeah." She sighs and walks inside, and just like that, the only girl I've ever loved gives me a small ounce of hope. I head up to my room and crack my laptop open. I pull up Serena Harding's name on messenger.

I'm sorry but we have to end whatever this is between us. No more hooking up. Remember how I told you about Jolie, the girl from back home? Well, it seems like our chance has finally come. I can't mess this up. I'm sorry. But I think we both knew this was temporary. All the best to you, Griff.

It's a little harsh but it has to be done. I won't let anything stand in the way of me winning Jolie Bryant's heart back.

Chapter 18

Jolie

It's early morning, and the house is bathed in darkness as I tiptoe in my sneakers toward the front door. I barely slept a wink, but my body craves the high of running, and I always do my best thinking on those runs. As I make my way down the stairs, I spot Mom sitting in the same chair she sat in yesterday, her silhouette bathed in darkness.

"You can't sleep," I say softly. Walking over to her, I place a kiss on her cheek.

She shakes her head and frowns. "Kip and I had some good times in this house. On the beach. It almost seems like a cruel joke that he's gone now. I was . . . finally happy." She exhales softly, and my heart hurts for her. Dad may not have been her knight in shining armor, but Kip was.

"You don't have to hide the fact that you weren't happy with Dad. I sensed it as a child. Logan and Jenn did too." My heart beats rapidly as I test the boundaries, trying to gain some sense of what Mom knew about Dad. Maybe she knew of his indiscretions, and was protecting us.

"I wanted to keep our family together. I did love your father. We just stopped making each other happy at some point. I don't know if we would have stayed together or not when he died. I never saw myself with another man until Kip," Mom explains, looking to me with guilt in her eyes. "Maybe it was the way I grew up. My father leaving Nana the way he did for another woman. I remember the hurt. I didn't want that for my children. And your father stayed. Despite everything, he stayed," she repeats. Mom didn't talk about Nana much. Nana died when we were kids, and we never met our grandfather.

"Kip was Daddy's best friend. Did you always have feelings for him?" I bite the inside of my cheek as the last words leave my mouth. I feel bad pressing her for information while she's grieving. I've had these questions on my mind for years. I just never had the guts to ask something so scandalous or inappropriate. Only now that I know of Dad's many indiscretions, do I wonder if Mom did too. Was their marriage an open one? I can't straight-out ask that question.

Mom's green eyes round as she looks at me as if I've grown two heads. "No! I didn't have the hots for Kip if that's what you're asking," she chides. "I saw him as your dad's best friend. When your dad died, and Kip started coming around more for moral support, I understood he had feelings for me. It took me time to return those feelings. Even though I wasn't happy with your father, he was still the only man I had ever been with. He was the father of my chil- dren . . . Kip though . . ." She says his name wistfully. A blissful smile curves her lips. "He was patient. He helped me heal and showed me love." She stops staring at the empty space in front of her. It almost looks like she can see Kip, but then she turns to me. In a way that type of love reminds me of Mason; he also tried to love me enough to heal me. "I'm sorry. You don't want to hear how your mom fell in love with another man," she says with a shaky chuckle, and I see her flush, even in the dark. She really fell hard for Kip. I loved Mason as a person but his presence didn't stir me the same way Griff's did. There has always been something magical between Griff and I. It's still there and it makes me feel guilty. Like I am somehow betraying Mason and all his efforts to mend my broken heart.

"I'm glad you're sharing this with me." I give her hand a squeeze. Last night, I couldn't stop *what if*ing. What if I had gone after Griff and made him tell me his reasons for leaving? Would I have still ended up with Mason? Is our fate predestined? I feel almost crazy with questions, but I know I wouldn't change a thing. When I was younger, I was a shy pushover. Today, I am an outspoken, strong woman. My life has formed me and made me who I am today, and I like me. The me of today would have demanded answers from Griff. The me of back then curled into a ball and had her heart broken. Why does hindsight always have to be twenty-twenty?

Mom blinks. "I'm worried about all of you. Jenn seems like she's a mess. You're shut down, and your brother has his face glued to his computer screen. We've been here close to two days and things are not right," she says. Her motherly intuition is spot on, making me think that at some point we will need to tell her that we know our father was a cheater who drove Griff out of town. Maybe she already knows, and we are freaking out for no good reason.

"I'm hoping to catch Logan for a talk today. Hopefully he and I can figure out what's wrong with Jenn. Don't worry, Mom, please. Maybe try to go up and get some sleep," I suggest, because I'm not ready to share my newfound knowledge, and Jenn's behavior may very well be linked to my dad's inappropriate treatment of her, which I hope to get to the bottom of.

"Good idea. I spent the last couple hours making gelato," she says.

My eyes widen. "Seriously? What flavors?" My tone is filled with a girlish excitement. Mom makes the best gelato. She would always experiment with new recipes.

"Blueberry cheesecake and hazelnut chocolate." She grins mischievously, knowing those are two of my favorites.

"Thanks, Mom. You're making me want to give up on my run," I say playfully.

"It's six o'clock in the morning. Who can eat ice cream now?

Besides it won't have frozen over yet. It needs a couple more hours. You go for your run. Just be careful out there." She stands and heads for the stairs.

I turn for the door.

With Airpods in my ears, my feet hit pavement while Mom's words resonate. She only fell in love with Kip after Dad died. She didn't have feelings for him before. Which means it was only Dad who had been the cheater, the deceiver. He knew something was going on between Griff and I and he went to such lengths to keep us apart. Why did he think Griff was bad anyway? Just because he made one mistake by selling the textbooks doesn't mean he wasn't a good kid. He'd always done well in school. Last night, I felt like my heart was breaking all over again, knowing he'd felt like he had no choice but to leave. When he was asking for friendship, it felt like he wanted a whole lot more. After everything I've been through, I never wanted to settle down again. Now my heart screams to run into Griff's arms and embrace whatever will happen. But my mind is cautionary. He's some hotshot Hollywood guy now. I can only imagine what that means when it comes to the ladies, and we might not have the same connection we once did. Although being close to him makes my body buzz, I remember why I made a vow to never be in a relationship again. They don't have fairytale endings.

The sun begins to rise over the water. I inhale a deep breath of sea air noticing a shadow behind me. I nearly lose my footing when I realize Griff is in jogging attire, catching up to me. I don't stop, keeping pace, yet he manages to catch up.

His lips move but I don't know what he's said. I pull the Airpods out of my ears. "I can't run and talk," I say before he has a chance to say something.

"Okay, I'll keep up beside you. I won't say a word." He winks.

When he said he wanted to spend time together, I assumed it would be later in the day.

I don't say anything as he jogs beside me. He's in good shape, he keeps pace effortlessly his long muscular legs moving gracefully.

The scent of expensive cologne and sweat wafts my way. I stop my jog abruptly, leaning forward to catch my breath. Having him this close affects me too much. I need to set him and me straight.

"I don't want a relationship. I'm done with those," I say, even though I don't know if that's what Griff is looking for. "I'm not programmed to be a one-night stand or hook-up."

"And you think I want you to be a hook-up?" His lips curve on one side, and he raises his brows. I've offended him—maybe stunned him? His shoulders sag.

"No." I shake my head. "I'm sorry. I just . . . don't have much to offer," I mutter, feeling so off-kilter. I'm no good at this relationship stuff—never have been. Mason and I didn't date; we were friends first, and Griff and I were also.

"Why don't you ask me what I'm looking for then. After everything I told you last night, I feel like I've been transparent. I told you I was okay with friendship, but I would be lying if I didn't tell you I'm hoping for more." He places each of his hands on his hips. His breaths are heavy.

"I can't do more." I purse my lips together, feeling bad.

"I'm willing to prove you wrong," he says, looking me straight in the eyes. With those aquamarines holding my gaze in challenge, he takes a step toward me.

"Don't," I warn. He can't chip away at the walls I've built. I won't let him.

"You have so much to give," he says with a warm smile that almost makes my heart burst.

"That was the old Jojo. She's gone. I don't want a relationship. I'm happy with the way my life is." It's not a total lie. I love my friends in New York. I'm headed back to school. I thought love conquered all when in reality it just conquered me.

"Give me two weeks of your time. Nothing heavy. Friendship, kisses . . . I'll take whatever I can." He raises a brow.

"Friendship I can do. Don't expect kisses." I hold up a finger. Aw! Who am I kidding? I want to kiss him now but that would lead to no good. We live on opposite sides of the country and lead different lives. And above all fairy tale endings do not exist.

"No expectations, Jojo," he confirms.

"Friends." I extend my hand to shake his.

He laughs sardonically, taking my hand and pulling me into his sweaty chest. "I think I deserve a hug, for old time's sake," he says. His skin is hot as my body collides with his. I'm sweaty and sticky from my run too but being in his arms again stirs old memories of good times.

"Is it okay if I continue jogging beside you then?" He pulls his head back and looks at me. "I'm used to working out regularly back home."

I can tell.

"Sure." I take a deep breath, filling my lungs with much-needed oxygen since having him this close sucks the air out of me, making me feel light-headed. I place my AirPods back in my ears and slowly start my run again. Griff picks up pace beside me.

I've always done my runs without a partner. This feels weird, but he doesn't talk, which at least allows me to focus on nothing but my feet hitting pavement. Time passes, and we run and run when I notice I'm in front of the same bakery I stopped at yesterday morning.

"We should stop in here." I pat his upper arm and we both slow down. He nods and begins to do some stretching. I follow his lead and stretch too. After about five minutes of cooling down, we enter the bake shop.

"It smells good in here. I didn't bring my wallet though," he says with a half grin.

"Guess your coffee and croissant are on me then, friend." I grin, reaching into a little pocket in my shorts for the twenty-dollar bill I stuffed in there before my run.

Griff doesn't hide the fact that he's checking me out or licking his luscious lips. If only I didn't have memories of the wicked things his tongue could do.

"You're cheeks are a cute shade of pink," he says and it feels like he's flirting.

My brows furrow. "The way you're checking me out is making me blush."

"Pink is a nice color on those cheeks." He shrugs and his nostrils flare.

My eyes widen as I startle. "This isn't keeping things friendly," I whisper and lean into him.

"You're right. I'll behave." He grins devilishly. My eyes move to his lips, and I think about what he said earlier about a little kissing. Would that be so bad? I haven't been with a man in so long.

Yes, it would be bad. That's the last thing you need in your life.

"You okay?" He gives me a look filled with concern.

"This all just feels overwhelming. I mean, everything I learned about my dad last night and you being back in my life," I admit.

"I've thought about you over the years. What you would be like all grown up. . ."

"Am I not what you pictured?" I ask, unable to read him.

"You're beautiful—breathtaking, really, but it just feels like you still have dreams to conquer," he says, reading me so well.

"I'm working on it." I smile, and I feel so much lighter now we have this easy banter between us.

"Good," he agrees. His gaze holds mine and saliva pools in my mouth. My chest warms and . . .

"Can I help you miss?" The woman's voice from behind the counter pulls us from the moment we were having. I swallow again trying to contain the heat in my body that's threatened to swallow me whole.

"Yes . . . uh . . . I'll take a chocolate croissant and uh . . . one of those chocolate almond milk drink boxes," I say. I look up to Griff to see what he wants. The amusement dancing in his eyes is annoying. He's toying with me and it's working.

"I'll have the same," he tells the woman with that gruff voice of his.

I press my thighs together. His finger comes up and touches my cheek, then slowly lowers to my jaw.

"I'm grateful we're here together," he says as the lady behind the counter prepares our order.

"Me too. I've had a lot of unanswered questions. It feels good to finally have answers," I say.

The woman gives us our order and we take a seat on the patio outside.

Griff takes a bite of the croissant first, steam rising from the pastry. The chocolate looks melted like it just came out of the oven. "Shit this is good. I could eat half a dozen of these."

"Me too. We should get more," I say.

"Really? You look like you don't eat much these days," he says.

I punch his shoulder playfully. "What is that supposed to mean?" My brows dip together.

"Come on. You and your mom were always trying to feed me when I was younger. Don't be surprised that I have concern for you too. After everything we've been through . . ."

"You don't need to worry about me. My appetite's just been mediocre. Plus, I run almost every day back home so what I eat burns off," I explain, because I see he cares. He's always cared about my whole family.

I stand. "I'll go get a few more. Any special requests?"

"Whatever you like. I'm easy." He winks. *Flirt.*

I pick up a napkin from the table and throw it at him. "Platonic, remember?" I walk away.

"Come on. Were we ever really platonic?" he shouts after me. He has a point but I'm not going there.

I return with four more croissants. He takes one and places it in front of my mouth for me to take a bite. He's taken a chocolate almond flavor. "Mmm that's really good," I say, chewing my bite.

"Take another," he says, placing it in front of my mouth. I take a bite. Why does he make eating feel erotic?

"I can feed myself." I grab the croissant from his hand.

"There's no fun in that," he says wryly.

"And are you all about fun?" I ask, then regret it. That information shouldn't matter.

"I work a lot, running my own company. I've had female companions but no one that I've ever loved, if that's what you're asking," he says seriously.

I shift in my seat. I always thought of him as the heart thief.

Even when Mason came along, it wasn't the same as it was with Griff.

"Why haven't you had a serious relationship then?" I ask, because I might as well find out everything I want to know. Why hold back?

"I see you aren't shy and hesitant anymore." He snickers.

"I'm not," I agree.

"I'm happy. You should always say what's on your mind, and to answer your question, I never got over you." He looks at me intently, his eyes the color of the ocean on a clear day. It stirs something deep inside me.

"I appreciate your honesty," I say, shifting in my seat again, wishing I didn't feel so uneasy about all of this. Knowing he could steal my heart in one breath again has me defending it fiercely.

"So, to clarify, you aren't dating anyone now?" he asks.

My cheeks burn. "No, but I'm not looking to date," I say hesitantly. Why do I hesitate?

"Well, yeah, I figure if you wanted to date, it would be easy for you." He nods. That's a nice compliment.

Am I supposed to ask him the same question?

No. I don't need to know. We are only friends.

"I'm not dating anyone. In case you are wondering." He smiles.

I cough. "I wasn't . . . wondering." My tone is a little too high.

"I have bed partners, but not relationships," he says, nodding his head repeatedly.

"What does that mean? Are you gay now?" I am clueless on current dating lingo, apparently.

"No." His brows scrunch together. "I have a female bed partner who is just that."

"Do you mean fuck buddy or just someone you hook up with? I'm confused," I say. *Am I really having this conversation with Griffin Campbell? It's freaking weird.*

"Yes, I guess it is someone I hook up with, but she knows there isn't a relationship and I texted her last night that we're done," Griff says, surprising me. It sounds kind of mean to text someone about a relationship being over but maybe a fuck buddy isn't really invested.

"You shouldn't have," I say with all seriousness.

"Don't, okay?" he says curtly. "Don't expect me to be with anyone else ever again."

He renders me speechless.

"Let's get back to no pressure. I want to be up-front. Let's leave it at that. Spend time with me as my friend. That is all I ask." He picks up my hand and places a soft kiss on the top.

My skin buzzes from where his lips connect.

"Is it okay if we cab back?" I ask, feeling like I'm holding my breath.

"Sure." He smiles warmly. "I'm exhausted. I didn't sleep a wink. That was a heavy night." He stands from the table.

"Me neither. And poor Jenn. Why didn't any of us see her eccentric behavior as a cry for help?" I say, looking to him. And just like that, we segue from the relationship talk and fall into easy conversation. My anxieties ease.

"I don't have an answer to that," he says, putting his hand on the small of my back as we walk toward the main street to catch a cab.

"I wish we didn't have to go back to a house full of people. I wish we could just sit and talk all day. I want to know everything about your life," he says, looking to me with longing.

"Maybe we can sit by the beach and talk there," I suggest.

"Sounds perfect," he says on an exhale. His appreciation beats like the sun, hot and penetrating, and it touches my frayed heart.

We spend the rest of the morning catching each other up on the minute details of our lives. I tell him about my girlfriends back home and what I do on Saturday nights when I'm not in pajamas on the couch. Griff tells me how his little movie trailer company became the hottest movie trailer company in Hollywood. How he meets with directors and famous actors and actresses. His life is surreal. I'm so happy he's passionate about his work. I can't honestly say I'm passionate about mine.

"But you should be passionate," he says.

"Not all of us get to work in jobs we love," I say.

"True, but you can. I think it's great you're going back to school," he says.

"Thanks. A large part of my love for history has to do with my father. We all looked up to him. He inspired a love for history in me and Logan, and now I just feel completely disappointed about the man he was," I say, looking out to the ocean.

"I don't know why he made the decisions he did. I've had a lot of time to think on this and a lot of therapy. The right thing would have been for your dad to divorce your mom and save himself the long list of indiscretions, but he didn't do that. Maybe he feared losing his kids. I don't know what his calculations were. All I know is that his decisions hurt us all," he says staring into my eyes. "That doesn't mean he didn't have the capacity to inspire you. You can love history on your own terms. Find your love and connections to it," he says with such conviction and assurance that he doesn't sound like the old Griff.

"You've changed. You're more self-assured, strong." I giggle. "Dare I say . . . wise . . ." I laugh.

"Wise, huh?" he chortles. "I'm older. I've had time to learn life's lessons the hard way. And you're right; my self-esteem is healthy today."

"I'm guessing very healthy," I joke, knocking him in the shoulder. When the heat of our skin makes contact, something shifts between us and the smile falls from Griff's face.

"I want to kiss you," he says, his voice heavy.

"I'm sorry." I pull away. *This is moving too fast.*

"Don't be; it was too soon. I'm sorry." He pulls his gaze away and stares at the water intently.

I try to gain control of my racing mind that repeats *guard yourself* while my traitorous heart beats fast, telling me I don't stand a chance. In the past, my heart always won but that was before I saw what love could cost. I'm not going to allow myself to fall again.

Chapter 19

Griffin

Jolie and me walk through the front door of the beach house just as Logan walks down the stairs.

"Were you two out running together?" His face scrunches up.

"Yeah, is that okay?" I ask, even though I don't need his permission to go for a run with his sister, but maybe I'm testing the waters. Seeing if I meet his approval.

"Uh, yeah, I guess," he mutters, like he hasn't given it much thought. "You good?" He looks to Jolie and his forehead creases. I wonder if she told him about us or maybe about her father. Jenn knows so it isn't exactly a secret now.

"I'm fine," she whispers curtly. "And you?"

He shrugs. "Fine."

Jolie laughs.

"What's so funny?" he asks her.

"Nothing. It's just getting any details about you or your life is like pulling teeth," she grins clearly playing with him.

"When I have something to share I will," he says with nonchalance.

Jolie eyes him. "Alright. Fine," her tone is playful. To her credit he has been behaving a little strange. I wonder if it's the woman he was telling me about. He seemed to get worked up when he was talking about her.

Logan claps me on the back. "Thanks for looking out for her," he says to me. He must think I joined her on the run to keep her safe.

I don't correct him. Instead, I nod and head for the kitchen. It doesn't seem like Jolie has said anything to him yet about his cheating father. He wouldn't be so cheerful if she had.

"Good morning," I say to Kathy and Kyle, who are seated at the kitchen table. Logan and Jolie follow me into the kitchen a minute later.

Kathy sits across from little Kyle, who is eating some French toast. I get that Jenn is messed up, but I hate that she isn't spending any time with him. It makes me wonder what happened to my own mother.

My dad wouldn't tell me much growing up. He said she couldn't handle the responsibility of having me. When he got really drunk, he would lash out in anger, saying it was my fault she left because she hated being a mom and he had to lose her because of me. I tried to convince myself that his cruel words were the consumption of too much alcohol, but my arguments were always weak. A part of me always feels unwelcome and not good enough, even with my success and years of therapy.

"Good morning," Jolie says cheerfully to her mom and Kyle. She grabs a cup of coffee and says she's going to shower.

"Hey! Wait a minute," I call out to her. We haven't made a plan to hang out today yet. Everyone at the table watches me expectantly. "Uh! Why don't we go to the beach?" I mutter, looking at everyone and no one in particular.

"That sounds like a good idea. I'll join you," Kathy says.

Jolie's eyes turn a light green and shimmer. "That's great, Mom."

"You going to join us, Jojo?" Kathy asks.

Jolie turns her attention to Kyle. "Only if Kyle is coming too."

"Yes, I had so much fun yesterday," he says with a mouthful of food.

"What does Grandma say about talking with food in your mouth?" Kathy gives him a disciplinary look that I remember her using on her own kids.

"Sorry, Grama," Kyle says, then swallows.

"I'm in too." Logan smiles to Kyle.

After breakfast, we all head back to our bedrooms to get ready for the beach, and then we head out together. Kathy lays a large sheet in the sand while Logan, Kyle, and I play beach racquetball. Kathy and Jolie sit on a sheet in the sand, taking in the sun. It feels like old times.

We spend the rest of the day on the beach. By lunchtime, Kathy runs back to the beach house to make sandwiches, and we have a little picnic as we reminisce about old times. Here and there, Logan shoots me a glare. I wonder if he's noticed how many times I've checked out his sister in her bikini.

Even though Jolie left Jenn a note to join us on the beach, she never drops by. By late afternoon, we've all had too much sun, so we head back to the beach house to relax before dinner. My grumbling stomach keeps me from taking an afternoon nap so after my shower, I head to the kitchen for a small snack.

I swing open the kitchen door to see Jolie by herself leaning on the counter, her chocolate-brown hair wet, her skin golden and shining. She's wearing a thin light pink tank top and a bra strap of a similar color peeks from under the strap. She only seems to notice me as she brings a spoon to her mouth and opens her eyes, maybe feeling that I've been watching her. Her green eyes turn wide and round.

"What do we have here?" I ask, my tone conspiratorial.

She puts a finger to her mouth, shushing me. "Mom made gelato. Would you keep it down?" she whispers, spooning another mouthful.

"I want in. You don't get to eat that stuff on your own. You know that." I grab a spoon from the drawer and dig in. Jolie and I spent many a night basked in the darkness of this kitchen sneaking as much gelato as we could, so we wouldn't have to share with everyone. "Fuck, chocolate hazelnut . . . You have no idea how many nights I've craved this," I groan as the cool, creamy dessert hits my palate.

She watches me with wonder, still digging into the other flavor. "This one is all for me. I swear I can finish this tub right now," she says.

"What flavor is it?" I ask. She digs her spoon back in the tub and brings it to her mouth, and her eyes practically roll in the back of her head.

"This. Is. Heaven," she answers.

"I'll bet." I reach for some, and she blocks me playfully with her arm.

"Uh-uh." She shakes her head.

"Oh, come on." I try to get my spoon around her hand, only she blocks me. I try another angle, and she blocks me again. "I'm getting some of that. Whatever it is," I say, putting the empty spoon on the counter. I reach forward and tickle her. She used to be one of the most ticklish people I know. She squiggles out of my reach without making a sound.

"If you make me scream, everyone will know we're in here, and then we'll have to share," she says deviously. It feels like déjà vu.

"And we definitely don't like to share. This is what is going to happen." I cross my arms in front of my chest for effect. Her green eyes glow with excitement. "I'm flipping you over my shoulder and holding you there till I get my taste," I warn. *The gelato isn't the only thing I would like to get a taste of.*

"You wouldn't dare," she says with challenge. Reaching back into the tub, she grabs another quick bite of gelato.

"I would," I say, daring her with my glare. It's too much fun to play with her like this. It reminds me of a time when we would sneak around just to be near each other. It was exciting hiding and filling our private moments with stolen kisses and eventually love. I lift her over my shoulder easily and a small yelp escapes her lips.

"Put me down. I swear I'll scream," she warns with a soft whisper. There is no way she'll scream. If Logan finds out there is gelato, he will grab the container and run out of here. I reach into the tub with a spoon but it's hard to scoop a good amount with one hand.

Jojo giggles. I have her perched over one shoulder. She's wearing a pair of cut-off jean shorts and my hands hold on to her smooth, silky legs. "Okay, fine, I'll share," she says with defeat.

I laugh quietly. "Really? Because I can hold you up here and eat this all on my own. It's called having my cake and eating it too." I manage to get a small taste. Fuck she's right. Heaven.

She begins to kick, adding an uncomfortable weight to my shoulder. "Cut it out."

"No," she rebuts, kicking harder.

There is no way I can eat the damn gelato with her legs flailing. It's killing my shoulder, the one I hurt playing college football. With no choice, I place her on her feet.

"We'll have to share." She bats her long lashes with a teasing glare.

"Touché," I snicker. We reach into the cheesecake flavor together. Kathy makes the damn best gelato I've ever had. "Sharing is caring." I wink.

"And he remembers something from kindergarten," she says sarcastically.

I throw my head back, laughing and happy that playful Jojo is back. "I remember the first time we kissed," I say, looking into her eyes. She swallows. Her earlier playfulness falls away and is replaced with a serious, heated stare. "I remember the first time we danced." My finger caresses the bare skin of her shoulder, and her green eyes go from shining emerald to a dark forest green.

"Griff," she whispers a warning.

"I want to kiss you so bad." My voice is gruff and filled with a need that far outweighs any craving for gelato. I don't wait for her answer because the way she watches me has me undone.

My lips press to hers slowly, a soft caress, a begging for permission. Her fingers come up and rake through my hair, tugging me closer. My tongue peeks from my mouth, begging entrance to hers as she opens willingly.

The kiss is slow and testing at first. I'm scared of pushing too hard and having her pull away. She says she doesn't want more, but the chemistry between us beats alive and strong. Her taste sets my body on fire as a million memories come crashing through my mind. Electricity sparks inside me, making me feel alive for the first time in what feels like forever. And now, with a simple kiss, I have come undone. My lonely heart beats in time with hers. My thumb brushes over the pulse point in her neck, and it thumps wild like mine.

"Jolie," I say her name like a prayer.

"What are we doing?" she murmurs into my mouth.

"What feels right," I answer into hers. Primal instinct begs me to take her on this kitchen counter and make her mine. My fingers pull at her scalp and she moans into my mouth, and my hard-on pulses to her sweet noises. The kiss intensifies until we are both breathless and panting when suddenly, she pulls away from me, pressing her hands to my shoulders.

"I'm sorry. That went too far," I say, immediately reading her distress.

"I'm just not ready. I can't do this, Griff. I don't know if I ever can." She walks out of the kitchen without giving me a second glance.

I pushed too hard. I didn't want to pressure her and somehow, my self-control evaporated. *Fuck!*

I need to be more patient with her. I can see she's hurting. She doesn't need me mauling her in the kitchen.

I don't go after her. Maybe I should, or maybe she needs her space. I don't know what to do.

I want to make things right between us but I'm not even sure how. She's familiar to me but we've also been apart for ten years. I don't know what makes her tick.

I place the leftover gelato back in the freezer, and then I look around the house for her. I hear her voice upstairs so I follow her up. There is no way I'm letting her slip through my fingers again. What happened to her big heart that loved so freely, as it now seems closed with a lock and key.

Chapter 20

Jolie

My pulse races as I take the stairs two at a time. I need space from Griff because he makes me feel things I didn't know I could feel again. My body is warm and tingly, and a stubborn ache burns between my thighs.

I told myself I would never give my heart again. The two serious relationships I've had have left me devastated, and even though I know Griff isn't to blame for his leaving, he also never came back. He could have made it to Daddy's funeral; he could have come and confessed the truth and yet he chose to stay away. My chest still burns as memories of my heartache surface.

"Hey! Hold up," my brother stops me in the upstairs hall. "What's wrong with you?" I turn around to make sure Griff isn't following me. He didn't.

"We need to talk," I walk past him into his room. I hate to tell him that our father was a lying cheater but he should know.

He follows me into his room. I close the door and take a seat on his bed only I need a moment to collect myself so my gaze remains trained on the floor. I try to push that kiss with Griff from my mind because my brother needs my full attention. Daddy was his role model. This will devastate him. "What's going on? You're acting weird." I look up to see him standing a few feet away from me with his arms crossed in front of him. He's wearing his glasses and he reminds me so much of my father.

"I found out that daddy was cheating on mom. And not just once, like a lot," I say hating to see his face fall as he processes my words. I go on to tell him about Griff overhearing daddy's inappropriate behavior and how daddy held the illegal selling of the Russian textbooks over Griff's head. Then I tell him about Jenn catching daddy on the phone and he turns green. Like I actually think he's going to vomit. Instead he takes a seat beside me on the bed. He removes his glasses and rubs his eyes.

"That is really messed up. She clearly needs our help. Something is wrong. She can't just stay in bed all day," he says.

"I know. I'm going to go and talk to her," I say.

"I'll come with you. . . Shit." He pulls on the strands of his hair. "I'm just so fucking angry. I can't believe dad would run Griff out of town for something like that. It doesn't make sense." He looks to me maybe for answers. I am not ready to talk about Griff and me. Not after that scorching kiss we just shared in the kitchen.

"No, it doesn't make sense," I agree with my brother.

"And poor Jenn," he stands. "That is seriously fucked up. How could he do something like that to his own daughter?" he begins to pace. "I'll come with you to talk to her. She needs to know she has our support whatever trouble she's in."

I stand from the bed and walk over to him placing my hand on his shoulder. "I think it's better I talk to her alone. You know how she's always on the defensive. I think if we go together it will overwhelm her. She'll feel attacked." I remove my hand.

"Yeah, you're probably right. Keep me posted," he says.

"Will do," I give him a hug. "I'm sorry."

"For what? It isn't your fault," he hugs me back.

"I don't know. . . that you had to find out at all," I say.

"It's really fucking messed up." He walks over to his bed and lies back on a pillow. "Please close the door on your way out." I figure he needs time to process.

"Sure thing." I close the door and head to Jenn's room. The scene of me kissing Griff in the kitchen all hot and bothered plays in my mind. I give my head a shake to clear it.

I peek into her room to see if she's here. I see her sleeping form under the blanket.

It isn't okay that she is spending an entire day in bed. Something is very wrong, and I need to get to the bottom of it.

"Jenn, you need to leave this room," I say, yanking on the string attached to the blinds, flooding the room with light.

"Leave me alone," she whines, pulling the blankets over her head.

"You can't stay in bed all day. You need to eat, and you have an adorable little boy who needs you to be his mother." I pull out all the punches. Whatever is going on with her has to end.

She throws the blankets off of her and slowly sits up. "You're mean." She rubs at her eyes, wincing as the dimmed light comes from the window. It's past four o'clock in the afternoon.

"You shared something pretty major last night." I remind her of her confession.

"Did that really happen? I was hoping it was a nightmare." She winces and stands. She sways a little.

I run down to the kitchen, get her a glass of orange juice, and bring it back up to her in her room. She gulps it down and thanks me.

"Dad put a burden on you that you should've never been asked to keep." I place my hand on her shoulder and attempt to catch her gaze.

"I don't need you feeling sorry for me. I'm tough. Always have been. I wasn't going to run to Mom and watch this family fall apart because I couldn't keep my mouth shut," she explains.

"That was a hard burden to carry. It was so unfair of Daddy. I feel like I didn't know him at all." I sigh and fall onto the bed where Kyle usually sleeps.

"That's how I felt at fourteen, only I couldn't be responsible for making you feel the way I did, and Logan looked up to him so much." Her words trail off. My stomach sinks as I think of the amount of times I thought my sister was a self-involved a-hole. She had been looking out for us the only way she knew how—by shutting us out.

"It was honorable but very unfair that you were asked to shoulder that secret," I say.

"It fucking sucked," she admits, and walks over to her suitcase and pulls out clean clothes.

"Let me help you unpack," I offer, standing to walk over to her suitcase.

"You really don't have to," she says, her gaze carrying a warmth I've rarely ever felt from her. As I reach into the suitcase, I pull out two one-liter bottles of vodka.

My sister mutters something under her breath.

"Is this a problem for you?" I ask softly, hoping there's no accusation in my tone.

"I'm beginning to think I may be in over my head," she admits.

"Let us help you. We're your family," I say, hoping to ease her mind. She seems fidgety and anxious as her left leg shakes up and down.

"I've made mistakes. Done things I regret," she says.

"Life is about moving past mistakes. Making amends," I say, and then a small bubble of laughter escapes me. It's nerves. "I have to tell you the craziest thing."

Her blue eyes look to me intently. "What?"

"Griff and I were in love as teenagers. We had a thing . . ." I sigh as she gasps loudly.

"No, I don't believe you," she says, and her voice doesn't sound so groggy.

"We did." I nod in confirmation. "I crushed on him as a young girl and when I was ready, we just fell into place together," I say so easily. It feels funny talking about boys because we never have before, and a part of me regrets not doing this with her growing up.

"Did Logan know?" she guffaws. "I imagine he would have lost his shit," she says, and there is a softness to her tone and demeanor I'm not used to.

"No, I never told him. Daddy found out though, and he black-

143

mailed Griff into leaving. That's why he hasn't come home for the past ten years." I frown.

I see the balls rolling in her mind. "You were so depressed your senior year."

"Yeah, it had felt like the world had ended. I don't even know why Daddy hated Griff so much," I say, looking to my sister for answers even though I don't think she will have them.

"He said Griff reminded him of himself. A small-town boy with big dreams. That's all I remember. I didn't know what he meant though. Daddy may have grown up a small-town boy but he became a Harvard professor. Nothing about him was small town, and Griff lived in the same neighborhood we did." She shrugs.

Now I get what dad meant—he grew up in a simple household to parents who didn't have much. He became a sought-after professor, giving lectures all around the world, and maybe that got to his head. He became a cheater. He was a man who took what he wanted. Griff could never be like that. At least the Griff I knew wasn't like that. I don't know the man he is today.

"Griff is nothing like Daddy," I say defensively.

"But isn't he? He's a big Hollywood guy now, Jojo. I lived in LA; I know what that means. I tried being an actress at one point. All those big Hollywood guys, they have ladies falling at their feet doing whatever they want.

"And you think Griff is like that?" I can't hide the surprise or disgust from my tone. Deep down I can't imagine he became such a slime bucket. He had girls chasing him in high school throwing themselves at him and it never went to his head.

"He knows all the big guys in Hollywood. At one point, I asked Logan if he could call Griff and ask him for a favor for me since I wasn't in touch with him. Logan called him, and Griff was able to hook me up with a producer to get a part. I got the audition. The guy also asked me to get on my knees." She scrunches her nose.

Bile rises in my throat. I knew Griff was famous and doing well, but in my small mind, I hadn't pictured what his fame really meant.

"D-did you? I mean get on your knees?" I ask, swallowing hard.

Her lips quirk on one side. "Do you want me to answer that?"

I frown. "I . . ."

"Stop being such a prude. Geez. You are a grown woman," she berates me.

"Excuse me if I think intimacy should involve feelings," I say.

"When is the last time you got laid? You are so uptight," she scoffs, and the emotional moment we just shared passes.

"I'm not answering that." I press my lips together, hating how crass my sister can be. "Besides, your life doesn't have to be like that anymore. Let us help you. You have Kyle to take care of."

"I want to stay here in the Cape with Kyle. I don't want to go back to LA. I have nothing there," she says.

"Your apartment?"

She shakes her head. "I couldn't pay rent. Kyle and I were staying with my friend," she explains. My chest aches thinking of Kyle as I try to imagine what he's been through at such a young age.

"I think it's great you want to stay, but Mom isn't your live-in babysitter. You need to take responsibility for Kyle. He should go to preschool maybe camp, and be with children his age." I don't want to sound like a bitch, but someone needs to make sure she doesn't take advantage of Mom and it seems like she doesn't know what her responsibilities are. "I don't want to lecture you," I begin.

"You don't want to, but you are. I thought things would be different now, but you're still perfect Jojo, dictating what I should do," she snaps, and walks out her bedroom door.

I've never dictated anything to her before. She barely ever gave me the time of day but fixing our broken relationship seems really important to Mom, and I would love to have my older sister in my life.

"Jenn, wait! I'm sorry," I shout after her. "I'm just worried about you and Kyle," I say as she walks over to the bathroom.

I chase after her, not wanting the conversation to end on a bad note, when she whips around. "Maybe you should worry about yourself. You have bigger problems than you think." She slams the bathroom door in my face.

"What is that supposed to mean?" I mutter, but I hear the water running and know the conversation is over.

"At least you got her out of bed," Griff says, standing at his bedroom door with a lopsided smile. I wonder how long he's been standing there and if he overheard mine and Jenn's conversation. Shit.

Jenn's words replay in my mind. I don't know what kind of life Griff leads out in LA. It seems like we are worlds apart now more than ever.

"Yeah," I sigh, and head down the stairs. I charge out the front door, grabbing my purse on the way out. My head is spinning, and I need time to think. I begin to walk toward the Frog's Den. I've never been much of a drinker, but I could use a nice glass of red wine before dinner. I also need to distance myself from Griff. Being around him is so confusing.

Chapter 21

Griffin

I didn't hear the whole conversation, but Jenn always has a way of stirring things up, and she sounded cryptic. I don't like it one bit. Jolie is trying to help her get her head on straight for the sake of her son, and Jenn has a way of flipping things upside down.

I head downstairs, bumping into Kathy as she leaves the kitchen. "Was that Jojo I heard leaving?" she asks.

"I'm afraid so." I rub the scruff on my chin.

"Do you know what happened?" she asks.

"She had it out with Jenn. She was trying to get her to stop behaving the way she is, and something must have gone wrong. I'm not sure." I shrug, but it's eating away at me. She just looked at me like I was a complete stranger, and how can that be possible after the hot kiss we just shared?

"I'm guessing she won't be back for dinner," Kathy says, pressing her lips together.

"I think I should go after her?" I say to Kathy, and it almost sounds like a question.

"I can't tell you what to do," she says. "You need to feel it in your heart."

"A part of me feels like it's too late. She has a life in New York; mine is in LA," I say, feeling like the list could go on. I'm a douchebag who has slept with too many women. How will she ever accept me?

I don't voice my thoughts.

"You have to do what feels right. Where you live is just a place on the map. What matters is where home is. I lived a very unhappy life with Gary in that old brownstone back in Cambridge, and yet when Kip came into my life, he made those empty four walls feel like a home," she says, her eyes welling with tears.

"I'm so sorry. I don't know what to say." I feel completely defeated.

"Just follow your heart." She pats my back.

"Jolie is my heart," I say. The answer comes to me without thought. "I need to go."

"Go." She nods and I leave. Jojo may think she needs time to herself, but she doesn't. She needs me to show her I can be the man she needs me to be.

▭

THE FROG'S Den is just as busy as it was the other night. After trying a few restaurants and cafes along the strip, I stop in, hopping she might be here. And there she is, nursing a glass of wine and laughing at something the bartender just said. The same guy I saw talking to her last night. He smiles to her. And I can just tell he wants her. Problem for him is that I won't let her slip through my fingers again.

"Hey there." I walk up beside her with a half smile.

"Oh, hi." She seems surprised to see me. Like last night, she looks over her shoulder, maybe thinking Logan is here with me.

"Just me. I was hoping we could talk," I say, shifting on my feet.

"What's on your mind? I kind of feel drained," she says, slouching on the bar stool. The bartender pulls away to help another customer.

"I kind of overheard part of yours and Jenn's conversation." I smile impishly. What am I supposed to say? Your annoying sister is right? I've made mistakes.

"I don't have any expectations where we're concerned. You don't need to worry about Jenn planting ideas in my head," she answers, her fingers wrapping around the stem of her wine glass. She brings the glass to her lips and takes a small sip.

"It matters to me. Will you please come sit with me at a private table?" I probably look like a puppy-dog, filled with hope as I gaze at her because she can't bring herself to reject me.

She sighs and stands. She's still wearing those cut-off jean shorts from earlier and the pink tank top. She looks simple, beautiful without an ounce of makeup. So very different to the women back in LA.

We slide into a booth opposite each other, close to the window.

"That kiss today meant something to me. It wasn't all in good fun. Things could never be that way for me when it comes to you," I say, wanting to reach out and take her hand, but both of her hands are busy fingering the stem of the wine glass.

She remains silent while I shift in my seat. The sweet smell of her skin makes its way over to me. She sips her wine a little faster.

"What Jenn said is true. I'm friends with famous people. Everything is pretty superficial in LA, and for a long time, I liked all the money, the fame, the ladies . . . because none of it meant enough to break me. Growing up, my father told me I was a worthless asshole, and I believed him. Then there was you. You made me feel special. You made me feel like I could conquer the world. You made me feel love, and when I lost you, I wanted to numb the pain. I didn't make the best choices. Your father banned me from your life, and I didn't see a way back to you. When he died, you were with Mason . . . I couldn't just walk back into your life." My hand comes up to my forehead, and I take a breath. "I've done things I'm not proud of, but I'm not your father. I don't want other women. I've only ever wanted you," I say, looking into her eyes while remembering my therapist's words—*I deserve Jolie.* I'm not the worthless shit my father said I was.

My resolve is paper thin. Coming back to Boston and being

back at the beach house brings back painful memories I've worked hard to bury. "Say something," I plead.

Her eyes water. "I'm scared, Griff. I've been through a lot. With losing you, but also stuff with Mason that I'm still working through." She pauses to look at me, and her gaze holds pain and uncertainty.

"You can tell me anything; no judgement. Whatever it is I can maybe help you work through it," I offer.

"I know." She smiles softly, sounding thoughtful but hesitant. "I can't lie to you. I don't know what we're doing here. We say we'll try to be platonic but somehow we end up kissing. I don't think we can be just friends. There are too many feelings involved and Jenn is right. We don't know each other today. You live a life that I'm so proud of but I don't think I would fit into. And would you want to move to New York?" She shakes her head. "I'm running away with my thoughts. You probably haven't thought that far ahead, and if I'm being honest here, I haven't either. I have no business getting involved right now," she says, exhaling a long breath.

"To answer your question, I have thought about what the future holds. I know you may not want to move to LA. I know things are complicated, but I also told myself on the way to Boston that I would be here to support your mom and leave. Only I can't leave and it has nothing to do with your mom. Seeing you again . . ." Words fail me. "I don't want to overwhelm you but I think we deserve this time. A second chance."

"Griff, I don't know what to say." She presses her lips together. Her chin tilts down and she looks away.

"Spend the day with me tomorrow. Let's get to know each other again," I suggest, hoping with everything in me she'll say yes.

She sits quietly.

"Please," I plead. Begging isn't beneath me right now. There is a reason we are here together in this moment.

"Okay." She nods.

"Okay?" I blow out a nervous breath.

Her agreeing to spend time with me eases the tension between us, and we spend the next hour talking about New York. She tells me about her friends Michelle, Ava, and Olivia. I tell her about my company and the trailers I've made for big movies. To my surprise, she's seen some of them since Logan told her to look out for them. It makes my chest burst with pride. Her father thought I was a loser but I'm not. He thought I would be a cheating asshole like him. That's not who I am. Now I need to prove that to Jolie.

At the end of the night, we walk back to the beach house and I kiss her on the forehead when we reach the door. I don't want her thinking my sole interest is to get her into bed.

"I'll see you in the morning," I say.

Logan walks up to the beach house. He's coming from the opposite direction we just did.

"I'm going to stay out here and talk to your brother," I say. She nods with a smile and disappears behind the door. I turn to face my best friend. This talk has been a long time coming.

"Were you out with my sister?" he asks, his tone accusatory.

"Yeah, we had a drink at the Frog's Den," I answer.

He nods repeatedly, like he's thinking something. "Is there something going on between you two?"

I run my fingers through my hair wondering how far back I go to get his approval to date his sister. Not that I need it, but it would mean a lot if he gave it.

I laugh nervously. "Well that's an interesting question."

His brows crease and he folds his arms in front of his chest.

"I've kind of always had feelings for Jolie," I admit, taking a shaky breath. As a teenager, I played this conversation in my head thousands of times but I always convinced myself he wouldn't think I was good enough. "Please don't be upset. I have the utmost respect for your sister."

He laughs.

"You're laughing?" I ask, flabbergasted.

"Well, yeah, you didn't date anyone in high school. There were rumors going around that you were gay. Then we got to college and everyone was fucking around except you. I told myself that if you were gay, it didn't matter. You were my best friend. I just had a hard time getting the guys on the football team to fuck off," he explains.

My mouth drops and I nod. His words process through my mind. I never heard anyone say or ask me if I was gay. Except . . .

"Holy fuck." I blurt. One of the guys from the team invited me over to his apartment one day. I thought a few of my teammates would be over too but it turned out to be just us. He got a little close to me and it made me feel uncomfortable so I told him I had a sour stomach and took off. "That makes sense now," I say slowly as the piece clicks into place.

"What does?" he asks.

"It doesn't matter." I don't want to out the guy if he never outed himself. It really isn't my business anyway. "Shit."

"Ah! Yeah." He chuckles but then it dies fast.

"I was with your sister. I was in love with her," I say, looking my best friend in the eyes and praying he doesn't hit me or worse, say I'm not worthy.

"What does that mean exactly? When did this go down?" he asks, seeming calmer than I expected. It makes me wonder if Jolie told him something about us or her father.

"It wasn't a quick fling. Jolie and I had become friends. There were many times I was at your house and you weren't around. I wasn't trying to go behind your back. Your mom invited me over because you know . . . my situation at home," I say. Where Jolie knew I had no food at home, I never came out directly and said that to Logan. The dynamic of our friendship was different, and I didn't want to come across as ashamed or weak even though I knew he knew.

"Yeah, man," he sighs.

"Our friendship grew into something more. We began dating secretly," I say.

He grits his jaw. "My father knew." He kicks the ground. "Why didn't she just tell me?" he mutters to himself. I'm guessing that Jolie spoke to him. "Fuck. Things are just so messed up," he says.

"You spoke to Jolie." It isn't a question.

He nods. "She told me about my dad kicking you out of town and that he knew about you selling those books. Fuck man. Why didn't you come to me?" He looks hurt.

"Because I was doing something illegal. I didn't want to drag you into my mess. The less you knew the better," I explain knowing it isn't enough for him. "When we got to Florida I felt free for the first time in my life. You know my dad was a big jerk. I just wanted to have enough money. I had the scholarship but my financial situation was tight. The books provided me with lots of money and it felt good not to worry," I squeeze my eyes shut then I look up to the sky. "It was stupid of me I know that today. Back then it made sense.

He moves his head up and down and bites his lower lip and then it's like a light goes off in his head. "Dad knew about you and Jolie. That's why he held the thing with those Russian books over your head." He spins away from me and curses.

"She's my little sister," he spews and I tense.

My mind races. Is he having the same reaction as his father? Does he not think I'm good enough for Jolie?

"I know. I never meant any disrespect. My feelings for her have always been genuine. I never cheated on her or anything like that," I mumble, unsure if it helps my argument.

He begins to pace back and forth.

"Say something," I urge. *Anything. Please.*

He stops and looks me in the eye. "Why tell me now? After all this time." He doesn't wait for me to answer. "You want her," he says blatantly, and his tone fills with accusation. "She's been through a lot, and what about you? The life you live out in LA isn't for my sister. You can't toy with her."

"Don't you think I know that?" I snap. "I was fucking in love with your sister when your father ripped her out of my life. I was broken for such a long time."

"This is fucking crazy. That's when you began screwing tons of girls? Because you were upset about losing my sister?" he says with disgust. "I was relieved you weren't gay but my sister deserved better."

"I agree she deserved better. I was scared your father would have me thrown in jail if I went after her. I had to let her go, and it tore me apart. I acted like an asshole but given the situation, I didn't see a way out." I try to explain. To defend my behavior, but my defense is poor. I should have come back sooner.

"I need to look out for my sister," he snarls.

"I get that, but seeing her again . . . man. . . ." My heart breaks as I picture her face. "Don't ask me to walk away a second time. I will give up everything I have for her."

"Fuck!" he hisses. "You're serious?"

"Serious? She's the fucking love of my life, Logan. I know it was shitty of me to keep this from you. Your dad had an idea that I liked her, and he would warn me away from her. He would threaten me. I didn't know how you would react. I didn't know if you would accept that I wanted to be with her," I admit, and it feels like I've sliced my arm with a knife and I'm allowing the wound to bleed.

He swipes a hand over his mouth. "You've been with a lot of chicks. And Jolie . . . she's a good girl."

"She's a woman now," I remind him, and he doesn't like that comment.

"Like I said, she's been through a lot," he says, staring me straight in my eyes.

We stand silent for what feels like forever.

"Look, I would like your blessing, but I am going after her whether I have it or not. Your mom gave me hers and—"

"Mom knows?" he asks, wide-eyed.

I nod. "Apparently she had a strong feeling back in the day. When I came back to Boston she mentioned it may be mine and Jolie's time since we are both single."

"No shit," he hisses.

We fall silent again.

"Okay, man." He reaches his hand out to me. At first, I don't know what he wants, but then I realize he wants to shake my hand.

I shake his hand and pull him in for a hug. "Thanks, man. This really means a lot coming from you."

He pulls away. "It's the least I can do after the way my dad behaved."

I press my lips together. "It really does mean a lot . . . Look, I was planning on taking Jolie away from here a couple days so we can get to know each other again," I say carefully because he's still Logan, and he's always been about protecting his little sister's virtue.

"I see. Well, you better not fucking hurt her or break her heart," he spits and then his anger fizzles and he forms a smile.

"Trust me. My plan is to make her happy," I say.

He claps me on the back. "I'm heading in."

"Thanks, Logan," I say.

He turns and waves before walking through the door.

I take a few extra minutes on my own. I stare up to the clear night sky, willing the powers that be to give me strength. After a few cleansing breaths, I head up to the guest room and open my laptop. I search for things to do in Cape Cod. It's already late evening, and I'm not sure what I can book on such short notice, so I make a phone call to one of my Hollywood friends.

An hour later, I have the perfect day planned.

Chapter 22

Jolie

"I'm going downstairs to get a drink." Mason leaves our bed, and I turn to look at the alarm clock. Shit. It's already seven a.m. I'm surprised he got up this early after returning home so late last night.

I head over to my walk-in closet to get dressed for work. I slip on a grey pencil skirt and an off-white sleeveless blouse, then I head into the bathroom to wash my face and brush my teeth. With a pair of heels in my hand, I head down the stairs of our very large home. When I get to the kitchen, I see him with his palms pressed on the counter and his head hanging between his shoulders. I walk over to him and press a kiss to the bare skin between his shoulder blades.

"Hi babe," I say and walk over to the coffee machine. "I'm sorry I didn't hear you come in last night. Did the bus arrive late?"

"Yeah. I went out for a bite with the guys when we arrived. I didn't want to come back home and have to make myself something," he says. That's weird; did he not read my text message? I had said that I'd left dinner for him on the counter. I turn to see the veal and mashed potatoes still sitting on the counter. I don't say anything though; he doesn't seem to be in a good mood. "How was the game?"

He finally lifts his head and looks at me. "We won," he says with no enthusiasm.

I notice a gash on his forehead. "Jesus what happened?"

"It's nothing," he shrugs it off. As a professional athlete he's used to getting banged up. I brush it off too.

"Congrats on the win." My tone is cheerful. The team has been winning a lot lately.

"Yeah," he says, and lifts a glass of orange juice to his lips. He takes a few sips and stares into space.

"What's going on?" My brows draw together with concern. When he has games out of town and then comes home, he is usually filled with excitement to see me. I'm kind of surprised he doesn't want to take me on the kitchen counter. He loves it when I wear my work skirts.

"Nothing," he snaps.

Whoa. Okay.

"Baby." I walk over to him and place my hand on his shoulder. Maybe I can give him a little massage to release the tension.

"Do you fucking mind?" he snaps. His hand comes up as if he's blocking me and he accidentally smacks the glass of orange juice off the counter. It breaks into shards all over the counter and floor, and orange juice is everywhere.

"What the hell is wrong with you?" I scoff, looking at him as if he's lost it.

His hazel eyes continue to look vacant and then something happens and he snaps out of his daze.

"Shit," he scolds himself. "Fuck. I'm sorry." He runs his hands through his shaggy brown hair.

"Um it's okay. Just be careful you don't step on glass. Let me grab the broom," I say. That was weird. What has gotten into him? I tip toe over to the pantry where I have a special cabinet for the broom. I walk down the hall to the closet and slip on a pair of flip flops when I return to the kitchen Mason walks up to me.

"I've got it," he wants to take the broom from my hand but I don't think he will do a thorough job of cleaning all the glass so I prefer to do it.

"That's okay. I got it," I force a small smile. Uncertainty over his odd behavior morphs into concern.

He wraps his arms around me from behind. "I am sorry," he repeats quietly into my ear.

I turn myself in his arms to look at him. The gash on his head looks worse from up close. "This doesn't look like nothing," I say. I had missed his game on TV two nights ago because I went out with a friend.

"It's nothing, baby. It's nothing, baby. It's nothing, baby." His voice echoes like he's far away. I'm not in his arms anymore but I hear his voice. It won't stop.

Make it stop. Make it stop.

"Jolie. Jolie. Wake up. You're having a bad dream." It's Griff's voice. "Jolie, you're okay. You're dreaming."

My eyes fly open and I see Griff hunched over me, concern etched in his eyes. I'm covered in sweat and my heart beats erratically. "W-what happened?" I ask, pulling the sheet over my bare legs. I sit up in bed and palm my chest. Slow breaths. I inhale slowly and exhale slowly like my therapist taught me. Griff takes the water off my side table and passes it to me. I feel like I've run a marathon. I sip the water slowly and he takes a seat at the end of the bed. He watches me carefully.

"Bad dream?" he asks, and he looks worried.

"It was nothing," I say, brushing it off.

"It didn't look like nothing. You were screaming 'make it stop,'" he says, his brows bunched together.

Shit. I look around the room.

"Um. Did I wake anyone else?" I ask. I don't need my family to know that I sometimes suffer from night tremors.

"Everyone is in the kitchen. I was the only one up here getting ready," he explains.

I blow out a breath.

"Um, I'm fine. Sorry if I worried you." I force a smile, but I can tell he isn't buying it.

"Do you get a lot of nightmares? Because you know, I suffered from nightmares for a long time. I—"

"I'm fine. I don't want to talk about it," I say, trying to keep my voice even. I place the glass on the nightstand, hoping to hide my shaky hands. "Um. I should probably get ready for our day." I stand and pull my nightshirt over my legs. It practically hits my knees. I notice Griff is freshly shaven and wearing a yellow polo and khaki cargo shorts.

"Jojo, if something is going on you can talk to me," he insists.

"Please don't mention it to my mom or Logan. I'm fine, really. I want to spend the day with you. Tell me where we are going so I know how to dress," I say, hoping he won't push for more or ask questions.

"Well uh . . . I originally thought we would spend the day, but then I got a really cool idea but it's going to take more than one day." He sounds unsure of himself. I think I've worried him. "We're heading out for two nights and three days, so pack accordingly," he says and he's not asking.

I open my mouth to object.

"Don't worry. I spoke to your mom this morning and told her. She's very happy. I also spoke to your brother, who is less happy and warned me he'd break every bone in my body if I hurt you, which are words you don't expect out of the mouth of your best friend, but hey, I respect him nonetheless." He chuckles. My mouth is agape. "Deep breath." He places a hand on each of my shoulders. "No expectations. Just spending time together," he says easily.

I nod. "Spending time overnight . . ."

"Uh-uh, I promise to be a complete gentleman. I just want to have you to myself," he says.

Oh!

"O-okay," I say slowly. I trust Griff. Always have, and that doesn't seem to have changed.

He tucks his hands into his front pockets and watches me. His lips are turned into a frown.

"Griff, I'm fine," I assure him. "Now please leave so I can shower." I nudge him playfully out of the bedroom.

I head into the shower. I slip on a yellow sundress and pack a bag. When I head downstairs, my mother's face is glowing. It's the first real smile I've seen on her since I arrived back home.

"You kids have fun." She presses both her hands together and brings them up to her face, as if she's bracing herself.

"Not too much fun, kids." Logan lifts a finger in a joking way, yet his tone carries a hint of warning.

"Very funny." I give my big brother a kiss on his cheek. "Where's Kyle?" I turn my head to look for him.

"Your sister got up early and gave him breakfast. They are already out by the pool," Mom says gleefully.

"Really?" My heart fills with hope. "That's amazing."

"I hope she's coming around," Mom says.

"I hope so too." I lean in to give her a hug. Griff hugs her too, and then I leave the beach house with the boy who stole my heart when I was just a little girl.

"Hey, wait up," Logan shouts, grabbing keys and heading out the door with us.

I look to Griff for an answer as to why my brother is coming with us, but all I get in return is a dashing smile.

Chapter 23

Griffin

"Thanks for giving us a ride, man." I clap Logan on the back.

"Sure thing." He claps me back, then we get the small suitcases out of the trunk.

Logan hugs his sister and says, "If you need anything, I'm a phone call away."

I clear my throat. "I'm not a stranger, you know?"

He nods and finally releases her.

"We're going to Martha's Vineyard?" Jojo asks her tone filled with shock.

"You're ferry awaits, dear maiden," I say, taking her suitcase in my hand. We are going over on the regular ferry—nothing fancy. I don't want to overwhelm her.

Logan gets in the car and drives off, and Jojo and I make our way over to the ferry. She's quiet as we board and take seats at the front of the boat. The sun is shining, and there are a lot of boats on the water. The view is beautiful, but she looks breathtaking.

"You haven't said much," I say, trying to get in her head.

"I'm a little nervous," she admits, wrapping her arms around herself.

"Are you cold?" The air feels warm, but a breeze rushes off the water.

"Not really," she says solemnly.

"Don't be nervous. I know I said this was supposed to be a surprise, but I will tell you where we are going. That will ease your mind," I say. She nods, liking that idea. "A friend of mine has a mansion over on Martha's Vineyard. I thought it would be nice to spend a few days there together. The house is big enough that you can have your own bedroom if you want it. Like I said, no pressure. I just want to spend time with you." I pick up her hand and bring it to my lips, pressing a kiss to her soft skin.

"Your friend is just loaning you his house?" she says with surprise.

"It's a vacation property. He isn't there all year. Just stops in for mini vacations. He has lots of houses all over the world," I explain.

"Is this friend famous?" She cocks a brow.

I laugh. "Yes, there are perks to having famous friends, you know?"

"Who is it?" She raises and lowers her brows. Curious Jojo. She's always been this way.

"Ryan Sonenberg," I say and watch her eyes widen.

"He's your friend? Holy cow." Her jaw drops, and she just stares at me. "That's crazy."

"Trust me. Sometimes I wake up in the morning and pinch myself." I chuckle. "He has a staff that takes care of things around the house year long. He asked them to stock the fridge and cook a few meals but I asked him to relieve them of their duties. I want time alone with you. Again, no expectations. I just thought having staff around serving us may get uncomfortable."

"I'll be staying in a famous director's house," she says almost to herself. "Did you make movie trailers for him?"

"I did. *Night of the Eclipse*. Did you see the movie?" I ask.

She thinks for a minute. "No."

"Well, we can rectify that. It's an epic film."

"Definitely." She smiles and even though she still seems nervous, I feel honored that she's willing to take this leap of faith with me.

As we talk about mundane things, the forty-five-minute ferry ride flies by, and before we know it, Ryan's driver picks us up from the pier.

As we sit in the back seat of a Lincoln, we both look out the window. It's a scenic view.

The driver turns off a main road and then there is a lot of greenery. The mansions along this strip are sprawling, each house nestled on acres and acres of land. I've never been here before but I'm not surprised by the opulence.

"Griff, this place is . . ." Her voice trails off and her green eyes are wide with excitement. We pass through a main gate once the driver enters a code. Each side of the driveway is surrounded by a long stretch of grass, and there are large trees in the distance. The driveway turns in a circle at the main house. The property is large enough that the house is hidden in a private enclave. I saw neighboring houses as we drove up but they were a fair distance away, given the size of the properties here.

"Um. . . wow . . . it's beautiful," she says, taking in all our surroundings. The house is on the water, and it's surrounded by perfectly manicured gardens.

The driver takes our suitcases and opens the house. His name is Daniel.

"Marie has your breakfast set up in the dining room. The linens have been changed. Mr. Sonenberg said to make yourselves at home. There are a few cars in the garage if you would like to take a drive. I will provide you the keys for each vehicle," he nods. He's a middle aged man with a kind smile. I am guessing he isn't only the driver but the butler as well. "Mr. Sonenberg mentioned you will not be needing our services the next few days. The house has everything you may need. You have the cars or bicycles in the garage for transportation. Marie and I are headed to the mainland. Our daughter just got engaged," he explains.

"Congratulations, that's lovely." Jolie grins.

"Thank you, madam," he says politely. "Well, if that will be all, we will get out of your way."

"Thank you very much." I shake his hand, knowing Ryan pays

him well and giving him a tip would just be insulting. He leaves with a woman who I am assuming is Marie, his wife, and Jojo and I walk deeper into the house.

"What a view." She sighs, looking out the kitchen window. The wide expanse of ocean with boats covering the water provides for a serene landscape.

"We have our own private beach. Ryan has a boat he said we can use. Well, he said he has a couple boats up here, I think, from the sound of it. But I wouldn't know how to drive something like that," I snicker.

"Maybe I would," she offers. "Dad used to rent boats up here all the time. He taught Logan and I a lot about boating," she says and then winces. "I'm sorry I shouldn't have brought him up. In light of everything, you must really hate him."

"A part of me hates him, I can't lie, but he was looking out for you. He made a lot of mistakes in his own life. I'm sure he had good intentions when it came to you. No one is all bad. We are just good people who make mistakes." I smirk.

"I like that."

"How about we eat? I'm starved." I need a change of subject. Talking about Gary Bryant still causes my blood to run cold.

I rub my hands together and we walk over to the dining room, which has a long, grey table covered in fruit and pastries. The smell of fresh bread fills the air, and the variety of cheeses and vegetables causes my stomach to grumble.

"This looks delicious," Jojo says giddily.

We take a seat at the end of the table where two place settings have been set. "The fridge is stocked with basics, and apparently seafood and meat, because Ryan said he has a wicked grill out back and it's really nice to have dinner overlooking the water," I explain.

"This place is dreamy," she says, and she seems more relaxed than earlier, but I still sense something is off. Her comfort level with me isn't what it used to be, but we need time to get back what we had.

After having a hearty breakfast, we slip into beach attire and walk up the beach. She tells me more about her life, but she leaves out important parts like the senior year of high school, college, and what her life with Mason was like. Still, I don't press. Instead, I offer more information about myself.

"I was a wreck after your dad pushed me out of your life. I went back to Florida and got a job working for Universal Studios. It was good for me, because it became a consistent place to work whenever I was on break from school. A number of guys and girls rented apartments in Orlando, and we shared the rent. Although the places were pretty crammed. Between the partying and work, I managed to stay busy. When school started up again, I had your brother, but he was a constant reminder of you so that became difficult." I go on as we walk along the water's edge. I focus on the waves rolling up to shore and the pull of the current as I bare my soul. "Logan had a lot of questions for me. I went from being this guy who laid low—no chicks, barely ever drinking—to a party animal. He wanted to know why I had left Boston without telling him. I hated lying to my best friend, but I had no choice. I told him I couldn't handle being home over Christmas with my dad. It wasn't entirely a lie. At the time Dad had a girlfriend, and they were both drinking and having sex together loudly throughout the house. I'm pretty sure she was an alcoholic like him, and it was a big mess." I wince at the memory as Jojo watches me, furrowing her brows.

"Why didn't you say anything?" she asks, and the hurt in her tone bleeds through.

"I wanted our time together to be about us. Not my shitty home life. I probably would have ended up mentioning it if our time hadn't been cut short," I explain, taking her hand in mine. We continue our walk. The smell of nearby flowers floats in the breeze. "Let me know if you want to turn back."

"I like walking with you like this." She looks at me, a small smile curving her lips. "Don't stop; tell me more." Her eagerness to know more fills me with happiness.

"Logan bought the story. He figured I was lashing out because of my shitty childhood. Then there were times he would mention you. Your mom would call him up and say that you seemed sad. She was worried about you. Logan would sit and try to figure out what was wrong with you," I say.

"There was a point my brother called me every day and asked me if I was depressed or if I wanted to kill myself." She laughs sadly, and my blood runs cold. Her words stop me in my tracks.

"Shit, Jojo." I wrap my arms around her so fiercely, I fear sucking the air from her lungs. Her head presses to my chest, and I take in the lavender smell of her shampoo as the top of her head hits my nose. I never want to let her go but I need to so we can talk more, and I fear I may be crushing her.

"I wasn't suicidal. Just really sad." She pulls her head off my chest.

I take a breath and release her, taking her hand back in mine. She gives it to me willingly. "And Mason? How did that happen?" I ask. My voice is shaky with the mention of his name, but I have to know.

I never got into a situation where I wanted to marry. No girl ever matched up to her. My heart sliced in two when I heard she had a new boyfriend just under a year after I left.

Jojo stares at me through watery eyes. "We began as friends. I knew he wanted more, but I had nothing to offer for a long time. We became close. The friendship grew into something else and we ended up together." Tears begin to run down her cheeks. "It wasn't that I forgot about you. I didn't understand why you would cut me off the way you did. I was hurt, angry. My heart was broken for a long time. And, if you remember, I wasn't exactly Miss Popular. I had less than a handful of friends. I was scared to tell anyone what happened between us because I knew people would talk, and I didn't want Logan or my family learning the truth about us. It was so hard keeping everything inside. I could trust Mason," she says, and I hate that I'm jealous of a dead man.

"He knew everything about us?" I ask as jealousy burns through me. I am the asshole who took her virginity and never spoke to her again.

She nods. "I had given you all of me and you left. I was so broken. A million reasons went through my mind. I questioned everything about myself. My self-esteem was shit, and then there was Mason, destined for stardom, who was interested in little old abandoned me, and he made me feel good. I can't apologize for being with him. I don't want to," she says, pulling her hand out of my grasp.

Shit. I'm losing her.

"I don't expect an apology. I've made my share of mistakes," I say. "I felt awful for leaving you. For not being there for you. It tore me apart."

"To clarify, Mason wasn't a mistake," she snaps. I have to tread carefully.

"I'm sorry. I didn't mean it that way. In a way, I'm grateful you had someone there for you even though I wish it were me. I didn't mean to say anything hurtful; if anything, I'm jealous of him." I sigh and look to her with such longing it feels like an elephant has taken residency on my chest.

"I'm sorry." She shakes her head. "Jesus, what a mess."

"I know." I rake my fingers through my hair. "At least we get to talk about it now. At least we are getting this chance," I say, unable to mask the hope I feel.

"This is all very confusing. I had a lot of stuff I was working through about Mason . . . I'm not in a position to be dating. I'm really a bit of a mess inside," she explains, swiping away tears.

"My chest is so tight right now I'm finding it hard to breathe," I confess, hoping to relieve her own stress and mine.

"Thank you for being open with me. After being apart for so long, I didn't expect us to be able to talk like this," she says, opening and closing her eyes.

I nod, feeling like if I talk anymore I'll break down and cry for so many things in my life but mostly for losing her.

"How about we head back to the house and do something fun? We need to just relax. I saw some Jet Skis by the dock. I'm sure we can handle that," she says, breaking the silence. "We can take them for a spin, maybe relax by the water."

"That sounds perfect." I take a long breath, trying to ease the pressure in my chest.

We walk back to the private beach area. We head into the house where Ryan has a small room off to the side of the garage filled with all kinds of gear from wet suits to life jackets and fishing rods. We grab two life jackets and a couple of beach towels and head out back. When Jolie takes off her sun dress, I try to will my dick to relax. Her red bikini is made up of triangles on top which show off her shapely breasts. The bottoms are held together with strings and her behind isn't fully covered, giving me a nice view of her skin. I try to wipe the visions of her riding me and me squeezing that fine ass of hers out of my mind. We are so far from having sex that I need a cold shower to calm me down. The cool ocean water will have to do. When she zips up the life jacket and covers her breasts, I take a cleansing breath because I don't know how much more I can take.

At the beach, we start up the Jet Skis. She warns me that I'm on my own if I go too far out. There are all kinds of boats in the distance, and she says it's a bad idea to get too close. Her sensibility tugs at my heart as I remember a young Jolie making cautious decisions.

We have some fun, circling each other. At one point, I accidentally spray water on her as I take a narrow turn. She returns the favor, spraying me back, that slight competitive edge to her personality coming through.

After a good hour, we break for lunch. Jolie makes us some grilled cheese sandwiches from the leftover bread and cheese from breakfast.

After lunch, Jolie spots a blender sitting on the counter.

"I bet we can make margaritas," she says cheerfully. Her hair is partially wet and hangs in strands down her back. Her green eyes blaze against her sun-kissed skin. It takes everything in me not to kiss her. It's too soon. I need to show her how much she means to me.

"I'm sure we can. There is a fully stocked bar over there." I point to the living room.

She yelps, "holy crap," and turns on her heels toward it.

She looks happy. The air between us is easy, light. The heaviness of earlier is lifted and we have a chance to just be us.

We blend drinks and head out to the beach area where Ryan has lounge chairs and umbrellas set up. We lie back as the sun beats down on us, sipping margaritas.

"I can't believe I have you here with me," I say dreamily.

"This feels really good." She confirms what I'd suspected, making my chest burst with pride. She's happy to be here with me.

We spend the rest of the day relaxing. Toward late afternoon, we head inside to shower. Each room in the house has its own private bathroom. She took her stuff to a separate room, and although I was disappointed, I know she needs time and I am willing to give her all the time she needs.

She comes out of her room.

"I got all the grilling stuff ready," I say as my eyes roam over her. In a pair of blue jeans and white t-shirt she looks relaxed. Standing in the kitchen barefoot. I wish I didn't find her so sexy. Picking her up and taking her on the kitchen island crosses my mind.

"I can make a salad or side dish," she offers.

I clear my throat. "That would be great. Come out back when you're ready." I grab the packages of lobster and steak and take them with me to a large patio nestled in more gardens. A large built-in barbeque is set off to the side with a large fridge I hadn't noticed earlier. The fridge is stocked with international beers. I crack one open and wait as the grill warms.

The air is warm and the ocean looks calm, like a big swimming pool. The sun begins to set as I watch the boats on the water giving me time to think. I remind myself to be patient. There is so much more I need to know about Jolie, but all in good time. What if I gave up my life in LA? The idea isn't an easy one. I worked hard to get where I am. I made friends and have a steady business that provides me with a very healthy lifestyle. I could move the location of my business elsewhere. It would make it harder to network and maintain friendships. . .

"Hi." Her voice pulls me from my thoughts, and I force a smile. She holds a bowl of leafy salad in one hand and a bowl of pasta in the other. She places both on the table. "Wow," she says, looking out to the water as the sun begins to set.

"It's a pretty amazing view," I agree. "Can I get you a glass of wine or a beer?" I ask. "Ryan has a fridge and wine cooler out here."

"This is how the other half lives." She laughs. "A glass of white wine would be perfect."

I open a bottle of white and pour her a glass.

She sighs. "It's a perfect night."

She inhales deeply and walks over to some rose bushes. "These are perfect." She leans in to smell them even though their sweet scent lingers in the air.

"You're perfect, Jojo." The words escape me before I have a chance to ponder whether the timing is right and I close the steps between us. She reaches up and gives me a quick kiss. I pat myself on the back for timing.

I finish grilling the meat and seafood, and then we sit for a meal. I pour her another glass of wine and crack myself open another bottle of beer. The conversation seems to be flowing easier now. Maybe it's the wine that's relaxed her. The warmth of her laughter washes over me, seeping into my heart. I want to claim her and promise her the world—if only life were that easy. There is still a wall dividing us. I push my thoughts aside to enjoy this moment with her under a starlit sky, the moon sparkling over the expanse of ocean in front of us.

When we finish eating, I lean back in my chair. "Would you like to take a walk?" I ask as she takes another sip of wine.

"I'd love to." Her smile is bright; her cheeks are flushed. She's definitely feeling the wine.

I stand and walk over to her, offering my arm. "Beach or road?"

"Beach," she says.

We walk down the stairs leading to the private beach.

"This place is perfect. Thank you for bringing me here," Jojo says.

"I'm happy you agreed to join me. There are things to do around the island at night, but I wanted you all to myself," I confess, staring ahead of us. There are boats on the water with lights on but other than the moon illuminating a path over the sand we are alone on a dark beach.

She grins with a shy smile. "You were quite demanding when you told me to pack a bag." She giggles.

"I knew if I gave you a choice you'd think too hard," I say.

"That's true and I kinda felt bad leaving Mom, but I know she worries about me being alone," she says. "I figured she'd want me to come here with you."

"When I first arrived to Boston, she told me she had a feeling something was going on between us years ago. She kind of blew me away when she encouraged my feelings toward you," I say, wondering how she will take the news.

"Mom's been trying to play matchmaker since I arrived home. It's just so . . ."

"Odd?" I offer.

"Completely. When Dad was around. he made sure to keep you away. I knew Mom loved you but she couldn't have been oblivious to the way Dad treated you," Jojo says.

I rub at my temples. I don't want to speak poorly of Kathy even though she admitted to me herself that she stayed with Gary because he was comfortable and she didn't want to rock the boat. "Maybe she wasn't oblivious but she helped me out in her own ways and that pretty much saved me. I can't hold your mother's decisions against her."

"I'm sorry, Griff. For everything you've been through." She looks up to me thoughtfully.

"I appreciate it but I don't want pity, Jolie. My life shaped me. Made me strong." I nod.

"Mine too."

"I want to know what that means. You give me snippets of your-self but not the whole picture. I want to know all of you," I admit.

Her features grow pained and she looks down. "Not yet. I'm not ready. Please understand." Her voice is soft as she kicks the sand around.

"I know losing Mason was hard but I'm here, a breathing, flesh-

and-blood man, and I want you more than I want my next breath," I say, my tone filled with emotion with ten years of heartbreak and yearning.

"I want you too. Lord, I don't think I ever stopped wanting you," she says, looking into my eyes.

"To hear you say those words . . . Tell me you want me to kiss you. Tell me you want my hands all over you." My heart beats fast and my body aches to touch her.

"Griff," she whispers my name like a prayer. "Take me. Accept me for the way I am now."

She reaches up on her tiptoes and her lips press to mine. Warm and welcoming, it takes me a half second to snap out of my daze and realize this isn't a dream.

My arms loop around her back as I kiss her, slipping my tongue through her lips and reveling in her warmth as she opens to me. She kisses me with such heat my body warms all over. Her fingers rake through my hair hungrily, and this kiss isn't like the first kiss we shared in the kitchen. That kiss had been more like a test to see if the spark we shared was still there. This kiss is pure ecstasy. Not only is there a spark between us, but our bodies press together and my need for her threatens to devour me whole. Through heavy breaths, we kiss hungrily under a moonlit sky. The fresh breeze tickles my skin. I buzz with awareness. I want her on her back in the sand while I hover above her. My hand slips under her shirt, caressing her soft skin. Her hands move to my shoulders and lower to my back. A feral groan from deep in my throat escapes into her mouth as my erection presses painfully against my jeans. Still, there is a part of me holding back. She isn't willing to tell me everything so it isn't fair I take her body. I wait for her cue to move things forward.

Chapter 24

Griffin

"Don't stop," she says threading her fingers through my hair. "I need you," she tugs on the strands and sparks shoot down my spine.

"I want you so bad but your holding back," I say into her mouth wondering how I am able to maintain any self-control with her pleading with me to take her.

"Please. I want you. We have time to figure out the rest." Her tone is breathless as she breaks our kiss. *Thank fuck.* Her hands work to remove my T-shirt.

I'm not sure if we have time but I can't deny her either. I've never wanted anyone this bad. I'm only a man not a saint. My cock presses eagerly against my jeans and any sense I have vanishes as she rubs the front of my jeans. "Here on the beach?" I ask, feeling too impatient to walk back to the mansion and claim a room.

"I'm feeling rebellious tonight." She giggles.

"Are you sure? I mean, you had two glasses of wine. If you're drunk or something I don't want to take advantage," I mutter because I know all about drunken mistakes. My insides cringe as I remember my last hookup. *Don't go there now.* I will my mind to shut off and just feel this moment here with her.

"I am tipsy," she admits, still giggling while working the belt on my jeans. "But I know exactly what I'm doing. I haven't been with a man since my husband. Two long years since I've touched a man. I want you. I seem to always want you." She pops the button on my jeans. Her hand wraps around my cock.

"Ah!" I watch her hands working me, and my cock swells even more. I grip at her T-shirt and lift it over her head. I suck in my breath at the sight of her white lace bra which leaves little to the imagination. I grope her breasts like a hungry, primitive man. She moans. My thumb rubs her nipples back and forth as we stare into each other's eyes. They harden beneath my touch, and her breathing picks up. A rational part of my brain says *wait*. *She's got secrets*, but another part of my mind says she needs time and she wants this as badly as I do.

"Griff. You're thinking too hard," she says breathlessly.

I laugh and bend my knees, closing my mouth over her nipple the lacey material adding a layer of friction. She grabs hold of my hair, messing her fingers through it, and I slowly move my tongue down her stomach.

"I want you on your back," I hiss. "How opposed are you to getting sand all over yourself?" My lip tugs on one side. My glare must be mischievous with all my dirty thoughts.

"I don't care about sand right now," she pants like I should have known this fact.

In one fell swoop, I lift her in my arms and lay her on her back. She gasps as her back hits the sand. "It's a little cold," she says, arching her back.

"Lie on this." I place my T-shirt on the sand beneath her. I can't stop watching her. The way her long brown hair splays across the sand; the way her breasts rise and fall with each breath. I run my hand from her neck down her chest to her belly button. I quickly work the button and zipper on her jeans, and she lifts her butt to help me slip them off. She is wearing a pair of lace panties that show her bare pussy.

"Fuck." I have to look away and take a breath because I am about to come in my pants. When I look back, her green eyes are

THE TRUTH ABOUT US

molten. "I want to take my time right now, believe me I do." I blow out a breath and climb over her.

Kissing her lips with our bodies skin to skin is intimate and so very arousing. She presses her hips into my groin and works on lowering my jeans. I help her get them over my ass and down my legs, then I take a quick sweep of our surroundings to make sure we really can't be seen. There is no one in sight. My cock springs free.

"It looks bigger than I remember," she says with a laugh.

"Yes, well your body has changed since I saw you last too. What hasn't changed is the fact that I may come too quick from just the sight of you," I say, and look down at my cock to see a bead of cum on the tip. She leans down and licks it off.

"Fuck," I gasp and move, pinning her on her back. I'm a savage, devouring her body with hungry kisses and little nips on her neck, down her breasts. My tongue circles her belly button. She squirms. I quickly remove her panties and my mouth connects with wet flesh. The taste of her has me unhinged.

This is happening.

She begins to moan.

"I'm going to come, Griff. Shit! It's been so long. I can't wait," she says all throaty as she whimpers beneath me.

My tongue works her up and down from her clit to her opening. Her hips gyrate against my mouth and she swells, coming so hard I fear she may black out. She screams my name and takes every lick and nip, her whole body convulsing with release. I don't stop taking her higher and higher.

"Fuck, holy shit," she curses. "Yes, yes."

I'm so close to coming that I need to breathe slowly and refocus. I give her a minute to relax but she doesn't want it.

"Do you want me to suck you?" she asks, her green eyes lazy and her body lucid.

"I'd love that very much but right now, all I want is inside you," I say. This is a dream.

"Do you have a condom?" she asks.

"Yes." I reach for my jeans, feeling like I owe her an explanation. Truth is, I always carry a condom. "I wasn't expecting anything," I begin to mutter. Shit. She must think I'm a douchebag.

"Hey." She touches my arm. "It's fine. You're a grown man; no need to explain," she says, but her comment doesn't sit well with me.

"Besides, I'm on the pill," she says.

All I want is inside her. I roll on a condom, then pin her back on the sand. Lifting her hands above her head, I hold them down with one hand. I kiss her hungrily and slide my cock inside her. Hot, wet, and pulsing around me, she feels so tight as I thrust inside.

Sweat pops on my forehead as I move hungrily in and out. In and out. She milks me so hard that sparks of light shoot up my spine. She meets me thrust for thrust.

"I'm going to come. Holy shit." She rubs herself against me and I lose it.

We come together in hot waves of bliss as I grind my dick inside her like an animal, humping and humping, as sparks fill my vision. I slow my movements as she continues to pulse around me, squeezing my cock.

"Holy sweet heaven," I groan, pulling out of her. I fall on my back to the sand, my breathing ragged. She pulls up next to me, tucking her head on my shoulder. We both stare up at the stars. "Do you know how many nights I looked up to the night sky and wondered where you were? What you were doing in that exact moment?"

She wraps her arms around me, not saying a word.

I hold her for a while until our breaths are under control. We scoop up our clothing and head back to the house. We take the left-over food from dinner up to the kitchen. I guide her to the room I'm staying in, and we shower together.

The only words we share are unspoken. I pin her to the shower wall, making love to her from behind. I take time to wash all the sand from her hair and she washes my body, her hands touching me everywhere. Besides us both being experienced adults, things are different because we don't need to hide.

After the shower, I take her to my bed and hold her in my arms.

She doesn't say much but I know she cherishes my touch. I finally force myself to sleep and I dream of her, laughing on the beach, looking to me with loving eyes. And even in my dreams, she doesn't feel like she's completely mine. Something is keeping us apart.

My eyes open with a startle. I look around, feeling the bed empty and cold beside me. *Was this all a dream?*

I head to the bathroom and grab a robe, and trudge out of the room to look for her. My heart beats frantically with fear. *Has she left?*

Relief washes over me when I see her making breakfast in the kitchen. She's wearing one of my plain white T-shirts that hits her mid-thigh, and she's singing a song. She doesn't see me, and I notice she has AirPods in her ears. I walk up to her from behind, and she yelps as I press a kiss to the side of her neck.

"Oh hey." She pulls out one of the AirPods. "My body doesn't let me sleep in. I hate it." She smiles. "We had a lot of leftovers from yesterday. I'm just setting it up," she says, taking a strawberry and bringing it to my lips. I eat half, and she pops the other half in her mouth. She seems to be in a good mood this morning and relief washes over me. I'm being paranoid but after everything we've been through, how can I not?

We eat breakfast sitting on stools at the bar in the kitchen, stealing glances at each other. We both have these smiles on our faces that can't be washed away. After we finish, I lift her on the breakfast bar and kiss her senseless. The kiss leads to more as I stand between her open thighs and slide a finger inside her. She moans and clenches around me. As our lips stay connected and our tongues tie, I slide my cock inside her, thrusting.

"I should get a condom," I say against her lips.

"As long as you're clean, I don't mind," she answers.

"I get checked regularly," I say, not adding that in LA, it's a must. Even though the thought of impregnating her and making her mine makes me even hotter.

She holds her hands around my neck, and my hands grip her waist, pulling her closer so I can thrust easily inside her.

"That feels good," she moans into my mouth.

"You feel like heaven," I answer, close to coming. I wrap my hands around her back and use the leverage to thrust deeper. Being bareback inside her makes me lose all reason. When she clenches around me, I lift her off the counter and hold her in the air. She wraps her legs around me and somehow manages to bounce on my cock.

"Ah! Yes." A loud groan comes from the back of my throat and I release inside her, shooting hot cum into her pussy. She continues to grind against me as we ride through the aftershocks of our climax.

When our breaths slow, she lowers herself off me, and I grab some paper towel and clean us both off.

"What are the plans for today?" she asks.

"You mean besides having as much sex with you as possible?" I smirk. *Keep things light, Griff. It's what she wants.*

"Besides that, yes." She grins back, her green eyes beaming.

"I may have something planned," I say mysteriously. I tell her to get dressed and wear a bathing suit or at least bring one along.

We go to our separate rooms. It doesn't take me long to have another quick shower and dress. While Jojo gets ready, I pack a backpack with some fruit, water and a blanket.

She meets me in the kitchen wearing a pair of jean shorts and a T-shirt. Her slim golden legs on display make me want to cancel our plans. But I know this trip can't only be about sex. We need to spend time together doing couple stuff.

"This way." I lead her to the garage. "I hope you're up for a bike ride," I say. I have no clue where I'm going, but I've been told a regular GPS works around here.

"I'd love to," she says happily and I'm relieved. Ryan explained that a lot of people use bikes around here because everything is close by.

We get on the bikes, and I set my phone to direct us to a harbor. "Are you going to tell me what we are doing today?" she asks from behind me.

"We're going sailing. Ryan has a sailboat on this harbor," I explain.

"You can sail?" she asks.

"I have no freaking clue how to sail. We will have a captain aboard," I explain with a chuckle, because I've made her nervous.

"That's what I thought," she says.

We park our bikes and I use a bike lock so they don't get stolen. I take her by the hand and guide her toward the harbor. Large boats are docked in lines. When we reach the dock where the Sapphire is docked, her eyes dance with excitement.

"Um wow . . . that's quite a boat," she says with a hint of laughter to her tone.

"Ryan doesn't go small with anything," I answer, and my gaze follows her line of sight to the name of the boat.

"The Sapphire?" She cocks a brow.

"I think he named it after wife number three." I grin impishly, because this just rubs LA life in our faces. She nods but I can tell the wheels are turning in her mind.

A man greets us by the dock and helps us aboard.

"Good day, sir." He shakes my hand. He has an Australian accent. "I'm Captain Alder; pleasure to make your acquaintance."

We shake hands with the captain, telling him our names, and he shows us around. Below deck is a huge living space with a full kitchen, bar, and two bedrooms with a bathroom. "The restaurant had your lunch delivered. It's in the fridge," he says.

"Thank you," I reply, and we move above deck.

"This looks like so much fun," Jojo says. "I've been on fishing boats, but I've never sailed."

"Me neither," I admit. "This should be interesting."

I take her hand and guide her to a long white leather bench above deck. The Captain leaves to prepare us to sail. I notice that one of the seats is open and looks kind of like a chest. I figure it's good to put our belongings inside so they don't shift when we pick up speed. I drop the back pack inside and close the seat over it.

"I'm really glad you agreed to come with me," I say and press a kiss to her forehead.

"This has all been very surreal. You were ripped from my life. I never had a chance to say goodbye. I came to terms with the fact that I would never see you again," she says, looking out to the water. The boat begins to back up.

"I truly believed the same thing. I didn't think your father's life would be cut short or your husband's," I say with a wince. It seems talking about her husband is a sore spot.

She doesn't say anything, and I get distracted, or maybe a little nervous when the boat begins to move forward.

"Oh okay. We are sailing," I say, my voice a little high.

Her head moves to the side as she assesses me. "Are you nervous about sailing?"

"Me?" I raise both my brows. "Maybe just a little." I pinch my pointer finger and thumb together. "I'm okay with air travel but I haven't really been on the water much despite the fact that my friends have yachts back home."

"They have yachts, huh?" she says, and I'm not sure what the far-off look on her face is, but it melts away. "Why did you arrange for sailing if you didn't like it?"

My face scrunches up. "Because I thought you would."

"That's sweet Griff. Thank you," she gives me a quick kiss on the lips then stands to look out at the water. "What a view."

There are lots of boats around us of all sizes, the Sapphire being one of the larger ones.

We move away from the crowded area of boats and head to more open waters. We also pick up speed, and I begin to feel a little queasy.

"Is your life in LA all about parties and an exuberance of wealth?" she asks, looking me steadily in the eyes.

"Whoa." I stand beside her and grip a railing. "I wouldn't say it's all about that. I do spend many hours working hard, but in the off time, yes." I sigh. "I attend a lot of parties I suppose."

She nods, and she looks like she's thinking too much.

"I need to know what's inside that head of yours," I say.

"This is all really great, Griff. Seeing you again. Learning the truth about why you left. There were obviously a lot of unresolved feelings between us, and if we're being honest, chemistry has never been our problem."

My cheeks heat. I smile. "What are you saying here?"

"What I've been saying to myself all along. We come from different worlds now. We aren't the same lovestruck kids. You made a life in LA; mine is in New York. So, what is this? What are we doing?" She looks at me and my heart bursts. She may be strong and willing to say what's on her mind today, but she still seems to put things through a grater.

"My feelings for you are still so deep. We may have grown up but the essence of us has stayed the same. I feel it and I think you can too," I say.

"I'm feeling it, but our lives are more complicated now. How would we ever work?" she asks and even though I have been thinking the same thoughts I don't voice them in fear I will send her running in the other direction.

"I said I would do what it takes to keep you in my life, and I meant it. I just don't have all the pieces worked out yet." My lips turn down and a wave of nausea washes over me. I try to shake it off. It's odd that I'm seasick now since I was fine on the ferry over. Although the ferry was slow and steady. We've picked up speed now. There's so little barriers between the open sea and me between Jolie's heart and mine and yet the rift between us grows.

"I can't go through any more heartbreak. I don't want to. I think that after this little mini vacation is over, we need to put a stop to whatever is happening. We can't get in too deep again," she says, and I know she feels the need to protect her heart, but I hate it.

"I was hoping these few days would show you we're meant to be," I say, and suddenly I feel vomit come up my throat. I turn my head away and look frantically around me. I grab a handrail on the edge of the boat and heave overboard.

"Shit!" Jojo screams. "Griff." She's by my side in a second, rubbing my back. I throw up again. "I'm going to tell the captain we need to head back to harbor."

She leaves me, and I can't even watch her walk away because I don't want to vomit all over this very expensive boat.

She returns a few minutes later. "Do you want to come down below? The captain said there is some sparkling water in the fridge."

I shake my head. This day is a royal fuck-up. Instead of showing her the real me, I've taken her on a fancy sailboat and rubbed my LA life in her face. Things couldn't get any worse. "I'll just hold on here." I grasp the side rail as the motion sickness makes me dizzy and nauseous.

Jojo stays by my side. "This kind of reminds me of the time you and Logan went to that party when Mom accompanied Dad to a series of lectures. I can't remember where they went but you and Logan were in senior year. You came home pissed drunk, and both of you were taking turns puking," she reminds me. Thinking back to that time makes my stomach roil.

"Geez, Jojo. I don't think this is the right time to bring that up," I say, feeling like I'm going to heave again.

"Just hear me out," she says, and so I take a slow breath and try to focus on her and not the nausea. The captain walks over, hands me a plastic bag, and says we should reach the harbor in the next ten minutes.

When he walks away, Jojo continues, "You were so drunk that night you kept confessing all these things to me. It started with 'Jojo, you are so pretty.'" She looks to me and grins.

"You still are." I smile.

"Then you said you wanted to kiss me." She laughs. "I told you there was no way I would allow you to kiss me with your vomit breath."

"I remember that too." I shake my head thinking of my younger immature self.

"Then you said, 'Fine, but promise me this. One day, you'll agree to marry me,'" she says and the memory of me, smelly and sloppy, enters my mind's eye. I smile. "Do you remember what I said, Griff?"

"One day, maybe," I say and smile at her.

"One day, maybe," she repeats.

"I really want to kiss you now," I say, and it isn't a lie. Those rosy lips of hers call to me.

"Not with that vomit breath." She giggles.

I laugh too and see that we are slowing down as the captain

guides the boat into the harbor. The captain parks the boat. We walk toward the dock and Jojo thanks the captain for the beautiful but short ride. She tells him to enjoy the lunch I ordered, and she helps me off the boat because I'm still dizzy.

"Should we head back to the house?" she asks.

"Nah." I shake my head. "Just give me some time. Being back on steady land and inhaling the fresh air feels good." I press my lips together. "Well, we know I'm not much of a sailor now," I say impishly.

"That's okay." She rubs my back.

"We can walk over to the lighthouse and relax a while," I suggest, not wanting this day to be a total write-off. Now that I'm back on land my queasiness is better.

"Sure, but here. You should drink some water." She pulls a bottle out of the backpack I packed this morning. I'm suddenly relieved that she remembered to take it off the boat because I totally forgot. She passes me the bottle and takes one for herself. The sun is warm now, beating down on us.

"Let me carry the bag," I say, extending my hand.

"I got it." She swings it on her back.

I take her hand, and we walk toward the light house. "We have lots of crazy stories," I say.

"We do. Like the time you saved me from the neighbor's possessed dog." She laughs.

"And the time you lied to your mom about going with one of your friends to a movie and we took the bus across town so we wouldn't bump into anyone we knew," I say. It had been a perfect afternoon of holding hands and making out in the back of the movie theater. We were cursed out more than once but we didn't care. We just wanted time together.

We both look at each other knowingly. There is a lot of history between us. With her hand in mine, we walk toward the lighthouse.

"Jojo . . ." I say her name and pause.

She squints when she looks over to me.

"I feel like you're holding back on me," I say hesitantly.

"I thought the sex was pretty good," she answers playfully.

"I'm being serious. The chemistry between us was always hot, but I'm not talking about that. Back in the day . . ." I rake my fingers through my hair, trying to find the right words. "Yeah, we made out a lot, but we also talked a lot too. Our connection was deeper than sex," I finally say, and her chin dips and she looks away from me.

"Hey." I touch her chin and guide her to look me in the eyes. "What is it?"

She pulls out of my grasp and continues to walk. "It's a lot of things."

"Such as?" I ask, urging her to tell me more.

"We were so close. You could have told me you got into trouble with school. Maybe if you did, I would have told you not to go to my father. I knew he gave you a hard time. Maybe I could have talked to Mom to help you, but you didn't trust me enough to share your problems with me," she says, and my stomach sinks.

"It's not that I didn't trust you. I was so deeply, madly in love with you I was terrified of what you would think of me. I thought if I would get thrown out of school, I'd end up stocking the super-market like my dad. Your father more or less told me that's where he thought I'd end up. I wanted you thinking better of me. I did some-thing illegal, and my self-esteem was shit. I fucked up. Your dad threatened me, and I bowed my head and walked away with my tail between my legs. I was broken." My voice cracks and tears well in her eyes.

"I'm sorry. I feel terrible about all of it. I hate that you were so worried about your finances that you made a bad decision. I hate my father for using your insecurities and situation against you. Gah." She shakes her head. "I want to scream at him so bad." Her tears fall and she swipes at them with her finger. "A part of me is upset you couldn't come to me when you were in trouble but I don't hold that against you. I get that you were in a tough situation and that you were scared." She stops walking and looks around. The area around the lighthouse is surrounded by greenery and a long walkway bordered with rocks. We're standing in a large patch of grass outside the lighthouse. The area is large enough that no one is close enough to hear our conversation. Most people are walking along the stone path that leads to the front of the lighthouse.

"So what is it? What's holding you back from me now?" I ask, looking deep into her green eyes. She's hurting, broken. A few tears run down her cheeks and I wrap my arms around her. Her cheek presses to my chest.

"This is such a mess." She pulls away from me. "You'd think I could keep my shit together in public."

"Everyone is far enough away," I say so she doesn't feel bad about breaking down. "There is something you're hiding. I can feel it. Something is weighing you down and after everything we've shared these last few days, I want to know what it is." I urge, as my emotions battle inside me. "It's like we are happy and having a good time but you aren't all in. Is it because of Mason? Do you feel guilty for being with me?" I practically choke on my words because if that's what's happening here, then I've truly lost her. Mason won her heart and I was the asshole who trampled it. If she can't get passed feeling guilty over Mason then we won't have a future. I walked away, but now I want it all back—the love, the passion. All of her.

"Not in the way you think," she says curtly. Taking her hand away, she wraps her arms around herself.

"You miss him; you loved him. I get it. I left and you found love again." I say those words and they pierce my heart like a dagger. I want to kick myself for not making better choices in my life.

Her brows draw together and it almost looks like she's holding her breath. "I've told you I've been through a lot."

"I want to know what that means because I care for you, and I know we don't have everything worked out, but I believe we'll get there," I say, hoping to convince her to confide in me.

"There are things that happened that even Mom doesn't know," she says and tears slip down her cheeks, and that's when I know it's bad, because she's close with Kathy.

"You can share them with me. You know I haven't had an easy life. I've struggled every step of the way. Maybe I can help you in some way," I say, hoping she will open up to me. I need to know what happened so I can find a way back into her heart.

"That's sweet." She laughs through her tears, looks up to the sky, and blinks while I wait patiently.

"I don't want to push but I feel a part of you is closed off and I want to reach that part. Does that make sense?" I say softly.

"It does." Her smile is sad. "It's not easy for me to talk about. Especially now. I pride myself on being strong, on saying what's on my mind, but you know I wasn't always this way."

"There's a small blanket in the backpack. How about we find a spot on the grass?" I suggest.

"Sure."

We find a spot away from the many tourists. I pull out a plaid flannel blanket I packed in the backpack, and we sit cross-legged facing each other.

"Whatever it is, you can tell me," I say.

"I know. It's just. . . I get panicked when I talk about it."

"I was panicking about coming back to Boston. I never wanted to return. I never wanted to see my father," I admit.

"But you came for Mom." Her lips turn up but her smile and eyes are sad.

"I came for you too. It may not be the original reason I was on the plane that day, but it's the reason I'm still here. I could never leave and wonder what could have been." I sigh.

She takes a few deep breaths and I prepare myself, because I can see that something very bad happened to her. It makes me angry I didn't come back sooner.

Chapter 25

Jolie

"Brace yourself," I say, taking a deep breath, and I'm not sure if I am talking to myself or Griff. I pull my hands out of his grasp and play with the blades of grass on the side of the blanket, threading them between my fingers. "My life came crashing down on me."

"Shit, Jojo." His deep baritone sounds pained as he stares at me through light blue eyes that look stormy right now.

"When I pictured telling you my story, I didn't picture telling it in a public place." I laugh nervously, desperately searching for the right words to begin this tale. I can't look him in the eye as the first words leave my lips. "Mason developed some anger issues, which I knew was common for ballers. Football is an aggressive sport. When Mason was home, he began to lash out. First it was verbally. Things he didn't mean would come flying out of his mouth. Meanness I had never seen in him began to be the ordinary," I say, and even though I'm not looking at Griff, I hear a loud hiss escape him. I persist, knowing there's no turning back now.

"One night, he came home saying he wanted me to join him and his buddies for a dinner party. He hadn't given me notice and I had a prior work commitment. I'd given up so much for him already that I was intent on standing my ground. Somehow, the fight spun out of control and he hit me not once but twice across the face." I pause and look up at Griff.

He wipes tears from his eyes. "I was scared you'd say something like that."

"Let me continue, Griff. This isn't easy," I warn.

"I'm listening." He nods, looking so torn. He has always been a crucial part of my life. He has always been super protective. I can only imagine what he must be feeling now.

"Mason was big and strong. Those hits marked my face, but the scariest part was watching his anger rise to the point he lost control. I just wasn't expecting it from him." I shake my head, telling myself I shouldn't be ashamed, but I can't stop that feeling from consuming me. "I left him that night. I didn't make it to my work function because, you know, I had a bruised face. I went to stay with my friend Tiffany Miller, who also happened to be a psychologist. I told her about his increasing anger issues and how he hit me. She asked me one question: how many concussions has he suffered? I had to think on that because there had been many, starting with a bad one while he played college football. I told her what I knew. That's when Tiffany mentioned CTE: chronic traumatic encephalopathy. She told me I would find lots of research easily because the NFL had made a statement about it a couple years prior, and many studies were being conducted. Tiffany was right; CNN and other main-stream media had breaking stories on the impacts of concussions on NFL players," I take a deep breath as I remember searching article after article and thinking how the facts matched Mason's behavior. "The disease had a slow progression, and some symptoms included aggression and impulse-control issues. To me, it was clear as the sky without clouds, but I was the only one who saw it for what it was. I didn't want to speak with him so I emailed him the links to the articles. I knew he had to see the facts. Football was his life. He wasn't going to buy into a theory."

"Did he go to the doctor? Did he try to get help?" Griff asks.

I shake my head. "While we were separated, Mason was persistent with calling me, leaving me messages, crying, and apologizing. When I finally answered his call he told me that I was way off base. That he was just under a lot of pressure. He laughed it off and told me I was overreacting. I hung up with him and called his mother. I told her he hit me, and she told me basically the same thing he did. That he was under pressure to succeed and it wouldn't happen again."

When I look at Griff, he's shaking his head. I can see that he wants to say something. "Please, please just let me finish." My voice cracks. It's so hard to continue because I feel like a fool when I tell the story even though I know better than to think any of it was my fault.

Mason and I had many good years together. He was suffering, but that isn't what people see. I'd always feared that when I tell my story, people will look at me like I'm somehow weak and broken, and even though my insides sometimes feel that way, I know I'm strong.

Griff nods.

"Mason didn't take the potential diagnosis seriously. He was making ridiculous amounts of money. He was able to help his family who had always struggled financially. He thought life was good."

"Please tell me you left him," Griff says, looking to me with unshed tears.

"I left him after that time yes. I rented myself a small apartment and told him I wasn't coming home until he got help." Problem with CTE is that it can only be diagnosed after death. "Mason said he was getting help for his anger and he'd never hurt me prior. He had always been sweet, supportive, and caring. We had been separated for a long time but I eventually went back to him. And for a while, things were good. I still noticed little changes in him with impulse control. His anger would rise and he'd maybe swear a little, but it was nothing major. He was doing his best. But when he began spending more and more time away from me I didn't understand why. At first I was hurt. Then I honestly began to believe that he felt like there was something wrong with him. One night, I confronted him about it, he beat me so bad he put me in the hospital. When I awoke, he was gone." I have a hard time looking Griff in the eyes. I hate to be the victim. I hate the guilt that runs through me for not getting Mason the help he needed.

I don't shed a tear because I've cried enough for Mason and how broken he left me. "He left a message saying he was going to be in Florida. I was heartbroken that he hadn't stayed to own up to the fact that he had a problem. I was upset with myself for believing he had gotten the help he needed. "One week later, he died in a boating accident-- Only I believe he killed himself. I told Mason's mother what I thought but she didn't want to hear any of it. She never did." I inhale and exhale. "A part of me lives with guilt. I should've tried to get him more help. The fact that he died on a boat with his friend from the team helped to strengthen the argument that it was an accident. Both men had high levels of alcohol in their system. They lost control of the boat. No one knows exactly what happened that day in the middle of the Atlantic Ocean. I wanted Mason's brain donated for research, but his mom was adamant it shouldn't be donated. I donated it anyway behind her back. Mason signed up to be an organ donor and deep down, I felt like the research would help others, and Mason had always been a kind and giving soul. He wasn't in his right mind when he died." It's hard to look Griff in the eyes. What he will think of me now? That I am a broken abused wife? That's not who I am. He remains quiet but I can tell that the balls are rolling in his mind.

"When the pathology results came back, I learned that Mason had a mild buildup of *tau* in his brain, something that was present in those suffering from CTE. It also made them more susceptible to suicide. When I told Mason's mom the news, she didn't want to hear any of it. She said I should stop making up stories about her son. In his will, Mason left me and his mother all he had but I didn't want any of it, so I gave all his money to his mother and donated a small fraction to concussion research."

"Jojo," Griff croaks as he leans forward, pulling my body into his and wrapping his arms fiercely around me. "I'm so sorry. You were by yourself and I'm so sorry." I feel him shaking as he holds me.

I rub his back to console him, knowing what my story must be doing to him. "I didn't tell you to have you feel sorry for me or to feel any guilt for that matter. I shared this with you so you can understand where I'm coming from. Mason wasn't to blame for what happened to him but still, I had to live with the consequences. You weren't to blame for leaving me all those years ago. I now know it was my father's hand that drove you away, but the reasons don't matter. My heart was shattered when you left, and my heart was shattered when Mason hurt me the way he did."

"Jesus. Jojo." He pulls back and watches me.

"I do feel like I should have done more to help Mason. He wasn't in his right mind, and I have to live with that."

"That wasn't your fault in any way shape or form," Griff says, sounding appalled at my words.

"I get that but because Tiffany had a theory about the CTE, I should have pushed harder to help him. He was a good man, Griff. I didn't love him the way I loved you, but he still had a special place in my heart." My voice shakes and my chest burns having to remember some of the worst moments in my life.

"Are you hearing yourself? You said you loved me more. Well, this is our chance." Griff looks to me with such hope that I hate to disappoint him.

"I don't want to hurt you, Griffin Campbell." I take his hands in mine. "I just feel like I've given up so much in my life, and things haven't gone my way one bit. Whatever is happening between us terrifies me. I would need to take things slow, and how is that even possible when we head to two separate ends of the country next week? And I want to go back to school in the fall. After everything I've been through, and Kip's recent passing . . . Life is too short. I want to achieve my own dreams," I say sadly. "I don't want to look back and have regrets."

"I get that. I do. But honestly, Jojo, there is no way I'm letting you walk out of my life," he says adamantly.

"I need time. I wasn't expecting this. I wasn't expecting an us."

"I'll wait for you," he says.

"It isn't that simple. Come on . . . do you really picture me living out in LA? I'm like the antithesis of a Hollywood starlet."

He laughs.

"I hate to disappoint you." I lift my hand and caress his cheek. "It's the last thing I want to do." As tears slip down my cheeks, I press my lips to his.

"I know," he whispers against my mouth. "I wish we could find a way to be together."

"In a way I was too, but I need to work on myself first. I hope that makes sense."

"It does. Believe me. I've been working on myself for a while. And a part of me wants to throw caution to the wind and say I'll come live with you wherever you end up, but I know you need to do this on your own."

"I still hope we can enjoy our time together. It means so much to me to have these special moments with you," I say.

"You're making it seem like we're saying goodbye." He swallows hard, his voice cracking. "I'm not letting you go so fast. This has been an emotional day, and my brain is swimming with everything you told me . . ." His brows crease together. "Why didn't you ever tell your mom or Logan about what happened with Mason? Why did you carry such a burden on your own?"

"Shame, and guilt. I have a therapist back in New York. We were working on me trying to share what happened with my family but I just wasn't ready to share." I say. "I didn't want to burden Mom, and I don't want Logan to feel like he somehow failed me as my big brother because you know how he can be." I laugh.

"Oh trust me, I know. He gave me the third degree," he scoffs, even though I know he isn't truly offended.

"Exactly. And I don't want people remembering Mason as a man who hit his wife because he was so much more," I say.

"You said he was a good man. That is very sad. I mean, you never really think about how the athletes' lives are impacted by their job. And so many of them get repeated concussions. That's messed up," he says, his face scrunching.

I lean forward and press a small kiss to his lips.

"What was that for?" he asks. "Not that I'm complaining."

"For being you." I smile. It feels like a weight has been lifted off my chest. I'm happy Griff understands that Mason was suffering from a health problem. It's important to me.

"How about we grab some lunch then check out the lighthouse?" He suggests, standing and offering me his hand. I give him mine and stand. The future between us is uncertain but he's still my own personal heart thief; that hasn't changed.

We head over to a restaurant and enjoy some lobster and shrimp. My chest feels lighter now that someone else knows the truth. Griff gives me small smiles that make my heart soar as we eat. How will I ever say goodbye to him?

It won't be a final goodbye. You'll see him again, Jolie.

"You ready for your lighthouse tour?" he asks, standing from the table.

"Definitely, and you're looking much better. Your coloring is back to normal." I grin.

He chuckles. "Yes, well, I'll have to make a note to myself: no more sailing. It's good this isn't our first date." He winks, knocking his shoulder into mine, and then he takes my hand and leads me to the lighthouse. "You know this isn't just a simple lighthouse with metal stairs that overlooks the ocean," he says, grinning wide.

"What do you mean?" I ask as we approach the lighthouse entrance.

"You think you can make it up all those stairs?" he asks playfully not answering my question. It makes me think he's got another something special planned for today.

I punch him lightly in the shoulder. "Hey, I'm not an old lady."

We climb the circular staircase until we reach the top.

"Check out that view," Griff sighs.

"Yeah," I answer, a little breathless from climbing the steps fast. I watch the large expanse of water with boats scattered about. Some of them look like mere specks from up here.

"So are you going to tell me why this isn't a simple lighthouse? Or are you going to make me guess?" I look around for a clue. This is the first lighthouse I've visited but it's what I would expect it to be.

Lots of old stairs, large enough windows to see the ocean and a lamp to light the way for sailors.

"Have you figured it out?" he asks.

"You're just playing me," I snicker.

"Never." He places his arm over my shoulder. "You know there's a lot of history to this place. I looked it up last night after you fell asleep. I figured after we went sailing and had lunch we would stop in here. I wanted to know a little about this place. Good thing I looked it up since my first romantic gesture was an epic failure." he says.

"It wasn't a fail. You wanting to plan everything out for us is sweet." His attention to detail reminds me of the Griff I knew as a boy. "Now tell me what you learned about this place. You've peaked my curiosity." I bat my lashes.

His lips spread wide and he gazes at me warmly. "Okay I won't leave you in suspense any longer. There was a lighthouse keeper living here in the late 1800s. He lived on this property with his wife and eleven children. Every night, he carried enough oil up here to shine light on the ocean. Apparently, this side of the island has some treacherous rocks, and the lighthouse was built here to prevent ship-wrecks," he says, looking to me with a serious expression.

"Do tell me more." I smirk, intrigued by the tale.

"One night, the lighthouse keeper became very ill. His wife was caring for him and so they asked their eldest daughter to carry the oil up to the lamp and keep watch because the north winds were stirring. The young girl, who was seventeen at the time, stayed awake all night, keeping watch and ensuring the lamp had enough oil.

"While she was keeping watch, she spotted a shipwreck off-shore. A tiny bass boat capsized and sank during a nor'easter. The girl quickly ran down to the edge of the dock and threw out a rope to a man and hauled him in. She brought him back to her parents' house, dried him off, and fed him, and he stayed with the family for a few days.

"The young girl nursed him back to health and they fell in love. Only he had to get word back to his family that he was okay, and he also promised to bring them back food. He left the next day on a ship destined for the mainland. He was a poor man and didn't know how he would keep his promise to the girl. Meanwhile, the father of the girl remained ill and she took on the job of lighthouse keeper. Every night she brought the oil needed to light the way for ships at sea, hoping one day her beloved would return.

"It took him one year to save enough money to build another bass boat and return to her. When he returned, he learned that he'd fathered a child. When he left on his last adventure, he had told his parents that he wouldn't be returning. He married the daughter of the lighthouse keeper and the father built them a small quarter on the property. Eventually the girl's parents grew old and moved to the mainland. The girl and her husband moved to the main house with their children. Each night, she and her husband took turns watching the sea because it had been the sea that had brought them together," he ends the story with a small smile.

"Griff." I hold my hands close to my heart. "That was beautiful."

"That's love, Jojo. What's meant to be is meant to be. I understand you're still healing and that you have goals you want to accomplish, but remember, I'll be here waiting." He kisses me hard, not asking permission. It feels more like he's taking back what's his, and before I can protest, my body and heart succumb to his lips, to his touch as he grips the back of my head.

We ease the kiss when we hear more people approaching up the stairs.

"You're mine. I'll always come back to you," he says, pressing another kiss to the outside of my hand.

I can't protest when my soul knows he speaks the truth. A part of me feels like I am the lighthouse keeper's daughter, waiting, watching, the dark hours passing while I hope for Griff's return.

"I want to take you back to the house and make love to you," he says. His gruff voice causes moisture to pool between my thighs.

"Yes," I say, and I allow him to lead the way.

We make love into the early hours of the morning, taking time to cherish one another. Griff is patient. He doesn't press me for more; he shows me with his body what lies in his heart.

It will be so difficult when we have to part again but I don't know what destiny has in store for us, but I know I'm not ready for more right now.

Chapter 26

Griffin

"You're awfully quiet," I say, looking to Jolie for answers about her somber mood. We are on the ferry back to the mainland.

Last night was intense. It almost felt like goodbye.

Our time alone together is nearing its end. Long-distance dating would be difficult but maybe we could give it a try.

"I'm not sure what to say. You know I've always cared about you. That hasn't changed. I honestly made a pact with myself the day we left the Cape that I wouldn't sleep with you on this trip because it would only complicate things." She exhales and shakes her head. "Clearly my self-control around you is non-existent."

"What can I say? I'm just so darn irresistible," I joke. "But seriously, we've always had this chemistry. Don't beat yourself up. You know you got under my skin so long ago. I was only a boy when I fell in love with you. Before seeing you in that airport, I'd convinced myself there was no way I could feel the same way about you after so long. Ten years is a long time." I blow out a breath and take her hand in mine. "But the moment I saw you waiting at that coffee stand, I knew . . . My heart beat differently when I saw you, and spending these last few days with you . . ." I search for the right words, staring into her eyes, and now that I understand what she's been through . . . it guts me. She's been hurt in such a deep way. She's scarred and guarding her heart but I need her to know I will handle her with the utmost care. "They were better than I ever could imagine—a dream really. I don't want it to end," I say, searching her face for some sort of clue as to what she's thinking.

She looks torn. "Griff . . . I'm not there yet. I'm still working things out in my head about Mason and—"

"I don't mean any disrespect to Mason. He clearly had a medical condition that caused him to behave the way he did," I say, feeling like I'm walking on eggshells. "But no matter the reason, he caused you to question faith in people and faith in love. I know I've had my own share in causing you heartache. But I was hurting too . . . and I never forgot about you. I need you to give me another chance. You need to know that when I make love to you, I feel things I've never felt before. There is an unbreakable bond between us. I can't let you slip through my fingers again."

She's wearing sunglasses and I wish I could see her eyes. "I don't want that either. This feels really good. Whatever is happening between us feels good."

"Then don't fight it," I say, willing her to see the depth of my feelings for her.

"I gave up so much for Mason. He got drafted into the NFL and I didn't continue to graduate school. Hell, I went to Brown to be close to him. I just don't want to be that girl anymore. She was broken." Her brows furrow deeply, causing a crease in her forehead. "I'm independent now. I work and support myself. I'm only just discovering who I am."

I take her hand in mine. "I think that's great. You need to know that I would never get in the way of your dreams, but I also want to be a part of your life."

"I want that too," she says, and I take a deep breath, feeling like I have been holding it underwater too long. "So what now?"

That's a good question. "We make plans. You tell me where you want to go to school," I begin.

"I quit my job in New York before I arrived," she suddenly blurts out. Her green eyes turn wide, as if she's terrified.

"Oh, why?" I wasn't expecting that.

"It didn't inspire me?" she says, and it sounds like a question. "Mom called and told me Kip died, and all I could think about was how I'm living this mediocre life."

"I get that. When your mom called it also got me thinking. I have a lot of material wealth back home; I even have good friends." I pause. "Well, some of them." I shrug. "But late at night, when I lie in my oversized bed, I'm lonely."

"Yeah," she sighs as if she understands me.

I lean forward and kiss her. I will never tire of kissing these lips. I want to say so much more but I have just made some strides with her. I don't want to scare her off by bending my knee and proposing.

Her hand comes up and caresses my cheek. "I'm scared, Griff," she says, and those words mean so much because she is finally opening up to me.

"Me too, baby. I haven't felt this way in so long. My dad said he broke when my mom left, and that always left me feeling vulnerable because what happens if I break?" I admit.

"Gosh, we are so messed up." She presses her forehead to mine.

"Tell me about it." I chuckle.

"We're going to be okay," she says, taking my hand.

We stay quiet for the rest of the ferry ride. We smile to each other and enjoy the sunshine. We steal glances and kisses and enjoy the scenic view.

When we reach the Cape, I grab our suitcases. We find a cab along the pier back to the beach house.

"Let me help you with that," Jolie says, offering to take her suitcase out of the trunk of the cab.

"I got it." I lean forward and press another kiss to her lips, knowing it will be weird to show her this kind of affection in front of Logan and Kathy.

With two small suitcases in hand, I reach the front door and turn the knob. Kathy has always left the door unlocked during daylight hours.

I hear loud yelling through the front door. Is that coming from the house? I freeze. I turn around, because I don't sense Jojo close behind. I notice she is still by the curb because her dress is caught on the zipper of her purse.

"You need help with that?" I ask a little loudly.

"I'm good," she calls out.

I push the front door open. "Hey, man. I wasn't expecting you back so early." Logan comes up to the door, out of breath. He looks frazzled.

"What's going on?" I watch as my best friend takes a deep breath. His hair looks mussed, and he looks like he's sweating or maybe as if he's been through a war.

"Jenn wanted to try and stop drinking yesterday. She asked me to take all the alcohol away, and now she's melting down," he explains.

"Fuck," I hiss. That would explain it.

Kyle walks up to the door. I bite my tongue. I do not cuss in front of children. "You think you can take Kyle and my sister for like a very long walk?" Logan says, shifting on his feet.

"Uh! Yeah. Let me just drop these suitcases upstairs." I try to take a step farther in the house but Logan blocks me. "What's wrong with you?"

He eyes me like he has unsaid words he'd like to share. "I need you to get Kyle and Jolie out of here like now," he whispers.

"Why?" Jenn's loud voice comes from the kitchen. She's loud and unhinged. "You want to hide what I have to say? You have to bury my secrets like you do Daddy's?"

Jolie comes up behind me. "What on earth is going on?" She looks around the house, wide-eyed.

"I need you and Griff to get Kyle out of here now," Logan snaps. I realize that he asked me to get both Jolie and Kyle away from here. I don't know why but I begin to think he has good reason.

"Hey guys, maybe we can take a walk to that bake shop. They

have amazing croissants." I smile to Kyle then look to Jolie. Her brows are furrowed and her forehead is creased, and Kyle seems pale and scared.

"Griff, it sounds like Logan may need my help. Would you mind taking Kyle on your own?" Jolie asks.

"You should really go too," Logan insists, placing his hand on Jolie's shoulder. He begins to guide her out the door. I can tell he's internally freaking the fuck out. I'm pretty sure Jolie is getting the same vibe.

"I'm good," she says turning back to look at her brother. "Would you stop pushing me out?" Now Jolie is getting irritated with Logan's attempt to get rid of her.

"Griff, can you please take Kyle? Something is going on here," Jolie leans in and says to me quietly.

I can't say no to her.

"I hate all of you. Fucking all of you," Jenn yells as the kitchen door whips open. She takes big steps, charging toward the front entrance of the house. "Please give me something to drink," she begs and Kathy trails behind her.

"Logan, I think this is too much. Go get the alcohol. I don't know how this works exactly, but she can't go cold turkey," Kathy cuts in.

"She made me promise her not to give her any no matter what. I'm just keeping my promise," Logan says to his mom.

Suddenly, Jenn turns on Jolie. "You bitch," she spits, looking at Jolie with disgust. Jolie takes a step back, staring at her sister like she's lost it. I'm pretty sure she has.

"What can we do for her? Jolie asks Logan. By the looks of it I don't think he has a clue. I'm clueless myself. My dad never quit alcohol.

"I'm standing right here," Jenn says. "What the fuck do you care anyway, Little Miss Perfect?"

"Griff, please get them out of here now." Logan grits his jaw.

"Jennifer Bryant. That is enough. Your son is standing right here. Now get upstairs," Kathy barks louder than I've ever heard her speak before.

Jenn's lower lip quivers, and she wraps shaky hands around her waist but doesn't budge.

I look over to Jolie and she is not budging either. I can't exactly lift her over my shoulder and haul her away.

"Logan, she should hear the truth," Jenn says quietly, rubbing her hands up and down her arms.

"Jenn, your son is standing two feet away from you. Think of your actions and what your words will do," Kathy says, placing a hand on Jenn's shoulder and guiding her toward the kitchen.

"Stop pushing me." Jenn screeches shimmying out of Kathy's grasp.

"Jenn you need to take a breath and get in the kitchen now," Logan barks. He has a hold of her arm now but Jenn is pulling in the other direction like an errant child.

"Mom's drinking too much," Kyle says, looking up to me sadly.

"You can't shut me up. She needs to know the truth. They all need to know the truth," Jenn yells, and then she punches Logan in the face. He almost falls backward but catches himself on a wall.

"What is wrong with you? You have your son here. If you need to sleep it off, then go do so," I say to her.

"You aren't a part of this family, Campbell. You should leave," she says dryly, as if I'm an afterthought.

"No, Jenn, you don't get to talk to him that way. He is part of this family," Jolie barks.

"He is," Logan cuts in.

I get a gnawing feeling in my stomach telling me something big is about to happen.

Chapter 27

Jolie

I hate that Jenn is attacking Griff. He's been through enough he doesn't need to take shit from her.

"You know you don't have to be mean right now?" I say placing each of my hands on my waist.

"Jolie, it's fine," Griff says quietly. He probably wants to say something along the lines of Jenn not being in her right mind. That would be an understatement.

"Fuck you." Jenn barks at me.

"That's enough," Griff turns pinning her with a stare that if looks could kill Jenn would be dead on the floor. His tone is demanding and eerily calm.

Jenn bursts into maniacal laughter. "Everyone always protects you from big bad demons. Always perfect, Little Miss Jojo Bear. Must be nice to be you. I always wondered. You know I fucked Mason first? You didn't have a right to him," she says, spraying spit on my arms.

I'm stunned into silence. I never asked Jenn for permission to date Mason but she never even looked his way after the night of the party when she took him up to her room. Suddenly, anger boils inside me. It wasn't like I stole him.

"Why didn't you say that it bothered you?" I snarl back.

"Did you see the way he looked at you?" She laughs. "Like you were his shining star."

"We were friends for the longest time," I argue.

Logan steps between us. "Things don't have to go down this way," he says quietly to Jenn.

"Don't they?" she asks, looking at him blankly, her eyes filled with tears.

"Tell me what's going on." I look between my brother and sister.

"Well, she's already told Mom about Dad's philandering," Logan chides.

"Mom." I walk over to her and wrap my arms around her neck. "I'm so sorry."

She pats my back. "I'm fine. It's my children I'm worried about," she answers, and her words cause a sinking feeling in my stomach. "I always had it in mind that it was possible your father was cheating. She admits, like she's had a lifetime to ponder and think about all of this.

I look between my mother and Logan. I'm about to look at Jenn when Griff takes two long strides over to me and picks me up, carrying me over his shoulder.

"We are leaving now," he says.

"Put me down." I hit him on the back. "Griff, please." I get that he's trying to protect me from whatever is happening, but I don't need it.

"Fuck. How many knights in shining armor does one girl need?" Jenn hisses.

"Don't." Logan warns her. "Mom, get Kyle upstairs now," Logan barks the order, and Mom takes Kyle by the hand but they only get so far.

"I fucked your husband. Kyle is Mason's child," she says, and Griff slowly lowers me to my feet. I look into his eyes for some understanding. My legs feel like jelly, and my mind feels like I've entered some alternate universe where I'm swimming inside a bubble.

Griff's face contorts.

I spin around. "What did you say?" It doesn't take me long to inhale a deep breath and get my wits about me. I take a few strides to get in my sister's face. I must have heard her wrong.

"I fucked Mason again. Kyle is his." Jenn tilts her head up to the sky as I stand in her face. I turn to look at my family. Maybe Jenn is just making this shit up because she's in some sort of withdrawal or having a hallucination, only Mom bursts into tears and Logan squeezes his eyes shut like he's in physical pain.

"How long have you known?" I look between Mom and Logan.

"We just found out. I'm so sorry." Logan sighs. Mom comes up to me and wraps me in her arms, only I feel numb. Like I can't breathe. I thought Mason was done hurting me but it seems that he has left behind some secrets of his own. Is this why he ended his life? Did he regret sleeping with Jenn? I will never know.

"I don't know what to say," Mom mumbles. "I feel responsible for her. I just never believed she would do something so . . ."

"Disgusting," I fill in. I break Mom's embrace and whip around to my sister.

"Why tell me now? Is this a lie? A way for you to hurt me?" I ask, stepping close to her. Not wanting to cower. My emotions swirl at hurricane speeds as my heart palpitates in an unhealthy way, but I've been here before. I've been shattered by words and my husband's fists. No one will break me again—not even my messed up sister. "Was it some sort of revenge? Explain it to me, because I would really like to know why and how you could be so disgusting?"

I don't think she is going to answer me as she bursts into tears. "I'm sorry. I'm so sorry. I was so messed up. I don't even know what's wrong with me. Please, Jolie. I didn't mean to hurt you. It's why I didn't come back home. I was ashamed. I was messed up. I got involved with drugs and I needed money. I'm so sorry. So sorry. If it's any consolation, I got down on my knees for him too but he rejected me." She tilts her chin at Griff.

"Are you fucking kidding me?" My jaw drops, and I look to the man in question.

"That's enough," Logan barks.

Jenn is a blubbering mess as she cries. A part of me hates her for sleeping with Mason but her behavior is just so gross that I feel sorry for her more than anything.

"When did you sleep with Mason?" I ask softly.

"Jolie," Logan says my name like I'm an errant child.

"I want to know," I say, lifting a hand to stop my brother, who looks like he is a beat away from throwing Jenn out of the house.

Kyle is four years old. Mason has been gone for two years. That means he slept with her almost five years ago. It must have been after the first time I left him. I went back to him after that. He said he had gotten help.

"Like you want details?" my sister croaks.

"I want dates," I clarify. Why in the hell would I need details?

She begins to mutter. It doesn't matter though; I can do the math.

"Why would you contact my husband in the first place?" I ask. "Were you purposely trying to hurt me?" I can't help the tears that slide down my cheeks. I think of Kyle, his hazel eyes and mocha skin. How did I not see it before?

"I needed money. I wasn't trying to hurt you. I asked him for a loan when he was in town for an away game and one thing led to another," she says, sounding sorrowful. She hiccups through her tears and uses the back of her hand to wipe her nose. She's a bloody mess.

"And Griff. Why were you on your knees for him?" I ask, and hear Griff groans behind me, muttering something.

"I wanted him to introduce me to one of his producer friends. I did what I do when I repay a favor. I got on my knees, only this asshole yanked me back up, gave me the phone number, and told me to get the hell out of his office."

As much as my heart is aching, her words about Griff provide some relief.

"And with Mason, I don't understand. He wouldn't have

expected you to pay back a loan on your knees," I say, realizing I knew little about the monster my husband had clearly become.

"If it's any consolation, he was already drinking when I got to his hotel room. He invited me in for a drink," she says.

"Is this really necessary?" Griff steps in.

"I want to know," I say softly, even though it feels like my legs are going to give out on me.

Jenn nods, walks over to the staircase, and falls back on a step. Her words are slurred. Her hair looks like a bird's nest. Her makeup is smeared. She looks scary.

"We had a drink and he gave me a look, like he wanted me. They had just won a game and he was pumped," she says.

"That's enough," Logan barks. "Jenn, get upstairs. I'm taking you to a rehab center. Do not go near Mom or Kyle. You've lost that right." Logan points up the stairs his entire body vibrating with anger and nerves. Jenn looks to him and bows her head as she climbs the stairs.

"What can I do?" Griff asks.

"Nothing," I say, feeling like I could melt into the floor and maybe curl into the fetal position. I take a deep breath, closing my eyes, and when I open them, my gaze lands on a sweet boy whose eyes are filled with tears.

Oh, dear.

My heart breaks.

"Kyle, how about we get out of here?" I say, extending my hand to him. He nods and gives me his hand, even though he continues to cry. His lips are turned in the saddest frown.

"I'll come with you," Griff says.

I don't answer him as I take my nephew's hand and leave through the front door. He just witnessed something that no child should see. He just heard words that no child should ever hear.

As I leave the beach house and walk down the boardwalk I feel spacey and hurt, but my attention stays on Kyle.

"I'm sorry you had to hear that," I say.

He nods and we continue to walk quietly as Griff trails behind us. I know he's here to keep us safe, to make sure we are okay.

"Did you know my dad?" Kyle looks up to me, squinting against the sun, and I see a small version of Mason. My heart breaks as I realize how much his career cost him.

"I did know your daddy. He was a famous football player, and a super-cool guy," I say. I know one day when Kyle is older, he will have a lot of questions about how he came about, but right now, he is a boy, and I think it's better he knows that his dad had been a hero.

"Really?" His eyes widen with anticipation.

"Yes, we went to school together. We were good friends. Your dad was a kind person, and he would have really liked to know you," I say, looking down at Kyle wondering if Jenn had told Mason about him or if he had no clue of his existence. If he did know I'd like to believe he would have wanted to be involved in his life. Suddenly Griff catches up to us and takes my hand. He gives me a small smile, and in that little gesture, he also gives me strength. I didn't think Mason could hurt me any more than he already had, but his betrayal stings right through me. It runs deep inside me, growing and festering, making my chest burn. I had grown up living in Jenn's shadow, wanting an inkling of the life she led, and to know that he slept with her during our separation hurts so damn much.

We continue to walk, and as I hold Kyle's little hand in mine, Griff's in the other, my chest warms because I love this young boy so much. I've only just met him, but I feel a part of him in some profound way I can't explain.

"You're a very special boy, you know that?" I give him the biggest smile I am able to muster right now.

"Thanks, Aunty Jojo." He smirks and continues to walk.

"Your mom isn't feeling well right now, and I know that can be scary," I say. After Jenn spluttered the truth about Kyle's paternity and Logan told her to get upstairs, my first instinct was to head up to my room, pack my bags, and leave. Until Kyle's sad face caught my eye, and I knew I couldn't. I knew he needed me. I've felt this bond with him from the start, but I couldn't place why.

Mason's sickness didn't happen overnight. The *tau* had been building in his brain for years. I know deep down he wasn't in his right mind.

As much as his betrayal hurts, I try to push my pain aside. For Kyle and for Mason, because I am guessing he didn't know about Kyle or maybe he did. It saddens me that Kyle will never get to meet his father or know the Mason I knew before the sickness set in.

"Mommy's been sick for a while. I try to take care of her, but it's hard. It's good we came to Grama," Kyle says. His words stop me in my path. A fissure runs through my heart.

"Oh Kyle." I take my hand from Griff and kneel down to Kyle's level. I embrace him in a hug. "I'm so sorry that you had to go through this." I take his small body in my arms and run my hands over his floppy brown hair. His head remains pressed on my shoulder. Feeling him in my arms, so small and vulnerable, makes me do something unexpected. "Kyle, I am going to stay here with you and Grandma. I want to take care of you until your mama gets better if that would be okay with you," I say, knowing my mom can do it, but she is older and hurting, and a part of me wants to make sure Kyle has someone who can give him a good time and do things kids like to do. Mom is just too tired for that.

Kyle pulls his head off my shoulder and smiles. "I'd really like that."

"Good." I smile. "Now how about we go get some ice cream?"

I look to Kyle and then to Griff. When my gaze connects with his, his eyes are watery. Oh, how my heart beats for this man.

"You are so damn special, Jojo Bear." He smiles and presses a kiss to my forehead, and that small gesture feels even more intimate than the alone time we've had these past few days. It shows me how deep his feelings run.

"Don't you think it's a little early for ice cream?" Griff asks, looking between me and Kyle.

"It's never too early for ice cream," I cheer, then I realize I forgot my wallet but I know Griff carries his in his back pocket.

We stop at an ice cream shop and Kyle eats ice cream outside on the patio. I take a few licks of mine but my appetite is non-existent. Griff tries really hard to make Kyle laugh by telling some really stupid jokes. Kyle's somber mood lifts, and we manage to get some giggles out of him.

I'm not ready to head back to the beach house or face Jenn. I don't know if I ever will be able to face my sister again.

When we are done eating ice cream, we head back toward the house. "I'm guessing you want to leave the Cape," Griff says.

"I need to get out of here," I nod. No way can I stay here. I need space. I feel like I've got whiplash.

"I can go inside and pack all your things. I can get Kyle's stuff too," he offers.

"Thank you. I really don't want to go back in there," I admit.

"Why don't you take Kyle to the beach?" Griff suggests.

Even though we don't have our bathing suits, I think that's a good idea. Jenn is a loose cannon. It's impossible to know what to expect from her.

"Thank you," I say softly. "It looks like my life just got a lot more complicated," I say, because we hadn't set anything in stone about what was happening with us and now I have committed myself to caring for Kyle.

"I like the way you've complicated it. I'm here to support you and Kyle. Whatever you both need." He smiles at me, and my heart breaks free of the chains that had been holding it hostage all this time. I don't need them anymore. Not with Griff.

"That means a lot," I say.

He gives my shoulder a squeeze. "I'll go get us ready to leave," he says and I can tell he doesn't want to leave me but I sure as hell am ready to leave the Cape. I don't know where Logan is going to take Jenn but the further away from me the better. I watch Griff walk away. I never thought that he and I would ever reconnect and here we are.

Kyle and I play in the sand while Griff heads back to the house. My mind swims with Jenn's cruel words as I try to make sense of my past. An hour later, Griff returns. He says our suitcases are all packed and waiting at the front door.

"Are you planning on taking him back to Boston?" he asks.

"I think that would be the best place," I say quietly as I watch Kyle play in the sand.

Griff squints against the sun. "I was thinking . . ." He pauses and bites the inside of his lip. He stares out to the ocean and then back to me. "Maybe you guys should come out to LA for a few days. I'd love to show you where I live, and maybe we could take Kyle to Disneyland and show him some fun. Take his mind off things. I spoke with Kathy back at the house and she thought it was a good idea too," he says, surprising me.

I swallow, thinking how even yesterday I would have been highly opposed to such a suggestion. I would have conjured up a million reasons as to why it was a bad idea.

"Say something," he urges. "You staring at me like this is making me hella nervous. Tell me what you're thinking. I really want both of you to come. I think it will be good for us and good for Kyle," he says. "I want to spend time with him. He's never had a father and I don't know, but since Jenn arrived with him, I feel this sort of kinship with him," he says, taking a breath.

"I saw that. It's both heartbreaking and sweet." I stand from the sand as Kyle runs back and forth along the shoreline. Griff eyes me like he isn't sure what to expect from me. "I'd love to come with you to LA." I press a kiss to his lips.

"Really?" He looks shocked. "T-thank you," he says, still pressing small kisses to my mouth. "You've made me really, really happy."

———

OUTSIDE THE BEACH HOUSE, Mom and Logan come to say bye. Apparently Jenn was listening when Griff suggested taking Kyle to Disney and broke down crying.

"Jenn says thank you," Mom says sadly. "She heard you're taking Kyle, and she really appreciates it."

"I'm not doing it for her," I snap.

"I know, dear." She rubs my back. "Goodness, Jolie. I expected this bad behavior from your dad, but Mason . . . he was a good man," she says quietly.

Griff eyes me and gives me a look that says it's time to come clean. It's time to share the burden I've been carrying too long on my shoulders.

"When I get back from LA, we'll need to have a talk. Right now, I think it's best we go," I say with my lips turned down and my heart heavy.

"You're right." She wraps her arms around me and I take comfort in her arms. "You are so strong. Don't ever question your strength and believe in yourself, Jojo Bear, because you have a lot going for you." She presses a kiss to my cheek.

"Thank you." I pull from her embrace and swipe at a stray tear.

She kneels down so that she's eye level with Kyle. "You have fun in Disney. Say hi to Mickey for me."

"I will, Grama," Kyle says, and gives her a hug.

Griff must have called an Uber because a car pulls up.

"That's for us," he says. He walks over to Mom. "Thanks for everything." He gives her a hug.

"Thank you, sweet boy. I haven't seen my daughter truly smile in a long time," she says to him. *Thanks, Mom.* Looks like her match-making agenda is working out after all.

"I hope to keep her smiling," Griff says thoughtfully, looking to Mom then back to me.

"You take care. All of you. Call me when you land," Mom says as we close the door on the Uber car. The driver pulls away and we all wave to Mom.

I know this is only a small trip, maybe a few days, but it means more time with Griff. Time to get to know him better and see what his life in LA is really like.

I just hope I like what I see.

Chapter 28

Jolie

"That was a great day." I sigh, leaning back into the seat of Griff's SUV. We arrived last night and woke bright and early to spend the day at Disneyland. Now, Kyle is passed out in the back-seat of the car seat Griff's assistant purchased hours before we landed in LA yesterday.

"It was." Griff lifts my hand to his lips and kisses me tenderly.

"I honestly can't feel my legs. I don't think I've ever walked for eleven hours straight," I say, lifting my ankle onto my other knee so that I can massage it.

"Me neither. I'm just grateful we could rent a stroller for the little guy," Griff says, taking a quick peek in the rearview mirror. I think he's checking on Kyle. He's been completely adorable with him.

"You were more excited than he was about the Mickey rides," I say playfully.

"I never got to do those things as a kid. I guess I could have gone to the parks on my own, but it didn't entice me. Now that I'm with you and Kyle, I'm thinking we go back tomorrow to see Universal

Studios," he says excitedly while staring at me for a brief second, maybe waiting for my reaction.

"Honestly, right now I need a warm shower and a bed. I can't feel my body, and the thought of doing this all over again makes me want to fall asleep." A loud yawn escapes me.

"Okay, so maybe the day after tomorrow then? Kyle was so excited all day. He didn't look sad at all. When we were back on the Cape, there were these times when he just went quiet, didn't talk, and kept his head down," Griff says.

"I noticed. It made me want to spend more time with him. No kid should look that sad or lonely," I say as I watch Griff driving. His jaw is wound tight. It hurts me so deeply that he was that kid. Maybe that's why I was able to forgive him for not coming back sooner to find me. He had been broken, and deep down, I know his feelings for me run deep.

I lean over and caress his cheek, wanting to pull him out of whatever bad memory he's thinking about. "Hey, I could use some company in the shower when we get back to your place."

"Jolie," he chides me, using a parental voice. "He may not be in deep sleep." He glances at Kyle again.

I laugh and turn back to check on Kyle. His head is tilted to the side and his mouth hangs slightly open with drool coming out the side. "He's definitely fast asleep,"

"Then that idea sounds perfect." He says about showering with me. It also buys me a Griff smile, and whatever heaviness was weighing him down lifts. His jaw relaxes and his eyes aren't creased anymore.

He pulls into his large drive and presses a button for one of the garage doors to lift. While I grab Kyle's backpack, Griff lifts him in his arms and carries him carefully through the house. My heart beats steady and strong as I watch Griff with him. Being here has me wanting things I thought I would never have. After Mason, I accepted I wouldn't fall in love again and that also meant I wouldn't have children. Now, new sparks of hope blossom inside me.

I follow Griff up to the second floor and open the bedding so that he can place Kyle right between the sheets.

I press a kiss to Kyle's forehead. Then I follow Griff out of the room. He takes me by the hand, leading me to the master suite.

"I'm not making any promises tonight. My body is so tired." I yawn again.

"Come. I'll fill you a bath."

It's still hard to believe that he lives in Beverly Hills. That he has this huge mansion with a personal assistant and a cleaning crew. Dressed the way he is now, in a worn pair of cargo shorts and an O'Neill T-shirt, he looks like the old Griff.

We head into the master bathroom. It's bigger than my bedroom back at my apartment. Which reminds me, that I better check in on Sasha tomorrow.

Griff fills the bath with steaming water and turns to me. I want him so badly but my body is just so wiped out.

"Come here," he says, his voice raspy, barely a whisper. His hands move up and down my sides from my rib cage to my waist once, twice. On the third time, he lifts my tank top over my head. My head lulls to the side, and he presses soft kisses along my neckline.

"Hmm, that feels nice," I murmur as my eyes close.

He continues to press soft kisses along my neck, behind my ear, and little goose bumps erupt down my arms and back. As he kisses me, he works to unclasp my bra, and as he sets my breasts free, he pulls back. The clear hue of his aquamarine eyes turn molten. A small rumble escapes him as he cups both breasts with each of his hands. I moan as he rubs my nipples with each of his thumbs, slowly, tenderly. Sparks of heat begin to erupt through my veins, igniting my sleepy body. I wrap my arms around his neck and kiss his lips. I'm too tired for any fast movements and so I move slowly, pressing kisses along his full lips while opening my mouth to taste him. He lifts his shirt over his head and my hands run up and down his chest over the hard plains of muscle on his back and then down to his shorts.

"Are you in the mood for a partner in the bath?" he asks.

I smile. "Yes."

I work on taking my shorts and panties off while Griff undresses too. I step into the bath first and he gets in right after me. It's a huge circular bath that has jets and little nooks to rest one's head. Griff gets in behind me, and I lean against his chest.

"I'm so exhausted. I'm sorry." I yawn again because the hot water is so relaxing it makes me sleepier.

"Don't be sorry. It's nice to be with you like this. To have you close again. Feeling your body next to mine is like a dream." He kneads my tense shoulders, working out the knots.

"Hmm, you're good at this. I'm used to being the one to give massages," I say, referring to my old job.

"I don't picture you as an aesthetician," he says.

"The money was pretty good. I liked the place I worked. My friend Michelle worked there with me. I guess it served its purpose for a while."

"And now, you're ready to head back to school? That's definitely a good thing."

"Thanks. I'm worried the schools won't accept my application for the fall semester this late in the year. Maybe I can try for the winter semester," I say.

"I hate saying this, but your dad had pull at Harvard, and if it's the history department that you're after, you should definitely make some phone calls," he suggests. "Your dad had lots of friends."

"I was thinking about calling the dean. He and Dad had been good friends, but now, in light of everything that happened with Jenn, I just . . . I don't think I want to stay in Boston anymore. I told Kyle I would be there to take care of him but I'm thinking it's better to find someplace new," I admit. I hadn't gone home in so long because of all the bad memories the place held. Now I feel like there are more to add to the list.

"Would you consider LA? There are top-notch schools here. Stanford is close to San Francisco but UCLA is like ten minutes away," Griff says. I turn to look at him and his brows are raised.

"I was thinking of Stanford." I cock one brow.

"It's like five and half hours by car, but we could manage," he says. "You look hesitant. Mind sharing your reservations?"

"I'm . . . not sure. I have a cat back home in New York, Sasha.

She is staying with my neighbor right now. My neighbor and I are really close. I also have a furnished apartment in New York. I thought of Brown, but I feel like I need a fresh start."

"Move here. With me," he says, startling me.

"Don't you think that's a little fast?" I say.

"Fast?" he repeats, looking at me wide-eyed. "It feels like I've been waiting on you a lifetime."

"I'm just not sure. I have Kyle to think about right now until Jenn gets her act together," I say. For Kyle's sake, I hope she does.

"For sure. I get that. Kyle is welcome to stay here too. I can find him a preschool. We can take care of him together, and it would make it easier on you if you had to attend classes. I know your family loves Ivy League, but UCLA has a good rep and honestly, even in traffic it wouldn't take more than twenty minutes to get there."

"You do make a convincing argument. Let me think on it, okay? I need to talk to Mom. We have to figure out Kyle's care. I don't think it's fair to have him bouncing around from place to place."

"Totally. What I'm suggesting gives him stability," he says.

"That's true," I say. "But moving in together is a big step. We've only been back together a week. I want to see what your life in LA is really like, not just when we are out having fun days at Disneyland. And we still need time to get to know each other again. And having Kyle with me does complicate things. From what I've seen, his life with Jenn was an unstable mess. I want that to change."

"Take your time and think on it," Griff says.

He reaches forward to turn on the water. There is a detachable showerhead attached to the bath. He sprays warm water over my body and then my head. I lean back and let him wash my hair and then my body.

By the time he is done I feel worn out. He washes his own body and hair, and then gets out of the bath first, wraps a towel around his waist, and then holds a big white fluffy towel for me. He wraps me up. It feels good to be cared for. Things hadn't been this way between me and Mason since before he got drafted. When he got drafted, he'd been a rookie player and had to show his worth. He'd always been busy working hard on the field. At home, he'd been tired and his focus had been elsewhere.

We head over to Griff's very large bed. He throws the thick blanket open. "Hop on in." He waves me in. Last night when we arrived, Kyle had been nervous about staying in such a large home and being in a new space so I'd slept with him in one of Griff's spare rooms. I was looking forward to sleeping beside Griff.

I quickly use the towel to dry off and then climb up on his high, very plush bed and melt into the softness of the pillows and comforter. Everything is so luxurious.

Griff walks around the bed and drops his towel as he climbs in. He lies next to me, pulling me into his arms as my back is pressed into his front.

"Sweet dreams, Jojo," he whispers against me.

"You too," I whisper back as my eyes lull shut.

Chapter 29

Griffin

"Rise and shine," I say, opening the shades with a remote. The room goes from complete blackout to sunshine, and Jolie squints against the light, bringing her arm up to cover her eyes. "I booked us in for brunch at the Beverly Hills Hotel, and then I thought we could come back here and lounge by the pool and just have a relaxing day."

"Yesss. Relaxing sounds good," Jojo says with a husky morning voice. I want to kiss the hell out of her and make love to her, but I'm pretty sure I hear Kyle awake and watching TV in the next room. So this is what having a kid is like.

"Good. I'll go check on him and get him some clothes," I offer.

"He's going to need a bath," Jolie says.

"Oookay. I'll get that set up in his room," I answer.

"Wait. Mom gave me a special soap for him. It's in his suitcase," Jolie says, sitting and holding up a sheet to cover her tits.

"I'll find it. No worries. I brought your suitcase into my closet so you can get dressed there. I want you writhing under me in my bed tonight, so I figure it's best I move you in here now," I say with a wink.

Her cheeks flush. "I slept so good." She rubs her eyes.

"Meaning you aren't tired and want to get busy before nightfall? Because I can call Annette. She's my assistant. She has a five-year-old son. Kyle would love him," I say.

"Griff, we are spending time with him. Me and you. You aren't passing him off," she says, sounding like a boss.

"No, sorry, you're absolutely right. It should be us. I was just thinking with my dick." I chuckle.

She takes a pillow off the bed and throws it at me. "I really like your dick, but with a kid, we need to be thinking with our heads and hearts," she says.

"You're right. Yes. I'm used to living like a bachelor, but Kyle is our focus now. I'm onboard," I say, feeling a little off. I'm used to doing what I want when I want, but Jolie is right. Kyle is what's important now. It doesn't matter who his fucked up parents are. He's a kid who needs us. I want to make him happy because he reminds me of a smaller version of myself and if I can help him in any way, then I'm damn well going to. "You get ready. I'll go take care of Kyle."

Jolie gives me one of her bright smiles where her eyes crease at the corners, and my heart bursts. Us playing house together makes me want to kick myself for not going to her sooner, but I know there is no point in dwelling on the past.

I walk into Kyle's room. He's found a cartoon channel. "Hey kiddo."

"Hi," he says shyly.

"Aunty Jojo wanted me to give you a bath, and then we are going to go for breakfast and swimming. Does that sound fun?" I ask cheerfully.

"Yes." He stands on the large bed and begins to jump up and down. "Can we see Mickey again and Lightning McQueen?" he asks.

"Aunty Jojo is tired today, but maybe tomorrow we can go to another special place." I lift him off the bed. I don't know much about kids.

I take Kyle by the hand, and he leads me into the bathroom. I fill the tub and pour the special soap into the water. Lots of bubbles begin to rise, and Kyle gets all excited. With the bath half full, he jumps in, and then we have a bubble fight. He throws bubbles at me and I throw them back. It's actually fun, playing with a kid. It makes me want to work harder to convince Jojo to move out here. I'm sorry she's hurting over her sister's betrayal but I'm not sorry she's here in LA.

I dump some of the soapy stuff on Kyle's hair and wash it quickly, then I wrap him up in a huge towel. He looks like he's in a cocoon, and I carry him over to the bed. I leave his clean clothes for him to get dressed on his own, since he says he can do it, and I head back to my room to check on Jojo.

"What am I supposed to wear to the Beverly Hills Hotel?" she asks as I stand behind her. She's throwing everything out of her suitcase.

"Whatever you want?" I shrug.

"Griff, just the name sounds too posh."

I lift the yellow sundress she wore the day we left for Martha's Vineyard. "Here—wear this. It looks beautiful on you."

"You think? It isn't ironed. I don't want to look like a slob," she says, stressing out. "See? This whole LA life isn't for me. New York is very laidback."

"Give LA a try. There are parts of LA that are laidback," I say. "Okay, so maybe San Francisco is a little more chill." I tilt my head from side to side. I want her staying here, not five hours away, even though it can be a quick forty-five minute flight. But I don't want to push her to stay here if she isn't comfortable. "I heard the house-keeper downstairs. Give me the dress; I will ask her to iron it for you," I say, taking it out of her hand.

"You don't have to do that. I can . . ."

I take her hand and pull her off the floor. "Hey." I press a soft kiss to her lips. "Relax. I got you. Now give me five, and I'll return with the dress. Kyle is just getting ready if you want to check on him."

"Okay," she exhales.

I head downstairs to see my housekeeper, Mrs. Garcia. I ask her to iron Jolie's dress. While I wait, I worry about how nervous Jolie suddenly seems. I need to find a way to make her feel at ease. I don't know how to do that.

My phone pings. It's Ryan.

Ryan: **Having a pre-release party at my place tonight. You back in town?**

I'm guessing he must have spoken to Annette or maybe his assistant. She is friends with Annette and she must have told him I was back in town. I can't exactly say no to him after he went all out with lending me his home in Martha's Vineyard and his sailboat.

Me: **I'm back. What time?**

Ryan: **8 sharp**

Me: **See you then. I'll be with a plus one.**

Oh boy. Jolie is nervous enough as it is. I just hope that taking her to one of Ryan's over-the-top parties won't be a complete fail.

Chapter 30

Jolie

"See? Lunch wasn't so bad, was it?" Griff asks. He had us seated in a corner off to the side in what seemed like a private room, since no one was sitting beside us.

"I don't know what I ate but I liked it a lot," Kyle says, referring to his crepe with fresh cream and strawberries.

"The food was delicious," I agree. I had some sort of fancy omelet and French bread. The waiter had been surprised when I'd asked for my bread with the omelet and Griff explained how the whole city is basically anti-carbs. I can't live without carbs, so whatever.

"Good. I thought you would both enjoy it here," Griff says, smiling like he's pleased with his choice of place.

"Can we go now? I'm bored," Kyle says.

"Me too." I laugh.

"They have a great pool here but I was thinking we could head back to my place and go for a swim. I asked my assistant to come over with her husband, and she has a five-year-old son. So you can have a play date too," Griff says, looking at Kyle.

"I love swimming," he says. I suddenly remember that Mom had him in a life jacket back on the Cape. I don't think Kyle is a strong swimmer. I make a note to mention it to Griff when Kyle is out of earshot.

"That sounds nice," I say.

Now that we are walking through the restaurant, I'm guessing a lot of these people are famous or tied to the movie industry in some way.

"Holy shit," I whisper. "Is that Taylor Swift?" My eyes widen and my heart skips a beat. I had seen Jennifer Anniston's old fiancé walking down the street once in New York and it wasn't really a big deal, but Taylor freaking Swift?

"Yes," Griff whispers. "I've met her before. She's actually quite friendly."

"Don't meet her now please," I say, feeling like I would blurt something stupid. He nods and we avoid her table.

As we walk deeper into the restaurant, I see another familiar face. "Griff, OMG." I grab his arm as my eyes widen and my whole body stills. "That's Channing Tatum," I say. Holy geez. If Mich were here, she would be having a freaking meltdown. We watched the hell out of those *Magic Mike* movies. That boy can move.

"I know him, Jolie. I'm going to have to say hi," Griff says, and walks over to Channing.

"Hey man," he says, coming up to his table.

Channing smiles and leans back in his chair. He shakes Griff's hand. "I heard you're doing the trailer for us."

"Yes. It turned out great. Ryan will be showing it tonight," Griff says. "I'd like you to meet Jolie," he says. "And this here is Kyle," he says, looking down at Kyle who has no clue who this man is.

"Jolie," Channing says, extending his hand. "It's a pleasure." His voice is as smooth as a good whiskey, and my body temperature rises.

I finally remember to extend my hand. "Pleasure to meet you," I say, trying to keep my voice even. I want to ask him for a picture but it doesn't seem like the right time since he is somebody Griff actually knows.

"And nice to meet you, Kyle. How old are you?" he asks.

"I'm four," Kyle says, lifting four fingers.

"Wow. Big boy." Channing smiles. "Give me five?" He extends his hand and Kyle smacks it really hard. "Ow! We got a strong one here," Channing says and Kyle smiles.

"Well, I'll catch you later, man. You going to Ryan's tonight?" Channing asks.

Griff opens his mouth to speak then closes it then opens it again. "I'll be seeing you later," he finally says, and I look to him for clarification but I don't get any.

"Cool, man. Later," Channing says, and he returns his attention to the man he's eating lunch with.

Griff puts his hand on the small of my back and guides me outside. He asks the attendant for his car. Kyle holds my hand as we wait.

I look to Griff for some clarification. Does he need to work tonight? He didn't mention it but it would be fine. Kyle and I could stay in and watch a movie or something.

"Is it just me or are you looking flushed over Channing?" he asks, cocking a brow.

"Oh stop it, you." I brush him off.

"Uh-uh." He shakes his head. "You are flushed and I am not sure I'm liking it," he says quietly but he has a playful hint to his accusing tone.

"Griffin Campbell, are you jealous?" I goad him.

"Me?" He raises his brows. "I've got more game than him," he scoffs, rolling his eyes.

"Did you see how that boy can move?" I ask, remembering how he rolled his hips in that movie.

Griff's face flushes and he takes a step toward me. My breath catches as he leans into my ear, and a shiver runs down my spine. "I would take you back into the hotel right now and show you just how much game I have. You want me to roll my hips, baby? Trust me, I can move. You haven't seen anything yet." His promising words cause warmth to flood between my thighs. I swallow hard.

"I guess I have a lot to look forward to then tonight." I wink.

He shakes his head as if I am a misbehaving child, and a sly smirk curves his lips.

"Oh baby. You have no idea what I have planned now." He gives my ass a strong squeeze and I yelp but I try to keep it cool, because Kyle is hopping up and down the sidewalk only about ten feet away. Damn.

The valet arrives with Griff's car, and I settle Kyle into his car seat.

"Do you have to work tonight?" I finally ask. Griff may have distracted me momentarily with his flirting, but I definitely remember something being mentioned about a party.

"Sorry. I was going to mention it. Ryan texted me just as we were leaving the house earlier," he says, eyeing me like I'm a skittish cat. "He's having a release party this evening to celebrate a new movie. I did the trailer and so I'm invited. I thought maybe you would like to come along," he continues with a hesitant tone. I wonder if he doesn't want me to attend for some reason.

"I can stay in with Kyle. You do what you need to do," I answer.

"Um . . . I'd actually like if you came as my date," he says, but it looks like he is wincing.

"Why do you seem so hesitant then?" I ask. If we are in a new relationship, I need him to know I will call him out on things. I can't guess what's going on in his head.

With Mason, I was hesitant to get answers, almost like I feared upsetting him, and that resulted in us growing further apart. I don't want to make the same mistakes.

"I'm not hesitant. Just that Ryan's parties can be over the top. I'd love for you to join me. I'd love for you to see what my life here is like—I just fear that you'll hate it." He gives me a bashful smile.

"What about Kyle?" I ask.

"I can ask Annette to stay with him. She's coming for a swim soon. I'm hoping she can stay to babysit after."

"Okay. I'd like to go with you . . ."

"But?"

I look down at my yellow sundress. It's the fanciest piece of clothing I have with me and it's pretty casual. "I'll need something to wear."

"I, um, can have my personal shopper drop a few items off for you to choose from?" he suggests again with a wince.

"Holy crap. You have a personal shopper?" The question flies out of my mouth before I can stop myself. I shouldn't be surprised, given the state of his house and the fact that he knows Channing Tatum, but I can't help my response either.

"Yes, I do. It makes life easier when I get busy. If we have time, I'd like to take you to my work and show you all the programs we use to make the trailers. It's pretty cool," he says.

"I'd like that." I gulp. How is it I end up with these famous men who live busy lives? Here I am, thinking of a happily ever after with Griff, but I bet his schedule is so jam packed he probably doesn't have time for a girlfriend, and definitely not one who is a temporary guardian to a child.

He runs his hands up and down my arms. "Tonight will be fun. There will be lots of famous people but it's no biggie. They are just people like us with private lives and families. We just make good money and lead comfortable lives," he says.

His words settle my nerves but only somewhat. I may not spend the money on trashy magazines but I see the headlines while waiting in line in the supermarket. These people do not live normal lives. "So what do you say? Will you come with me?" He looks into my eyes with such hope that I can't say no, but before I answer, I look down to Kyle.

"Kyle, would you mind if I go out with Griff tonight? He has a nice assistant who has a boy your age. They would keep you company," I say, trying to hide the guilt I feel over leaving him out of my tone.

"That's fine, Aunty Jojo," Kyle says quietly.

I look up to Griff. "Okay, I'm in."

Chapter 31

Jolie

We spend the afternoon hanging out with Annette, her husband, Jacob, and their son, Chris. Kyle and Chris have become best buds since they spent the afternoon jumping into the pool, then running out and jumping in again. Annette and her husband are super-nice and down to earth. Not what I was expecting from a couple who live in LA, although maybe my ideas have been distorted by the media. Plus, they are from the Valley.

After a light dinner by the pool, Jacob bids his son and wife farewell, since they are sleeping over and he needs to be at work bright and early since he installs air conditions.

"I'll take the boys up to shower," Annette says.

"Oh, you don't have to do that. I can come and bathe Kyle," I say.

"Don't be silly. We are friends; that is what friends do. Besides they've been inseparable all afternoon." She smiles.

"I noticed that. I'm happy they are getting along so well."

"Me too. They are so adorable." She rubs her hands together.

"Thanks Annette," I say. I've made lots of friends over the years in different cities. We've gone out and had fun. I even confided a little in some of them. They worried about me being alone and tried setting me up on dates but they didn't come to my house when I was sick to bring me chicken soup or move in for the night when I wanted to go out like Annette is doing for Griff now. When he mentioned her running all his errands for him, I figured it was because she was his assistant, but I see now that Annette is his family. She's good-hearted and watches out for Griff. I'm glad he has her.

The doorbell chimes. I head to the fridge to get a bottle of cold water and Griff goes to answer the door.

"My personal shopper is here to help you find a dress," Griff says. My stomach sinks. I feel so out of my element right now. We spent a lovely morning and afternoon together, but the thought of going to this party makes me nauseous.

"As in, she is here to pick me up to go shopping?" I ask, confused. "I can go myself. Honestly, just tell me where the closest department store is." I hug his torso. I'm used to living in new cities and venturing out on my own. This really isn't a big deal.

Griff places his hands on my shoulders, then rubs them up and down my arms. I release the hold I have on him.

"Relax, sweetheart. This is normal for here." His gaze is sympathetic and warm, and his term of endearment melts my heart. "She actually has the dresses and shoes here with her now," he says apprehensively.

"That sound's super-expensive. I can't afford that," I say. "I would rather just cab it to the mall. Kyle is busy now anyway."

"Jolie, this is a party I've invited you to as my guest. It would really be my pleasure if I could buy you the dress. I know you can go out and get your own dress, but this is how things are done in this neck of the woods. I'm trying to show you what my life here looks like while I pray on my knees you don't hate it completely. Humor me and allow Janet to dress you. She dresses a lot of actresses and actors. She basically takes care of most of my wardrobe." He looks down at himself. "Well, at least she takes care of my suits," he says with an impish smile.

"I like you dressed this way," I say, referring to his simple T-shirt.

I run my hand along his chest, and he inhales a deep breath as his nostrils flare. "I can't wait to get you up to my bed but first, please meet with Janet."

I cave. "If it means that much to you, then okay," I say. My deceased husband had been a famous NFL star but it was a different lifestyle. He had an abundance of money but we didn't need personal shoppers. We weren't walking red carpets.

"Thank you." He gives me a quick kiss. "I'm going to order some pizza for the kids. Janet will meet you in the main dining room." He turns away toward the kitchen. I sigh. What have I gotten myself into?

Griff's personal shopper is exactly what I was expecting her to be—thin, with curves in all the right places, blonde, beautiful, and chic. After she presents me with five different dresses all in my size, I find the right one.

"I definitely think you should wear this one," she says of the emerald dress. I stand in front of a mirrored wall and gaze. It does bring out the color in my eyes.

Griff walks into the dining room, and his eyes remain plastered on me as he takes me in from head to toe.

"Griffin, so good to see you." She saunters over to him in her four-inch stilettos, swaying her hips with each step, and gives him a peck on the check and rubs his bicep. Only Griff's gaze remains trained on me while he gives her a brief nod.

"Thanks Janet." He walks over to me and his eyes simmer with heat. "I love that on you. What do you think?"

I run my hands down the dress to smooth it out and take a look in a big mirror hanging on the wall. It's simple but sexy. "I think I like it." I nod.

"You're beautiful, Jolie." Griff wraps his arms around me from behind so he is now looking into the mirror with me. As I gaze in the mirror, I see Janet has both her brows raised, and she looks taken aback. I wonder if he's bedded her. I internally berate myself. *You can't be thinking this way.* He has a past, and I can't go to the party tonight wondering which actresses he's slept with. It will drive me crazy.

"Boys just went down to the home theater in the basement with Annette," he whispers.

"Jolie looks lovely," Janet says. She walks up to us and stares down at my feet. "Griff wasn't sure what shoe size you were," she says, and as she walks by Griff, she brushes herself against him. I recoil.

"I'm a size eight," I say, not wanting to show her that whatever she's doing to get Griff's attention is bothering me, even though she's failed to capture his attention.

"I guessed between a seven and nine. Let me head out to my car. I have something in mind that will be perfect."

She leaves the room and I look to Griff. "Did you have a thing with her?"

"It was very short-lived. I told her I don't want to mess up, since she was my personal shopper, but reality was she wasn't you," he says. "I'm sorry. I feel terrible."

"You shouldn't. You had a life and so did I," I say, and Griff gives me a small, chaste kiss.

Janet walks back into the room holding a few shoe boxes and clears her throat.

"We can try these," she says, placing a pile of shoe boxes on one of the dining room chairs. "Try these first," she says, opening up a Louboutin box with a black stiletto strappy sand al.

"These are nice." I slip them on, and it looks beautiful with the dress.

"What do you think, Griff?" Janet says with a seductive voice, cocking one of her brows. She runs her hand up his bicep.

"That's highly unprofessional of you," I say, placing my hands on each side of my waist as I stare her down.

With wide eyes, she removes her hand swiftly as if she's touched hot coals. "My apologies, Jolie."

When I look at Griff, he has a crooked smile.

"These will do," I say coldly. I don't give her a second glance as I turn out of the room, dismissing her. Griff follows me up the stairs and to the master bedroom.

"That was fucking hot," he says.

"Hey." He stops me and crouches down so we are face level. He pushes out his lower lip. "I'm sorry about that but geez, Jolie, if I had any doubts about you handling this town, you just put every doubt to rest."

I don't know what to say. "Will I be faced with a lot of women whom you've bedded?" I ask, not looking him in the eyes.

"I haven't been a saint. I'm sorry." He sighs.

"You don't have to be sorry. I'm just frustrated." I wrap my hands in front of my chest.

"Maybe I can help you work out some of that frustration. The home theater has special soundproof walls. They won't hear a thing."

I laugh, but then realize he's serious.

Oh.

"Come." He pulls me by the hand into the master suite and closes the door behind us, and then he wraps his hands around me and kisses me hungrily. I return the kiss with the same fervor, but then he drops to his knees and his nose and lips pave a trail of kisses down, down. Sparks ignite in my body. I can feel his touch everywhere, sending burning, hot need through my body. He lifts the dress up my thighs and over my behind, and gives me a small smack on my behind that I feel between my thighs, and then his nose is sniffing me.

"Hmmm," he groans as he slowly lowers my panties. "Keep the shoes on," he says. I'm too overcome with lust to even think of my shoes.

He walks me back a few steps. My back presses against a wall for support and then oh, dear. He licks me between my thighs, and my knees almost buckle. I splay my hands along the wall as if it will help hold me up as Griff's tongue devours me. I let out moan after moan.

"Griff . . . I . . ." I can't stand. My legs begin to shake in these four-inch stilettos. My core begins to contract as he flicks my clit with his tongue. Once, and my eyes shut. Twice, I'm seeing colors. Beautiful colors.

"Yesss," I moan. He continues the torment, and suddenly, hot lava shoots through my body. I fear falling but Griff grips my waist with each of his hands and holds me in place as my hips rock against his devilish tongue. This is possibly the hottest thing I've ever done. I grab his shoulder, and he places one of my legs over his shoulder. "It's . . . too . . . much . . ." I pant.

"I've got you," he says.

My climax racks through my body, causing my skin to dampen and my heart to beat rapidly. It's so intense that I think I'll black out and fall to the floor, but suddenly, Griff lifts me in his arms and walks me to the bed. "Lie on your stomach," he says, and I do, panting and out of breath.

His hand grips my ass and rubs me. "Griff, please."

"What do you want, Jolie?" he asks. *I want all of you.*

"I need you inside me," I say breathlessly.

In one swift movement, he enters me. "Ah."

He rocks himself inside me and then leans forward and rubs my nub with his finger. "Holy fucking hell," I whimper.

"I have you cursing," he says through gritted teeth. He slams into me over and over while rubbing me, and my hips begin to rock with his, up, down. As he thrusts inside me and rubs his fingers along my nub, I am lost in sensation. Lost in him. Another orgasm hits, even though I still feel breathless from the first. I pant and cry out as my body erupts with pleasure, and then I feel him stiffen inside me, and a loud, guttural groan fills the room. His sounds of pleasure make my core clench and my heart happy. He falls forward on top of me without putting his full weight over me.

"Fuck, you have me undone. I want to stay like this with you all night. No, scratch that. I want you in my bed forever. I never want you to leave." He turns and falls beside me, and I see his forehead brimming with sweat.

"Hmm." I smile, still feeling speechless. I turn on my back and catch my breath as I stare up at the ceiling. "That was . . ."

"Fucking amazing," he finishes my sentence.

"Yes."

"We are magic," he says.

That was truly magical. He moves in closer and nips my ear. A wave of goose bumps erupts over my body.

"We are," I reply. He looks past me at the clock on his bedside table.

"We better get ready," he says. "I need a shower."

"Me too," I say.

"If you come in that shower with me, we will never be on time."

I stand and finally remove the heels I'm wearing. They look very expensive and I try not to think about their price. It's important to Griff that I get a sense of his lifestyle here and I can't do that on an aesthetician's budget.

I turn my back to him. "Will you unzip me?"

He groans. "We are going to be so freaking late."

I follow him into the shower with a grin.

Chapter 32

Jolie

"An hour late for a party isn't too bad." Griff grins. He looks relaxed and happy after all the sex we had. I am walking on a cloud. Nothing can get me down.

"You look beautiful," he says for the umpteenth time.

I smile again. Living on cloud Griff is blissful.

A driver drops us at the front door of a very large mansion. I take a deep breath, feeling my nerves getting the best of me. What if I don't fit in here? Into his life? The thought makes my stomach turn.

"Hey, this will be fun," he says, pulling me from my turmoil.

I nod but my chest feels tight. He said there will be a lot of famous people here tonight. When I said I would probably melt down into fan mode, he said to just treat them like normal people. Yeah. Okay. Sure. Not.

As we enter Ryan Sonenberg's house, my heart beats fast as I take in the sheer opulence, from the fancy waitresses serving colorful drinks to the beautiful artwork that adorns the walls. Griff's house is large and fancy but it's understated, like the man himself. This home is flowing with riches, from the gold trim on the furniture to all the beautiful people who don't have a hair out of place. How is it even possible? Griff is shaking hands with all kinds of people while introducing me as his girlfriend from out of town.

We've not had a discussion about what our relationship is. We went from the seclusion of Martha's Vineyard to the hailstorm that is Jenn. With all the craziness, I somehow ended up here in LA with him instead of heading back to Boston with Mom or back to New York. I don't know what I would have done if Jenn hadn't dropped her bombshell. Yet, here I am, and things couldn't be more perfect. It makes me feel like fate is finally on our side.

We walk through the house and I smile as Griff introduces me to movie producers, directors, camera personnel, actresses and actors. Some ask where I am from and some keep it short and quick with a brief hello. Some faces are familiar. I keep telling myself they are just people, like Griff told me to do. Luckily, I don't make a fool out of myself.

As we walk toward the backyard, Griff and I have a moment to ourselves.

"Girlfriend, huh?" I giggle.

"You are so much more than that but for tonight and these circumstances, it seems like the best explanation," he says, and his words make my belly flip.

"I like the sound of girlfriend. It sounds so high school." I cock my brow and give him a seductive look.

"Don't remind me of high school now. You have no clue how I burned for you back then. Having you here, makes me want to take you again," he whispers against my ear and a gush of wetness hits me between the thighs. I rub my legs together, trying to relieve the ache his words cause.

"You looked flushed," he says with a deep, raspy but quiet tone.

"That's because your words are getting me hot and bothered," I whisper.

"I like the sound of that," he says, and then he pulls me to the backyard where there is a swimming pool and a large tent. Random bars are set up every ten feet or so. The property is sprawling. Some people are swimming in the pool; some are just drinking and chatting it up.

A loud, irritating noise comes through the speakers. It sounds like someone is adjusting a microphone, and it hurts my ears.

"Ladies and gentlemen, may I ask you take a seat at your tables." A man's voice comes through the many large speakers set up around the property.

"Ryan is probably getting ready to give one of his speeches," Griff explains. "He usually talks our ears off about the upcoming movie, and then plies us with delicious food and alcohol."

Griff takes me by the hand and leads me to a table. After a set of introductions, we take a seat. I lean over and whisper in his ear, "Do you think now would be a good time to use the ladies room?"

"Yes, of course. Would you like me to take you there?" Griff offers.

"It's okay. Sit and relax. I think I saw something off to the side of the tent," I say.

Griff leans forward and gives me a kiss. He keeps his eyes trained on me as I walk away from the table.

It's a warm summer night, but I find the lack of humidity in the air appealing. New York can get so muggy in summer. I notice a sign for the ladies room and am surprised to enter a small cottage-like house that has at least five bathroom stalls. I'm guessing that Ryan really is a big entertainer.

I push one of the doors open and flinch when I notice someone inside. Sheesh. Why didn't she lock the door? Before I can turn to move, I see that she's sniffing white powder off the toilet seat.

"I'm sorry," I apologize and turn to leave.

"No worries." The woman looks up to me. "Would you like a bump?"

Geez! I hadn't realized that people were so friendly about sharing their cocaine. I'm barely a drinker. Drugs is something that doesn't appeal to me at all.

"No, thank you," I answer politely, even though unease has taken up vacancy on my chest. I quickly skitter to another stall, this time opening the door slowly. I paper up the seat before getting my business taken care of. Who knows what's been on these toilets?

I feel like I've handled this party well using Griff's advice. I have been able to make small talk with these famous people without making a fool of myself. I internally pat myself on the back.

I exit the stall, wash my hands, and dig into my purse for lipstick when a blond woman comes up to the sink beside me. She's beautiful. Everything about her is perfect, from her shiny hair to the curves of her body. Everyone here is mere perfection; it's a common theme tonight.

"You are here with Griff. Right?" she asks.

"Uh yes . . ." I answer timidly. I'm not sure if she is a friend or a previous conquest.

"Griff and I go way back. Name is Serena," she says, and it only takes a moment for her face to enter my memory. She was in that movie that took place during World War Two. I'm pretty sure she won an Oscar for her performance.

"Jolie. It's a pleasure to meet you," I say, rubbing my lips together to even out the lipstick.

"Pleasure is mine," she purrs. "Griff has told me so much about you," she says, surprising me.

"He has?" I ask with a small snicker. "I hope all good things."

"He said your father threw him out and that you ripped his heart out when he found out you moved on from him so quickly." Her words are said so easily with no harsh tone. It's as if she said it was a lovely evening, and yet they make my world tilt sideways and cause my head to swim. I grab the sink counter to steady myself. "You look surprised," she continues. "Why are you here anyway?"

"That isn't any of your business. I don't know who you are, Serena, or what your problem is, but I'm here with Griff and he's never mentioned you. You are acting like a jealous girlfriend and it isn't becoming." I pop my lipstick in my small handbag and turn to leave the ladies room.

"Jolie, wait," she calls my name and walks up to me.

"I think we are done here," I say and turn to leave.

She grabs my arm. "Not quite. I heard you came to LA with

your son. That you have some imaginary idea that you and Griff will sail into the sunset and live happily ever after."

I internally guffaw at her words. Griff isn't sailing anywhere with his sea sickness, and where the hell did she hear all this? "Lady, you're honestly crazy. I don't have the patience for this nonsense." Once again, I turn to leave.

"I'm pregnant," she blurts after me. "The baby is his."

I stop in my tracks as my heart sinks into my stomach. Wide-eyed, I turn and watch her to see if there is any humor in her tone. She must be joking. The woman who was sniffing coke off the toilet leaves her stall, smiling and looking high as a kite.

"OMG, congrats, Serena." She wraps her arms around the actress and hangs on her.

"Thanks, Tori," Serena answers tapping Tori's arms. She removes them. "I need a minute, doll. See you out there?"

The woman nods and waves to me as she walks away.

When it is just me and Serena again, she says, "I'm twelve weeks along. He doesn't know yet," she says softly.

"Why tell me then?" I ask bitterly.

"So you will know you don't have a chance. If you know Griff as well as I do, then you know he will want to be a father to this baby. He will want to give this baby a home," she says, holding her belly, which looks completely flat.

I don't say another word and walk away. She must feel like she's said enough because she doesn't call after me. My chest feels tight, and as I look around the opulent grounds, I realize how much I truly don't belong and Serena is right. If she is carrying Griff's child, he will do anything to keep his child safe and happy. Kyle is not even his, and he wants to give him the world. He didn't even mention having a serious girlfriend. I would think that Serena was blowing smoke if it weren't for the fact that she knew such intimate details about his past. About me. The way she painted me as the villain causes anger to boil inside me.

Numbness overtakes me as I make my way back to the tent. Fate has an evil way of fucking with me. First Mason, and the news that he fathered my sister's child, and now Griff—the love of my life. I began to allow myself to believe he would be my forever. We haven't used the words *I love you* but they've been sitting in my heart, resonating while I've tried to figure out if LA life is for me. I've felt truly happy these last couple days. Hope, which had seemed destitute inside me for so long, had begun to blossom anew inside my heart.

Now what?

Take Kyle. Leave?

A part of me is sick and tired of running, and poor Kyle has had to experience enough change already.

I don't head back to the tent. Instead, I use the Uber app on my phone and call a car, grateful that I remember Griff's home address.

I head out front and wait for the driver. I've been through so much heartbreak, loss, and disappointment that all my emotions feel spent. I can't even cry. Why didn't Griff mention Serena? He sure as hell mentioned me to her. My phone buzzes and his name lights up the screen. I send it to voicemail. Damn where is the driver? I don't want to have to face him here and have such a personal talk around all these people. A few seconds pass and he's calling again. I suddenly wonder if Serena is even telling the truth. Regardless I'm too worked up to stay here now. My need to fight or flight kicks in and I am ready to run.

The driver pulls up to the end of the driveway since it is filled with cars. Ten minutes later, he stops in front of Griff's long driveway and I get out. I want to run and hide. I can't face him, only I can't take off because Kyle is sleeping upstairs. Regardless, I know I have to stop running when the going gets tough. I'll avoid him tonight and face him tomorrow.

Chapter 33

Griffin

I look at my watch for the umpteenth time. It's taking Jolie a mighty long time in the ladies room. I'm about to get up from my seat, since Ryan finished his long-winded speech about the epicness of the new film, when Serena takes a seat beside me, in Jolie's seat. She leans in to give me a kiss, and when I see she's aiming for my lips, I turn my head and her lips land on my cheek.

"Hello darling," she says, placing her hand on my upper thigh.

"Serena please." I lift her hand off me and move it to the table, which buys me a pout.

"Oh, come on." She moves it back to my thigh, and slowly moves up my leg to my . . .

"Jesus." I jerk my chair back and stand, which garners the attention of the people sitting with us. I turn around to look for Jolie again. Where is she? Anxiety begins to build inside me.

"Are you looking for her?" Serena asks, still sitting in Jolie's seat. She looks smug, and I don't like it.

"Yes," I snap, getting ready to walk away and find her.

"I think she left," she says, looking at her manicured hand.

"You think? Why would you think that?" I ask, feeling the blood inside my veins simmering. Serena and I have hooked up over the years, but she is a friend and fuck buddy. Nothing more. When I arrived to Cape Cod, I sent her a message confirming that things between us would only be platonic from here on out. I know it is shitty to send something like that by message, but I felt things progressing with Jolie. Serena and I weren't even in a relationship and I very well know she's had other lovers.

"I saw her head out front," she says, and I begin to take off while dialing her number. It goes to voice mail.

"Hey, wait up," she calls out as she tries to catch up to me in her very high heels.

"I need to go," I snarl. I dial Jolie's number again. Where the hell did she run off too so quickly?

Voicemail.

Fuck.

"Oh, come on. I need to tell you something. Can we maybe go somewhere private?" She runs up to me and places a hand on my shoulder to stop me. I lift it and throw it off me.

"Don't touch me. I told you we are done."

She smiles sadly. "We are far from done."

"What does that mean?" I ask.

"You know exactly what it means. That night we were both drunk and you forgot to use a condom . . ." She reminds me of my stupidity and my worst nightmare. *Fuck! She can't be. . .*

"It's not possible," I mutter, but I know that what she may be suggesting is possible. It was one fucked up night months ago. A mistake I regretted when sobriety took hold. "We're over."

"We are far from over, Griff. I'm pregnant." She holds her belly, and the air gets sucked from my lungs. My heart picks up pace and begins to beat too fast while sweat breaks on my forehead.

"Excuse me?" I take a step back, wanting distance from her.

"Griff. You know it's true. We messed up, and now I have a baby growing inside me . . . *our* baby." She takes a step toward me. I take another one back. She takes another and holds my arm. "We are going to be a family." She smiles as if this is the greatest news. What a fucking disaster.

"I'm with Jolie." I pause, and my brows furrow as realization hits. "You told Jolie you were pregnant with my child?" I ask, my tone filled with disgust.

She giggles. "Of course, silly. I figured she should know the good news."

I rip her hand off me. "What else did you say?" I need to know how much damage control I need to do.

"That she ripped your heart out and that she doesn't deserve you. It's the truth. I didn't lie," she continues to act all innocent. It feels like an act, even coming from an award-winning actress.

"You shouldn't have done that. I'll figure things out with you later, but I am with Jolie. I've made that clear," I say.

"Things change," Serena says, her tone sounding like a melody.

"Not this time. I plan on making her mine forever. I'm sorry, Serena. I'll take care of the kid but nothing is getting in my way again. I have Jolie in my life and I won't lose her," I say.

My mind spins as I think of Serena carrying my kid, and I feel dizzy and nauseous. I give my head a shake and turn away from her. I have a good six months to deal with her before the kid comes. I need to get to Jolie.

Chapter 34

Jolie

I walk up to the front door of Griff's house. He never uses this entrance, but I don't have a key. I'm not sure how to get in. I knock again and again. It's late. I don't want to ring the doorbell and wake Kyle and Chris.

I pace back and forth and knock some more.

Annette finally opens the door in her SpongeBob SquarePants pajamas. She looks adorable with her red hair up in a messy bun on her head.

"You're back early. Where's Griff?" She looks past me, then eyes me. "Oh dear. What happened?"

I burst into tears and walk past her, deeper into the house.

"Shit. What happened? Talk to me," she says, following after me.

"I met Serena," I turn to say, and watch as Annette's face falls.

"She's a bitch but don't worry about her." Annette waves me off. "I don't want to sound crude but they've only ever been fuck buddies, and honestly, I've never seen Griff look at a woman the way he looks at you."

"Fuck buddies? She's carrying his baby. Or so she says. Who

244

knows what goes down in this crazy town?" I flail my hands in the air and walk past her.

Annette winces but takes a few steps to catch up to me.

"I need to get out of here. I can't stay with him. As it is, I was so uncertain about coming here and . . . I need to leave." My sobs cause my body to heave but my chest feels so tight, constricted, and my heart hurts.

"Kyle is sleeping," Annette reminds me.

Shit. Right.

"Aunty?" Kyle's sweet voice comes from the staircase. I quickly swipe at my tears, feeling so foolish. How did I end up here? How did I manage to put my heart on the line when I promised myself I wouldn't?

"Hi sweetie," I say to Kyle. I don't have something better. I don't know what to do. I feel like taking him in the middle of the night and running off somewhere. I'm guessing that is what Jenn would do in this situation.

But I want to do better for Kyle's sake. He walks downstairs, holding the railing. He looks completely adorable in his Superman pajamas. A small man.

"Is everything okay, Aunty? You look sad," he says, and I take him by the hand and guide him to the kitchen. Annette follows us. I take a seat by the breakfast bar and Annette leans over the counter.

"Can you hold me?" Kyle asks, and his question makes my heart skip a beat. *Oh, sweet boy.*

"Of course." I open my arms and he climbs on my lap. He's so mature for his age. I wonder how much he's had to endure, having Jenn as his mom. I wrap him up in my arms, and it's so soothing. He presses his head against my chest and through the pain, he makes me smile.

"I'm okay." I rub his back.

"Would you like some warm milk?" Annette asks Kyle. "Sometimes when Chris has a hard time sleeping, I give him warm milk, and then he sleeps through the night."

"Yes, please," Kyle says. His polite manners bring another smile to my face.

Annette gets to work frothing milk using a frother attached to an espresso machine.

We sit quietly. I'm sure Griff has realized I left the party by now. He will probably come after me and try to explain himself, but I am sick and tired of explanations. I came here to get away from all the drama and heartache my sister caused, and now, I'm faced with another problem that makes me want to run.

"Can I make you a warm tea?" Annette asks, looking to me.

"That would be great. Thank you." I sigh.

I want to ask her more about Serena, but I need to get Kyle to bed first. She passes him the milk, and he drinks it down swiftly, leaving him with an adorable milk mustache.

"Come on, munchkin. Let me get you back into bed," she says, placing her hand on his shoulder. She turns to me. "The boys wanted to have a sleepover so he has Chris in bed with him."

"It's my first ever sleepover," Kyle says, his voice filled with enthusiasm and his hazel, Mason-like eyes gleam with excitement. His happiness seeps into me.

"That is awesome," I say, hoping my tone doesn't sound bland.

I don't have it in me to take him away from here just yet. But what should I do?

Annette leaves the kitchen and I head up to Griff's room. I want to change out of this ridiculous dress, which is so not me, and these expensive shoes. I want to move my stuff out of his room and back into one of the spare bedrooms. I can't leave tonight. I don't want to do that to Kyle, but I also don't want to face Griff now. He's having a baby with another woman. Yet back on the Cape, he said he wasn't tied to anyone. That he wasn't in a relationship. He may only be Serena's fuck buddy, but they created a child.

The thought causes spiteful jealousy to rise inside me. I want it to be me. I believed Griff and I were finally going to get our happy ending.

I quickly grab my things and find an empty room. I lock the door and head into the shower, wanting to wash away my fancy hair and fancy makeup. After my shower, I slip on one of my old T-shirts and climb into bed.

A few minutes later I hear a knock on the door, and I jolt in the darkness.

"Jolie. Please open the door." His voice is soft, pleading, and broken. I'm guessing he must have spoken with Serena.

I need space from him. Time to think.

"Please let me explain," he continues to mutter as I lie in bed under a warm blanket. A shiver runs over my body. The bed is cold and empty, and my dreams feel shattered. I'm not even sure when I developed new dreams but somewhere between Boston, the Cape, Martha's Vineyard and LA, I clearly dared to dream of a future with Griff. Now, this fantasy has been washed away like all my others. It's like something goes well in my life for a while and then something bad always has to happen. Gah!

"I'm going to sit here by your door all night. I'm not leaving," he warns, and my heart aches. Why does love have to feel so painful?

Hot tears roll down my cheeks. Oh, Griff. Serena was right. You are going to want to give that child the world, and it can't be me who stands in your way. You will only regret me later if I do. I would never want that for you. You are going to make an amazing father.

I'm not brave enough to tell him to his face what I feel in my heart. My tears fall freely as I mourn losing him all over again. This time, things are different. When I was a teenager, there was so much about life I had to learn. As a grown woman, it felt like the stars had aligned for us. We were open about our feelings, past and present. I told him about Mason, for goodness sake. That was so hard on me, and yet I was willing to take a chance on us by coming here. I know it's only been a couple of weeks since we've reunited, but he is still Griff. The boy I grew up with may be a man now, but I still knew him so well. He was honest with me and told me about his past, and I know he didn't cheat, but just knowing another woman carries his child stings me right through my heart. My soul. He may think he wants me now, but once he really grasps what this all means, that will change.

Chapter 35

Griffin

"Griff . . . hey." A soft, throaty voice pulls me from sleep, but I'm too tired, and my body hurts too much to move. My neck feels broken in two.

"Come on, big guy, let's get you up." Someone nudges my shoulder.

My eyes open and Annette stands crouched over me wearing a silly pair of SpongeBob SquarePants pajamas. It reminds me of the time we lived in an apartment together in Orlando. There had been seven of us living in a two-bedroom. She used to wear the silliest pajamas.

Her features look drowned in worry, and that's when the events of last night resurface in my mind and cause a stab to ache through my chest. "You should go to your bed. The boys will be up soon," she says.

I'm wearing the clothes from the party last night: a pair of light beige dress pants and a white linen button-down shirt that is now rumpled and creased. I must have fallen asleep while waiting for Jolie to open the door.

"I'm not leaving this spot. If I do, she'll leave, and I won't be

THE TRUTH ABOUT US

able to explain," I say adamantly. The fear of her walking out of my life threatens to swallow me whole.

Annette frowns. "She told me what happened."

"I fucked up." I run a hand through my hair. All the years I had practiced safe sex. One night. One fucked up drunken night, and now I'm paying the price. I feel like an asshole because Serena is pregnant with my kid, but it's the wrong fucking woman carrying my child, and I can't do anything about it.

"Maybe it's not yours," she suggests.

"I'm pretty sure it's mine," I say solemnly. "The dates add up and we were friends first. She wouldn't lie to me. I don't know what to do. I don't want to lose Jojo."

"I know, big guy. I think you'll find a way. I really like her too. I'd love for her to stay," Annette says.

"She is something special," I agree, thinking how beautiful she looked in that emerald-green dress last night.

"She is." Annette nods solemnly. "I'll get the boys up and make them something to eat. Jacob is on his way over."

"Thanks for staying the night. Sorry about all this drama." I try to smile, but I have a sour taste in my mouth.

"Of course." She walks off and I hear her say something along the lines of 'rise and shine' as she wakes the boys.

"Jolie." I knock on the door. "Jolie, please open up. You can't stay holed up in there forever." I knock and knock.

"Good morning," Kyle says as he walks by me.

"Oh, hi boys. Good morning." I clear my throat and fake a smile. "I hear Annette has something fun planned for breakfast. Why don't you go check it out?" I tilt my lips up feeling like my face is going to crack.

"Are we going back to Disney today?" Kyle asks, pouting. I adore him and he's not my flesh and blood. Surely I'll feel the same way about the child I created with Serena. "You said we can rest and go back. Has it been one day?" Kyle pulls me from my intense thoughts. The hopeful look in his eyes makes it difficult to say no, but I don't know what to say. How do I answer him?

The door swings open. Jolie stands with her hair rumpled and swollen eyes. Her nightshirt hits her knees and hides her figure, and yet she looks breathtakingly beautiful.

"Kyle, you and I can spend the day together in Disney or we can try another cool place called Universal Studios," Jolie says, not even glancing down to look at me. I probably look like road kill, and I feel worse.

"Universal?" Chris asks. "That is the best place ever," he says, looking at Kyle. He then turns to look at me. "Can Mom and I come too?"

"Um . . ."

"Mom! Mom!" Chris begins to scream.

Annette climbs the stairs. "Why are you yelling?" She gives her son a berating look.

"They want to go to Universal," Chris says.

"My son is obsessed; we have a season pass," she explains, looking at me. "I don't know if we can go. I need to ask my boss." She smirks to Chris, then looks down at me.

"By all means. Enjoy the day." I grin. It's the least I can do after she gave up her evening to babysit and stay over.

"Thanks, boss." Annette gives me a wide grin, which quickly turns into a frown. She then turns to Jolie.

"Ah. . . I can head to the office. I have some things to take care of," I say figuring Jolie needs space. She clearly doesn't want to talk to me right now. She can barely look at me.

"I'm happy to drive us there?" Annette offers.

"That would be great," Jolie says. "Let me get ready and I will be down in a bit."

I'm relieved and quite surprised she isn't running away. I got the impression that running is what she does when the going gets tough. Is she willing to stick by me and work things out? I'm doubtful. Her staying probably has more to do with Kyle. She doesn't want him bouncing around. What a colossal mess.

I quickly stand, and my back aches all over. "Jolie, please. Can you give me a minute to explain?"

"What for, Griff? We both know where you and I are headed."

"I want to believe that we can work around this," I say softly.

She moves a step closer to me. I don't know what to expect. "You are having a child with your lover. There isn't much to discuss," she whispers.

She turns and slams the door in my face. I wince and head to my bedroom. I need a hot shower, and Jolie clearly needs some space from me. If she's headed to Universal with Annette, it means she isn't leaving LA, which gives me time to think of a way to get through to her. Now I need a solid plan, but how can I have one with everything so up in the air?

Chapter 36

Jolie

"Thanks so much for spending the day with us. It's been really great," I say to Annette as we walk side by side at Universal. The place is amazing. My parents took us to here when we were younger, but the rides have come a long way since then.

"It's my pleasure. Trust me. A day out of the office, and Chris loves it here," Annette answers.

"Mommy, Mommy, can we show Kyle the *Despicable Me* ride?" Chris asks, practically jumping up and down. It appears that he knows all the rides. He explains everything to Kyle and gets him super-excited. Kyle is even eating better now than he did on the Cape, thanks to Chris.

"What do you say?" Annette asks.

"Lead the way." I try to smile but it fails me. I'm tired and completely burned out, maybe from life. I had been processing the fact that my husband had cheated on me while we were apart. The fact that it was with my sister makes me feel so much worse because they had a history, even though it was brief. And since I've felt like I've lived in Jenn's shadows all my life it's a pretty big freaking deal.

For Mason to be so careless that he not only slept with her but got her pregnant is . . . cruel and disgusting.

"You've been awfully quiet all day," Annette says, pulling me from my spinning mind.

"I'm sorry. My head is swimming."

She looks over to Kyle. "He's your sister's son, right?"

"Yes," I sigh. As much as I abhor Jenn, I have come to care deeply for Kyle. He is an innocent in all this mess.

"I don't want to overstep, but Griff and I are best friends. Or at least, I am the most reasonable friend he has." She giggles, but her laughter dies fast and her face falls to a more somber look. "He said he can't tell me everything about you, but he did say that your deceased husband fathered Kyle."

I hiss, "Jesus."

"Don't be upset with him. He tells me everything anyway even though I signed a non-disclosure agreement when I began working for him. Regardless, I would take his secrets to my grave. I just brought it up because you have clearly been through a lot and I want you to know that you can talk to me. I've been told I'm a good listener." She grins. "And you don't need to worry. I would never share with Griff anything you wouldn't want me to."

I nod, appreciating Annette's candor. "I've had a rough go in general. I hadn't planned on things moving so quickly between Griff and I. Denying all my old feelings for him became impossible because they still beat inside me, alive and thriving. Everything in my power wasn't enough to control what I felt. The whole revelation with my sister just gave me the nudge I clearly needed to explore our feelings further, but now in light of this news. Serena carrying his baby. . ."

"Don't give up on him. You can't shut down love. You just said it yourself. The heart is powerful and love is an inextinguishable flame," Annette says.

"Hmm, that sounds very poetic," I say, contemplating her words.

"I write poetry as a hobby." She shrugs. "When Jacob and I

were dating, things got really messy. He comes from an affluent family. I was the poor girl his parents would never accept. We had to fight to be together. He walked away from a very large trust fund, and now, we live this simple life, but we couldn't be happier."

"Simple in LA? Nothing here feels simple." I sulk.

"Griff deals with a lot of the big Hollywood guys. He's done well for himself but he came from humble beginnings, and he hasn't lost the sense of who he is, unlike most people in this town," she says, and I like hearing that about him. But what does it matter now that I know Serena is pregnant?

"You know, Griff and I were working in Orlando when I met him?" Annette says.

"Oh, really? So you are from Florida?" I ask.

"Born and raised." She nods with a smile that falls. "Griff was hurting back then. We became fast friends. We stayed in touch, and I would go to him for advice about Jacob. When he moved out to LA, I came along to be his assistant. Jacob was originally from New York. He was studying at a private college in Florida. His family cut him off and stopped speaking to him because of me. He dropped out of college and moved out here, and the rest is history." She smiles.

Her eyes warm every time she says Jacob's name and a pang of jealousy runs through me. I hate feeling this way. I should be happy for her. All those years Griff and I spent apart, he didn't fight for me or us. He stayed away. Fate brought us back together in Boston, and now fate is tearing us apart once more.

"What about Griff and Serena?" I ask, because I've had a million questions running through my mind since last night. I know this question should be directed at Griff, but it is so much easier to talk to Annette.

"He's never been serious about her. He's told her as much. My guess is she's been hoping for more for a long time. From the outside, it looks like he was just having fun with her," she says, and it feels like a sharp blade has cut through my heart. "Sorry." Her lips turn down.

"It's fine. I asked." I wave her off. The line for *Despicable Me* is long but we are soon approaching our turn, and that means I need to ask everything I want to now.

"He never brought her over when he'd come to hang with Jacob and me. We live in the Valley, and Griff comes by every Sunday. We usually barbeque and hang with friends and their families," Annette explains. "See? That's what I mean. He's never brought a girl over, and we are his family, his home, but he called me right away before you guys left Boston to make sure everything was set up and ready for you and Kyle."

"Thanks for saying all this." I take a deep breath.

"It's the truth." She reaches over and hugs me. I really like Annette. If things had worked out with Griff, I could have seen her and me becoming fast friends. I even like the sound of her family Sunday barbecues.

It's our turn for the ride, and we all hope on, Annette beside Chris, then Kyle and me. Kyle's beaming, and my heart, which has felt so raw and pained, warms. He's happy. At least I could give him this time.

By evening, both boys are exhausted and sitting in a double stroller Annette rented. There is still so much more to do but I think we need to call it a night. What now?

I have to go back to Griff's place. He cares for me, I know he does, but I also know what becoming a father will mean to him. I can't stand in his way.

It's probably best that I go back to New York. My neighbor has been more than kind about taking care of Sasha, but I can't take advantage. Kyle and I can head to New York and from there, I will see which college I can get accepted into.

Annette drives us back to Griff's. "Do you need help getting Kyle into bed?" she asks. The boys passed out after we ate burgers and fries for dinner. "There's a special technique to lifting them out of cars."

"Explain it to me. I might as well learn." I smile.

"Just lift him slowly, and then cradle him into your body. That way, when you lay him in bed, you only need to lean forward and slide your fingers out from beneath him."

"Got it." I lift Kyle in my arms when I realize I don't have a key. My eyes widen.

"I texted Griff. He knows you're out here. He's coming to the door," she says quietly.

"Thanks so much for everything." I smile again. I feel so appreciative. With my hands filled with carrying a four-year-old, I can't hug her.

"Stay in touch. Okay?"

"I will. Bye. Take care, and thanks for everything."

I walk along the driveway and up the stairs to the front door. It's large and overwhelming, just like this house.

Griff opens the door with a sad smile. "Hi. Oh, here. Let me help you with him." He takes a step toward us.

"I've got him. I need to learn how to do this," I say, and Griff's lips turn down. He looks so sad.

I walk Kyle up the many steps to the second floor then into his room. I lean forward on the bed, placing him down softly just as Annette told me to. He turns over and continues to sleep, and I breathe a sigh of relief. It's been a long day. All I want is a shower and to get on my phone and book some airline tickets.

When I leave Kyle's room, Griff is standing in the hallway.

"Can we talk?" he asks softly.

"What for, Griff? We both know where this is going," I say.

"That isn't fair. I didn't plan for this. What happened with Serena . . . it was a mistake." He winces.

I pause to look at him. Even her name out of his mouth hurts. Still, I give him my attention.

"We were never anything really. She was a friend I hooked up with," he says.

"If you call her a friend, then you like her as a person. The woman I met at the party last night was calculating and vindictive," I say.

"She's a Hollywood diva." He shrugs as if it's explanation enough.

"She's having your baby," I remind him.

He rubs at his eyes. "I know. It was a drunk night three months ago, Jolie. What am I supposed to do? I didn't foresee you coming back into my life. When I got to Boston and I thought we could maybe have something, I ended it with her. Not that there was something to really end. We weren't exclusive; she had been with other people and so was I. That's how my life was because I didn't care enough about those woman to settle down."

"Griff, she's carrying your baby. You need to go to her and figure things out. I've been through so much. I just . . ." I shake my head. "This is too much for me. This city is overwhelming. I want to go back to New York with Kyle. I just need time for myself. I was still dealing with all the Mason stuff when Jenn blew me out of the water again. I feel like I've been fighting for so long and I'm tired, so freaking tired." My shoulders slump. I'm exhausted from this day, but also from my life. All I want is some peace and quiet.

"I need to see Serena. I need a paternity test, but I don't plan on being with her regardless of the results," he says. "I know I have a responsibility to the child but not to Serena. I don't want to be with her. I want to be with you."

"Wait until her belly starts to grow and your child arrives. Are you telling me that you won't want to be there every waking moment to care and love him or her?" I ask, and Griff takes a step back like I've knocked him over with something. His face falls and he looks confused.

"This is exactly why I can't stay here with Kyle. You have to figure out your life. You have responsibilities now that will last a life-time. I don't plan on getting in your way," I say. Deep down, I want him to fight for me, for us. He never did fight for me. To my dismay, he seems to be cowering all over again. "I'm going to schedule a flight for Kyle and me for tomorrow afternoon so we can take it easy in the morning and pack," I say.

"Jolie. Please don't do this." He takes a step toward me, lifting his hand up to my face. I move before he can touch me.

"Please don't," I whisper.

I turn and walk into the spare bedroom that I slept in last night.

With the door closed, I fall to the floor and cry. I thought I was all out of tears. Maybe I still want to believe Mason was out of his right mind. I don't know. What I do know is that Griff has gutted my heart once more, and I don't know how I got here again. I did everything in my power to prevent it.

Chapter 37

Griffin

I don't want to let her go, but I have some things to work out with Serena. Jolie knows me well. I want to be the best father I can be to that child. I want it to know that it is loved and wanted.

I've guessed I was a mistake. At least, to my mother I was—maybe even to Dad, too, and I never want a child of mine to feel that way. Even if I don't love his or her mother.

Jolie leaves for the airport. She gives me a swift hug and wishes me luck. It takes everything inside me not to wrap my arms around her and never let her go, but I have a responsibility to my unborn child, and Jolie has been through so much that I hate to cause her any more heartache.

"I need to work out some things with Serena," I say as she pulls out of my arms.

"I know," she says too quietly.

"We aren't over. This isn't over. Look me in the eyes and tell me," I say with utter desperation.

When she looks into my eyes, she gives me a cold stare. She's shutting down. I hate that this is happening now. She doesn't say anything, and her lack of words speak volumes.

"I hate this."

"I know." She rubs my arm. "I'm sure everything will work out the way it's meant to be," she says. Is she referring to me and her? I hope so, because her words feel cryptic.

The Uber driver pulls up.

"I could have driven you both to the airport," I say, rocking on my heels. I really don't want her to leave. Should I get on my knees and beg? It isn't beneath me. Then I remember I have Serena to deal with. What a colossal mess. After the way things went down at the party with Serena, I can see that she is volatile, and I don't want Jolie standing in the crossfire.

"It's better this way." Jolie leans up on her toes and gives me a peck on the cheek. Seriously?

My hand wraps around her waist. I don't want to let go but I have to.

"Okay," I whisper and remove my hand from her waist. I kiss her cheek and cherish the moment my lips touch her skin. "This isn't goodbye," I repeat.

She gives me a short smile.

I hug Kyle and tell him I hope to see him soon, and then they enter the car and drive away. I want to run after them and tell them to come back, that this can all be fixed, but I don't know if it can be. I am so confused that my head feels like I'm in a constant state of vertigo.

My cell phone rings, and Serena's name lights up the screen. I guess I will be facing her sooner rather than later. "Hello."

"Griff? Oh, thank goodness. I need you to come. I'm at Cedar Sinai in the ER."

"What happened? A-are you okay?" I ask. Her troubled voice makes my heart rate kick up a notch.

"I, yeah, I don't know . . ." she mumbles.

"Serena, is the baby okay?" I'm holding my breath. I've felt so messed up since she told me the news. I didn't even work yesterday. "Serena." I raise my voice, and suddenly hear a whimper.

"The baby is fine, Griff. I was onset. I had some bleeding, and they called an ambulance for me. They did an ultrasound. The

THE TRUTH ABOUT US

baby is fine. Heartbeat is strong. I need you to come get me," she says.

"On my way. Hold tight. I'm glad to hear everything is okay," I say, and it's the truth. It may not have been my plan to have a baby, but I am ready to be a dad. My child will not go through what I did. He or she will never feel like a mistake.

She sighs. "Yeah." She sounds about as unsure as I do.

I head back up to my house and open the garage door. My Aston Martin Vantage is easily accessible. I grab the keys and bolt out of the driveway, aware that I need to take it slow but with my heart gunning in my chest, I can't get to the hospital fast enough. Serena's words ring in my mind. *The baby is fine. Heartbeat is strong.* Those simple words cause something to click in my mind.

This. Is. Real.

This. Is. Happening.

My heart expands. Jolie is right. I will do everything in my power to protect that child, but not at the expense of my feelings for her. I will find a way.

I pull up to the ER at Cedar Sinai, relieved there is a spot out front close enough to the entrance. I jog toward the sliding doors and ask a triage nurse where Serena is. She directs me to her room. When I see Serena, my stomach dips. Her eyes are rimmed red and her makeup is messy. She looks nothing like the put-together starlet I'm used to.

"Griff," she exhales my name. "I'm so glad you're here." She looks to the doctor. "This is the baby's father."

The doctor, a middle-aged man with grey hair and glasses, gives me a pinched smile. "The ultrasound is okay but I would like her to follow up with her obstetrician as soon as possible. Until then, she should probably stay off her feet," the doctor explains. He then turns to Serena. "I'm sorry, but you will need some time off work," he says to her, and I get the feeling that Serena probably tried to convince him otherwise.

"Of course, doctor. Thank you. I will make sure of it," I ensure the man.

"Perfect. Let me just take care of the paperwork and give her a list of instructions and she's free to go," he says.

Twenty minutes later, and I have Serena in my car.

"This isn't the way to my house," she says.

"That's because I am taking you to mine. I need to keep an eye and make sure you stay off your feet," I say. I haven't even had a proper talk with her about the baby and here we are, faced with a crisis.

"Griff, that's sweet of you, but honestly. I need to go home, have a bath, and change out of these clothes. My pants have a blood stain," she says, and her cheeks turn pink. She is vulnerable in a way I've never seen before.

"Shit," I hiss. "You shouldn't be pushing yourself so hard. Especially now. You can call your housekeeper and ask her to pack you a bag. I can send an Uber or something to pick it up."

"Fine." Serena makes the call, giving her housekeeper a list of all the things she will need.

When she's off the phone, I ask, "Have you eaten something today?"

"Some fruit onset, but that was it." Her face scrunches.

"You need to take better care of yourself and eat properly," I say, feeling like I'm lecturing her. "Please tell me you haven't been drinking or doing coke." I eye her from the side of my eye.

"Since I found out I was pregnant I haven't, but I didn't know I was pregnant, Griff. I'm sorry."

Jesus fucking hell . . . I swipe a hand over my mouth. "Okay, well lay off everything from here on out. Do you have vitamins or something to take?" I ask, as if that will help set off her previous lifestyle.

She nods. "The doctor gave me some just last week."

"When did you find out you were pregnant?" I ask.

"Last week," she says.

"And you are sure it's mine? You've been with other people since that night," I say, because lucky for me, the paparazzi follows her, and shots were taken of her leaving the Beverly Hills Hotel with her current co-star.

"I'm three months along. Three months ago, it was only you and you know I'm careful . . . We fucked up that night, Griff, and now I don't know . . ." She shakes her head and tears fill her eyes. "I didn't plan on having a child at this point of my life. I'm terrified of gaining weight and fear what my body will turn into. Will I get more jobs after this? Will I be employable?"

Fuck. Fuck. Fuck. Her doubts nauseate me. I keep my thoughts to myself.

"Why were you so mean to Jolie?" I ask. Serena and I had been friends for a long while. I'd shared intimate details of my past with her. She knew how important Jolie was to me and yet she set out to sabotage my relationship with her. I don't want to be an insensitive prick but I can't help being angry with her for ruining my chances with Jolie.

"I . . . was scared. I'm sorry. I just found out last week that my life is going to change in this dramatic way, and I needed you, but you were out of town, and you sent me that message the week before about us being over permanently. Then you show up with her," she spits, "on your arm at Ryan's house. Everyone was talking about you two. How beautiful she is. How perfect you both look together, and it angered me. I'm carrying your child. Dammit." She hits her hand on the arm of the car door, then covers her face. I think she's crying.

"Please don't cry. It's not good for the baby," I say softly, and take her hand. She is my friend.

"Is that all you care about? The baby?" She turns to look at me with tears streaking down her cheeks.

"Of course not. We go way back as friends." I give her hand a squeeze and force a smile. I'm in so deep over my head.

She gives me a smile and leans her head back on the headrest.

"Everything is going to be fine," I say, more to myself than to her.

"Yeah," she sighs.

Who the hell am I kidding? My ex-bed partner is carrying my child, and the love of my life is raising her dead husband's love child with her sister. To top it all off Jolie has left me to move to the opposite end of the country.

This is a fucking mess. . .

Chapter 38

Jolie

"Thank you so much for taking care of Sasha, Mrs. Montgomery." I give my neighbor a hug.

"Why don't you come in and have a cup of coffee and tell me about your trip? I have some sugar cookies for Kyle," she says, smiling down to him.

I just want to go back to my apartment and mope over Griff, but that won't be an option with Kyle around. "Sure. Sugar cookies and a sound ear are a winning combination right now," I say, and she grins.

"Perfect." She waves us into her apartment. Kyle follows Sasha toward the family room area, where there is a couch and television.

Kyle looks up to me. "Will she bite me?"

"She's been declawed, and she's friendly. Try patting her head and back. She likes that," I say.

"Here, take this." Mrs. Montgomery passes Kyle two sugar cookies on a floral tea plate, and the television remote. She winks at me. "That will keep him busy for a while. Now, tell me what on earth is going on, and why you are suddenly a parent to that boy," she says quietly as I follow her towards the kitchen. She turns on the kettle. I take a seat at her table. We've had many intense talks here in the past.

She watches me with kind eyes, and I suddenly break. I tell her everything, from my life with Mason to meeting Griff in the airport to Jenn having an affair with my late husband and having his child. Mrs. Montgomery places a tea in front of me. "Careful it's hot," she warns. "It's chamomile. After what you just told me I thought you needed to relax."

"Thank you, I do." I take a bite of a sugar cookie. "It's delicious."

"Thanks dear, now go on and finish your story," she says with a blink. I go on to tell her about Serena's awful behavior and the revelation about her carrying Griff's baby. I lift the tea cup and take a sip of tea since it has had time to cool.

"Oh, sweetheart. I was hoping that heading home after so long would provide you with some closure. I'm sorry you've had to suffer through so much and carry such a heavy burden, holding these secrets in your heart. You shouldn't feel ashamed about any of it." She says sitting across from me at her old kitchen table. She places her hand over mine for a brief moment. "You know, my Stan and I didn't have the perfect marriage either. Sure, we had good years, but we also had some tough ones too. There were years when the economy was in a recession and we were just scraping by. The pressure was intense, and I hate to say we grew apart. I even found out that Stan cheated on me," she says.

I gasp. "I'm so sorry. How did you deal with it? Did you separate from him?"

"I faced him head on. Told him I knew what he was up to. My kids were teenagers by then, and divorce wasn't as common as it is now. He apologized and we stayed together for the sake of the kids, but things weren't the same. We lived out the rest of his days in a loveless marriage. I couldn't trust him after that," she says with sad eyes.

"I'm so sorry you had to go through any of it. I left Mason. We weren't together when he fathered Kyle, but then we reconciled. He said he couldn't think of being with another woman during our time apart," I scoff. His treachery burns me so deep. "My own sister. How could she do that to me?"

"You said it yourself. She's had problems with your wayward dad, and probably her own demons too. She's an alcoholic. That's a tough sickness to combat. My brother-in-law was an alcoholic. My sister put up with him until the end. Caused all kinds of crazy in her life, and he ended up dying of liver failure."

"Geez."

"Yeah, you young kids expect this perfect life. This easy road. I know that because I have kids your age, but life isn't easy. No one promised us a perfectly paved path. There are bumps in the road sometimes, big ones, but I can tell you this: you are strong. I see fire in your eyes. You are a survivor, and I may not have had my happily ever after, but I think you will get yours." She nods, so sure of it.

A laugh escapes me. "Yeah, right," I snicker. "He let me go. Again. He let me go. He isn't willing to fight for us, and he's probably gone to her, the actress."

"Look, I don't know him, but it sounds like you guys share something special. He was just as surprised about the news of the baby as you were. The bitch told you before she told him because she wanted you out of the picture and it worked." Mrs. Montgomery takes a sip of her tea. "Let me tell you this. Men are slow." She giggles. "Honestly. Maybe he'll still come around and if he doesn't, then he isn't worth your time. You are special, girl. I'm telling you, and I'm old. I've met my share of people, and you are kind, beautiful, and smart. A man would be lucky to have you, and if it isn't going to be Griffin, then someone else will come along. You're young; you have time."

I take a long gulp of the tea. I want to say that I want Griff. I've only ever wanted him. Yes, Mason helped me get over him in a way, but the passion between Mason and I didn't even come close to what I felt, what I still feel with Griff. That knowledge scares me because what if I never have it again?

I stand and hug Mrs. Montgomery.

Kyle walks into the kitchen. *Perfect timing.* I'm hoping the TV was loud enough to drown out my talk with Mrs. Montgomery.

"Thank you for the cookies." Kyle smiles.

She crouches down. "You're a polite boy."

"Thank you," he says. He's one thing that my sister got right. I don't voice that thought out loud.

"Come, Kyle. Let's get you showered and into bed." I ruffle his hair and take Sasha in my arms. "Thank you again, Mrs. Montgomery. I don't know what I would do without you." I smile and she smiles back.

I head over to my apartment with Kyle. After all the upheaval he's been through growing up with my sister as his mom he's this ray of sunshine beating warmth into my life. I may be in a funk over Griff but watching Kyle thrive gives me the strength to believe that one day I will thrive too. Problem is my heart truly beats for one man. Is it too much to want my prince charming to run after me for once? I don't believe Griff will come for me. And where does that leave me if he doesn't?

Chapter 39

Griffin

Serena went straight for the master ensuite. She sits in my bathtub and I really wish I had told her to take one of the spare rooms. An Uber driver comes to the door with her bag, and I'm glad to have some time away from her. I take it up to my bedroom and head back downstairs. While I'm in the kitchen, I pour myself two fingers of whiskey. Why the hell did she go to my room? She surely can't think she's going to sleep in bed with me?

I make a call to a restaurant and order food. When I end the call, my cell rings. It's Annette.

"How you holding up, big guy?" she asks, her voice filled with concern.

"She's gone. She went back to New York with Kyle," I say, using my thumb and forefinger to squeeze my temple. I throw back a long haul of the whiskey.

"Yeah, she mentioned that being the plan," she says.

"Serena had bleeding. She went to the hospital. Everything is okay, but she is here now in my house. Doc said she needs to be off her feet. She's taking a bath in my fucking bathtub," I say, grinding my jaw while a headache sets in.

"Um . . . I'm sorry to hear she was having trouble," Annette says, her tone a little high-pitched. "I hope everything is okay with the baby."

"The ER doc said she'll be fine, but we need to follow up with the obstetrician. Do you think he wasn't telling us something? Does the bleeding mean something bad?" I'm talking too fast as my mind conjures up all these negative thoughts about something being wrong with the baby. Just remembering how Serena was talking about her body becoming distorted by a pregnancy causes nausea to roll over me. Jolie wouldn't be like this. I picture Jolie pregnant, and my heart expands and warms.

Fuck.

"Probably not. I mean, when Jacob and I would have sex when I was pregnant, I'd sometimes bleed," she says.

"For crying out loud. That is too much info," I bark, and throw back more whiskey while Annette laughs at my expense.

"Sorry! I couldn't help myself," she says.

Suddenly, I wonder if Serena was having sex in her trailer on set, and that's what caused the bleeding. Fuck, thinking of some dick touching my baby or someone else's cum inside her touching my baby makes my head spin. How the hell did I let this happen?

I think back to the careless night we conceived our child. Serena had gotten news her aunt died. She had raised Serena, and Serena was super upset. I didn't make a habit of it, but we both began drinking heavily, then we fucked our brains out. It was what we did.

"Griff. You still breathing?" Annette breaks through my thoughts.

"I'm not sure. I think she thinks she's sleeping in my bed. I don't know what to do. All I want is to get on a fucking plane to New York and get Jolie back, but those words alone make me feel like the world's worst parent. Serena is having trouble. I can't leave her and the baby. I need to take care of them and make sure they're okay. No matter what, I need to be part of my kid's life."

"I get that, but Jolie isn't going to wait on you. This whole situation is messed up and you clearly didn't do enough to keep her here with you. I just hope you haven't lost her," Annette says, making my world spin.

"No fucking way. I know I messed up. I was trying to wrap my head around this baby thing, and I was in shock. I didn't know what to do, and I know Jolie needed to know I was on board with her, but I fucking don't know if I'm coming or going. Now I clearly can't leave," I say.

"Serena is in a fragile state. As much as I dislike her, she needs you. You're in a bad situation with no easy way out," Annette confirms my exact thoughts.

"No shit." I pour myself another two fingers.

"If you need me, call me. I'm just saying, figure yourself out, and fast."

"Thanks, Annette." My tone is dry and bland.

"Bye," she says and the call ends.

The doorbell rings. I place the glass of whiskey down on the kitchen counter and trudge toward it. Must be our food. I ordered it from a posh restaurant nearby since I want Serena to eat something healthy. Not that that's a problem in LA. Everything is healthy.

I collect the food and sign the bill, then head back to the kitchen and leave it on the counter. I head upstairs to check on her. I walk into my own bedroom slowly and hesitantly. I don't want to chance seeing her naked. The bathroom door is slightly ajar.

"Food is here," I shout from outside the door.

"You can come in, silly. You've already seen all of me," she says. I don't feel comfortable looking at a naked woman who isn't Jolie. Now that I've had her, I only want her.

So do something about it.

I fucking can't.

I feel crazy.

"You should get out of the bath. The bag with your stuff arrived, and I placed it by the bed," I say, since she clearly figures she's staying in my room.

"Thanks." She sighs.

I head into my walk-in closet and grab some pajamas and

clothes for tomorrow. If Serena is sleeping in my bed, I will stay in one of the guestrooms.

She comes downstairs dressed in a silk pajama top and bottom. Her hair is pinned on top of her head, and she isn't wearing makeup. I don't think I have ever seen her without her face made up. I am pretty sure she was wearing makeup to bed all the nights we spent together. Not that it matters. She is beautiful regardless. She just seems more vulnerable now, and it confirms that I need to stay put.

"Michele's. I love their food." She smiles happily. She looks a lot more relaxed now.

"I know." I smile too. She's going to be the mother of my child; we need to get along.

I pass her the salad composée; it has fried green tomatoes in it. Blah! "I also got you the duck breast with parsley root and tarragon. I know it's your favorite. I got myself the lamb saddle with black garlic custard and king oyster mushrooms, but we can switch if you want."

"This is perfect. I've been having an aversion to seafood so I'm glad you chose the duck," she says, and we both eat quietly. I've barely eaten all day so my appetite is hearty.

We eat in silence, which is unusual for us. We've never had a problem with conversation. She was far from being my best friend, but we have acquaintances in common. She's been in films I've done trailers for. There has always been something to occupy the quiet space that lingers between us. When I texted her a couple weeks ago to end our friends-with-benefits situation, I didn't feel an ounce of sadness or loss. I realize it was because our friendship was superficial. This is so messed up. Is this how my parents felt about me?

Guilt washes over me like a thick coat of honey, and it's suffocating. Fuck. I don't finish my meal. Instead, I fill another glass of whiskey.

"None for you," I joke with her. I can't show that I'm freaking the hell out.

"Very funny." She rolls her eyes playfully.

After dinner, she sits on my couch, wanting to watch a movie.

My head is filled with Jolie to the point where I don't even know what movie we are watching. After the movie, she takes me by the hand and I pull out of her grasp. She frowns and looks taken aback, but then shrugs it off. We walk up the stairs together, and I turn into the spare room.

"Good night, Serena," I say.

"Are you not coming to bed?" She pushes out her lower lip. Shit, she's a good actress. I almost believe she cares about me.

"I'll be sleeping in here. You can have my bed."

She nods and I turn in to sleep.

Chapter 40

Jolie

I've been up all night researching different schools I may apply too. Kyle is asleep in the little car bed I ordered for him online. I'm suddenly kicking myself for quitting my job so fast. I spoke to Mich earlier to tell her I was back in town. She wanted to go out tonight, but I have Kyle. Mrs. Montgomery would probably love to babysit, but I feel bad leaving Kyle so soon when my apartment is still new to him.

For the past week, I've shown Kyle around New York. I've taken him to Times Square. He wasn't too interested in it. I took him to the big M&M store, which he actually liked, and to Central Park, which he told me wasn't a real park, although he did like to watch the ducks swimming in the pond. New York City isn't all that exciting for a kid.

My cell rings and Annette's name lights my screen. It's two a.m. here, which means it only eleven p.m. there.

"Hello," I say, trying to hide the surprise from my tone.

"Hey, it's Annette. I hope I'm not calling too late," she says, and she sounds a little nervous or maybe unsure.

"I'm up. I was just researching schools," I say, wondering the real reason for her call. She's Griff's friend, not mine. She wouldn't call me for small talk so late at night.

"I think it's pretty cool that you're going back to school," she says lightly.

"Thanks. I was all excited about the idea at first, but now I don't know. It feels a little daunting," I admit.

"Griff said you are super-smart," she says, and my stomach turns at the mention of his name. When I don't respond, the line remains quiet for a bit. "Look, I don't want to meddle," she begins, and pauses, and whispers I think to her husband. "Okay, Jacob just forced me to admit that I do want to meddle, but I mean well." I hear her take a deep breath. "I'm guessing he hasn't called, and it's not that he doesn't want to call you, shit . . . He's going to kill me," she mumbles. Then I hear a male voice whispering something.

"Hi Jacob," I say.

"She says hi," Annette says, and Jacob's voice comes through the phone.

"Hi Jolie. My wife is losing sleep over you and Griff. I told her not to meddle but I am tired and, well, I want my wife beside me in bed and not sitting on our family room couch, pondering a way to get you and Griff past, well, you know . . ." His voice trails off.

His declaration causes a giggle to bubble up my throat. "I'm sorry."

"It's fine. Don't listen to him," Annette chides.

After everything Annette told me about their relationship, I envy them. They had to fight to be together but they were both persistent and made it through. Now, they have a family they can be proud of and a love that seems sweet and intense.

"Griff is in over his head. It's going to take him a little longer to get to you than originally planned, but he will come for you. I know it," she says, and her words confuse me.

"Um, I don't know what you mean by all that. The last I spoke to Griff, it was pretty clear he wanted to be there for Serena and their baby. I get it. Griff is an honorable man, and I saw how he was with Kyle. I can only imagine he would go to the ends of the earth for his own child," I say. It's one of the things about him that melted my heart and made me reconsider a future with him. The way he took an interest in what was happening with Kyle. The way he took time to play with him because he knew he wasn't getting the attention he needed. An array of things made me fall for Griff all over again, but they don't matter now.

"I don't disagree with all that except he truly loves you, Jolie. He told me himself," Annette says, and it really feels like she is not telling me something. I'm not sure why. I feel weird to ask her what is going on. It isn't my business anymore. Right now, I have Kyle to worry about and a school to choose.

"That's irrelevant. His long-standing whatever-you-want-to-call-her is carrying his child." The words burn as they leave my throat.

"I called because I wanted to help but I don't feel like I've done any good," Annette says bleakly.

"I appreciate you trying, but there is nothing to be done." I feel like this conversation is going in circles.

"She was bleeding. The pregnancy is at risk, okay?" she blurts, sounding completely stressed. "I don't know if she's up to something or if she is really at risk, but Griff feels like he has to take care of her. If something happens to the baby, he would never forgive himself," she finishes followed by a . . . "Shit, I'm sorry."

I feel winded. My head falls into my hands, thinking of how difficult this situation must be for him. "I feel terrible, Annette, but there isn't much I can do. He made his choice, and we are all going to have to accept it," I say. "I should go." My eyes suddenly feel very heavy.

"I'm sorry," Annette apologizes. "I just . . . I know how much you mean to him, and sometimes guys are slow. I know he'll come around. I was just hoping to give you both a nudge," she says. I know her heart is in the right place.

"I appreciate your efforts, but sometimes it just isn't meant to be," I say sadly. "You have a good night," I say, and she wishes me the same. We end the call and I realize I may not get my second chance with the only boy I've ever loved because fate clearly has other plans.

Chapter 41

Griffin

I'm awake before my alarm again. I can't seem to get a good night's sleep, and I've been relying more on whiskey than I'd like to admit. I was never a heavy drinker because of my dad. I've always worried about having a gene that would pull me toward addiction.

It's been a full week of having Serena in my house. We saw the obstetrician, who assured us that the baby's heartbeat was fine, although she did mention being concerned about the actual size of the fetus and said she will monitor the progress of growth the next appointment. I get the feeling she was trying to brush it off so that Serena wouldn't be nervous.

It's been really hard having her here. I feel like a selfish prick for even thinking it, but all I can think about is Jolie. What is she doing back in New York? Is she thinking of me the way I am thinking of her? I've had my finger on her number more times than I would like to admit but at this point, I don't think she would accept a declaration of love over the phone. I fucked up. I was faced with this life-changing situation, and Jolie needed to be assured that I wanted her. I was always sure, but I wasn't sure about dealing with Serena or a child. The guilt alone has been consuming me. Bringing a child into the world when I don't love its mother weighs heavy on me. Serena reminds me of my own mother and doesn't truly want the baby. The way she talks about the baby changing her life in negative ways gets my stomach tied up in knots. Jolie was right though; I will be there for the kid. I will be its mother and father if I have to. I give my head a shake unsure how that would work. My mind has been spinning. I'm clearly losing it.

I have to force myself out of bed. Serena needs me to drive her back to the obstetrician so we can get another ultrasound and check that the baby is growing the way it should be. So far, there hasn't been any more bleeding this week.

I sit up and turn my body so that my legs hang off the side of the bed. My head hangs between my shoulders and my fingers come up to my hair and brush through it. Another day . . .

Suddenly I hear a shriek. It's Serena. I am on my feet, running toward her in my boxers. My heart beats frantically as I reach the door to my bedroom, which she always leaves open. My eyes widen when I see her sitting on the bed. The cover is flipped off. Her white nightgown has a bloodstain on it.

"Griff, oh no. Griff, something is wrong." She holds her stomach like she is in pain.

"Okay, let me get dressed and I will get you to the hospital," I mutter. Sweat pops on my forehead as I think of something happening to my baby. My poor, helpless baby. I throw on a pair of jeans and a T-shirt and lift Serena in my arms.

"What are you doing?" she asks frantically. Shit. There is a lot of blood on her nightgown and my head gets woozy.

"You shouldn't be on your feet," I say.

"Grab my robe. I can't leave the house like this," she says, always the Hollywood diva.

I walk over to the chair at the corner of my room where she's thrown it. She grabs hold of the robe and I head down the stairs. With Serena in my arms, I walk to the front table at the entrance to my house where I keep some keys. They aren't there, and my arms begin to ache from carrying her.

"I have cramps." She holds her stomach and groans.

Shit. What am I doing? I find a set of keys at the door to my garage and rush out. I've only walked a few steps when I realize my feet are bare on the cool concrete.

"I'm going to put you in the car, then head back in to get shoes," I say.

When I look at her face I realize she's crying hard. Shit.

"Everything will be okay," I try to reassure her, but who am I kidding? This looks bad. "Should I call an ambulance?" I ask. I don't want to scare her but it may be best.

"No, please, no. I'm freaking out as it is. An ambulance will only spike my anxiety," she says.

She presses her lips together while stifling her cries.

"No ambulance." I say and give her shoulder a squeeze. "Be back in a sec."

I run in the house, grab a pair of her slippers from the front door, and slip on a pair of leather flip-flops I had sitting right next to them.

The drive to the ER is brutal. Morning traffic in LA fucking sucks as I swerve between cars. Serena is holding a roof handle above her head. My heartbeat is erratic as I will myself to completely focus on the road.

"We're almost there. Hang tight," I say. I pull into the front drive of the ER. There is no way I can park the car in a marked spot and carry her all the way in.

With Serena in my arms we enter the hospital. A nurse runs up to us. "Let me help you sir," she guides me to a wheelchair. I place Serena in the wheelchair. "You should go check her in. I will take her to see a doctor right away." She wheels Serena away, and I feel like I can barely breathe as I provide her info to the triage staff. With Serena checked in, I head outside to park my car in a legal spot. When I head back inside I go straight for the main nursing station to find out what room Serena is in.

When I reach the room, there's already a doctor in a white coat talking to her. Everything feels blurred like it's happening too fast. They roll an ultrasound machine in. Serena is now wearing a blue gown, not the white one from home. The doctor takes the wand.

"I'm going to squirt some of this warm jelly on your stomach," he says.

Serena nods.

The wand moves over her belly. The doctor is quiet. Too quiet. Dammit. I wish he would say something. Anything.

His lips finally press together, and by his grim expression, I know what he is going to say. I suddenly feel faint and grab on to Serena's hand. I hadn't noticed the chair by her bed but I somehow fall into it. The doctor's words sound mumbled. Something about no heart-beat. Something about the size of the fetus not matching how far along she is.

There is buzzing in my ears as Serena breaks down and cries. The doctor stands and says, "I'm sorry. I'll give you both a minute alone." He leaves the room. My head falls forward and I cry, hard. My shoulders shake. Serena's little sobs fill the room. I lift my head and stand up and I reach over to hug her. An emptiness washes over me.

"I'm sorry," I say.

"This is definitely not your fault," she answers through tear stained cheeks.

My head is cloudy as we check out of the hospital. Serena wants to go home. I walk her up to her front door but she doesn't want me coming in. She wants to be alone. Does she feel the guilt seeping through my pores? Is it seeping through hers? I was so unsure about how having a baby with her would work and now it's gone. I somehow feel responsible, and Serena and I barely communicated all week while she was staying with me. I have nothing to say to her. There is no love between us, only loss. Whatever attraction we felt toward each other has died out. At least, for me it has.

I respect Serena's space and tell her that if she needs anything she should call, but I don't think she will. She looks hurt. Maybe she wanted more from me. I don't know. I don't even remember the drive back to my house or how I get into bed. I only feel the sting of tears—a relentless stream of pain as they fall wet and cool against my cheeks.

"GRIFFIN. GRIFFIN." Someone is shaking me.

"Hmmm." I want to sleep. Sleep is good. Blissful.

"Griff, wake up." I hear Annette's voice in my room. That can't be right. "Griff, what's going on? Did you take something? Should I call 911?"

I try to open my eyes and wince against the light. I see Annette with a halo around her. Her red hair is in a high ponytail and her lips are turned down.

"Leave me alone." I swat her away. I have a splitting headache, and my mouth feels like sandpaper.

"Answer me now. Did you take something? Do I need to call 911?" she repeats. *Fucking LA.*

"No, I don't use," I say.

"Phew, okay." I hear her blow out a breath and mutter something in Spanish. "Where the hell have you been then?"

I suddenly have the greatest urge to pee. I throw my blanket off and am relieved to see that I am wearing jeans and a T-shirt. I run to my bathroom and slam the door shut.

I am pretty sure it's the best piss of my life. My mind begins to clear and everything comes rushing back to me. I press the heal of my hand into my eyes, as if it will stop the pain of losing our baby.

I wash my hands with soap and splash cool water on my face. When I look in the mirror, I see a few days of stubble on my cheeks.

I leave the bathroom, and Annette winces. "What time is it?" I ask. Did I sleep through the day?

She looks at her phone. "Two p.m."

Okay, not so bad. I shrug and take a seat by my bed and look at my phone. "Oh, fuck," I blurt.

"Yeah, oh, fuck," Annette repeats.

"It's fucking Tuesday?" I ask.

"You didn't show up to work yesterday, and your phone was off. I can put up with twenty-four hours without hearing from you, but now we are almost going on forty eight," she says.

Right. I had been to her house Sunday afternoon for her regular barbecue shindig.

"Sorry. I . . ." The words are harder than I thought. She must sense my distress because her tone softens.

"What happened, big guy? I see Serena moved out?"

"Yeah, uh . . . she lost the baby." I swallow past the lump in my throat.

"Shit." Annette gasps and then she is hugging me and consoling me and telling me that everything will be okay, but how can it be when I am sad over my baby and feel very uneasy about the relief this news has provided?

"Okay, this is making sense now. This happened yesterday?" she asks.

"In the morning," I say, realizing that I was sleeping in the bed. The blood is gone. The sheets are clean. My housekeeper must have been here while we were at the hospital yesterday.

"Griff?" Annette's voice pulls me back to reality.

"Sorry." I shake my head. "She began bleeding. I took her to the ER. When the doc checked her, the baby didn't have a heartbeat." I frown and look at the floor. I hear Annette let out a loud sob.

"I'm so sorry." She sits beside me on the bed and hugs me. "What can I do?"

"Thanks but I'm good." I smell my shirt. "I need to shower, then I need to call Eric Vance and apologize," I say. He's a new client, and we had an appointment to meet this morning.

"I can call him," she offers.

"That's okay. It should be me." I try to force a smile.

"I'll head back to the office to check on things. I'll send you an update," she says.

"I'll shower and dress and head over," I say, even though my mind is still reeling.

"I know it isn't easy, but it does get better," she says, and I know she is talking from experience. I remember when she miscarried before having Christopher. She was early on, but her and Jacob were so excited they had told all their friends.

"'Kay, big guy," she whispers.

"Thanks Annette."

She leaves my room, and I text Serena to ask her how she's doing. I wait for an answer but it doesn't come.

I hop into the shower and then I shave. My instinct is to fuck work and hop on a plane to New York. Without complications in my life, I can go to Jolie. Fuck, the thought hurts. I feel terrible for even thinking it. What kind of person am I?

I head into the office and finish some work on a trailer. I come home and drink whiskey. I fall asleep on my couch, and the next morning, I wake wearing the same button-down shirt and slacks. I head up to the shower, then I shave and put on fresh clothes. I meet with Eric Vance and we agree on a price and schedule. I let Annette know to send him a contract. I head into the office to work on another trailer. On my way home, I stop for a burger and fries. Not my usual food of choice, but my stomach is so empty I feel like a hole is burning through me. I head home and drink some more whiskey. I realize I have a lot of alcohol that I have been collecting over the years. I try a single-malt, followed by some vodka, then more whiskey. I'm pissed drunk, and it feels good.

I wake in the morning with a splitting headache and a stomach ache. I trudge into the kitchen and realize it isn't morning; it's night. The alarm on the front door beeps, and Annette walks in. She walks toward me slowly like I'm a skittish cat.

"Are you alright?" she asks, walking on tiptoes.

"Yes, of course." I wince from the pain in my head.

Annette's eyes are wide as she walks around my house. I follow her line of sight, and my own eyes widen. There are a good twenty bottles of liquor sitting on my kitchen island. There are a bunch of empty ones, and there are pieces of glass on my floor. Fuck. I look at the clock. It says nine.

"It's nine p.m.?" I ask, and ruffle the hair on my head.

"Yeah, you missed a whole day. I helped Tara with some footage. I tried calling you and you didn't answer. I . . . I don't know what I thought . . ." When her eyes meet mine, I see hers are watery. "This is becoming a problem."

I can't argue with that.

I call my therapist and he makes some calls. I'm not an alcoholic but I am in a dark place. An hour later, Annette is driving me to a rehab and mental wellness center. It isn't a place I thought I would ever end up in, even if it is popular in this town. Growing up with my alcoholic father made me very cautious around liquor. I would party, but not too much. I would drink, but not too much. Right now, my life is spinning out of control, and I know I need help before I get in too deep.

Chapter 42

Jolie

I'm on my way into work. Mich gave me my job back. She actually never submitted my resignation request, which I am now grateful for because I won't start school until January.

I didn't want to use my father's influence when I applied to a program, and it was too late to submit an application with September being around the corner.

While I'm at work, Kyle is at a day camp. It's a routine we've settled into these last couple weeks. I've registered him for kindergarten here in Manhattan, which Mom will be footing the bill for. I've sent out applications to NYU, and on a whim, I also sent one to UCLA. Not because I think anything will happen with Griff, but because Kyle has been talking about his old friends from preschool. LA was his home for the first four years of his life, and I liked the way Annette described her life in the San Fernando Valley. It's just a back-up plan anyway. I don't think it will work out.

Mom said Jenn is getting help but she's still living at the rehab center outside of Boston. Mom spoke to the counsellors there and they aren't sure when Jenn will be up to caring for her son, and honestly, Kyle and me have become a team. I will have to part with him eventually, but for now, I am enjoying our time together, and he seems truly happy. One thing has crossed my mind though, and that is telling Mason's family he has a son. I'm sure his mom would want to know. Mason was an only child. She should meet her grandson. I just don't want to talk to Jenn at all. I have nothing to say to her. Mom said she can't pressure Jenn now with that kind of decision, which leaves things up in the air.

With a block left to walk to work, I stop into Starbucks for a coffee. As I am waiting in line, my cell rings. I'm pretty sure it's Mom's routine morning call to check in on Kyle and me but when I look at my screen, Annette's name shows up. I let out a heavy breath. Talking to her just causes my chest to constrict. She means well. Her last call, when she told me about Serena having problems and Griff being in a jam, just made me feel like shit. It reinforced how much Serena needs him and how he's going to be there for her, leaving me out of the picture. He hasn't even called me to see how me and Kyle are doing. What does that say about him?

By the third ring, I'm still contemplating if I should even answer. Gah! Who am I kidding? My curiosity wins. "Hello."

"Jolie, oh good. I'm glad I got a hold of you. How are you?"

"Good, but I will be heading into work in about five minutes, so I need to make this short. What's up?" I say, a little too cheerfully. I don't want Annette to tell Griff that I sound like shit just because he chose Serena.

"Well . . . not much. Chris is at a day camp close to home and . . ." She pauses. It's a quarter to nine in the morning, New York time, which means it's a quarter to six in LA time.

"What is it?" I ask, because she sounds a little distressed.

"I know I shouldn't meddle. Trust me, I know. Please forgive me in advance, because I really like you and I love Griff. I just want to do what's best for him. He's like family to me and . . ."

"Annette, what's going on?" I snap, and squeeze my eyes shut. She's making me nervous.

"Serena lost the baby. I know it should be him who tells you but he took the news really hard. I'm not sure Serena wanted the baby. I think it dredged up all kinds of issues from his past," she says, followed by an "oh dear," and a deep breath. "I . . . he . . . began drinking too much. I got worried, and he's in a rehab center."

"What?" My heart sinks. I press my palm against my chest. *Poor Griff.*

"Jolie?" Annette's voice pulls me from my state of shock.

"I'm here," I croak, and realize tears are streaming down my cheeks. I can't imagine what he must be feeling. How horrible. "I don't know what you want me to do, Annette," I say with all honesty. He chose Serena and the baby. After everything we had been through, he chose them.

"I don't know," she says, sounding broken. "I just want to help him. For him to turn to drinking the way he did . . . He's not a drinker," she says, and I know all this.

"I feel terrible," I say. "Wish him my best," I say, then I shake my head. Where did those words come from? They feel so cold and detached.

I end the call and head into work. Mich is her bubbly self.

"Hey there." She smiles, then turns back to the client she's checking out.

"Hey," I mutter, ducking my head and rushing straight for my room. Phew! Thank goodness she's busy because I am a shaky mess. I go over my schedule and set up my table for a massage. I drop the towel on the floor and have to replace it with a new one. While setting up the oil jars, I drop the lavender scented one, and the glass breaks on the floor. I have no idea how I am going to get through this morning.

My clients keep me busy, but it's the quiet time between appointments that has my mind wondering to Griff and our time together on Martha's vineyard. My mind then skips to the day we returned to find Jenn breaking down and confessing about Kyle. Griff was there for me. He didn't let me break. He gave me strength through a very dark moment. Then I remember the night he told me the truth about us. I'd never understood why he left over the years, but I felt betrayal from his abandonment, and with the ache of loss also came anger. Why didn't he come back for me? What was keeping him away? Now, I had all the answers, and it was so easy to fall for him all over again—or maybe I just never fell out of love. As I think those words, guilt seeps in. I married Mason, but I didn't love him like I loved Griff. I'd conceded to the idea that no man would ever make me feel the way he had. I'd never thought he would be back in my life, and then he was.

I have to stifle my tears as I take care while I massage my client. I feel bad for not having complete focus. Maybe I should leave, but what should I tell Mich? I don't want to share what happened between Griff and Serena. Just thinking about it makes my chest hurt. I check my schedule to see that I only have two more clients. Then I have an hour to pick up Kyle from camp. I push through the last couple hours.

"I'm heading out," I say to Mich two hours later.

Her brows furrow. "You okay?"

I can't lie to her. "I have some things I need to figure out but I don't really want to talk about it."

"Gotcha. Well I'm here if you need me," she says.

"I appreciate that." I give her a hug. "See you tomorrow."

"Bye, babe."

When I leave the spa, warm air hits my face and I take a deep breath. I need to hop on a bus to pick up Kyle. I might as well head there now. I want to call Logan or Mom to ask for advice, but how can I do that without revealing this current mess? Mom is dealing with Jenn, and I don't want Logan getting angry with Griff for ripping my heart out again.

I get on the bus and take a seat by the window. What should I do? What does Annette think I should do? The thought of Griff drinking too much and having to go to rehab makes my stomach roil. He must feel so alone. I remember back to those nights on the Cape when he told me the truth about my father's betrayal. He was alone and so confused when Daddy pushed him out of my life. I'm glad he has Annette now, but she has her own family to worry about.

I get off the bus one stop before my usual one for Kyle. There is a quaint piano bar I know of nearby. I enter the bar and order a glass of red wine. The music playing sounds melancholy and matches my mood. I sit by the quiet bar, grateful I am the only one here.

Do I go to Griff? No matter what, he is family. Thinking of his heartbreak over the baby makes my chest tight. I take a breath. *He's family.* Even if we don't work out—that is what Mom would say, and she is right. But I have Kyle to think about. He just got settled into camp. How can I drag him across the country again? It wouldn't be fair. He's happy now. I don't want to disrupt his life. And what would happen after I showed up in LA? Would Griff even want to see me? My doubts make my head spin but deep down I know I'm leaning toward going. Griff has had to face so many things in life on his own. He threw that in my face when he said I could have come after him all those years ago. What if I had? I would have known the truth much faster. Maybe I wouldn't have married Mason. I've never regretted that decision until Jenn confessed that he was Kyle's father. It makes me feel like I didn't really know my husband as well as I thought I did.

I pay the bartender for my glass of wine. I'm a little more relaxed now. I walk the extra block to get Kyle and dial my mom's number.

She picks up after one ring. "Hey there. What's going on?" she asks, her tone on high alert. I don't usually call this time of day.

"Mom, I think I need to go back to LA. Is there any way you can come to stay in New York with Kyle?" I hold my breath.

"What's wrong? Is Griff okay?" she asks. I told her we broke up a couple of weeks ago but I didn't have it in me to tell her why. I just said that our lives were too different.

"I need to go to him," I say. As the words tumble from my mouth, I feel them with the utmost conviction. I have to be there to give him my support.

"Okaaay. I need to let Jenn know I am leaving. I guess I can probably pack a bag tonight and go online for a ticket. I can try for Thursday. Does that work?" It's three days away.

"Yes, Mom. Thank you."

"Of course. I hope everything works out," she says. I want to correct her and say I am going as his friend. I have zero expectations for us. The fact that he checked himself into rehab must be serious. I can't . . . no, I won't let him face this alone.

Chapter 43

Griffin

The nurse calls me out of a therapy session to tell me I have a visitor. Before I have a chance to respond, my therapist cuts in.

"Who is it?" she asks, looking to the nurse. I'm guessing it is very unconventional to be interrupted mid private-therapy session. Whoever it is must have put up a really good argument.

The nurse and therapist whisper between themselves. Did Logan show up? I can't imagine Annette causing this much trouble, even though I sometimes think trouble is her middle name. It sure as hell can't be Serena.

The nurse smiles to me as she leaves the room, and I draw my attention back to my therapist.

I've been here for about a week. I came to get my head on straight. Detoxing from alcohol was never the issue. Through group therapy and private sessions, I have been working through the loss of my baby along with the horrible feeling of relief that flowed right after. The therapists are helping me detach my present feelings from my past. They are getting me to see that I am nothing like my mother or father. I did the best I could for Serena and the baby, and at the end of the day, what happened was out of my hands. I feel ready to leave but given my extreme reaction to what happened, the head doctor feels it would be best I stay here a little longer to work through things.

My therapist sits back in her seat. "Griff, take a seat," she says with her soft, smooth voice. It soothes me.

I sit and wipe my hands along my thighs. Why do they feel so clammy? I need to know who is here to see me. I know who I wish it was, but I blew any chance with her.

"Griff, Jolie is here," my therapist says, and my eyes widen. I suck in a harsh breath and stand.

"Where is she? I need to go to her," I say, getting ready to leave Dr. Sandler's office. She knows everything about what happened between Jolie and me. I've even managed to tell her childhood stories.

"Let's wait a second, okay? Please take a seat." She waves her hand for me to sit and I do.

"Did she say why she's here?" I ask.

"No," she answers, and my heart begins to beat fast. If she's here, it must mean something.

"I need to go to her."

"I know," she answers. "Just remember what we discussed. You need to say your piece and that is fine, but you also need to listen to her without pressuring her," she says. I wonder if it's because I basically didn't leave Jolie alone from the second we arrived to the Cape. I followed her to the bar, on her runs early in the morning . . .

"Yes, I know," I say nervously. "No pressure," I repeat. But she's here. The words sing in my mind and euphoria washes over my body. Excitement ignites in me; I haven't felt this way in a long while.

"Okay, go ahead. Nurse Jones is by the door waiting to take you to her," she says.

"Thank you." I sigh and get to my feet. I follow Nurse Jones through narrow halls to the main entrance, which looks more like a hotel lobby than a drug rehab and emotional health facility entrance.

I see her from afar. Her brown hair is messily tied on top of her head. She's wearing a simple white T-shirt and a pair of ripped jeans with yellow Converses. It reminds me of the time I saw her at LaGuardia airport after ten years of being out of her life. Fuck, she's beautiful, and she's alone. Her eyes connect with mine, and I watch her throat bob. She is so damn perfect.

"Hi," I say, tucking my hands into my jean pockets. *Give her space, Griff.*

She throws her hands around me. "I'm so sorry, Griff," she cries. It only takes me a second to pull my hands from my pockets and embrace her. She's always been so full of heart. She gives me a tight squeeze before releasing me. "Annette called. Told me what happened."

"Remind me to kill Annette," I joke with a hint of laughter.

"She cares for you. Don't be mad." She turns her head toward the entrance door. "She's waiting out in the car." She looks through the sliding doors then back at me. "Can we sit somewhere?"

"Of course." I lead her to the side of the lobby where there is a set of empty couches, thankful people aren't sitting around right now. This time of day is usually reserved for therapy.

I take a seat, suddenly feeling very broken. I hate that she knows I am here. That I'm weak.

"How are you doing?" she asks.

"Better. It was all very overwhelming." I rub my hands over my face. The doctor's words about not pressuring her run through my mind, but my heart is in overdrive and I have too many things to say. "Jolie, I never wanted to be with Serena. After you left, I told myself that I would find a way to be with you. That I would care for my child while being in a relationship with you and not Serena. I wanted to come to New York. I planned on coming to you, but—"

"Griff, I'm here as your friend, a member of your family. I don't want you to feel alone. I want you to know that even though things didn't work out between us I want to be here for you. You were such an important part of my life. I uh . . . just wanted you to know that you aren't alone. That I'm here," she repeats, and my heart sinks. *Have I really lost her?*

"I appreciate those words." I swallow. Not what I wanted to hear but we will get there. I look down to her hands and want to hold them in mine. Instinct tells me to hold back. "I fucked up with Serena, I know that, but the night we were together was way before I even imagined returning to Boston. I planned to come to you but then there were complications with the pregnancy. I couldn't leave her. She was staying in my house," I say, and Jolie slightly flinches. I think it means those words bother her. She's maybe jealous. I pray that she still cares enough to feel any of those emotions. "She slept in my bedroom. I slept in the spare room. I was never intimate with her. She was with me so that I could take care of her and the baby —that was it. I made that much clear to her. I want you to know that. I don't want there to be any secrets between us," I say, looking into her emerald eyes that are now rimmed red. "I wanted to come to you but I didn't know how, and then everything happened so fast. She lost the baby and I felt this immense amount of relief and it sickened me. I thought of my parents and wondered if they had wished I was never born and things got crazy. . ." I explain and rake my fingers nervously through my hair. "Say something please." I practically beg because she is too damn quiet.

Chapter 44

Jolie

He's unshaven and his hair has grown out. His pupils have dark rims around them, and my chest clenches as I can only imagine what he has been through. He wants honesty. He doesn't want to have secrets between us. Those words alone are music to my ears.

"I-I've been through so much," I stutter. "Jenn's confession about Kyle gutted me, and I wanted to run away but you were there for me, and I don't know . . . we moved too fast. It was too much too fast." It's the truth. He shakes his head. "I had my guard up when we arrived to the Cape but you disarmed me almost immediately. I don't have it in me to resist you," I admit, against my better judgement. I came here as a friend, but nothing about this conversation feels like friendship.

"Then don't. Don't fight us anymore," he says, his voice gruff, and if I'm not mistaken, he's filled with hope.

He stands from the couch and kneels, taking both my hands into his. "I love you so much. You are my heart. I will do anything for you. You need time and space. I will give you that, but please don't tell me it's over. It will never be over between us and you know it," he says, his blue eyes glistening.

"It will never be over," I agree. What I feel for him beats inside me, loud and strong. There is no way of purging Griffin Campbell from my system.

"We can take time and date. Whatever you need," he says, still on his knees. "Just please tell me we have a chance." The desperation in his voice guts me and all my broken pieces fall back into place.

"I'd like that very much," I say as tears begin to stain my cheeks.

"Don't cry." He cradles my face in his hands and peppers small kisses over my lips, nose, cheeks, and the corners of my eyes.

"I'm sorry." I laugh a little from feeling embarrassed over my tears.

"Don't be. It shows me how much you care," he says so gently, like I am breakable glass, and maybe I am. I've tried to stay strong through so much. I built up a shield around me and I didn't allow myself to break, but now sitting here with Griff makes me feel fragile.

The tears begin to flow faster. They turn into hiccups, which turn to sobs.

"Hey, now." He takes a seat beside me and wraps me in his strong arms. He holds me close to his chest, close to his heart, and I break in his arms.

"Oh, Griff, everything has been so messed up," I mutter.

"I know, baby, I know," he says as I continue to cry and cry, and as I cry, it cleanses. Like I am ridding myself of all the damage and grief I've been through. "You are so strong and resilient."

"You are too." I pull my head off his shoulders. My tears leak down my neck.

"That's why I'm in here," he says with an eye roll.

"It was responsible of you. You've been through so much too, and look at everything you've accomplished. The fact that you can even afford this place is an accomplishment," I say playfully.

We both crack up laughing. Through our tears, we find joy.

"I love you so much," he says.

I stare into his gaze and my heart melts. "I love you so much," I answer, because he has given me so much in the short time we've been back together. He's shown me I can trust him; he's shown me what a good and honorable man he is; and he's been completely transparent about everything, which for me, for now, is very much needed.

He takes a deep breath and holds me in his arms, and for the first time in a long time, I have hope that everything will be okay.

Chapter 45

Jolie

Six months later

I light the candles on the cake. "It's so pretty." Annette claps beside me. Neither of us are good in the kitchen but since it's Mom's sixtieth birthday and she is coming out to LA for a visit, I wanted to make everything special.

"Can I lick the frosting, Aunty?" Kyle asks, standing on a chair beside the counter.

"Absolutely not. Grandma needs to see what a great job we did." I smile down to him and scruff his shaggy brown hair. He helped us bake the cake too.

"Okay," he whines.

It took Jenn a long time to get herself together. She's still struggling though, and that's why Kyle is staying here with me. We've developed a routine here in the San Fernando Valley. He goes to kindergarten while I attend UCLA full-time. I hadn't planned on renting a house this size, but Mom insisted she would help since she wanted Kyle to have a nice yard to play in and Annette is only minutes away.

"Go out back and wait with Chris." Annette nudges him away

from the cake since he is still eyeing it suspiciously, and we don't want to risk ruining it. It's a two-tier cake with pink frosting and purple and green flowers. *Happy 60th Birthday Mom* is scrolled on the top.

With the candles lit, I take the cake in my hands.

"Don't drop that thing," Annette jokes.

"Quiet, will you? We don't need bad karma." I laugh shaking my head.

Annette opens the screen door for me. Everyone is seated around my long patio table: Mom, Logan, and Annette and her husband, Jacob. The kids are hanging on each side of Mom, and Griff sits beside my brother, watching me the way he does, with loving eyes. We all sing "Happy Birthday," and Mom blows out the candles. She closes her eyes. "I don't know what to wish for." She opens her eyes and smiles.

"Come on, Mom. You can think of something," I say.

"I've had it all. And my kids are finally happy," she says, still squeezing her eyes shut. The wax from the candles is beginning to melt on the cake.

"Wish for a dog, Grama," Kyle cheers.

"Hmm." She cracks one eye open and looks at Kyle, then quickly gazes at me. "I got it," she says, and she blows out her candles. We all clap, and then Annette cuts the cake for everyone. I walk back into the kitchen to get extra forks.

"Hey, you." Griff sneaks up behind me and wraps his hands around my waist. He presses his lips to the side of my neck. "Hmm, you smell good," he moans.

The sound hits me between the thighs. "I better get these forks out there," I say, lifting them up in the air.

"No." He spins me around and presses his lips to mine. The kiss is firm and demanding, just like the man himself.

Six months ago, I went back to New York so that I could make arrangements for a cross-country move with Kyle. Griff checked out of the rehab facility. He came to realize that some things in life aren't in our control.

The loss of his baby was painful. He began to open up to me

more than he ever had. When we were younger, he gave me snippets of what his home life was like but he didn't share everything. When I returned, he explained to me that he was trying to protect me from the horrors he faced daily. Through therapy in the center, he learned that he needs to share what he feels with me, good or bad. And to me, it means everything. It isn't easy for him to open up but the process has been healing and has brought us closer than we have ever been in the past.

As his lips move with mine, familiar heats licks my body all over. He presses his firm groin into my belly, and I whimper. "Griff," I say into his mouth. "It's my mom's birthday party. We can't do this now."

"Oh don't stop on my account." Mom laughs. I jump away from Griff, feeling my cheeks flush with heat. She pulls the forks out of my hand. I forgot I was even holding them.

I swat at Griff's chest, and he winces. The rest of the world melts away when we are together.

"Sorry, Mom," I say, taking a breath. How embarrassing.

"Sorry, Kathy," Griff adds, but he isn't sorry at all.

"I'll just head on back. You two get back to it. I just wished for another grandchild; I want that wish to come true," Mom says, shocking me.

"Umm." I stand frozen.

"Is there a thing about saying what the birthday wish is and it not coming true or is it the other way around?" Mom asks with a mischievous grin, standing at the sliding door.

"I-I'm not sure," I murmur, feeling like I am going to die of embarrassment. Did my mom just insinuate Griff and I should get busy?

Mom smiles devilishly and closes the door. She has been a staunch supporter of our relationship from the start and after everything we've been through, it means so much.

"I have some news," Griff says. His light blue eyes sparkle.

"Oh yeah?" I watch him intently.

"The offer came through on the house. Sold. Firm deal," he says, referring to his Beverly

Hills mansion.

"Oh wow." I throw my arms around him. We had talked a lot about moving in together since I basically arrived to LA. I wasn't big on moving to Beverly Hills, but I've come to love living in the Valley. Annette and Jacob have welcomed me into their friendship circle, and Kyle has Chris. Since I wouldn't move to Beverly Hills, Griff decided to put his house for sale. "That is such great news."

"I know. I finally get to move in here." He smiles at me. Standing in my little kitchen makes him feel so large.

"You're excited about leaving a mansion in Beverly Hills to move into this place?" I ask, and my lips twist.

He shrugs. "Well, yeah. You know I can't wait to have you in my bed every night. Besides maybe we can buy something out here together. A property that has more than two bedrooms." He winks, followed by, "I mean so we have space in the future," he corrects.

"You know we have time for that," I say. "But I am happy you're going to be moving in." I kiss him again. I make it quick because we have a tendency of getting carried away.

"Come. We are being rude." He takes me by the hand, and we join everyone outside. Everyone is raving about what a good cake we made, how it tastes so much better than a store-bought one.

"What do you think, Mom?" I ask, because she is the expert baker.

"It's light and fluffy, and the icing is delicious. Creamy, not too sweet," she answers.

I eye Annette, who is sitting on Jacob's lap.

"We did well, my friend," she says, and I walk over to her and we give each other a high five.

I turn around to see my brother and Griff huddled in a corner. They are talking quietly and then they give each other a bro hug. Hmm, that's weird. I turn to the table and take a few bites of cake. "Hmm, this is really good. Wow." I pat myself on the back.

When I turn around, Griff is standing in front of me and he drops to one knee. My mouth is full of cake, and yet my heart manages to skip a beat. Annette gasps and cheers, and Jacob shushes her. I look over to Mom, and her smile is wide as she gives me a nod and blinks once. She knows something about this, and by the look on my brother's face, he does too.

"Jolie Bryant, I have been in love with you ever since I can remember. We have had our share of love, our share of heartbreak, and our share of pretty much everything in between." Griff chuckles and his cheeks flush. Small bouts of laughter ripple around us. "I want you to be my forever, baby. We've worked long and hard to make it to this point, and since you've been here, it's all been so easy. Loving you is simply a part of me, just like you are a part of me. Let me make you happy every day. Agree to be my wife," he finishes and opens the small box in his hands. Inside is a simple solitaire diamond. It's large, but not ridiculously so. It's classy and simple.

Tears erupt in my eyes, making my vision fuzzy. My hands come up and cover my mouth as emotions overwhelm me—love, happiness, admiration. I see forever in his eyes and I hope he sees it in mine.

"Baby, this is when you say something," Griff urges with a laugh, but I can tell he's nervous.

"You didn't ask," I say.

He laughs. "Always busting my balls, this one." He pauses and his features straighten. He licks his lips. Oh, how I love those lips. "Will you marry me?"

"Yesss," I scream, and he gets off his knee, lifts me up, and kisses me breathless. Everyone around us cheers. He slips his tongue in my mouth and our lips move in rhythm. I hear Annette's distinct voice say, "Okay, we got kids around here."

Griff and I break away, and everyone takes turns hugging and congratulating us.

"This is going to be a birthday to remember," Mom says.

I briefly think of Jenn. When I am alone studying or sometimes at night just before I fall asleep, I think of her, my older sister. I remember wanting to be just like her when I was little, and even as we grew older, there was so much I envied about her. Now I pity her. Our lives were moving forward, and she was stuck in her string of bad choices, even though Mom said she was holding down a job now and she was clean. I still didn't want to see her. I had nothing to say to her, even if a part of me ached I didn't want her to be part of these special moments in my life.

"Hey." Griff comes around and puts his arm over my shoulder. "You good?"

"I'm great. I was just thinking of . . ."

"Jenn," he says.

"Yeah," I sigh.

"Maybe one day you two will work things out," he says.

"Maybe." I shrug. I pull my mind away from her. There is no point in dwelling.

I spend the rest of the evening listening to Griff making plans about buying a house in the Valley. Kyle cuts in and asks if Griff can build him a treehouse in the new place. Griff promises him he will, and Kyle beams.

I've come to love him as a son. I don't know when and if Jenn will be ready to be a mom, and the thought of Kyle leaving us is heartbreaking. But I choose to focus on the now, and right now Griff and Kyle are my family.

After Annette, Jacob, and Chris leave, Mom gets Kyle ready for a bath. Logan took off somewhere with my car, and Griff is helping me clean up.

"I love you so much," he says.

"I love you," I answer.

"Leave the dishes. I will get them in the morning," he says, taking me by the hand and leading me to the master bedroom, which is right beside Kyle's room, where Mom will be sleeping with him.

"Griff, the walls are thin," I warn.

"I just asked you to marry me. I want you now," he says, his tone demanding.

Excitement spikes inside me as needs swarms my body. We enter the room, and Griff locks the door. When he turns to me, his baby blues are blazing. He walks over to me briskly, and we grab onto each other, kissing with such fever it's like we are long-lost lovers who have been reunited. Our desperation for each other shows. As our lips entwine, he rips off my shirt and unclasps my bra dropping them on the floor as my hands move to the hem of his shirt. I pull it over his head and kiss his neck and lower my lips to his nipples. He groans, low and guttural.

"Fuck, baby, I am so turned on," he says.

I laugh. Isn't it always the case?

He pinches my nipple between his thumb and forefinger, and heat floods between my thighs. I get to work removing my leggings while Griff unbuttons and unzips his jeans. I stare at his naked torso, so strong, the planes of his stomach a perfect eight-pack. I lick my lips.

"See something you like?" he asks with a devilish gleam in his eyes.

"Very much." I nod.

"On the bed," he demands. I climb on my knees and he swats my ass. A moan escapes my mouth.

"Oh, this ass," he says, giving it a squeeze. "I wanted you on your back, but now I've changed my mind," he says. "Stay like this."

I turn my head to see what is happening, and he drops to his knees on the floor. He takes me by the hips and guides me so that my ass is at the edge of the bed, but I am still on my knees and my behind is still very much up in the air. His tongue connects with my flesh, and I moan into the dark room.

"Cover your mouth," he urges, and then his tongue is back on me, moving up and down through my opening. When he licks my clit, my body shudders, and I begin to move my hips along with the motion of his tongue.

"Oh, oh," I moan. "I don't think I can keep quiet."

He ignores me and picks up speed. I am like a loose cannon, lost in sensation, rolling my hips against Griff's sinful tongue. When I feel my orgasm nearing, I grab a pillow and bury my face in it. Sparks of white light fill my vision as my body shudders from the orgasm. I fall on my back, and Griff lies beside me as I recover.

When I do, I climb above him, peppering kisses across his chest and down his torso. His breathing picks up pace. I lower myself until my lips wrap around his cock. He moans, and it's so sexy. I love watching him coming apart beneath my touch. My mouth takes him in and out. In and out. His hips begin to move in rhythm, and I feel him strengthening and lengthening. I wrap my hand around the part of him I can't take in my mouth, and I pump him in a similar motion.

"Fuck, baby, yeah. Just like that. I'm so close," he groans, coming apart. As hot liquid hits the back of my mouth, I try my best to suck it down. Then I lie beside him and watch a relaxed Griff coming down from his high.

We lie for a while, tangled in each other.

"I sold the house with the furniture," he says, his voice raspy as his fingers run through my hair. "I figured it would be better that way. You can decide what you want to buy later on."

"Are you still okay with moving in here?" I ask. He knows that I love this house. It's small but it's felt right since the moment the real estate agent brought us to see it.

"I was actually thinking . . ." His voice trails off, and when I tilt my chin up to look at him, he has a sly grin.

"You were thinking what?" I ask. He's trying to pique my curiosity on purpose.

"I was thinking we could buy this house, since you love it so much. It has a huge yard. I mean, it could use a renovation, but we can do all that in good time," he says.

My eyes widen. "What? Are you serious? That would be amazing." I can't hide my glee.

"I thought you would like the idea," he says, proud of himself.

"I like you," I say.

He frowns. "I thought you loved me."

"That too," I add with nonchalance. Griff flips on top of me and pins my hands above my head, and my breath hitches. His hard length is settled between us, and just the thought of him moving inside me is enough to get me wet.

"Say it," he urges.

I know what he wants. I squirm beneath him, but just for fun, I tease him. "Say what?"

"That you love me." He pinches my nipple lightly and twists.

"Ah!" That feels so painfully good. "I love you, Griffin Campbell."

"Damn straight." He kisses the air out of me, and I wrap my arms around his back. He enters me in one swift movement, and I'm already wet for him. His hips move in and out, and I'm building. My eyes fall shut as my own hips move along with his thrusts. We give and take, give and take, and I've never experienced anything so beautiful in my life.

"I can't wait to make you my wife," he grits out as we fall together, Griff and I, two beats of one heart.

Chapter 46

Griffin

Twelve years later

I reach the drive with my heart beating fast. I'm almost as excited as I was the day I married Jolie. Okay, maybe not that excited, but still, my happiness is ramping pretty high right now.

I run up to the house and throw the front door open. I know everyone is home this time of day.

"What has gotten into you?" my wife asks. She's just as beautiful as she was the day I married her. Maybe even more beautiful now. Since she had Maddy and Jake, her hips have filled out a bit and her breasts are larger, which is all the better for me.

Her brows knit together as she gives that look. The *what have you gone and done now* look. I may have given up my Hollywood lifestyle to appease her, but what she's given me means so much more—a family and love. Even though now and then I've been known to throw some money at something she doesn't approve of, she always comes around, like I know she will today.

"Kyle, get yourself outside," I yell down the hall.

Jenn never truly got her shit together. She had times she was clean and times she wasn't. When a couple years had passed and she still wasn't ready for Kyle, Jolie asked her if we could adopt Kyle. The process was long but well worth the wait, and he became our son just before Maddy our daughter was born. Jake came after. We named him after Jacob, Annette's husband. I actually wanted to name our daughter after Annette but Jolie wasn't having it. She fell in love with the name Madeline and wanted her to be called Maddy for short. With Jake, she conceded. Now our kids are eight and ten, and Kyle is sixteen and a half.

I wait impatiently for everyone to get outside, but it's taking them time. Jolie steps out the front door first and gasps. "Griffin Campbell," she says in a chiding tone. "I can't believe you." She shakes her head as her eyes land on the SUV I bought Kyle.

"What?" I say. "I wanted him in something safe," I say of the Yukon. It's a big, strong car in a midnight blue.

She presses her lips together and smiles. She can't stay mad at me for long.

Maddy rushes outside, holding a doll. "What is it, Mommy?"

Jolie whispers something in her ear.

"Where's your brother's?" I ask.

"Jake is playing Fortnite and Kyle is listening to loud music," Maddy answers as she begins to comb her doll's hair. She reminds me of a little Jolie but with my eye coloring.

I take a step in the house.

"No, it's okay. You wait here. Let me get him. You should at least see the look on his face when he sees the car," Jolie says, sauntering into the house. She wears eye glasses now. After all the years she spent reading books and researching, her eyes became weak. Now she is an assistant professor with tenure at the History Department of UCLA.

"Thanks, doc," I say as she walks away. It became my nickname for her when she earned her PhD.

She smiles and sways that fine ass of hers as she heads into the house. Her hair is pinned in a bun, and she's wearing a pantsuit. It's fitted to her body, and she looks sexy as hell. I still have to adjust my dick in my pants when I see her. Even after all this time, we are hungry for each other, and I hope that never changes.

Jake comes barreling out the door, looking a little pissed that we pulled him from his game.

"Hey, buddy," I say.

He still runs up to me and gives me a hug. "Hi Daddy."

I kiss the top of his head. "How was your day at school?"

"Same old," he answers. Sometimes, I think he's eight going on thirty.

"I'm going to be doing a trailer for a superhero movie. Do you want to hear which one?" I ask.

His green eyes turn round. "Tell me," he pleads.

"Nah, you don't want to know," I say, playing with him a bit.

"Dad, come on," he whines.

"It's a cross of Superman and Spiderman. It's a new script. Original storyline. We'll get to go to opening night, and you can come into work and help me with it."

"Seriously?" He beams.

"Yeah." I nod.

I sense Kyle reaching the front door, and my heart gets that nervous, excited feeling again.

"Dad?" he questions. He started calling me Dad soon after I moved in, before Jolie and I married. He was small and said he didn't have a dad, and he asked me if it was okay. My heart broke in the best possible way that day, and he's been mine ever since. Even before the adoption came through.

"It's all yours." I lift the keys and dangle them in front of him. He deserves this.

He hugs me fiercely. He's a big guy with broad shoulders, just like me.

Jolie told him all about his dad. She also told him that they were once married. We figured it was better coming from us than him researching his father and Jolie's name popping up, since their marriage was public knowledge. He met with Mason's parents a few years back but they don't have much of a relationship. For some reason they have bitter feelings toward Jolie. I don't have a clue what that has to do with Kyle but it doesn't matter. My kid is a happy one and that is all that matters.

"Should we take a drive, son?" I ask.

He looks to Jolie. "You coming, Mom?"

Jolie wipes tears from her eyes and nods.

"You too, squirts," he says to Maddy and Jake.

Jolie and I share a glance and burst into laughter.

"What's so funny?" Kyle asks.

"I used to call your mom squirt when she was little," I say.

"You guys are so mushy." Kyle makes a sour face.

We all get into Kyle's car. I sit in the back with the kids, and Jolie takes the front seat with him.

"Let's go get some ice cream," I say.

"That'll ruin their dinner," Jolie chides. She gives me a look and smiles. "Let's get ice cream."

Jolie had once been a big planner, and after life threw her some sour lemons she tried to control things even more, but over time, we've learned we can't control everything. Life is hard.

When Jenn died of an overdose, we attended her funeral, and Jolie cried on my shoulder. When Kathy got sick, we helped her through, and when Logan married, we all went to Iowa and stayed on a farm. Not my cup of tea. We've had our ups and downs over the years, but we've also had each other.

The truth about Jolie and me is that we are fighters and lovers. We are winners and losers. We persevere. I live life to the fullest with my family by my side and my wife in my arms each night. It isn't my money that makes me a wealthy man. It's the love that surrounds me that makes me rich, and I wouldn't have it any other way.

STAY TUNED FOR LOGAN BRYANT'S STORY COMING 2020. TURN THE PAGE TO READ AN EXCERPT FROM MY BEST SELLING MILITARY NOVEL HALO!

Prologue

Rogers Park, Chicago
Christmas morning 2002
Thomas

I lie in bed waiting for Halo to wake up. I know Christmas was a big deal around her house when she was growing up. Even though her parents are gone I still want her to feel the magic of the holiday. When I was a kid Christmas was another shitty day in my life. Nothing to celebrate. Another mark on the calendar moving me closer to the time I could leave my father and my dirty past behind.

Halo begins to stir in bed, shifting toward me with her eyes shut. A sweet smile plays on her pink, lush lips and my chest bursts with love for this woman.

"Hey." Her morning voice is raspy and thick. She opens her eyes. I couldn't love this woman more even if I tried. She's my everything.

"Hey yourself." I grin as my eyes roam over her rosy nipples. The memory of making love last night gets me all hard again. I would take her right now if I didn't have something planned. I let out a grunt.

She stretches out her arms and her body moves into a delicious curve. I lean down and close my mouth over her nipple. Damn, she tastes good.

I groan. "Baby, you can't be teasing me now. It's Christmas morning and I got stuff waiting for you under the tree downstairs."

"Stuff?" Excitement grows in her eyes. "Like presents?" She instantly pops up to her knees, bouncing on the bed. She's too cute. It's taking everything in me not to claim her right now. I want to give her Christmas.

Seeing her smile means everything. Not too long ago she was drowning in darkness. The healthy gleam in her eyes tells me she's feeling good now. It will make my news a little easier to deliver.

"Yes, baby, the stuff is presents." Before I can say anything else she pops out of bed and grabs her T-shirt off the floor. I must have thrown it there last night during our lustful attempt to actually make it to the bed as opposed to having sex on the floor again.

There's nothing wrong with floor sex but it can get hard on the back and Halo's knees. Halo throws on the shirt and darts down the hallway. I hear the small patter of her footsteps as she makes her way down the stairs. I slip on my boxer shorts and follow her. I placed a number of presents under the tree and she won't know which to open first.

I swiftly walk down the stairs to the living room where our Christmas tree is shining bright. I look out the window to see a small dusting of snow falling from the sky. Halo seats herself on the floor in front of the presents. This is my second year with a Christmas tree and her second year without her parents—bittersweet.

"Which one do I open first?" she asks like a little girl rubbing her palms together. It makes me laugh. I mean we are young. I'm twenty and she's nineteen. We were both forced to grow up too quickly. I guess it's memorable times like this that we cherish.

"If I knew presents made you this excited I would try to get more." I chuckle.

"It's not just the presents, Thomas. It's Christmas. Do you feel that? It's magical." She stares out into space with a peaceful look on her face.

"Sure baby, I'm feeling it." I look down to the chub in my shorts from this morning's perusal of her body.

"Thomas," she chides, punching my shoulder.

I chuckle again. "I'm just joking, this day is special for me too." She's too cute. I lean in, pressing a soft kiss on her lips. I pull away and lean toward the first box I want her to open. "This one." I pass her a little red box wrapped in pink ribbon. She opens it in a hurry. It's a thong from Victoria's Secret. It's not meaningful, but I couldn't help picture how hot she would look in it.

"Thank you." She leans forward and places a kiss on my lips. Then she rises to her feet and walks over to the closet by the front door. She retrieves a box from the closet and comes back to the tree.

"This is for you," she says, extending the box with one hand. I pull her toward me, guiding her to sit in my lap. Then I open my gift. It's a dog tag. Engraved. "I will always love you. You are the light in my darkness." My chest grows tight.

I enlisted in the navy and went through SEAL boot camp, passing with flying colors. Then I was shipped out to Coronado, California a year ago for more training.

Becoming a SEAL was a dream I had all my life. Originally I wanted to be a SEAL to get away from my father. Then I met Halo. She was only fifteen and perfect. She made me want to be a SEAL for an entirely different reason—I wanted to prove myself worthy of her.

I haven't told her yet, but I'm deploying. I was putting it off until I knew the depression was better. I also know that she could feel me itching to leave. My friends from boot camp had already been assigned to teams that had left for Afghanistan. Being a newlywed meant I could put it off for a while. Now I was deploying. I worried she would take it hard. That's another reason I wanted to make Christmas extra special for us.

"Halo, it's perfect, baby." I lean over and give her a kiss. "You are the light in my darkness. I know you know I need to leave. I wanted to talk to you about it, but…"

Her finger presses to my mouth. "I know…I know you need to

go. I've known for a while. I guess I was selfish trying to keep you here all this time."

"There isn't a selfish bone in your body. You were having a hard time and it was completely understandable. You're stronger now. You're going to be okay. You're busy with school and you have Jenny. You will be fine without me, Halo. I don't think you realize how strong you really are." I pause for a minute because I want her to open her next gift. "Here, open this." I pass her a little silver box; this one has a little gold bow on top. She turns on my lap so she is sitting with her legs wrapped around my waist. She opens the box and her jaw drops.

"Thomas, it's perfect," she gasps taking it out of the box. It's a silver locket.

"Here, let me." I take it out of her hand and show her the engraving on the back.

You're my Halo, my ray of light.

I will always find my way back to you

She laughs.

"We clearly think alike." She nods, proud of herself. It's true her name is quite original. We've used "halo" as a term of endearment many times. It's a reminder that when a person is drowning in darkness, another person can show them the light.

"It's perfect, Thomas."

"It opens up. You can put two pictures inside," I explain, showing it to her.

"I will have to get some pictures made."

I place the necklace around her neck and her palm closes over the locket, holding it close to her heart. I place the tags around my neck.

"Baby, I ship out tomorrow. I've known for a couple of weeks, but I didn't want you walking around sulking for my last days at home. I thought it's better we had a quick goodbye." I speak the words softly, but inside I'm cringing, hoping she isn't mad.

"Thomas…" Tears roll down her cheeks. "I know this has been coming. I know you need to go. It's okay. I've told myself it's okay since we had our first date four years ago. I've been preparing myself mentally for this. You will be great and you will do good in this world." She leans forward and places a wet kiss on my mouth. I can feel her tears on my face. I love her so damn much it hurts.

"Baby, I love you. I'll probably be gone for a while. I'll try to stay in touch as much as I can but I've been told that I may be off radar for long periods of time…" I pause because my next words aren't easy. I take a deep breath. There really is no easy way to say this… She's young and beautiful and we fell in love and married young. If something were to happen to me she needs to know that she needs to move on.

"Don't say it, Thomas." Her tears continue to fall and she nods. "You're it for me, baby." She says it adamantly and I believe her. I was her only boyfriend and her first everything.

"Halo, listen to me." My thumb grazes her cheek, wiping away her tears. "I'm a SEAL now. We go on high-risk missions. I need to know that if something happens to me that you won't check out. You need to find yourself a new husband and make a life. You are nineteen years old and the most beautiful thing I have ever seen walk this earth. I know I'm asking for a lot here, but I need to hear you promise me you will. Now that being said, I promise you that I will do my damnedest to come home to you. I will find you in the dark; you can trust that. Just in case, please say the words." I beg her as if it's my least breath. I know she would always keep her promises to me and this one is important. My own tears spill.

I'm a realist. Living a difficult life makes you into one. There are no ifs about it. I wipe gently at her tears and look at her with pleading eyes, chipping at her stubborn walls until they are fully broken.

"I promise." She nods then claims my lips hungrily. The thought of her being with another man makes me crazy possessive. I know deep down I need to do everything I can to stay alive, but the reality of being a SEAL doesn't always allow for that. The heat between us ignites and within seconds I yank down my boxer shorts and have my cock buried between her legs as she rocks on top of me. I need to own every inch of her because that conversation about her moving on has just done crazy things to my insides. As I bury myself inside her, I cleanse my mind. There is nothing else—just me and her. The way it should always be.

Chapter One
    Five years later
    January 15, 2008
    Rogers Park, Chicago
    Halo
    It's happening... This. Is. Real.
    Shit! I lean over the side of my bed and brace myself. *Slow breaths, Halo. You can do this. Everything will be okay.* I take a slow breath, but the pain is too intense.
    I'm losing it. What should I do? It's too soon. This baby wasn't meant to come for another three weeks. Jenny and Dave aren't back from Florida yet. Who the hell should I call?
    Fuck! Here comes another one. Holy hell, it feels like my insides are being squeezed to death. This can't be good. My contractions are five minutes apart. Little beads of sweat trickle down my forehead and my heart accelerates.
    I never anticipated being alone for something like this. For this I was supposed to have a partner by my side.
    Thomas had stuck by my side. He'd put his own dreams on hold. I knew with everything in me that he would always be by my side.
    The contraction subsides. I rise from the bed, huffing out slow breaths as I wobble over to the window facing the backyard. I place my hand on the cool glass, which feels nice on my heated skin. The sky is a midnight blue and the stars are sparse. I watch the clouds slowly moving and concentrate on breathing slowly through my nose and exhaling out of my mouth.
    I'm on the verge of panic. Being alone means I don't have the luxury of melting down. "*Even darkness must pass,*" I whisper the wise words of Tolkien, keeping my eyes glued on the large backyard covered in at least two feet of snow, anything to distract my mind from the fear that threatens to swallow me whole. Thomas and I had shared a love of books. We quoted Tolkien's words all the time.
    I look back to the clock on the night table. It's three a.m. Even though Thomas has been gone for just over seven months, I still sleep on my side of the bed. It's messed up, but when someone like

Thomas makes a promise to come back to you no matter what, you believe it, you breathe it and it enters your soul. People like Thomas are loyal. They don't make promises and then break them. They sure as fuck don't walk out on their pregnant wives. When he left on previous deployments I always missed him when he was gone and waited for his return. This time was different. I waited for him to make contact. It never came. Then the divorce papers were delivered and I understood...

Fuck! Fuck! Fuck! I usually don't swear, but I can't stop cussing. This pain is maddening. I'm going to lose it in a minute. Maybe it's good Thomas isn't here for this because all I can think about right now is gripping his balls and twisting so he can understand my pain.

Flakes of snow begin to fall from the sky. Usually I love watching the snow fall. It relaxes me on a good day. Right now it's only adding to my anxiety. I'm worried about driving myself to the hospital with the snowy roads. My car is more of a death trap than a vehicle. I turn away from the window and walk over to the closet. I grab an orange beach bag off the floor and I begin to fill it with pajamas and a change of clothes. I thought I had more time to prepare.

My best friend Jenny was overdue for all three of her children. I thought going beyond the baby's due date was the norm. I was hoping Thomas would sense my broken heart and walk through our front door when I needed him most.

I tried reaching him through all the routine channels. I even called some of the wives of his fellow SEALs on his team. I figured they would be sympathetic to my situation and they definitely were. They asked their husbands about Thomas. Avery, the wife of one of Thomas's fellow SEALs, said that Thomas had seemed pretty messed up but that he was definitely on active duty. I then asked her to send the message for him to call home since she was in contact with her husband. That call never came. A couple months later I learned his team had gone dark and they were expected to stay that way for a while.

I step into the bathroom and with shaky hands throw my toothbrush and some toothpaste in the bag too. I planned to take off school a week early and buy diapers, get sleepers and fix the truck. With being a teacher I didn't want to leave the classroom while in the middle of a unit. I wanted to wrap things up. With the baby coming three weeks early my plans have been quashed and I am now unprepared. Unfortunately for me none of my plans ever seem to work out.

Ow! Shit! Here comes another one. The bag slips out of my fingers and my hands go to my swollen belly to brace for the impending contraction. My face scrunches up. I can't do those damn slow breaths I was taught to do, because these damn contractions are owning my ass.

I think that was four minutes. I hunch forward as the contraction rips its way through me. I close my eyes and pray. I pray that Thomas will walk through the door this second, or that Jenny will for some unforeseen reason end her vacation in Florida early.

"Charlie what should I do?" I ask, looking into the brown eyes of my Golden Retriever. She stares back at me and I can tell she understands what's happening. I'm sure she'd try to help if she could speak. I don't know how I would have gotten through these last months without her. She has cuddled me and let me cry on her more times than I care to remember.

"What do you say, Charlie? Ambulance or a taxi?" Charlie tilts her head to the side and lets out a cute little moan followed by a louder bark. "Taxi it is then." I pat her head. An ambulance will make me even more anxious than I already am. I'm about to lose my shit in another minute.

I walk over to the phone on the nightstand and call the cab company. A man with an East Indian accent picks up and tells me he could have the cab here in five minutes. I bet that's even faster than the ambulance. My heart is racing a mile a minute and my hands are clammy. I hang up the phone and try to focus. I'm not sure I will make it through this on my own. I always had it in my head that somehow he would come home for this. I really believed that when he left it wasn't final. I was his Halo. He promised me that I was his fucking Halo…

Acknowledgments

This book took me such a long time to write. I was so invested in Jolie and Griff that I had to make sure they overcame their obstacles and pursued their dreams in just the right way. I hope you fell in love with them as much as I did.

To all the readers thank you for choosing this book it means the world to me.

Thank you to my wonderful editing team. My wonderful beta readers, I couldn't have figured the story out without you. Thank you to Lauren Clarke my editor and Renita McKinney my proof-reader. Your dedication, suggestions and grammar fixes are always so much appreciated.

To Sarah Hansen my cover designer. You knocked this one out of the park. I'm so in love with the cover.

To my publicist Christine, thanks for all that you do. And to my wonderful agent Stephanie at SBR Media, thank you for promoting my books.

Thank you to all the bloggers who read and reviewed. You all just manage to make my heart melt each time I release a book. You are so dedicated and selfless. I think you all rock.

To my children, I love you so much. I thank you for being so understanding when I'm deep in my cave writing. They remind me daily that I can do anything I set my mind to. Apparently, they got that advice from me.

To my husband, thank you for your continued support. I appreciate and love you so much.

About the Author

R.C. Stephens is a top 100 Amazon best selling author. She has written ten romance novels and plans to continue to write many more.

When she isn't in her writing cave she is raising three lovely children with her adoring husband.

Her books are filled with humour, heartbreak, emotion and true love.

Born and raised in Toronto, she loves the winter, but Spring and Fall are her favorite seasons.

Keep up with R.C. by signing up to her newsletter-http://rcstephens.com/newsletter/

facebook.com/rc.stephens.8

twitter.com/rcstephensbooks

Also by R.C. STEPHENS

<u>STANDALONES</u>

DICK

HALO

FRAUD

<u>BILLIONAIRE ROMANCE SERIES</u>

MR. ALL WRONG

MR. SO WRONG

<u>SPORTS ROMANCE</u>

BIG STICK

BUTT ENDING

POWER PLAY COMING FALL 2019

www.ingramcontent.com/pod-product-compliance
Lightning Source LLC
Chambersburg PA
CBHW020403260626
47156CB00007B/2215